Faithful

S.A. Wolfe

For my family

One

I glance back to see him following me as I run. I like the sound of his voice as it releases my name over the buzz of the party.

My breath escapes in misty pants as I sprint around the maze of tall hedges, chasing five-year-old Toby, one of the neighbor's rambunctious boys. I'm laughing at the ridiculousness of the situation—a little boy running away with my sandal.

My bare left foot digs into the cool damp soil as I turn corners, trying to remember the way around the garden maze that has been a focal point of many parties at Lois's, one of the grand dames of Hera, a sixty-something who excels in hosting parties. I mastered her garden maze before I was a teenager; however, the endless glasses of champagne tonight have left me bewildered, as though I'm disoriented in an unknown forest.

I hear Toby's giggle up ahead and laugh loudly in response as I get closer to my prey. I am becoming more light-headed as I hear the sounds of party guests and music playing in the distance. Dylan and Emma must be dancing or maybe they've already departed for their surprise honeymoon, the same way they surprised everyone at tonight's outdoor party with an impromptu wedding service.

My mouth was full of potato salad when Lois told everyone to shut up, and then Dylan and Emma approached the front porch of the house where a judge was waiting to preside over their vows. I had looked around, just as startled as everyone else. Although happy, I was also

1

somewhat sad to be losing more friends. Yes, that was how it had felt, like I was losing something.

My single friends are getting married and caught up in their newfound blissfully wedded lives of creating homes and being spouses. Meanwhile, I'm being left behind.

Therefore, I did what any normal woman would do. I grabbed the first bottle of champagne Lois had opened and got busy, pushing that tinge of sorrow and jealousy so far down my throat all I could feel was a complacent numbness.

Now I'm losing the cute, little runt, and I'm lost, stuck in the maze. I stop running and put my hands on my hips as I catch my breath while Toby's giggles continue to grow farther away.

"Imogene," a deep voice purrs my name, smooth and rich like sweet liquid on his lips.

When I turn around, he smiles. Man, he is handsome. I've always thought so, but tonight, the moonlight captures his tall, lean form in an unearthly sight of mythical beauty. His shoulder-length golden hair shines, and his gray eyes stalk me like a wild cat. Being drunk takes my imagination to thoughts I have been dismissing for months. Inebriation is also what makes it easy for me to walk quickly towards him and fling my arms around his neck. Then I pull him down for the kiss I have long fantasized about.

Strong and solid, he resists my brazen behavior before giving in and kissing me deeply. The smoothness of his movements comes from experience and confidence and, hopefully, excitement for me.

One of his hands presses against my lower back, pulling me tightly to him while the other reaches under my skirt and firmly holds one of my butt cheeks.

I grab fistfuls of his thick hair as I stand on tiptoes to kiss him. When we unlock our lips for air, I feel him smile against my cheek, and then I bury my face against the warm skin of his neck.

"Imogene," he whispers, his breath tickling my ear and sending a shiver of tingles through me.

I close my eyes and hold on to him. "I think I drank too much."

"I've got you."

I feel my feet leave the ground as he lifts me up. My head is about to roll backwards before he adjusts me so my face rests against his hard chest. My arms are still wrapped around his neck as a sleepy contentment takes over my body. I sigh, and his chest rumbles with a laugh.

This is an unexpected turn of events, one I don't want to end.

Two

Regret sets in the minute I hear Lauren pounding up the stairs, shrieking for me to wake up. She's the prison matron for Cell Block H. Sure, we live in a nicely renovated Victorian house, courtesy of our friend Jessica who rents it to us rather cheaply, but it's still the place I have to work day and night on the struggling jewelry business I run with Lauren. When I'm not here working or sleeping, I'm at my family's diner, Bonnie's, breaking my back with those heavy, oversized serving trays.

With the exception of my four years at Syracuse University with Lauren, I've spent my whole life in Hera, a miniscule town in the Catskill Mountains, a town that barely eclipses Horton's Whoville. We're far enough from New York City to offer countryside solitude and close enough for me to realize how mundane my life is compared to those in the city. However, I'm also a lifer; it's in my bones. I don't think I could ever move away from the family and friends I've known since I was in kindergarten. Hera is lacking in excitement and available men, but I'm still holding on to my last shred of hope that things will improve for me.

Two years ago, I was full of optimism and courage to start my business venture with Lauren, designing one-of-a-kind repurposed jewelry from vintage pieces we find by scouring estate sales and online auctions. Despite being labor intensive, we're rather proud of our unique style that has been picked up by a few high-end boutiques in New York City. We've even generated a small but steady following for our online web store. Our price point, which

4

averages between eighty dollars for a pair of earrings and four hundred dollars for a necklace, makes our line too expensive for mass retailers yet affordable for the shabby chic crowd who shop at specialty stores.

In the beginning, my math said we would only need a few hundred retailers around the country to allow Lauren and I to quit our waitressing jobs at the diner and settle into our dream career. Boy, was I wrong. Start-up costs, selling, advertising, and gaining footing in a crowded market are killing us. Essentially, I have the same income as when I started while I'm working more hours, seven days a week. Cell Block Hell.

Opening my eyes to the sundrenched room causes a stabbing pain to whirl around my head. With this unwelcome pitchfork in my face, I'd like to greet Lauren's loud morning enthusiasm with a meat cleaver. Unfortunately, she enters my room where I have the energy and muscle tone of a sponge.

"Time to get up, party girl!" Lauren bounces into my bedroom like the effervescent cheerleader she was and will always be. She's a tall, skinny, blond, the opposite of me and my shorter, curvier figure and long, dark hair. Lauren's sunny disposition is unnerving when things like stomach viruses and hangovers roll around.

For a moment, I think I'm having an out of body experience, watching as she hovers over me, her long, blond ponytail swaying back and forth as my lifeless arms reach up to strangle her. Of course, it's wishful thinking; no part of my body has moved an inch unless you count my eyelids.

"Stop moving," I hiss through my dry lips. "You're making me nauseous."

Lauren smiles and swings an open bottle of water towards me. "You look like shit."

"I feel worse." I swat my arm at the water bottle like a sad imitation of Frankenstein with his meaty, ungraceful

5

paws. It takes everything I have to latch onto the bottle and guzzle that sucker until it's empty without throwing up first.

"God, wasn't that amazing?" Lauren beams dreamily at me.

"The amount of champagne I packed away last night or the fact that I'm still alive today?"

"The wedding. Dylan and Emma. I can't believe they kept it a secret until the last minute."

"The best part is we didn't have to wear bridesmaids' dresses or even buy gifts."

"Oh, you. I would have loved it if they'd had a real wedding. No one has the big weddings anymore. At least, not in this town. Jess and Carson did the same thing."

"I like these no-frills, honky-tonk weddings with ribs and three kinds of Jell-O. Between our failing fantasy business and our waitressing jobs, we're living on a sinking ship. We don't need more expenditures because I'm pretty sure we can't afford life boats."

"You've been awake for two minutes, and you're already pissing and moaning again."

"Lauren, we have a real problem. We have to do something drastic, or we have to give up on our business. Seriously, I cannot keep waitressing full-time and then run home and work through the night on the jewelry. Even if we stop sleeping, we still can't produce enough inventory to make a profit at this rate."

"That's the hangover talking."

"No, we've gone over the numbers. You and I have to make some real decisions soon."

Lauren's smile disappears and she sighs. "I know. You're right. We've been winging it for too long. Carson said we need structure and to follow a real business plan. It's probably time to sit down with Archie and go over our options."

"Sounds a little scary." I know we should meet with

our friend Carson; he has a mind for business. And Archie, our lawyer, who is older than the sun and always meticulous in a three-piece suit, will guide us through the business dealings and contracts with care as if he were our grandfather. It's all still ominous, though.

"Yeah, well, I need to go unpack our new boxes, okay? The stones and the copper findings you ordered came in, so I'm going to set up the project trays. When Leo gets back, we're going out for lunch in Woodstock, and then I'll come back and work with you on the new pieces. We can talk about it then."

"Where's Leo?" I'm used to Lauren's live-in boyfriend making coffee and toast for us every morning. I could really use one of his hangover cures.

"He drove Dylan and Emma to the airport early this morning. They're spending a week in Mexico."

"Nice," I say, thinking of our friends dashing off on their honeymoon.

I push myself up to sit and wince as the blob of pain and queasiness sloshes forward with me.

"Take a shower and eat something," Lauren urges as she heads for the door. "I'll be back soon."

I suddenly notice I'm on top of the bedspread, still wearing the same tank top and skirt from last night, and the bottoms of my feet are black with soil.

"Lauren? How did I get home last night?"

"I drove you and Leo."

"Did he help me up to bed? I don't even remember walking up the stairs to my room."

"God, no. Leo didn't help you. He was so sloshed he fell asleep on the living room couch the minute he walked in the door. I was just going to leave you on the back seat of the car. You were snoring away, but Cooper insisted on bringing you in."

"Cooper?" I ask sharply. "You mean he actually helped me walk up the stairs?"

"He was the one who put you in the car. Then he followed us home on his bike and *carried* you up to your bed."

"Cooper," I groan.

Lauren laughs. "Accept it; you finally have to be nice to him. At the very least, you have to thank him."

She leaves, laughing all the way down the stairs.

Cooper.

I touch my lips and remember part of that rather sensual dream I was having. One minute, I'm chasing a little boy, and the next, I'm kissing a gorgeous wall of muscle. Oh, fucka-doodle-doo, that was Cooper. In my dream, I was getting hot and heavy for the very guy I've been avoiding for the past year.

I have to put Cooper's sexy lips out of my mind and will myself to walk to the shower. I have to face some cold, hard facts about my life, my business, and setting a firm resignation date from the diner. My grandmother has owned the diner for decades along with my parents, and leaving the security of an established, successful business that has supported my family and me for years to make pretty necklaces for a niche market sounds really foolish at this moment.

However, if anyone can help Lauren and I sort this out, it will be Archibald Bixby, town lawyer extraordinaire and one of the few people who will help us for free, no strings or invoices attached. Yet the thought of sitting in Archie's law office while he explains the cost of business expansion, loans, investors, and hiring people, thus increasing our overhead and payroll, gives me the willies.

I'm not as sure-footed and determined as our friend Carson, who started the furniture company in town. Between his high-end furniture business and his foray into building eco-friendly homes, he employs over one hundred locals. He's become the favorite employer, generating enough in sales to pay far above the average as well as

8

offering bonuses and premium benefits packages. I'm not sure Lauren and I have the fortitude to carry our business that far, to put ourselves out there with a high risk of failure and the fear of a huge debt.

Sometimes, I imagine us moving our little workroom from the second floor of this old house to a real studio and having several very talented employees assembling the necklaces, earrings, and bracelets Lauren and I design. In my scenario, it's a comfortable, bright studio where we happily chat while we work, orders piling in, bills paid on time, and naturally, our business, brand, and income growing.

Then there's the reality that most businesses fail. Lauren and I could take out small business loans to expand the abandoned garage at the end of the main street and hire a few locals who have been out of work for years. They won't have any real skills or talent for beading, but we could teach them the basics so we can increase our inventory just enough to break even each month. We won't have money to renovate our space; it will be shabby and gray with a few permanent oil stains on the concrete floor. While we work, we'll all drink cheap coffee Lauren will provide with her Mr. Coffee machine she still has from our college days, and we'll keep our conversations guarded, worried that each day brings us closer to bankruptcy. It's a lousy scenario I revisit each day.

I'm not sure we can be as successful as Carson. I don't know if we have his drive, although his came in part from a serious desperation and will since there were no other options besides success. He had been taking care of his younger brother Dylan for so long since their parents' deaths, and Dylan needed medical help—his bipolar disorder had put him at risk for every possible horrific outcome. Carson Blackard is the most ambitious, determined person I know. He took on his new business and managed his brother like the shiny new steam engine that rolls into a horse and buggy town and shouts its arrival.

Carson helped revive our little town. He also put a lot of good people back to work and brought in some new people, too. Not only did he get Dylan help, he has him running the sales division of Blackard Designs, which is shipping furniture to high-end retailers all over the country. Carson also hired one of my dear friends from college, little Miss Mobster Emma, as Lauren and I used to call her. I guess it's not so funny now that her father was arrested in an FBI takedown of several high-profile mobsters last year.

Emma's life is better now with her marketing position at Blackard, working with her new husband to boot. That's right; she married our lovable, once mentally unhinged Dylan. In fact, both Dylan and Carson, the two men I expected to be lifelong bachelors, got married.

I love those two guys to pieces. I grew up with them, and they are like brothers to me, but how in the holy hell did they manage to find their soul mates and get married before me? Carson was all work and no play, avoiding women altogether, and Dylan had a terrible reputation as a womanizer, not to mention being crazy as fuck sometimes, while *I* worked hard at the dating scene.

I mean, I *really* worked it like it was a legitimate career from high school all through college, and I ended up in relationships with Mr. Douchebag-Who-Accidentally-Sleeps-With-The-Girl-In-My-Dorm, Mr. I-Care-For-You-As-A-Friend, Mr. We've-Had-Sex-It's-Time-For-New-People, Mr. I-Have-Needs-And-One-Woman-Isn't-Enough, and Mr. I'm-Leaving-Town-Without-Telling-You.

Yes, indeed, I've had my share of shitty men. I don't know how it's still happening since my resolution years ago to stop dating pretty-boy jocks or unbelievably good-looking, rugged hunks seemed like it would weed out the ones who were sure to disappoint or, worse, hurt me. I thought I had perfected my new no-wanker vetting system, but Jeremy somehow got through my firewall of protection.

That wanker.

To fly under Grandma Bonnie's cursing radar, I've adopted slang from British romantic comedies. My grandmother has pitch-perfect hearing when I mumble *fucker* or any variation of the word. So now, when I'm sizing up men at the diner, the pool hall, or any social event, I have my Wanker Radar on full alert. Apparently, I will be dateless until the end of time because, so far, every single guy I meet registers as a wanker.

And, although we've never dated since he moved here over a year ago, I had Cooper penciled in as a wanker, too.

Cooper, my brain murmurs.

Three

After a shower and a half-assed attempt at blowing my thick hair out, I stumble into the kitchen for coffee to make me feel human again and a slice of untoasted bread to stop my stomach from rumbling.

Leo left a note on the fridge, saying he'll make us dinner tonight. He's not a wanker. Lauren actually has a nice guy. Gangly, sweet Leo. In the humidity, his short, brown hair curls make him look like a young teenager. He moved in a year ago when he sold his home to Dylan, which is where the newlyweds now reside.

I don't mind having Leo around, helping with expenses and upkeep. So far, the house feels large enough to avoid intruding on each other's space. They have the master suite on the third floor, and I'm at the other end of the hall with several empty bedrooms between us. Aside from our workroom, we have an actual formal library we've designated as the TV room. This is where Leo escapes from us and spends most of his time, either on his computer or playing video games on the TV. The first floor living and dining rooms are rarely used since we don't have all those great parties we imagined hosting when we first moved in here. Other than eating in the kitchen and sleeping in my bedroom, I live in the second floor studio, beading every chance I get.

I'm not always so negative or cynical; I absolutely love designing and creating our jewelry. It's the business end that has me in a constant state of distress, worrying if we can succeed or if I'll have to learn how to love Spam and powdered milk.

Once I'm suitably awake, I plant myself at the large craft table that can seat more than a dozen people and takes up most of our studio space. Starting with the new beads that were delivered, I begin sorting the gemstones and silver beads into their proper bead boxes. It's the kind of tedious work that sucks up our time and slows down our productivity. We've discussed hiring a high school girl to come do some of the grunt work so we can work on the craft and business details, but even a minimum-wage employee is too steep for our non-existent budget.

As I begin filling bead trays for individual necklaces we'll make today, I hear vehicles rumbling up our dirt driveway. Then I hear Lauren and Leo in the downstairs front entryway. They trail off down the hall, heading towards the kitchen, but I also hear heavy footsteps on the staircase.

I look up from my beads to see Cooper filling the doorway. My insides quake with a little tremor, either at being found or suspicious of what will follow his appearance.

Cooper looks as good as always; no hangover, no sallow, tired skin. His shoulder-length, straight blond hair is tucked behind each ear and looks perfect against his tan, handsome face. I've seen that knowing grin of his so many times I've learned to look away to avoid being swayed by his magnetic charisma. Everyone thinks he's charming and gorgeous if you listen to the women gossiping at the yoga studio when they have their asses in the air and their heads low to the ground as they rate local men in hushed tones. He's a regular ol' chick magnet, the last thing I need.

"Imogene." There's that deep, rumbling purr again. He always says my name with a slight smirk on his face.

"Hi, Cooper." My eyes sweep over his physique quickly before settling back on my work.

I didn't miss a single detail: the relaxed jeans that hang from his narrow waist; his thick biceps reaching up as he places his hands on both sides of the doorframe, pulling his white T-shirt up enough so I see his flat stomach; and his broad chest that seems to get bigger every time I see him. The heavy, physical work he does at Blackard Designs has definitely done wonders.

Cooper was promoted to operations manager, and I've watched him helping the crew load furniture into the delivery trucks and unload timber delivered to the factory. He looks like he does it all, and it looks amazing on him.

"How are you feeling today?" he asks with a little smugness.

I continue beading, though I see him out of the corner of my eye, slowly walking around the studio, checking things out. "I feel like I have sharp boulders rolling around in my head. How about you?"

"I didn't drink last night, so I'm good. You look great, by the way."

I snort a laugh and look up at him. "Honestly, Cooper, you don't have to lie to make me feel better. I feel like crap. I actually got winded brushing my hair today. But I'm fine. I'll recover."

"I'm being honest." Cooper's gray eyes catch mine, paralyzing me for a moment. "You always look good, Imogene. No bullshitting."

"Oh," I manage to say then look down again. Usually, I have a sarcastic comeback or a mean dig for Cooper. This time, nothing comes to mind.

"Well, look at that. I made you blush." Cooper's slow, rich chuckle feels like a caress.

Damn, he's good.

"Thank you for carrying me to bed. I'm told Leo was too drunk to help and Lauren was too tired to care."

"It was my pleasure." He leans against the opposite side of the table from me. "I wasn't going to let them leave you in the car, and I finally got a chance to show you I'm not a jerk."

"I never said you were a jerk," I snap and immediately wince at my sharp tone.

"You didn't have to. You've been treating me like I have the plague, and you take every opportunity to walk in the other direction from me." He tilts his head slightly, waiting to see how I'll talk my way out of this one.

"True. I haven't been the most pleasant person over the last year. Sorry. Now you know why I'm not on the board of the Hera Welcome Wagon Committee."

"Does that exist?"

"Not officially. It's really just Lauren."

As Cooper laughs, I take a breath and laugh along with him. Perhaps this is a first—us being together alone where I can't use the presence of others as a safe buffer. I'll admit, this moment with him is surprisingly nice.

Said Little Red Riding Hood about the wolf.

"So, you really do work all the time," he says, lifting his chin at the wire crimper in my hand and the elaborate display of beads in the tray in front of me.

"Yes, but I love doing this. I wish I could do *only* this and make a living at it."

"Lauren told me you two plan on quitting the diner soon, and you need to put more into your business."

"She did?"

"Yeah. She and I talk a lot. She's not afraid that I'm contagious, and she is living with my best friend, after all."

For a silly, stupid moment, I think he's referring to me, but of course, he means Leo.

"Ha. Funny. I guess I didn't think you two talked much." I sort through my bead tray, concealing the fact that I've completely forgotten to use two beads and screwed up the sequence on the necklace.

"She's even eaten dinner at my house, with Leo, of course," he continues.

While I only stare at Cooper as if I'm meeting him for the first time, he laughs at my stunned silence. "What's

15

wrong? I never see you speechless. Are you surprised that we share the same friends?"

"I suppose I haven't given it much thought, but I guess I have missed some of the things going on around here. I always assumed Lauren and Leo were going out to restaurants or movies. It never occurred to me that they went to your house."

"I always ask her to invite you, too, but Lauren thinks it would be uncomfortable for you," he explains with a sly smile. "Something you want to tell me?"

"Um, no. I'm good. I kind of stashed the social life for work and sleep. I'm a little bit more concerned about our setup here than Lauren. She's better company than me, anyway."

"She told me you're a little stressed out."

"Wow, you two do talk a lot." *About me.*

Cooper studies me for a moment, his eyes giving away nothing, seeming to casually assess me and everything around him. Sometimes, when he watches me, I sense he can see right through the defenses I've put up when I can't tolerate small talk or casual, flirty behavior from customers at the diner or men who think buying me a beer at the pool hall will put them in good favor. With a slight nod or a questioning tilt of his head to the side, I know Cooper's thinking about something that's out of the ordinary. Do I know this for certain? No, but a guy doesn't leave an extraordinary career without having mastered some kind of unique skills, even if he's secretive about his background.

I don't know much about his old life before he moved to Hera other than he was an FBI agent, involved in some mob dealings that had to do with Emma's past. At some point last year, he resigned from the agency and went from being an undercover, gun-toting character du jour to leading a rather simple existence in a management position at our local furniture factory. It's all a little peculiar, especially since he comes across as a leather-clad, easy-

16

going biker.

Seeing him ride around our sleepy, little town on his Harley makes me wonder why a young guy like him would give up his adventurous career in the city for table saws and daily lunches at Bonnie's diner. It's not like everyone sitting around, eating meatloaf sandwiches and burgers while trying to drum up the most scintillating town gossip that rivals the local weather report is very interesting.

I'm not a pushover, I'm not easy to get to know, and I've been less than friendly with Cooper for the past year. Maybe it's because I really do think he has a sixth sense about people, about me. Today, he studies me like he knows I have a peach-colored bra and panty set on underneath my green tank top and shorts without ever looking at my ample chest.

The first three things men notice about me are that I have a curvaceous body, which they like; big, brown eyes that stare them down; and wavy, chestnut hair like a 1940s pin up model. I'm average height with a small waist that blooms into real hips and a real ass. It's all about how you carry your weight, and I carry mine with enough confidence because I discovered a long time ago that boys and men appreciate a curvy, hourglass figure. One boyfriend used to refer to me as *Vavoom* and others liked to compliment me on my boobs and ass. It gets old fast. I'm a little soft and squishy, but I wear it well. I'm also not past using it to my advantage, although lately, I've lost interest in the dating game in general. When it comes to Cooper, however, I've always been rather self-conscious.

Regardless of my assets, he always stares at my eyes before producing that sly smile of his and turning away. I give him credit for not doing the classic head drop where a guy's gaze locks on a woman's cleavage when he's talking to her. In a way, it's more disconcerting to wonder what is going through that former G-Man brain of his than if he were outright ogling my body.

He turns back to the display cases against the far wall where we keep our finished pieces ready for sale. I pretend to work, though I can't concentrate with him in my space. I notice he takes a necklace off a display bust and holds it out, draped across both of his hands. It's my best piece, the one I'm most proud of and definitely the most expensive because of the components and labor involved in creating it.

"This one," he says firmly, holding it out to me with an urgent seriousness. "I'll buy this one."

"Excuse me? Why do you want to buy one of my necklaces?" I stand quickly and bump the table, jolting my bead tray and the alignment of the loose beads. "Fuck!"

Cooper grins. "Aren't these for sale?"

"Well, yeah, I want to sell everything, but you can't buy that." I walk around the large table to meet him. "I put a lot of work into that necklace and it has some pricey components. That silver locket attached to it is from 1880, and some of those vintage beads are—"

"So I'm not worthy of this necklace?" He raises an eyebrow.

"It retails for seven hundred dollars, Cooper. Who would you buy this for? The Pilates instructor you're banging?" As that last part comes out before I can stop myself, I cringe inwardly.

It doesn't faze Cooper one bit. "I thought I'd give it to my sister. She'd really like this."

"Oh," I respond awkwardly. I didn't even know he had a sister ... because I haven't been neighborly in any way. It's uncharacteristic for Hera residents not to be hospitable and learn everything about new residents. That ship sailed over a year ago when Cooper moved here and I decided he fit into the Wanker Hunks category and must be avoided. "I should give it to you at the wholesale cost. Three fifty."

"No, I'll pay retail. If you could put it in one of those gift boxes you have with your card, that would be good."

He puts the necklace on the table and pulls a wallet out of his back pocket. I put my trembling hand out, palm up, expecting a credit card. Instead, he begins peeling off hundred dollar bills and places them on my palm while I stand there like a statue. I should be thrilled with this sudden monetary injection into our business revenue, which is barley sustaining on life support, yet I feel more like a charity case.

"Did Lauren put this idea in your head? Did she tell you how much the business is struggling, and you thought you'd help the sad, little bead girls?"

Cooper scoffs. "Yes and no. She told me about the problems with the business, but I don't think of you two as the sad, little bead girls." He smiles at that. "There's nothing sad about you, Imogene."

"Huh," I reply with suspicion as I look at Cooper. His eyes narrow at me in turn, mocking me as they crease at the edges with a … a fucking twinkle!

I crumple the bills in my fist, take the necklace, whip around, and walk briskly to the area where we keep packaging supplies. Cooper follows and stands close behind me, watching over my shoulder as I wrap the necklace in tissue and a customized Imogene & Lauren box donned with a silk ribbon woven through our pretty business card. It only took us fifty potential attempts after our preliminary L & I Creations to come up with our not-so-clever business name. While Lauren decided my name was too unique not to use as the headliner, I'm egotistical enough to love it.

"There." I turn around and hand the box to him. "Thank you. Come again," I add without thinking about how it sounds like a sexual innuendo when it's said outside the diner and between a man and a woman in a quiet, private place. This is the perfect opportunity to say something crude. I usually do, so why am I behaving like a virginal mute?

He merely smiles at my sudden gawkiness. "I'm not banging the Pilates instructor, by the way. I stopped seeing her a couple of months ago."

"Okeydokey. None of my business." I scoot him out of the room and then pass him to lead him out of the house.

"I thought you should know since you got a little angry when you mentioned her," he says softly from behind me as I jog down the stairs to get him out the front door as quickly as possible.

"Nope. Not angry," I reply as we reach the first floor where I throw open the front door and walk out to the porch with him right on my heels.

"Really? Because your body language says otherwise."

"How so?" While I internally admit I sound pissed off, I won't say it to him.

"Obvious signs. Your lips are curled under into a thin line, which is hard to do when you have full lips like yours." Before I can react to the comment about my lips, he continues, "And your body went rigid, your arms and hands moving directly in front of your torso, which is a defensive reaction. You scrunched your eyebrows at me, and then your chin went out. You probably didn't notice, but you also took one step back, away from me, at the same time. You were showing anger and distrust towards me. They're little signs and they happen fast, but I'm very good at reading signals."

This is such an odd conversation; I've never heard Cooper talk like this. "Who are you?" My tone sounds disgusted. I can't seem to control myself today.

"Cooper MacKenzie," he laughs. "I'm a regular guy, Imogene. But when I was with the Bureau, doing undercover—NARC, round-the-clock actor, whatever you want to call it—I could profile anyone down to a T. Even though I've switched careers, profiling people, reading them, is still a habit."

"You've never told me anything about your FBI work

20

other than what happened with Emma's father last year."

"You never asked," he says in all seriousness this time.

"I did tell you that Lauren is the official one-person welcome wagon in this town. I'm not known for being … welcoming."

"That's all right." He walks towards the porch stairs and then turns back around. "I have something for you. Wait here."

I watch his perfect butt and bold swagger as he walks to his Harley. He puts the jewelry box in a leather satchel on the side of the bike and then retrieves another object. He walks back to the porch with the same assuredness and smiles as he holds up my lost sandal, letting it dangle from his finger.

"My shoe! I was wondering how I came home with only one. Where did you find it?"

He takes the stairs two at a time, and within seconds, his chest is so close to my face the familiar scent of the laundry detergent on his T-shirt shocks me. *That sexy dream had the same scent.*

"It was in Lois's fountain. After you got tired of chasing Toby through the hedges, I put you in Lauren's car. That's when we realized one of your sandals was missing. I went back to the party and found Toby using it as a boat in the fountain."

Toby, the hedges, the maze … oh, no.

"Did I do anything embarrassing besides needing you to carry me to my bed?" I ask hesitantly, slipping my sandal off his long finger. His hands are large, tan, and rough from working in the factory and on that fixer-upper house of his I've heard about through the grapevine.

"No." He shakes his head.

"Whew, good." I playfully swipe the back of my hand against my forehead.

"Although, you did maul me. Of course, I didn't mind that one bit." He grins, his eyes lighting up as the heat rises in my cheeks.

"Oh, God," I mutter, bringing my hands along with the smelly, dirty sandal up to cover my face.

When I peek at him over my fisted hands, Cooper smirks. "I have to get back to work," I say, annoyed.

"So, we're not going to talk about what happened?" he asks with amusement.

"No. I was drunk. It doesn't count as anything. But thanks for helping me, and I hope your sister likes the necklace."

His smile fades as he nods. "She will."

He stares at me for an extra beat then turns and makes his way back to his bike. Instead of immediately going back inside, I stand there and watch him again because it's just so damn easy to watch a hunky guy stride to his Harley like he has all the time in the world. He knows I'm watching him, too.

"And the answer is no!" he shouts as he turns around and puts on his sunglasses.

"No, what?" I shout in return.

"After you had your tongue down my throat and before you licked my ear, you asked if I had a tattoo on my ass."

While, from behind me, I hear Lauren gasp, I'm mortified again, and he's enjoying this.

Cooper swings a long, muscular leg over his bike and sits back into it like a seasoned pro. That confident posture is amplified with the Harley between his legs. He's smiling and loving the fact that he's shocked me.

"The answer is no," he reiterates as he straps on his helmet.

I stand on the porch, mute and thankful he didn't shout this in the diner or in some other crowded venue.

"And, Imogene," he says. "I enjoyed it."

Fortunately, the roar of the bike's engine breaks the silence as Cooper peels out of our front yard, leaving a trail of dust in his wake.

22

"That was exciting," Lauren exclaims from the doorway.

I turn around and hold up my filthy sandal. "He was just returning my shoe."

"Oh, he was doing more than that," she laughs. "It's like Cinderella."

"Yeah, it's just like Cinderella," I respond with a sneer. "Except there's no glass slipper and no Prince Charming."

"Apparently, there was a whole lot of tongue, though," Lauren responds gleefully.

Four

For the next two weeks, I'm ruthlessly pragmatic in terms of not facing my own humiliation. I decide the best way to save face is to refuse to wait on Cooper during every shift. I astound everyone with my sudden zeal to serve and bus any table that isn't his, completely breaking character from my usual wisecracking, mopey presence. It all comes down to maintaining a vast distance between myself and Cooper, who keeps a watchful, amused eye on me the whole time.

I pretend to be the most attentive, caring waitress to everyone other than him, and it has got to be some of the best acting I have ever done in my life. When I'm not giving one of my Oscar-worthy performances at the diner, I'm holed up at home with Lauren, working and going over prospective business objectives from Archie.

"Hey, remember Yadira Saldana?" Lauren asks, looking at me over her shoulder. "I just got an email from her. She's having a party tonight."

"Yadi?" I put down the necklace I'm working on. "We haven't seen her in at least two years. I thought she moved to Chicago for a job."

"The company went under, so she moved back here. She says she's renting a house with Kimberly Baker."

"Is Kimberly still a librarian?"

Lauren opens the library website on her monitor and reads from it. "She's the Director of Stone Hill Public Library, and it looks like she lined up a job for Yadi, something clerical to help her out. Kimberly works with historic preservation ... documents and buildings according to her bio. It's a little library, so I doubt they pay well, but it sure is a nice title."

"Well, Kimberly was the brainiac in tenth grade English. She was the only one in our class who got an 'A' on her essay of *A Separate Peace*."

Lauren laughs and swivels in her desk chair to face me. "Mr. Enger was so angry at us that day. He said we all turned in sloppy papers. It was June, none of us could think straight. You were the worst, though. You said the characters were elitist, whiny, prep school boys."

"Enger was so pissed at me. It was his favorite book. He said I had no right to disparage great literature. Then he made me memorize the first ten pages of *The Catcher in the Rye* and recite it to the class. I got in trouble again for adding a little speech to the end, saying how much I despise whiny Holden Caulfield. That set Enger off again. I couldn't wait for that school year to end. All I wanted to do was put on a skimpy outfit and head to the Potato Mash to scope out cute guys."

Lauren giggles. "I can't believe we raced out to that place every night to meet guys."

"Nothing says sexy desperation like inappropriately dressed teenage girls at a roadside food stand with giant paper cones of French fries. Gah, we have to go to this party just to see some of the old gang."

Leo decides to meet some friends at a local biker bar, The Rack, where the pool games have the celebrity status of *The Voice*. Clean-cut Leo looks out of place with the hairy, tattooed clientele, but he's earned a lot of respect for his skills in billiards and a spot on the hotshot roster posted on the wall. Honestly, when Leo wears his wire-rimmed glasses, sometimes it's like watching *Harry Potter* go up against the *Sons of Anarchy*. As long as he doesn't come home with a painful wedgie or a broken leg, Lauren lets him put money down on his games.

We arrive at Kimberly's house a little after eight to find people I don't recognize are already spilling out of the house onto the front lawn.

"Lauren! Imogene!" someone screams from the crowded living room as we walk through the front door. Yadi bursts through the people and sandwiches us into a hug. Her black hair has been styled into a pixie cut, showing off her long neck and strong features, dramatic cat eyes with heavy eyeliner, and a wide smile with bright red lipstick.

"You look so different," I say, remembering the girl from high school who had hair down to her butt and didn't wear a stitch of makeup.

"When I moved to Chicago, I decided to reinvent myself. I decided to be braver and put myself out there the way I always dreamed of doing in high school but was too afraid. I finally grew out of my awkward stage."

"It suits you," Lauren adds.

"You look more sophisticated," I nod. "Exotic and pretty."

"Thanks. You two look great, too. I heard you have a serious boyfriend, Lauren."

"He lives with us," I explain. "I'm going to have to find a new home soon."

"His name is Leo and he's wonderful, and Imogene does not have to move." Lauren frowns at me.

"So you're working with Kimberly?" I ask, scanning the crowded room for her.

"Yeah. When I lost my PR job in Chicago, I couldn't afford to live there, so Kimberly gave me a decent administrative job. I like it and the people are so much nicer than the cutthroat PR world. The paycheck is seventy percent smaller, but it's something. Kimberly was already renting this house, so she doesn't charge me much."

"What are the male prospects here?" I ask bluntly.

Yadi sighs. "We're a little low on nice hotties. There

26

are three groups of guys here from what I can figure. There's group one, the immature idiots who wish they were still in high school because they don't want to grow up. Avoid them. Group two is the married guys who are out, pretending they are still single and trying to escape from wives or babies or both. Avoid them. Then there's the third group. They are the nice guys who can actually carry on conversations. They're scattered around here somewhere and about as hard to find as a gold-plated toilet. I have to go stock more wine and beer in the kitchen if you'd like to get a drink."

"I'll help you," Lauren offers and gives me a pointed look.

"Not me. I'm going to check out the guys."

I regret saying that the minute I see Brian Torrance telling some poor, unsuspecting woman a joke about pigs that ends with him asking her to pull his finger. The woman looks around uncomfortably for an escape, and I cover the side of my face and zoom by so Brian doesn't notice me. I squeeze through a group of people and end up behind a tall potted fern. It gives me a moment to scan the room, and that's when I see Cooper.

His back is to me, but I'd know that sexy, shoulder-length blond hair and long V-shaped muscled back anywhere. It's the perfect topping to a nicely packaged butt. Hidden behind him is my old friend, Kimberly. She's a petite woman with an adorable smile framed by honey-colored corkscrew curls. She throws her head back and laughs at something Cooper says.

"Here you are." Lauren pops in next to me, behind the fern. "I got you a beer. Why the hell are you hiding behind this plant?"

"It seemed like a good place to check out some of the guys at this party." I take a swig from the bottle.

"Ugh, I know. I just saw Brian Torrance." Lauren sips from a mini seltzer bottle. "I bet he still picks his nose in

27

public. But there are some nice looking men here, too. Oh! There's Cooper. Look."

"I saw. He's talking to Kimberly."

"Why aren't you going over to say hi?"

"I don't want to interrupt their conversation. Maybe it's private."

Lauren looks at me in disbelief. "We're at a very crowded party, no one is having private conversations. We're supposed to interrupt people and say hello. It's called mingling."

"What if they're dating? How else would he know her?" I sneak another glance at Cooper and look away. The image of him tooling around town on his Harley with Kimberly hanging on to him gives me a stab of annoyance.

"Maybe he was invited by some other friends and met her tonight. I don't know. Let's go talk to them."

"No," I mutter. "Do you know who he's dated? Was he serious with anyone? Leo would tell you, right?"

"Good grief. What has gotten in to you? Why don't you go ask him? The Imogene I know would walk right up to a guy and be very direct with him."

"That was the old me. I don't want him to get the wrong idea."

"What idea? That you're interested in him?" Lauren grins.

"I haven't decided if I am. I have been down this road too many times with a lot of Cooper look-a-likes."

"Oh, blah, blah, blah." Lauren huffs with exasperation. "I have a great idea. I'll pass a note to Cooper and ask him to check the yes or no box for if he likes you."

"This may seem like sixth grade nonsense to you, but I already know he's interested in me. The issue is whether or not this is just about sex, and it more than likely is."

"What has happened to you? You never had dating dilemmas. If you liked a guy, you would let him know. You never sat around, worrying about these kinds of things."

"I'm a little older and wiser. I don't want to spend my time with a guy who isn't serious about me."

"How can anyone be serious about you if you don't date them? Honestly, you're all mixed up lately."

"Okay, how about that guy?"

Lauren follows my gaze to a tall, handsome guy standing across the room with a group of men. He has short, dark hair and a nice build, filling out his jeans and T-shirt perfectly.

"Who is he?" Lauren asks, eyeing him.

"I have no idea, but he's hunky and has a great smile, and there's a plus side to hitting on a guy who isn't known in town and doesn't hang out at our neighborhood diner."

"Really? You're looking for a one night stand now?" Lauren gives me a judgmental glare.

"I'm going to go flirt and see if I'm interested in him."

"Why?" she snaps as I pull her arm and drag her off with me.

"You're my wing girl."

"Yeah, I'd like to wing you," Lauren mutters.

As we approach the group of men, Tall-dark-and-handsome flashes a grin and big brown eyes at me. I smile and he steps forward, pushing a couple of his friends aside.

"Hi, I'm Imogene."

Out of sheer habit, my body language changes. One shoulder dips forward as I take a more poised stance with a hand on my hip and a slightly bent leg with one foot pointed out as if I'm about to pirouette in my platform sandals. I dangle the beer bottle in the other hand, giving maximum stretch across my generous scoop-neck top.

"Oh, brother," Lauren mumbles behind me.

"I'm Anton." His voice is deep as his eyes sweep over me from my red toenails up to my face. He didn't pause at my cleavage before meeting my eyes again. It's an unfair test since my bosom is on display, but I still like to play the little game, if only to humor myself. Some men can't help

29

blinking or staring too long at my chest; however, Anton, like Cooper, must be very experienced at this game.

"This is Lauren." When I point to her with the beer bottle, she reaches out to shake his hand.

"Do you know Yadi and Kimberly?" Lauren asks Anton.

"Yadi is my cousin."

"Really?" I'm surprised since I've never seen him in town. "We went to school with Yadi. You're not from Hera, are you?"

"No, I grew up in Westchester, but my construction firm relocated out here because of the boom in vacation homes. I built a place for myself between here and New Paltz." He has the self-assured grin of a man who has no problem getting women. At least I know exactly what I'm dealing with here.

"One of our best friends is also in the home building business. Have you heard of Blackard Designs? They have a furniture company, and they build these amazing houses." I lay the coyness on a little too thick, but I have Anton's rapt attention.

"I know Carson Blackard. We bid on the same projects. His houses are more expensive because he uses all that high-end *green* material," he says with a dismissive shake of his head.

"Hello, ladies," says a familiar voice from behind me. Then I feel Cooper's strong arm around my neck as he pulls Lauren and me in for a semi-head lock, making me stumble and grab on to his waist, which makes him hold us more securely against him.

This is not the smooth move I was going for in front of Anton. Lauren laughs as I give Cooper a sideways kick to the shin with my platform sandal.

"Hey, Anton. I see you've met two of my favorite people." While Cooper sounds defiant, Anton frowns.

"We were just getting to know each other." I push

away from Cooper to stand up straight again, but he keeps his arms wrapped around the back of our necks, his hands dangling protectively next to our faces. I look sideways at him to see his gray eyes challenging mine.

He smells fantastic, and I can't complain about how good it feels holding onto his hard body, but I don't like getting manhandled when I'm in the middle of my flirting schtick. He's intentionally blowing this for me.

"I'm loving this town already. Hera has some beautiful women," Anton says, smiling at Lauren and then letting his gaze settle on me.

"Yeah. This has been fun." Lauren plucks Cooper's hand off her shoulder. "You'll have to excuse me. I'm going outside to call Leo."

She whispers something in Cooper's ear and then wades through the crowd. There's obviously some bad blood between Cooper and Anton; they look like they are about to duel, and I doubt it's because of me.

"Anton, try my new creation!" Yadi suddenly interrupts with a pink cocktail in her hand, shoving it under his nose.

"Excuse us," Cooper says, moving his arm down to my waist. "Imogene and I need to have a little chat."

Anton scowls as Cooper turns me around forcefully and yanks me by the waist through the crowd until we have a private spot in a hallway.

"Why the hell were you coming on to Anton Pierce?" The anger comes through clearly as he gets in my face.

I look at his lips and back at his eyes as I flatten myself against a wall. "I wasn't coming on to him. We were talking, kind of like what you were doing with my friend Kimberly."

"What?" he asks in disbelief.

"How do you know her?" I shoot back.

"I'm a customer. She talks to everyone."

"A customer? Are we talking about the same thing?"

31

"I don't know what the hell you're talking about, but I actually use the public library. That's how I know Kimberly."

"I heard my name," Kimberly says, rounding the corner of the hallway with a wide smile. "Imogene!" She gives me a big hug, feeling soft and cuddly and sweet, like her disposition.

"I was asking Cooper how he knows you," I say glumly.

"Oh, Cooper comes into the library almost every week." Cooper gives me a smug look. "He likes to go through the old blueprints we have on historic houses, and he checks out a lot of non-fiction. Philosophy, right?"

"Philosophy?" I snort.

"Hey, I have to go help pass out some pink drinks Yadi made. Would you two like some?" Kimberly asks.

"No thanks," Cooper responds. "We're fine."

Kimberly bounces off with her curls bobbing along with her.

Cooper stares at me and leans in with his hand braced against the wall behind me. "Satisfied?" he asks. "Were you talking to Anton about library books? Doubt it. Do you have any idea how sleazy that guy is?"

"No. I didn't get to talk to him—you showed up."

"Good. You're lucky it was me and not Carson. He'd pummel the shit out of that guy if he saw you with Anton."

"He's my friend's cousin; he can't be that bad. You're jealous because he's a business competitor. He said you guys bid on the same projects."

"He doesn't do the same work as us, so he comes in with lower bids. Blackard is doing something unique and it costs money. Our niche market will pay for it, so I wouldn't really call Anton a competitor. But he does sleep around. Word gets around fast. He sleeps with clients, his staff, and every woman he can hit on. He changes partners so fast I'm sure he doesn't bother to ask their name."

32

"I was striking up a conversation; I wasn't planning on sleeping with him."

"Why don't you strike up a conversation with me for a change? Then I wouldn't have to save you from those creeps." As Cooper puffs up a bit, I see that he's not kidding.

"Are you jealous of him?" Normally, this isn't something I would need to ask, but a little doubt is making me wonder if Cooper has an issue with Anton's construction business rather than seeing me with other men.

"Yes," he says emphatically.

"Is it his business that pisses you off?"

"No. Christ, Imogene."

"Well, it's a fair question. I find it hard to believe that you're jealous about me. You say he's a sleaze, but in some circles, women speculate and say the same things about you."

"Oh, really?" Cooper barely smiles. "I think that must be the circle of Imogene and everything Imogene makes up."

"And I'm supposed to believe you check out library books on philosophy and ..."

"Sometimes other things," he replies. " *'He must speak and act openly because it is his to speak the truth.'* "

"What?"

"Aristotle."

"Oh. Huh. Well, you could have gotten that off a bar napkin."

Cooper sighs. "I'll always be honest with you, Imogene. I'm pissed that you'd spend any time talking to that guy. I'd rather you talk to me."

He takes my full beer bottle and places it on a hall table. "Come on." He then takes my hand and leads me through the crowded living room.

"Where are we going?" I ask, trying to keep up with his long stride.

33

"I'm going to have Lauren take you home."

"Wait a minute." I jerk my hand back. "I want to stay. I have friends here that I haven't had a chance to talk to yet."

"You can call them on the phone." He picks me up and cradles me in his arms, much like I remember from that night a few weeks ago. "Coming through!" he yells, and the people part to let us out the door.

"This isn't embarrassing at all," I mutter. Startled by his sudden jog down the porch steps, I fling my arms around his neck.

"Don't worry,"—he smiles at me—"I have you."

"I'd let him cart me off anywhere he wants to go," a young woman remarks as Cooper carries me through a group of people.

"Hear that?" He arches his eyebrows at me.

"The question is why are you doing this?"

He deposits me at Lauren's car which is only a few feet from his bike.

"I'm doing this so you don't make a mistake," he replies, opening the passenger door for me.

"What did I miss?" Lauren shoves her cell phone in her pocket.

"You need to take Imogene home. She's had enough to drink, and she shouldn't be anywhere near Anton."

"I had two sips of beer. I'm painfully sober, and I was only talking to the guy. Who made you the dating guru?" I refuse to sit in the car, so I edge away from the door.

"The last party I saw you at, you jumped me." He puts his hands on either side of me, against the car's roof. "I would hate to see you mistake Anton for me."

"Oh, snap," Lauren says dryly, adding a belated snap for effect. "I'm getting really bored with this tug of war you two keep playing. Get in the car, Imogene. We'll go pick up a pizza." Lauren slides in and starts the engine.

"I have to go to The Rack to make sure Leo isn't

34

getting clobbered by sore losers, so please get in the car," Cooper insists.

"I'm only going because Lauren wants to leave, and I would hate for Leo to be pinned to the dart board by angry bikers."

"You're so thoughtful." He smiles and leans in closer to kiss my cheek. "And, I am jealous enough to make you leave this party. Anything to keep you away from Asshole Anton. I don't trust him."

"And I'm not sure I trust you."

Cooper steps back. "I'm going to work on that, but you have to give me a chance and stop comparing me to other guys."

After I slink into my seat and reach for the door, he doesn't let me close it until he gets in the last word. "And maybe you could stop pretending that I'm invisible when you see me at the diner." He winks and then closes the door.

As we drive away, I watch him put on his helmet and straddle his bike. Before we make it out of the long driveway, Cooper's bike roars ahead of us and loses us on the road home.

Five

"I can't do this much longer," I remind my mother as she gathers laminated menus together.

We're standing behind the long counter, scanning the packed diner. I am, of course, ignoring my tables. I assume they have everything they need, and my regulars are used to my lollygagging lately. The tourists are probably scouring their table for a comment card, something where they can post a lengthy write-up on their inattentive, smart-mouthed waitress. Fortunately, thanks to me, those wretched, little opinion cards had a sad little mishap one day when the whole box of freshly-shrink wrapped cards ended up in the dumpster out back under a pile of discarded produce. Also, my tables are mysteriously missing all of the paper muffin cups we fill with peppermints for the customers.

My parents and grandmother are hopeful that I'll power through this mean phase of mine and either become my usual, crusty self or have a financial boon with the Imogene & Lauren business, enough so that I can hand in my resignation.

"I know it's hard for you," my mother says, "but until the other girls can pick up the full-time hours and your business takes off, these are the breaks, sweetie. Now get to work." She swats my ass with the menus and heads back to the hostess stand.

"Oh, crap," I groan as I watch my section fill up. "I'm so tired of this and so bad at it. I should be fired," I say to Kelly and Samantha, the two high school girls sitting at the counter.

"How is your jewelry business going?" Samantha asks as she slurps on her soda.

"It's going great if you like a life of poverty," I respond, leaning against the counter.

"Your stuff is fabulous," Kelly, the cute blond, says. "Someday, we'll see actresses wearing them on the red carpet at the Oscars."

"Oh, honey, that's sweet. But they wear Harry Winston at the Oscars."

I'm only seven years older than these high school seniors, but I feel ancient.

"Harry who?" the girls ask in unison.

"Diamonds," I reply. "I don't do diamonds. They're out of my league."

"I still love your funky jewelry, and it's so cool that you have your own business," Samantha insists. She's that naïve eighteen-year-old I once was.

"It's a fucking dream come true," I mutter.

"Imogene," my grandmother snaps from behind me. She's sneaky like that. She's supposed to be sitting down and letting my mom handle managing the restaurant, but Grandma Bonnie can't seem to let go of the diner life, the customers she visits with daily, and the general hubbub that goes on. She keeps moving around from the hostess stand, the tables, the kitchen, and to the back office, making sure everything is running the way she wants.

"You're supposed to be sitting down." I point to the stool behind the hostess stand.

"You're supposed to stop cursing. These are impressionable, young women. They don't need to hear the foul things that come out of your mouth, Imogene." My grandmother plants a quick peck on my cheek and ambles over to my mother at the hostess stand.

"Shit," I say and quickly cover my mouth. "Sorry."

The girls giggle.

"Just say the words backwards, then you'll still feel the

joy of swearing without offending anyone. They won't know what you're saying," Kelly explains.

"What?" I half-heartedly listen to her stupid idea while I look out at my tables, wondering if my presence is needed anywhere. Every single person in my section seems to be chewing. That's good enough for me.

"Say *kcuf*! Or *Kcuffing-A*!" Kelly is smiling at my confused expression. "See? I'm saying it backwards, so no one knows I'm swearing."

"Because you're not. It sounds like some kind of nutty language you invented."

"It is," she says with pride.

"So what's the point if you don't get that same immediate satisfaction from letting a curse word rip?" I question.

"You do. Just try it, and you'll feel like you're cursing, but no one will get mad at you for saying it," Samantha continues.

"No, but they'll think I'm crazy."

"So, what else is new?" Kelly says with a laugh.

I'm about to respond when Leo walks in the door with Cooper.

"Oh, kcuf," I snap.

"That's it. See how easy it is?" Kelly asks then swivels in her stool along with Samantha to see what I'm looking at.

"Oh, it's Mr. Yum." Kelly is delighted.

"Mr. Double Yum," Samantha adds.

"Who are you talking about?" I ask testily. They aren't swooning over Leo. It's not his lanky, boy-next-door sweetness that has them enraptured. It's Easy Rider, as Dylan likes to refer to Cooper.

When the guys from Carson's factory come in for lunch, they usually turn heads. Building and hauling furniture gives them very nice, muscle-toned bodies, and the way their dusty jeans show off their cute butts doesn't hurt, either.

Cooper is in the special league, the one with Dylan and Carson. They have the extra potent touch that goes beyond good looks. Women have always adored the Blackard brothers. Carson was adopted so they look nothing alike, but they both tower well over six-feet. Carson with his shoulder-length brown hair and blue eyes, and Dylan with a shaved head riddled with scars that don't deter from his boyish charm. Their good looks do nothing for me, but Cooper is another story. *Kcuf!*

Cooper's hair looks more golden today, as if he's been spending a lot of time in the sun. It frames his sculpted features, giving him a Norse god-like appeal. He's a *kcuffing* Viking. I was never good at geography, and I doubt Mackenzie fits into the Viking surnames, but who gives a *flying kcuf.* I'm getting good at this.

"Cooper is delicious," Kelly says dreamily as she watches him being escorted to a booth by my traitorous mother.

"He's at least ten years older than you. Stop looking at him like that," I hear my mother's voice coming out of my mouth.

"Why?" Samantha laughs. "He's gorgeous. Like a—"

"Like a guy that's too old for you. Seriously, stick to your high school boys," I say bitterly and swipe the counter in front of them with a wet rag.

"That's the problem, they're immature *boys*," Samantha responds.

"I've got news for you, men are just as immature. Most of them are wankers." My riveting lecture doesn't end there. "Didn't anyone teach you about the famous *Just Say No Campaign*? It works on every person and every topic. Stay in school and just say no."

"You lost me at wanker." Kelly sighs.

"What's a wanker?" Samantha asks.

"It's a male kcuffer," I reply dryly.

39

"Oh, please. You dated Cody Aasland, the god of the football team. You went to homecoming and prom together. He must have been a good guy if you stuck with him for your whole senior year." Kelly points her straw at me.

"Yes, I did date Cody, and he was as dumb as a sack of hammers. No offense, but teenage girls aren't always the brightest bulbs when it comes to boys. In college, I dated more beautiful, stupid hammers."

"Hammers and wankers." Kelly rolls her eyes.

"Listen, if there's anything I've learned from my mistakes with men, go for the intelligent ones. Find the guy who is smart and kind."

"Like Jeremy?" Samantha smirks.

"Right," I sigh at my pointless symposium on finding Mr. Right. "Jeremy was intelligent and … kind."

"Last week, you called him a twat," Samantha adds.

"That's because he broke up with me from two thousand miles away, so yes, he's a kcuffing twat." That has the girls giggling. "He was spineless. You need to be selective and date the ones that are smart, kind, and have a spine. And just say *no*. There. That will get you through college. Where are you going by the way?"

"We're both going to NYU." Samantha beams.

"Okay, well, in the city, you really need to learn how to say no."

"Hey," Cooper says to me, suddenly appearing behind the girls.

They both turn and stare at him, saying "Hi!" in unison with frozen smiles plastered on their faces.

Cooper smiles and nods at them.

"Yum," Kelly whispers to herself, yet we all hear it. Cooper glances at her and then back at me with a concerned frown.

"Well, you two just wasted my time," I mutter to them and then give Cooper a shrug. "Sorry, we're real busy. I'll send Lauren over to your table."

"No. I'm sitting in your section. I'll wait for you. I just came over to see how you're doing, but I see you're busy corrupting the next generation." With that, he flashes a smile and walks back to his booth.

My teenage students are still in a foggy rapture from Mr. Yum's presence.

"Imogene," Lauren says angrily as she rounds the counter with an empty tray. "I ran food to three of your tables. I'm in the weeds! Bust a move and get out there, *now*."

"I need you to take Cooper's table."

"No way. He paid me a hundred dollars so you'd wait on him."

"What? Why?"

Lauren pulls the bill from her apron and snaps it in front of my face. "Don't know, don't care. I love you, but today, I love this more. Now get to work."

I walk over to Cooper and Leo's booth, pull my ticket pad out of my apron, and click my pen. "Hi, Leo."

I am every customer's worst nightmare: the disgruntled waitress they fear will spit in their food.

"Hey, Imogene," Leo says as he peruses the menu.

I want to get this over with, but sweet, stupid Leo, who has been ordering the exact same lunch for two years, has his head buried in that damn menu and is ruining my plan to use him as the point man to keep from having to look at Cooper.

"Does it make it healthier if I substitute the bun for a wheat one?" Leo asks.

Goddammit, Leo!

"Of course not," I say, grabbing the menu out of his hands.

I give an annoyed glance at Cooper who is refraining from laughing. Even reclined against the back of the booth, he's tall and fills out the bench. He crosses his arms, stretches out his legs, and then crosses his ankles. As his large, heavy-duty work boots stick out, almost touching my leg, I have the sudden urge to kick them back under the table.

I don't even recognize myself when I'm around him. It's like I'm turning into a twelve-year-old. That, of course, makes me think someone should have been smart enough to come up with a snappy, smartass nickname for me years ago so I wouldn't have to go through life with a deceased relative's old-timey, three-syllable name.

"Imogene, it's quite possible that you are the crabbiest waitress," Leo states, causing a short laugh to escape from Cooper.

"I know, right? I should be fired. So, you guys want two burgers with the works and Cokes?"

When Leo contemplates this for a moment, I want to smack him. The guy hasn't broken his routine in two years, and now he wants to think about it? I'm ready to jam the jumbo laminated menu down his throat.

"Leo?" I ask sharply.

"God. Yes. Burger. Coke. Geesh."

"Wait," Cooper says. "Imogene, I'll have an extra order of fries with mine."

I jot it down, making a point of stabbing the pad with my pen. I'm still not making full-on eye contact with Cooper because I'm reliving the terrible little speech about men I gave moments ago to Kelly and Samantha. I would make a lousy teacher. Probably a lousy mother, too. I wish my parents or grandmother had the balls to fire me today so I wouldn't have to live with this indecision about waitressing anymore, and I wouldn't have to serve Cooper.

"And Imogene?" Now Cooper is just intentionally fucking with me.

"Good Lord, what?" I glance at him quickly.

When Cooper smiles, his gray eyes that screw with my mind finally win over, and I really look at him hard this

42

time. He's incredibly calm about the obvious breakdown I'm having in the middle of the lunch rush. If Dylan were here, I'd beg him for some of his anti-anxiety meds. I have a good mind to march over to Lois's yoga studio, Beyond the Pants, and score some pot from her. She may be sixty-something, but she has more experience than me in the area of drug-induced relaxation. I'm sure she'd be happy to teach me how to use her bong.

"Take it easy, I just want you to ask your dad to make the fries extra crispy. You know how Mark—"

"Yes, I know... -Mark-my-father-fries-crispy-extra... Got it." As I fumble with my pad and pen, the menus shoot out of my hands, smacking Leo in the face. After all my self-control, poor Leo got whacked anyway.

Cooper smiles and collects the menus then stands up and puts his arm around my shoulders and hands them to me. I stiffen under the warmth of his arm.

"Don't scream," he says in a low voice, "but I'd like you to add two slices of cherry pie to that order."

"Do you think, if I put a fork in your eye right now, my family would finally fire me? Today?"

"Let's try it without the fork," he says as he slides back into the booth.

"Let's see if Imogene can make it through lunch without murdering anyone," Leo adds.

"Huh, funny. By the way, I think I need a nickname. Nothing too cute, but something fun and cool. You know, something different to motivate me to start a new career. Why don't you two work on that while I'm gone?"

"Well, that's random and weird." Leo makes a fish mouth, making me realize he's absolutely correct. I need to sit down and take a breather, maybe give Kelly and Samantha more pointers.

"We'll work on it, baby," Cooper says. "Taking that one for a test drive."

"I'll bet *baby* works on all those twinkies you bag," I

43

say, shaking my head.

Leo laughs. "You're going to let her get away with that one?"

"I don't like twinkies, Imogene." Cooper winks at me.

"Don't do that," I retort pointedly.

I leave and make my rounds to the other tables with apologies for my absence. *I got locked in the walk-in freezer!* I'll say anything at this point.

After I serve decaf coffee to everyone who asked for regular and regular to all those who asked for decaf and give away free ice cream to all the kids whose parents said *no sugar!*, I return to Cooper's table with a huge tray and an obnoxious amount of food for two people. The *Bonnie Burger* is more than half a pound of beef, piled with guacamole, bacon, and sides of truffle waffle fries and regular fries. Watching the big dudes from Carson's factory scarf these things down every day has sworn me off them forever.

"Don't worry, I ate seven of the fries off your plate to make sure they are perfect," I say to Cooper.

"Good girl."

"Don't say that," I demand, wedging the tray under my arm.

"Sit down with us and take a break," he insists.

"I've been on a break all day. I need to make my rounds and at least put some effort into ignoring my customers. Why are people always so hungry and needy?"

A whoop from another table causes me to turn around. Archie is walking into the diner with a rifle propped on his hip.

"Holy crap. Why is he carrying a gun in here?" I ask no one in particular.

"That's an antique musket. It's probably older than those vintage lockets you like so much," Cooper says, rubbing a hand over the blond stubble on his chin.

"Are you sure?"

"Yeah, I think I know weapons. I worked a case where these arms dealers were moving tons of illegal … never mind. That musket looks like it's more than a hundred years old, and it's missing the hammer and trigger, so it's not operational."

I scoff and storm over to Archie.

"Isn't this a beauty? I just bought it at the Murphy estate sale. The place is incredible," Archie says, posing with the relic across his chest. "It's from the Civil War."

"I don't care if it's from War of the Worlds. Arch, you can't bring that thing in here; you're scaring the customers."

We both look around at the diners who are nonchalantly enjoying their lunch.

"Really? You're not afraid of a lawyer in a three-piece suit?" I address the crowd. "Not even when he's holding a gun? You should be scared. He's a lawyer with a gun!"

The customers laugh and someone says, "It's a musket."

I scowl and walk back to the kitchen, catching Cooper watching me with that hideous, disgusting … sexy as all hell grin.

I do the bare minimum of clearing dirty dishes and helping Lauren serve the rest of the lunch crowd, who I had decided are all her customers. After avoiding their booth for a good forty-five minutes, I make it back to Leo and Cooper.

"I hope you're aware that I had to go re-fill my own Coke," Leo says, holding up his glass. "I think you've lost it, Imogene, and your grandmother is in full agreement with me."

While Cooper is biting his lip to keep from laughing, I notice he has polished off every morsel on his plate. Even the empty French fry dish and the two pie plates are wiped clean. Where do these guys pack it away? They don't have an ounce of fat on them.

"Thank you for your highly qualified medical diagnosis, Leo. You're not telling me anything I don't already know."

"Here, you beautiful ball buster, you." Cooper hands me their bill and a wad of rolled cash.

"Nope. That's not going to work as a nickname." I take their dishes and Cooper's money, walking back to the kitchen where I dump the plates at the dishwasher station. Then I sit at the employee break table to make change for Cooper's bill.

I pull out the trucker's wallet from my apron. Cooper and Leo's lunch ticket is less than forty dollars, but when I unroll the money Cooper gave me, I count three one-hundred dollar bills. This guy is too much. I walk back out to the dining area, prepared to give him his exact change back, all two hundred sixty-seven dollars and thirty-eight cents of it.

The booth is empty.

"Be back in a few minutes," I say as I walk by Lauren and out of the diner.

I walk a few yards up the street to Blackard Designs. When I pop through the front door, I receive a big, friendly wave from Daisy, the receptionist.

"Where's Cooper?" I ask, not stopping because I know exactly where he is.

"He's back in the factory." Daisy motions with her hand.

I nod as I continue down the hall and past the management offices until I come to the factory window. The factory is an extension the size of an airplane hangar. It houses a lot of timber and hardware that is eventually transformed into furniture and has a couple of large, open fire ovens used to weather the wood to give it that aged look. It also has some incredibly loud equipment.

The place is buzzing with employees: men and women hauling wood, working table saws, and guys who are

46

baking wood. This is Cooper's territory.

I'm gazing through the enormous, industrial window to the factory, looking for the manager of operations—that Viking I'd simultaneously like to slap and kiss—when the door to the factory opens. Carson enters my quiet, observation space, removing his safety glasses and heavy work gloves.

"Imogene, what are you doing here?" he asks, tossing the glasses and gloves into a bin by the door.

"I'm looking for Cooper," I reply, my eyes roving the large factory for him. "Bingo. I see him."

"Ah, crap," Carson mutters. "You look angry. You're not going to kill him, are you? It took years to find someone who can run this place better than me."

"I'm going to have a word with him. Well, maybe five words. There will be no blood shed, though."

"Put on the safety gear before you go in there. And no crossing the blue lines," he orders.

"Yeah, yeah."

"I smell French fries," he says, wrinkling his nose.

"It's me," I snarl. I generally don't walk around in my diner duds; the black T-shirt and jeans with hair that smells like a deep fat fryer after every shift.

"I need lunch," he says absently and exits down the hall.

I put on a pair of the clear, plastic glasses and the large gloves that feel like oven mitts and then barge into the factory, weaving around workers and equipment, making sure I don't step over the areas marked by blue tape.

Cooper is talking to a group of employees, examining wood they've pulled from the oven. I stand at the edge of the blue tape and wave my hands like one of those airport ground crew members that holds the orange paddles to help navigate an airplane as it taxis in. I sure could use a pair of those paddles to get Cooper's attention.

I'm about to shout over the noise of the machinery

when he finally looks at me. He says something to the men and then comes my way with an easy, long gait and a smirk.

"Are you trying to get my attention?" he asks as he approaches.

"You need bullhorns in here."

"I could spot you a million miles away," he responds. "You're like a Trident missile coming in."

"You're hilarious, and here's your money back." I whip the bills and coins out of my apron and pick up his hand to slap the money in his palm in a dramatic fashion to make my point.

"That was meant for you." He lowers his voice, sounding disappointed as his fist closes around the money.

"I know what you're doing, Cooper. It's nice of you, really, buying my jewelry and throwing bills at me and Lauren at every opportunity. But this has to stop. This isn't going to change our situation. Lauren and I have to deal with our business and our current finances. I think we can both agree that I don't deserve this huge tip, and this sudden interest of yours to give us wads of cash makes me feel like a charity case."

"I want to help you," he says, shoving the money in his pocket.

"And I appreciate it. I do. But Lauren and I have a handle on this. So, thanks, but no thanks." When I turn to leave, Cooper takes my elbow and presses close to me.

"That's the problem. You don't have a handle on your business, and you're too afraid to quit working at the diner, so you're in limbo," he says roughly as he walks me to a side door that leads outside to the employee parking lot.

Pulling me into the bright sunshine, he takes his safety glasses and gloves off. I stand there dumbly, watching him, thinking of something clever and possibly rude to say. However, I'm mostly enjoying the view of how his broad chest and nicely developed biceps fill out his T-shirt.

He quickly yanks my glasses and gloves off and pushes me backwards against the brick wall of the building. I'm about to reprimand him for unnecessary roughness, but then his mouth is on mine, kissing all of the snarky sense out of me. His tongue roves around mine like it owns me, causing a small moan of approval to escape me for his excellent kissing skills. Without caring that we may be on exhibition to anyone walking by, my hands slip around his waist as his hands slide up my arms before cradling my head firmly in place for a deeper kiss.

Brushing his lips against mine, he then lets his beard stubble caresses my cheek before his head drops into the crook of my neck and he sighs.

He just made my day with that kiss.

"Damn, you smell good," he says into my neck. "Like French fries."

I pinch his side hard.

"I love French fries," he adds, laughing.

"Stop doing this, Cooper. I have to get back to work." I push him off me.

"Hey, I'm just reciprocating. You were the one who kissed me at the party.

"We both know I was very drunk that night. I probably would have made out with any guy that crossed my path."

"You're perfectly sober now," he retorts, holding me in place by the waist. "And we both know you enjoyed this kiss."

"I'm pretty sure I'd enjoy kissing Wolverine, too, but I don't have time for him today, either. Now let me go," I say as I try to wriggle from his grasp.

"Wait," he commands. I stop moving because my hormones are signaling my brain to listen to the sexy Viking. "What time do you get off work?"

"Why?"

He drops his head down so his nose is almost touching mine. "Imogene, answer the question."

"I'm going back to do the shift clean up, and then I'm heading home in about a half hour. Why?"

"Good. I'm leaving here at four. I'm going to run home and shower, and then I'm picking you up at five and taking you to that estate sale Archie mentioned."

I look at him in confusion. Since when do Cooper and I go shopping together? Since when do we do anything together other than these two unintended make out sessions?

"Arch said they have a lot of jewelry there, and Lauren said you two need more pieces because your inventory is low."

Between staring at his eyes and his perfectly kissable lips and hearing him talk about taking me to shop for jewelry, I'm quite dumbfounded at the moment. It takes me a few seconds to gather my thoughts.

"Cooper, our inventory is low for a reason. We don't have the funds to buy the good pieces right now."

"It's a catch-22. Whether you have the money or not, you need new pieces to make the jewelry, right? So, if you don't purchase more stock, you can't make more things and the business dies. So I'm taking you there to stock up."

"Stock up? This isn't like buying canned goods at the grocery store. Those antique lockets and beads are expensive."

"Right. I have to get back inside to deal with a minor problem, but be ready at five. Five o'clock. I'm always on time, Imogene." With that, he tweaks my chin lightly before heading back through the side door.

What just happened? I kissed the guy who's the type I'm not supposed to kiss, *ever again*. Then I made plans with him, or rather, he made plans *for* me.

I head back to the diner and finish my clean up before the night crew arrives. As I turn in my sales, I realize the enormous tip Cooper left me is back in my apron. Somehow, the sneaky bastard managed to slip it back in my

apron pocket while we were kissing.
That kcuffing, sneaky, sexy bastard.

Six

After freshening up and getting rid of the infamous grease stench from the diner kitchen, I put on some clean jeans, a sleeveless blouse with a modest neckline, and a pair of flats since I'm assuming Cooper will be picking me up on his Harley. I'm pretty excited about that; I even caught myself with a goofy grin thinking about it while I was putting on mascara.

Yes, I'm actually sprucing myself up for Cooper. Maybe it was the kiss, maybe it's because I've spent a year being pissed off at Jeremy for taking a job in California and moving away, only to fall off the grid like a fugitive.

Jeremy was supposed to be my reform boyfriend. After all the shitheads I dated, I was done with falling for the gorgeous assholes. Jeremy was my unassuming, rather average-looking boyfriend who, for several months, treated me like I was a precious gift.

In hindsight, that was part of the problem; I was happy to be in a different kind of relationship, and Jeremy was just happy to have any kind of relationship. I should have known we were headed nowhere. I had felt it in my bones. I was hanging on to a guy who was gentle and intelligent, and we started out with the kind of sweetness that happens when a bashful guy gets up the nerve to ask out a woman he thinks is out of his league. Perhaps it's egotistical of me to say that, but it's true, and yet, I still tried to make it last, ending up shocked that he could break up with me. Also egotistical yet true.

I assumed it was the excitement and stress of starting a new job thousands of miles away that kept Jeremy from talking about our future. Therefore, we didn't discuss details about where we were headed; we kept saying we'd do long distance for a while and then the conversation would always end there.

It certainly ended, and what a role reversal it was for me. After I hugged and kissed Jeremy goodbye, I received one text that he'd moved into his new apartment, and then blip, the guy was gone, never to be heard from again, never returning my calls or texts.

More than heartbroken, I was humiliated over being dumped. Naturally, I was sad, and then I was *mad*. After Jeremy, every man who attempted to ask me out met my sharped-tongued alter ego, a mean bitch who'd ram a hot poker up their ass if she were given the opportunity.

I can't explain why I was so angry, except that I thought I had carefully selected a better man this time around. Plain guys like Jeremy weren't supposed to turn into spineless shits. Obviously, my sweeping generalizations about men and dating have been off the mark, and my failed relationships have resulted in making me cynical more than anything.

I can't even say that I've actually experienced real heartache. You have to fall wildly in love first for that to potentially happen. I have had many lust-filled crushes that ignited and burned out before the calendar would be flipped over to the next month, and it never bothered me. I was that type of girl: crush on him, swoon over him, have sex with him, fight with him, get bored with him, then dump him. That seemed to be the only type of relationship that could be fostered in high school and college, at least for me.

Then Cooper came to town, all six and half feet or whatever of him. He's taller than Jeremy. I know because they had one week where their schedules overlapped at Blackard Designs, and I remember sizing Jeremy up to Cooper. That should have been a red flag to me.

Jeremy came into the diner with Cooper for lunch, and

while Jeremy rambled on about this elusive interview Carson had hooked him up with in California, I was eyeing Cooper. Not in an obvious way, but you can't *not* look at the guy. He stands out that much. For the love of God, a hot guy moved to town who wasn't like a brother to me. However, I wasn't about to become friendly with Cooper, even after Jeremy fled with his shriveled pecker between his legs, because I was still working off my dumb theory about men.

Cooper has paid dearly for my prickly personality over the last year, but after these recent events—a drunken kiss, a sober kiss, and an upcoming social outing—maybe I can try to be friends with him after all.

I'm attempting to play it cool in front of Lauren, and for my benefit, she's acting like it's no big deal that her favorite biker, whom I have portrayed as my nemesis for many months, is taking me out to peruse an estate sale.

"Don't forget the business credit card," Lauren says as I pop into the workroom to see her current project. "It's still in the freezer."

"I can't use it if it's frozen."

"Imogene, people put their credit cards in blocks of ice so they can't overindulge with them. You put ours in the freezer next to the vodka. The card may be cold, but it works. You can spend up to two thousand. That's affordable in terms of payments and interest."

"I hate that."

"I do, too, but we need the good stuff to make the next twenty designs we have. If we can get them done in the next two weeks, Sasha's will buy them all. So please don't back out of this auction like you did last week at the Goodman estate."

"Maybe you should go to the Murphy place with Cooper. You're more pragmatic about this stuff."

"Oh, no. I'm still doing the bead designs," she says, holding up a fistful of colored markers. "I want all the design sheets done by tomorrow so we can start filling the trays. That's going to take fucking forever."

"Then let's make some less elaborate necklaces."

"No, Sasha's likes our big three-tiered ones with the showy lockets and the drop pearls. If you can get some jet pieces, do. I'd love to put some Edwardian beads into these new designs."

"I'll do my best." I sigh, thinking of the cost, even at estate sales where they are highly motivated to negotiate a price down.

Lauren pauses in her work and regards me for a moment. "You look different. Nice."

"Didn't I look nice at Yadi's party?"

"Yes, but today you look better, more relaxed or carefree. Something is different, and it kind of lights up your face."

That's because a Viking reminded me what it's like to have worn out, bruised lips from a passionate kiss. I admit, the irony of the situation has made me happier than I've been in a long time. I did not expect it to come in the way of Cooper Mackenzie.

"I have no idea what you are talking about. This is nothing special. Archie started this whole thing by telling us about the estate sale and mentioning the jewelry, so we're going to check it out. That's all this is."

"Okay," she replies softly and smiles as though she doesn't want to set me off on one of my unflattering Cooper rants. I can't blame her there.

"Okay, then, so I'm going to go get our very cold credit card out of the freezer," I say, checking the time on my phone. "And I'm going to meet him out front. He said he's always on time."

"He is." Lauren nods her head. "He's very punctual. And tidy. Very tidy for a guy."

"Now you're being weird. I'm going."

"All right, but don't kick Cooper in the balls, it

wouldn't make for a good date. Have fun. He's a nice guy."

"It's not a date. Cooper insisted on taking me to this because he wants our business to do well. He's doing this for you because you're his friend … and Leo is his best friend."

"All righty. If you say so." She smiles and quickly goes back to her various drawings.

I huff and leave her to her work. I don't want to discuss this new wrinkle in my stay-away-from-Cooper plan.

I retrieve the frigid credit card from the freezer, grab my purse, and head out the front door in time to see Cooper arriving. He comes up the dirt driveway, straddling his hog with the whole package: sunglasses, black helmet, faded jeans, and a white T-shirt. On top of that, he's got a sexy, wide smile. What woman wouldn't want this man picking her up for a … a friendly shopping excursion?

Seven

Cooper gets off his Harley in one sleek motion of grace and power and hands me an extra helmet from the back of the bike.

"So, you don't mind riding on my bike?" he asks, lifting his shades and studying me from head to toe before settling on my face.

He's noticed that I don't resemble the French fry girl from earlier. My ponytail is gone, and my hair has been freshly washed and styled in long, loose waves. My skinny jeans show off my nice ankles, the only part of me that never gains weight, and I'm wearing my ballerina flats which are more flattering than the black running shoes I wear at work. And, yes, I have highlighted my eyes with liner and eye shadow and worked some magic on my chapped lips. No cleavage, but from Cooper's reaction, I've managed to transform the pissy waitress into a more pleasant, feminine version of that chick.

"Why would I mind riding on your bike?" I ask, strapping the helmet on.

"Some women get nervous on my ... on these things. They're loud and ..."

"Pfft! Your bike is the only reason I agreed to go with you to this auction."

Cooper smiles. "I told you to be ready, but I don't think you ever agreed."

"Well, I'm ready, so let's go before I change my mind."

Once Cooper swings his leg back on his bike, he revs it up for show. "Hop on and hold on tight, baby."

"Don't call me that," I say as I slip on my sunglasses.

He chuckles seductively, and just for that, I wrap my arms around him extra tight. Although, instead of holding his waist, I have one arm across his stomach and the other across his chest. It's sort of an erotic stranglehold.

Sometimes, I like to call guys on their flirty behavior, and for the most part, they're generally surprised. Cooper's no exception. I feel him startle under my groping hands, and then he exhales slowly as if to calm himself.

When we hit the county road at top speed, I lean as close as I can to his ear. "Oooh, I'm so scared!" I shout into the wind then feel Cooper's booming laugh under my hands as every hard muscle vibrates.

It takes us a good forty minutes to find the stately home outside of Woodstock. Whoever lived here had money; the Victorian house and immaculate grounds have been well preserved.

I let go of Cooper's warm body and swing myself off the bike, which is not easy to do in snug, skinny jeans. My legs still feel hot and wobbly from the reverberations of the bike; as a result, I do a full-length stretch and arch as I take in the surroundings of the home; the landscaping; and all the cars that are parked in the large, semi-circle driveway. As I stand up again, Cooper is suddenly in front of me, gently removing my sunglasses. It's a completely innocent, helpful gesture, but as his fingers graze my face, my eyes pause a little too long on his.

"That wasn't so bad, was it?" he asks in a low voice.

"The ride was fine," I reply, my gaze going from his eyes to his lips. I must have a dazed expression because Cooper begins unfastening my helmet.

"Let me get this for you." His voice draws my attention back to his beautiful eyes.

Of course, everything about him is gorgeous in the setting sun on a glorious spring day. This guy's assets shine: the tousled hair; the sun-kissed skin; the tall, hard body that apparently I've already had the opportunity of climbing.

After he takes the helmet off me, I'm about to reach up and run my fingers through my hair to fluff it when I see that tenacious look in his eyes. He's going to kiss me again.

"No, we …" I'm cut off by his lips that lightly graze my own.

"Yes, we can," he mumbles and pushes into my eager mouth. His hand wraps around the back of my neck as he kisses me thoroughly until I'm well acquainted with his tongue … again.

When he pulls back and studies my sated expression, his mouth curves with satisfaction.

"See? We can do that. We do it very well."

"Cooper, we're starting to become friends. I think. I don't want to be the kind of friends that screw around with each other, though. I have no interest in that."

He sighs, annoyed. "I never said I wanted to be friends with benefits."

"Okay … good. Then we're on the same page," I add, nodding my head. "And I have something for you."

When I open my small wristlet purse and pull a wad of cash out, Cooper's expression visibly darkens. "It's your cash. I can't keep your tip, and I can't sell my friend a necklace at my retail prices. I can't take your money because it makes me feel like a failure."

Cooper is silent as he looks at the cash I'm holding out to him. He's not making a move to take it; therefore, I grab his hand and put it in his palm. It's a replay of what happened earlier in the day, and at the time, Cooper was more generous, maybe a little miffed yet laughing about it. However, now he appears to be quite pissed off.

"If we're really *friends* as you put it, then this wouldn't be a problem because friends help friends."

"I gave you the necklace at cost because, when friends start loaning or giving cash to other friends, it becomes weird and uncomfortable. I am very uncomfortable with this," I explain.

"Then it appears we have a serious fucking problem with our *friendship*," he punctuates with disgust.

"Please, keep the money this time. Lauren and I are handling the business, and we have Archie coming onboard. I can do this without taking money from you, but I really appreciate—"

"When you started the business, you accepted money from Carson, right?" he says, cutting me off in a clipped tone.

"Ah ..." Boy, this is not what I wanted. We went from fun, social banter and a few stolen kisses to accusations and hurt feelings.

"Lauren told me," he explains. "So, you don't have a problem accepting money from your friend Carson."

"That's different. It was a small loan, and he's practically my brother," I say in my defense. "It's not weird between us."

"Okay, so it's me." He steps closer and blocks out the remaining sunlight as he towers above me, observing my silence. "I have my answer," he says as he removes his wallet from his back pocket and puts the bills in it.

"What answer?"

"Accepting money or help from me is awkward for you because I'm a different kind of friend to you. I'm the friend you're actually interested in."

I scoff while I think of a clever comeback, but words evade me because this guy is on to something I have not been willing to admit to anyone else. I am attracted to him, although he's another distraction from what I'm supposed to be doing—working hard at running a business.

"A few kisses doesn't mean I want more than that. We're friends," I reiterate, as if it makes it truer.

"Yeah." He puts his arm around my shoulders and guides me towards the house. "Let's go buy stuff, friend."

While Cooper gets lost in the living room where the military artifacts are on display, I head into the enormous dining room where the jewelry is being sold. The expensive pieces include diamonds that are encased in locked table vaults and being sold as individual pieces. The less expensive, antique jewelry is showcased on velvet trays and being sold off in numbered lots.

I walk around every table, studying the stunning jewelry which even includes some broken or incomplete necklaces and earrings from the Georgian, Victorian, and Edwardian time periods. This is exactly what Lauren and I look for—vintage jewelry we can disassemble and repurpose into our own designs.

"Hey, look what I got," Cooper says from behind me.

I turn around to see him brandishing a large sword. Now he really does look like a Viking, and he's got the attention of every woman in the room.

"Oh, God, not you, too. What is with you men and weapons?"

"This thing is so cool," he says as he puts an arm behind his back and swings the blade upward, ready to duel.

"Stop it. You're going to get us kicked out of here," I whisper loudly to him.

"I don't think so. I'm advertising their products. Besides, I dropped a nice little bundle on this beauty."

"You bought it?"

"Hell, yeah." He smiles, looking pretty proud of his acquisition.

"What are you going to do with that?" I ask, imagining him cruising around town on his bike with a swashbuckling sword strapped to his side. Oh, good grief. I have to stop thinking of him like that.

"The blade is completely dull and useless, but it'll be nice for party tricks."

"Perfect."

"What did you find?" he asks, sheathing the sword and stepping forward to look at the table I've been salivating over.

"Everything here is fantastic. They have the jewelry set up by the period it's from. The family that lived here collected some incredible pieces."

I feel Cooper's warmth as he presses against my side to view the velvet tray in front of me.

"Lauren wants me to get the jet jewelry. Those are these black, Edwardian beaded pieces in this lot. I really want the Victorian silver lockets over there. They're similar to what you bought for your sister."

"Great, let's buy all these boxes," he says, and one of the middle-aged auction women standing behind the table gets a little giddy, either over the idea that she thinks he's buying the whole table or that she has a smoking hot guy standing two feet from her. I'm betting it's the hottie factor.

"Are you cuckoo for Coco Puffs? Each one of these trays is anywhere from six hundred to three grand. You're not buying anything for me, and I'm only buying one lot because that's what Lauren and I agreed on."

Cooper looks at the auction attendant, nods his head to the side towards me, and rolls his eyes, causing her to give him a little laugh. He's very practiced at winning the female population over, so I smack his side to make him stop.

He leans down to whisper in my ear. "If you do things like that, people will think we're more than friends."

"Thanks for the heads up." After I push his face away from my cheek and inform the woman which tray I want, she hands me the lot number and purchase card.

"I'm going to go pay for my goodies," I tell Cooper. "Be right back."

Heading into the foyer where they have cashiers set up, I turn over my lot number and credit card. After they ring me up and give me a receipt, I return to the dining room to collect my purchase. Cooper is talking up the auction attendant and has her in stitches over something. *That kcuffing charmer.*

After I hand her my receipt, she turns over my packaged items to Cooper! I immediately take the bag from him. "I'm ready to go. Lauren will be excited to see this."

"Are you sure? There's more here, and I know you love this stuff." He sounds so thoughtful and concerned. I have to glance away when a blond lock falls forward, and he has that adorable questioning look along with the ridiculousness of a ginormous sword at his side.

"I'm sure. I've spent my max. And how are we getting that thing home?" I ask, pointing to his sword.

"They're holding it for me. After I drop you off, I'm going to bring Leo's truck back to pick it up. The auction will still be open."

"Okay, so can we go?" I shrug.

"Whatever you want," he says as his hand rests on my lower back and he turns me away from the table. At that moment, I catch him give a quick wink and smile to the woman who just helped me.

"What the hell was that wink for?" I ask as we leave the lovely home. "Did you hit on her?"

Cooper laughs. "No, I was just being friendly since she was so friendly in assisting us."

"You mean assisting me. Man, you sure are *friendly*." I overemphasize the word with a deep, snarky punch. "You should take over my shifts at the diner, what's left of them. The customers would love you."

"Imogene, I'm teasing you. Sometimes I like getting a rise out of you. You're sexy and lethal," he says and hands me my helmet.

The ride back is easier. I feel less tense about our situation. I think I clarified the friend set-up fairly well, and

I bought some vintage jewels without completely stressing myself out. Having Cooper along to reassure me and to lighten the mood definitely made it easier. Being all cozy and warm, snuggled up to him on the Harley didn't hurt, either. Unfortunately, those are the kinds of things that blur the friendship lines, and I'm notorious for blurring things, so much so I'm practically blind.

When we return to my house, Leo walks out onto the porch and tosses his truck keys to Cooper.

"How did he know you needed the truck?" I ask, attaching my helmet to the back of his bike.

"I called him while you were paying for your stuff." He takes off his leather bike gloves and then pulls my jewelry bag from the satchel.

"Good thinking."

"Are you happier?" he asks as he hands me my bag.

With it being kind of a loaded question, I don't know how to respond. I begin running the scenarios of the past few days through my head: my behavior with Cooper; divulging my concerns about the business; potentially quitting my most reliable source of income; defining boundaries for an emerging friendship between us; and then, naturally, dwelling on those hot and heavy kisses that negate all my previous arguments I thought were so rational.

"I love this," I finally respond, waving the bag. "Thanks for insisting I go, and thanks for taking me. I had a really good time."

"I know you did. It's written all over your face. And I had a great time, too. So when's our next date?"

After all that, I laugh. "It wasn't a date. You're something else."

"I'm something you like. Remember, I'm very good at reading people. My former job used to depend on it."

"Even so, it wasn't a date."

"Call it what you want," Cooper says with a shrug. "So

when are we going out again as friends?"

He is tenacious and I'm flattered, but I can totally envision a relationship with Cooper as the kind that ignites in a lusty frenzy and burns out just as quickly. As such, he's probably not a wanker, but the thought of having a potentially destructive fling with a guy who is part of my circle of friends is enough for me to keep him at arm's length. Apparently, however, that arm is very short if I keep kissing him. Yes, that's a problem.

"Lauren and I have to buckle down and really get to work on some necklaces that a store will purchase if we meet their deadline. So I don't really have time for any social outings. With anyone," I emphasize.

Cooper glances at Leo's truck as though he's ready to bolt without another word.

"Hey, Coop!" Leo returns and suddenly shouts from the porch. "Wait up!"

Leo runs down the steps and jogs over to us.

"Is something wrong?" Cooper asks.

"No, I need to talk to you, so I thought I'd take you to get your sword thing."

"Okay," Cooper replies with that shrug again. He then looks down at me with an indecipherable expression.

"I'll see you around. I'm going to get some work done," I say joyfully in a rehearsed manner. That's not like me, making me fully expect my phoniness to cause a little fire and brimstone action; perhaps my hair will start smoking or my head will turn into a swarm of hissing snakes.

"Humph," Cooper grunts and grabs my shoulders, pulling me in for a quick kiss, enough to nip my lips.

Hot damn.

Eight

How does this keep happening?

Is it really possible that my one drunken episode has caused this domino effect so that every time Cooper sees me he feels entitled to kiss me? It's not like I'm fighting back or cursing him out. I realize I'm letting this happen. I keep talking friend-zone shit and boring myself to death with my pithy rationalizations, and then I let my tongue do whatever it wants when Cooper touches me.

Leo looks unperturbed by the incident as he jumps in the truck and waits for Cooper.

Cooper cups my cheek. "You'll probably see me sooner than you think."

"I guess," I concede since he's clearly outmaneuvering me at every turn.

While they drive off to go back to the Murphy estate, I trudge into the house, replaying the last few days with Cooper over in my mind. It *was* my kiss and bold behavior at the party that started this whole series of events. I changed our relationship from that of a standoffish acquaintance on my part to something more potent that's brewing in both of us.

I drop my purse on the front hall table and kick off my shoes before walking upstairs to the workroom where Lauren is finishing the designs. She's quite a talented artist when it comes to drawing the details of each necklace pattern. She lays them out like a blueprint where each bead is marked with a code that correlates to a specific bead size and color. Her drawings look like paint-by-number pictures in that respect, and it makes it very easy for us to fill the bead trays and see what the actual necklace will look like before we string them on the various jewelry wires and add the hooks and closures.

"You're going to love what I got," I exclaim as I take the items out of the bag and reveal the exquisite pieces to her.

"They're gorgeous." She picks up the necklace with the largest black, faceted teardrop and fifty smaller carved black beads. It has some engraved silver balls interspersed and some muted, chipped gemstones. The clasp is broken and some of the beads are missing, but we'll remove the good parts and incorporate it into some of Lauren's new designs. That's how each piece of jewelry we design becomes one-of-a-kind. We can't replicate a single necklace with the exact same beads because we only have one of everything when it comes to the vintage pieces. When they are strung together with new Swarvoski crystals or vibrant gemstones, they become our own little masterpieces.

"The broker there gave me this whole lot, all ten pieces, for seven hundred."

"You did great. I'm so excited about this new batch of designs. Sasha's is going to love it. Seriously. I bet business will take off."

"I hope you're right." I sit down next to her, ready to get to work.

"There's something I have to tell you." Lauren's eyes have sort of glazed over, hiding whether she's about to tell me something sad or if she's holding back enthusiasm.

"Is it bad?"

A smile spreads slowly across her effervescent face. "No, it's really good," she beams. "It wasn't planned, and it wasn't exactly prevented, but now … I'm pregnant."

My jaw drops, a joke about protection immediately coming to mind, but then I see she is serious. My best friend is pregnant. Lauren is going to be a mother. If anyone plays her cards right in life, it's Lauren. She doesn't do anything half-assed, and frankly, I'm lucky to have a friend like her giving me advice and confiding in me; as a result, I have to be happy for her.

Her face watches me with concern because I'm taking much too long to react. The longer I gasp in silence, the more it comes across as judgment.

"Oh, Lauren," I utter softly and reach over to hug her.

She exhales in relief and squeezes me hard. "You're going to be an auntie."

"Okay, let's not get ahead of ourselves. I'm going to be a step-sister," I correct her, and she laughs against my shoulder.

"There's more."

"Oh, my God, you're having twins?"

"Leo and I are getting married in a month. We wanted to have a wedding at the end of summer, but the baby news has pushed it up. Since it's early, we don't want to tell people, other than our closest friends and our parents. So I want to get married before I start showing. We have four weeks to get it planned and organized, but I think I can pull it off."

"Jesus! I'm still on the *'I'm pregnant'* part!"

Lauren bursts out laughing. With her being overjoyed, I must tread lightly when it comes to my cynicism. A baby and a husband and a little business with me—she has everything she has dreamed of, and I feel genuinely happy for her. If she weren't pregnant, I'd call in the reinforcements for an alcoholic celebration.

"You're having a baby and getting married ..."

"Wedding first, baby six months after, and I want you to be my maid of honor."

"Yes, I'd like that." I laugh, trying to think of what those duties entail.

"We're skipping over the little parties. I don't want you to plan anything like that. You're my best friend,

Imogene. I just want you by my side when I marry Leo and when I have this little human." She's almost in tears.

"I can do that. I can." I nod vigorously as if I've been asked to join a special task force. Truthfully, before this, I've only been a tipsy bridesmaid. I have never been asked to be the maid of honor, and I haven't had any friends give birth yet. We're entering a new phase in our adult lives, and it's time for me to step up to the plate for my friend.

"It's going to be fine, right?" Lauren asks me, the least knowledgeable person on marriage and parenting.

"Yes, just tell me what I need to do."

"Leo is telling Cooper right now. That's why he decided to go with him tonight, so he could ask him to be the best man."

"Cooper is the best man?" I ask, envisioning him standing in a tuxedo at the altar with a sword.

"Yeah, and we're going to call Carson and Jess and Dylan and Emma when Leo gets back. We want all of you to be in the wedding party. We already told our parents this afternoon."

"Uh-huh," I reply, realizing the others are married couples, and once again, Cooper and I will be the only single people in the group, except this time, we'll be matched up with duties.

"Since we're pressed for time and you and I have a big deadline, the wedding plans will be simple. Leo wants us to do one last outing together before we get married, like a camping trip," she explains, and this is where my mind goes into a foggy state of *'oh fuckerooni'!* Lauren rambles on about dance classes and some state park, and I only hear verbs: dancing, grilling, and hiking.

"Did you say dance classes?"

"Yes, we want to have a quartet at the church and to open the reception. Our first few dances will be waltzes, so Leo and I decided the wedding party, our best friends, will take dance classes together. It'll be a blast!"

"You don't want to take the easy way out with a DJ and let people shake their booties any which way they want?" I ask, hopeful.

"That will happen later. But I want to have classical music and start the dancing with that, and …" she trails off. "I see your big noggin spinning, Imogene. Can you handle being paired up with Cooper for this? He's Leo's best friend, and you're my best friend."

It's not like I can say no to her. "Yes, Cooper and I can boogie the night away and handle a little waltzing. Anything for you and Leo."

"Thank you." Lauren hugs me. "I'm getting married and having a baby!" she squeals.

"Yay!" I reply with some extra punch. As nervous as I am, I manage to drum up some enthusiasm. "So who's delivering the baby, me or Cooper?"

Lauren laughs. "This will be a hospital baby with all the highly qualified professionals on duty. I'd like you there when it happens, but we can talk about that later. Let's deal with our big order for Sasha's and the wedding first."

"Good." I nod. "Excellent plan."

The more I think about it, the more a lump catches in my throat and tears pool in my eyes. I'm losing my best friend to that exclusive club of married people. Married people with babies is even more discriminating, too. I will be the pathetic outcast, invited to parties and questioned at length about my single status. I'll have to start declining invitations and hang out with the senior crowd: Archie, Lois, and Eleanor. It won't affect Cooper. There are plenty of single women who will escort him to parties as well as Pilates and yoga instructors who will want to bang the living daylights out of him to prove their prowess in bed and in all things domestic in hopes of snagging the most eligible bachelor in Hera.

Kcuf!

"Did you tell Imogene the great news?" Leo shouts, barreling through the door.

"Oh, she sure did," I exclaim. I stand up to give him a loving embrace, giving myself a chance to wipe my runny eyes and nose on his shoulder.

"I told Cooper and gave him the run down on our plans," Leo says to Lauren.

I grab a tissue and blot my eyes then toss the box to Lauren who is blubbering away. As Leo hugs her, I take in how perfect they look together.

They've been dating for a year and a half, living together for most of that time. I've never seen these two hold a grudge or say cruel things to one another. No flying dishware or dramatic exits from the house. Their disagreements have been civil, miraculously always ending in compromises and sealed with embraces. A marriage ceremony and a child are the next logical step for people like them.

I compose myself and sigh, exhausted.

"Oh, I forgot," Leo says and bolts out of the studio. He runs downstairs and returns with an armload of velvet trays. My heart has a spasm as I recognize the black velvet shadow boxes holding the treasures I was coveting earlier at the estate sale.

"What the...?" I say, standing up as Leo places all the trays on the worktable.

"Cooper bought all of this. He said you were eyeballing them."

"I thought he just bought that stupid sword," I say, reaching for an expensive Georgian locket.

"He told me he paid for all of this while you were buying your things, but he didn't want to tell you. He said you'd blow a gasket, so I'm supposed to tell you both that this is a wedding gift for Lauren's share of the business," Leo says apologetically to me.

"Oh, really?" The snark is back.

"My God, this must have cost a small fortune," Lauren whispers, touching as many beautiful beads and lockets as she can.

"He bought six lots. This cost a few thousand dollars," I snap. "They even gave him the kcuffing trays!"

"The what?" Leo asks, confused.

"She's trying not to curse," Lauren explains quietly as an aside. "Kcuf is fuck backwards. Don't ask."

"Oh, all right. Good for you," Leo says warily.

While I lean on the table, studying the assortment of jewelry, the only thing missing is the steam coming out of my ears. "That sneaky ..."

"It's a gift, Imogene," Leo reminds me.

"Don't start a war with Cooper, at least not until after our wedding," Lauren warns in an authoritative tone. "This was very generous of him, and you and I both know this is really going to help."

These are non-returnable items. How clever of him, I think. He's put me in a position once again where I feel appreciative of his benevolence, although then there's the downside in that I'll have to thank him and continue to be charmed by him. He is good friends with Lauren; therefore, maybe this was all for her benefit. However, the part of me that is a little enchanted with Cooper is telling my ego that he's on more than a friendship crusade with me.

"I'm going to call and thank him," Lauren announces.

That feels wrong. It is my responsibility to thank him since I was the one ogling all the jewelry at the auction.

"No, I'll do it," I say. "Put his number in for me." Pulling out my phone, I hand the phone to Leo, who quickly obliges.

"Well, that's new," Lauren says, eyeing me with suspicion. "You're not going to give him a hard time, are you? You two have to dance together, and you have to look happy," she demands. "I don't care if you have to fake it for the next month."

I sigh, take the phone from Leo, then head downstairs for some privacy on the front porch where I settle into one of the wicker chairs and call Cooper.

"Hey, sunshine," he answers in a sexy, deep voice.

"Don't call me that. How did you know it was me? Or did you think it was one of your acrobatic girlfriends calling?"

Even through the phone, his velvety chuckle tickles my ear. "I figured you'd be calling to chew me out."

"I thought about it, but Leo and Lauren seem to think you're *fantastic!*" I say mockingly. "So I'm supposed to thank you."

"I knew you'd be a little angry at first since you don't like me giving you things, but I thought you'd get over it and feel relieved to have some work." He sounds guarded and maybe a little hurt by my reaction.

"Cooper, I'm sorry. I was rude, and you have been … You've been very nice and extremely generous, and I really do want to thank you," I say into the phone, a slight, nervous tremor zipping through me. This guy is starting to go to my head. I may end up in another ignite and burn situation, which would be bad for the wedding, the business, and me.

I hear him exhale slowly. "Imogene, I know you're stubborn and strong and resilient, but my gift doesn't diminish your strength in any way. It's just a gift. I like you, and even if you don't want to admit it, you like me." I can hear the smile in his tone.

"I don't know where you come up with these ideas, but for the sake of Lauren and Leo, I'm going to be nicer to you. We're going to stick to this wedding agenda they have planned for all of us, and then we'll be free to go back to being ourselves."

"Jesus, woman. You're so hard on me," he laughs. "First of all, I've always been myself with you. And, secondly, it's not just a wedding, baby. You and I are walking down the aisle together, we will be dance partners, there's the camping trip we'll have to discuss, and you and I will probably end up in the delivery room with their newborn." He's laughing, but I'm still thinking about the way he said we'll be *walking down the aisle together.* Camping?

"Wait, did you say camping? What camping trip do we have to discuss?"

"Ah, you didn't hear about Leo's grand plans for the wedding party? Since Lauren's pregnant and can't really party, he wants to do something different and decided we're all going on a camping weekend together. Carson and Jess, Dylan and Emma, Leo and Lauren, and that leaves you and me, so—"

"Are you kidding? I'm not a camping person. Exactly how is this going down?"

"I'm pretty sure it's tents, which means couples in tents, doll."

"Blech, don't call me doll. Couples in tents? What about you and me?"

"Exactly," he says smugly, his grin clearly evident once again.

Nine

I missed my opportunity to interrogate Leo on this camping trip idea of his because he and Lauren were already in bed by the time I got back upstairs. I didn't want to walk in on any embarrassing celebration sex, so I went to bed and stared at the ceiling most of the night, concocting various excuses to get out of this camping debacle.

The next morning, Leo was still asleep when Lauren and I left for the diner; as a result, now my plan is to corner him at lunch or at the furniture factory and get this issue of me, tents, bugs, and Cooper resolved.

"Why camping?" I drill Lauren on the way to work.

"Because Leo loves it. He grew up in a family that went camping all the time, and he thinks it will be a nice way to bring us all together for a relaxing weekend without phones and other electronic devices. It will be really fun. Campfires, walks in the woods, fishing—"

"Fishing? Who fishes? Not me." I'm not a morning person, and putting on my grease-stained apron from the day before, which I forgot to wash, only makes me crabbier than usual.

"You don't have to fish if you don't want to. We'll make s'mores, sit around, and gossip with the girls."

Lauren parks her dumpy little car behind the diner, and when we enter through the back kitchen door, we're greeted by my parents and grandmother. All three are standing expectantly at the door, fairly jubilant for six in the morning before the arrival of the demanding breakfast crowd.

"Surprise!" says my mother, Pam. "Nina and Garth

told us the wonderful news!"

"My parents are pretty thrilled." Lauren shines with the news that her parents have been calling everyone about the wedding yet discreetly leaving out the pregnancy bit.

My grandmother gives Lauren a big, squeezy hug, the painful kind. "Girls, we've decided we're giving you your notice. Your last day is this Friday."

While Lauren's face drops, I don't know whether to be happy or cry.

"I don't think we're ready to leave," Lauren says desperately. "I have wedding expenses, and Imogene and I can't live off our business yet."

"We've taken that into consideration," my father adds. Mark Walsh is a quiet man, a sweet father who makes decisions after giving them a lot of thought. I trust him, but at this moment, he's scaring the shit out of me. I wonder if dementia is setting in early in his forty-nine-year-old brain. "We're giving you the break you need, the kick in the pants to get you moving along."

With that, my mother holds out two envelopes to us. Lauren and I reluctantly take them and rip them open.

"It's a check with four zeros," I say, looking at them and then at Lauren. This is a shitload of money for me and my family.

"Mine, too."

"It's just enough to get you through the next two months so you can work full-time on the jewelry," my grandmother adds. "And Lauren's parents are paying for her wedding since it will be small."

"And Leo's parents are going to help with the wedding expenses, and of course, he has a good job with Carson, so you have living expenses covered," my mother assures us. She married my father and had me when she was younger than I am now; therefore, she must have some sense about these things. She regards us for a moment, waiting for us to look excited.

"It's a really big check," I say, looking down at it again and then turning back to Lauren, gauging her somber face for a reaction. She's my barometer by which many things are measured. If she's thrilled about this, I'll feel more certain.

"Yay!" she blurts out, and then the cheerleader smile spreads across her face.

I breathe a sigh of relief. "Yay," I laugh nervously.

The end of my lunch shift doesn't come soon enough. I'm at the counter with my regular teens, Kelly and Samantha, gabbing away while I fill salt shakers when Leo, Carson, and Cooper finally walk in the door for a late lunch. As they pass the girls to sit on the other side of them at the counter, both girls giggle to each other.

"Mr. Yum's got swag," Kelly whispers to Samantha and me.

"Mr. What's got what?" I ask loudly, seeing Cooper smirk at me before he settles onto the stool next to Kelly who is about to have a heart attack at his proximity.

"Swag," Lauren adds as she comes by with napkins for the dispensers.

"What the heck is that?" I ask Lauren.

"Swagger, I guess. I think it means he's cool." Lauren smiles at Cooper who's enjoying this little drama over him.

"You should be worried if Mr. Yum has an STD," I whisper loudly and wave the back of my hand at the girls.

"Hey, not my fault if they're talking about me. Man, you're cruel," he says jokingly to me with a little smile that makes the girls gasp.

"Yeah, it's not his fault the girls think he's yummy," Lauren pipes up.

"God, I do not want to hear this," Carson mumbles as he scrolls through his phone.

Red-faced, the girls pretend to be studying the ice cream menu.

I lean on the counter in front of Cooper, close to his face. "I bet, if you cut your hair short, shaved, and wore khakis and a polo shirt, those girls wouldn't give you a second look. You'd be just another old yuppie dude to them."

"Maybe so." Cooper leans on his forearms towards me. "I really don't care, Imogene. You're the one who seems bent out of shape over what they call me."

I scoff. "You care."

"Really? Okay, I'll go for the clean-cut look on one condition. You go on a hike with me this weekend. It will be a little practice run before the camping trip."

"Why would I do that?"

"Why would I want to cut off my hair and wear nerdy clothes? I'm willing to test your little theory if I can get something out of it."

"A hike with me? That's what you want?"

"No, the hike is part of the deal. You have to complete the hike with me, and if you fail, you have to go on an actual date with me. It's kind of a win-win for you," he says then turns to give Samantha and Kelly a wink.

"Oh, so you're assuming I can't complete the hike? I'm in awesome shape." I step back from the counter and hold my arms up like a victorious prizefighter who knows how to pose to show off my voluptuous assets.

Cooper's eyes trail lazily over my figure. "I agree," he says, sounding like he just had a shot of whiskey.

We are totally corrupting these teenagers.

Lauren works around me, taking the burger orders for the guys because I've already checked out, barely doing any work, and I won't let Cooper beat me at this game.

"There would be conditions and time limits," Cooper continues. "I think you'll bail, but then you'll win a date with me. I hear I'm known as Mr. Yum."

Samantha and Kelly huddle together and giggle.

"Stop that," I say to them, annoyed. "I don't think I

like this lame bet."

"That's because you know you'll lose, and you're scared to go out with me."

"No, I just don't find the prize that enticing."

"Ouch," all three men say in unison.

"You're insane," Samantha says, pointing a finger at me.

"Right?" Cooper nods to her. "Imogene is terrified to go on a little hike in the woods with me." He shakes his head at me with a wicked grin. I see now what the girls are seeing, a beautiful man who looks sexy hot when he runs his hand through his hair. *If only I were holding a pair of sharp scissors.*

"Kcuffing-A," I hiss and the girls laugh.

"What?" Cooper asks.

"Nothing. You're good at this. I'll give you that. And I'll see your lame bet and raise you. Not only will I go on a hike with you, but if I can't complete it in a reasonable time, I will pay for our date, as long as it's a dinner out and nothing else."

"Oh, no," Leo mumbles under his breath.

"No, this is great," Cooper says. "I'm going to pick out a restaurant and make a reservation today."

"Reservation where?" Lauren asks as she comes out of the kitchen, delivering their hamburgers.

"Imogene is going on a date with Cooper," Kelly adds matter-of-factly, as though this is a done deal.

"Slow down, Easy Rider." I glare at Cooper, and Carson bursts out laughing. That surprises everyone because Carson doesn't really *burst* at anything. "You haven't won yet, and we're doing the hike on my schedule because Lauren and I have a huge order to take care of first. So your fun and games will have to wait until I have time for your nonsense."

"*Easy Rider*," Carson repeats, laughing. "Dylan would be proud of you, Imogene."

79

Cooper grumbles something then takes a bite of his hamburger, Kelly and Samantha watching him chew. Silly, naïve, high school girls, fascinated for all the wrong reasons. As if he senses their intense gaze, he swallows and turns to them.

"Imogene is a little stressed out, but I'll take care of that. She'll be fine." He says this directly to the girls, who both nod their approval.

"Don't start acting like a wanker." I lean in and take three fries off his plate, chomping on them with renewed frustration and fury.

"What's a wanker?" He pushes his plate closer to me so we can share the fries.

"It's a male kcuffer," Kelly replies.

Carson and Cooper look at each other with blank expressions.

"Ha!" Leo laughs.

"What is she saying?" Cooper asks Leo.

"Male fucker," Leo whispers. "Geez, Imogene, you are a terrible influence on these girls."

"Stop referring to us as girls," Samantha snaps in a more formal voice, one she must be practicing for college.

Carson over-exaggerates a shiver. "Sam, let me know if you want to fill in for Daisy when she's on vacation. You'd make a perfectly terrifying receptionist, exactly what we like."

"Do you want more ketchup for the fries?" Cooper asks, ready to pour more on the plate as I absently eat most of his food.

"No." I push the plate back at him.

"She won't be so testy when we start going out," he says to Kelly. "She needs to get her dating legs back."

"Stop it. Really." I dump their empty plates in the bus tub under the counter.

"Hey, you're my wedding partner for the next few weeks, whether you like it or not. And I'm pretty damn sure that you're going to love it, sweet cheeks."

"Don't call me that."

"I thought that one was pretty good," Cooper says, "but I'll keep thinking of more endearing nicknames until death do us part."

"That may be sooner than you think," Carson mutters, slowly shaking his head.

"I think it's sweet," Kelly throws her opinion in.

"Ugh. Have you two not listened to anything I have taught you? Get back to school. Lunch break is over." I take their beverages and shoo them away. "Get going."

"Good luck," Samantha says to Cooper and gives him a thumbs up.

"See? They're on my side," he gloats.

"Of course they are. You could be a gorgeous serial killer and they'd fawn over you. There are stupid women everywhere who send love letters to guys in prison, men they have never met. Men who have committed murder have lovesick, crazed fans, so don't think you're so special."

"I don't want to hear this," Carson sighs. "Let's get back to work."

In complete agreement, they all stand and put cash on the counter. When Cooper sees me watching his bills for any excessive tipping, he tilts his head in exasperation. "Is twenty percent safe?"

"Fine. I'll give it to Lauren."

Carson and Leo head to the door while Cooper lingers behind.

He leans slightly over the counter so only I can hear. "At some point very soon, I'll have you saying more than *fine*." His tone is oozing with sexual flirtation, leaving no doubt that this is his bedroom voice.

"Promises, promises," I respond coyly, and then I can't contain my laughter any longer.

He grins at his victory. Yes, Cooper has a way of

breaking me; his determination to make me laugh puts a smile on my face.

He reaches across the counter and cups my chin, holding it firmly. "Your tough exterior is for show, Imogene. You don't have to do that with me. I'm the good guy."

Ten

The rest of the week flies by because I'm a lazy waitress and cut my shifts short, only doing the breakfast rush and skipping lunch so I can race home every day to string beads.

The thought of living without my weekly diner paychecks is a great motivator to work harder and longer on the beading to the point that my fingers are sore and my hands are riddled with cuts from the sharp tools and some of the antique metal coins we've been reshaping. Lauren and I are beading maniacs, yet we're still not caught up on the work we promised the Manhattan boutique, Sasha's.

I still have Lauren's twenty-four hour companionship; however, I find myself missing that moment each day when the guys walk through the diner door for lunch. And by guys, I mean Cooper. He won't let me escape that easily, though. He sends me wildly inappropriate texts, which I absolutely love.

"Miss me? Shady Pines Motel is running a special. $15 per hour. I'll book 6 hours for us to be safe."

I think about my new *friend* pretty much non-stop. It always starts with the memory of one of our kisses and continues with our teasing banter, and then it segues into the murky area of something more romantic. It's dangerous territory—getting romantically involved with someone who is a trusted colleague and friend to many in my small circle. However, the former impression of Cooper I held to firmly for many months has been replaced by someone else entirely.

Although our conversations have only been the lighthearted variety, those moments occupy my mind much of the day since I work in a solitary environment. For the sake of productivity, Lauren and I often work with headphones on so our talking doesn't decrease our speed; however, on occasion, Lauren interrupts me and asks what I've been thinking about because I sometimes break into uncontrollable daydreaming smiles. Well, if that doesn't just shoot my ball-busting image to shit, I don't know what else would.

As I tidy up the worktable and set up for tomorrow's marathon beading session Lauren and I think we can perform, Lauren pops her head in the doorway.

"Can you believe we're never putting on those aprons again?" she asks, referring to our last shift this morning.

"Are you scared or excited?"

"Excited. Yep." She smiles. "Dinner is ready, so quit fussing in here and come on down."

"Be there in a minute," I reply, admiring the stunning lockets Cooper purchased for us.

Lauren leaves, and I find another cloth, polishing a silver locket until it's gleaming. Using an excuse that it's Lauren's wedding gift was clever. This guy is incredibly generous, and I like it.

When I get downstairs, I see that Lauren has set the formal dining room instead of the kitchen table we usually eat at. She went all out with the good porcelain dishes that Jess left stored in the buffet for our use along with crystal candleholders on the table and buffet. White tapers are already lit and provide the only source of light against the dark woodwork of the room and table.

Leo places two roasted chickens on the table as Lauren enters with some side dishes.

"Lauren, you really outdid yourself," I say, taking in the romantic atmosphere at the same time I wonder if the dinner is really for those two and if I should excuse myself.

"It's about time we had a nice meal in the dining room.

Leo, the wine."

"Right," he says, and then there's a knock at the door. "That's Coop."

"Cooper's having dinner with us?" Part of me is thrilled; the other part is shouting every obscene expletive that crosses my mind. It's going to be very difficult to keep this in perspective and not consider more if Lauren is going to push Cooper and I together at every opportunity.

"It's my 'thank you' dinner for him, for the jewelry," Lauren explains.

"Yeah, two chickens should about make us even," I snort.

"Hey, honey pot," Cooper smiles, addressing me as he saunters into the dining room.

"Hate it."

He looks fantastic. *Kcuf.*

He's wearing black jeans with a black, button down shirt, and his hair is slightly damp, pushed back off his face and tucked behind his ears. He looks absolutely sexy and *clean*, and I look incredibly dumpy in my baggy jeans and tank top that has splotches from a tube of adhesive that attacked me this afternoon. To make things worse, my hair is in a ratty ponytail. The only thing missing from this hideous picture is one of my mother's hair scrunchies. Regardless of my less than optimum appearance, I melt a little at seeing him.

"Hi, Cooper." As I feel my cheeks involuntarily inflate with joy, I can only hope I'm wearing a pleasant smile and not a deranged one.

He absently hands off two bottles of wine to Leo without taking his eyes off me. I really wish I could excuse myself for a ten-minute power glam session, but that won't happen without me looking positively desperate.

"I've missed seeing you at the diner. The other waitresses don't know how to deliver insults and eat food off my plate."

85

"Well, I do have many talents." I look down at my bare feet. My toe nails have remnants of a nasty red polish from two weeks ago and are so jagged they look like a rat has been gnawing on them.

"Dinner!" Lauren announces.

"It looks great," Cooper says, trying to decide which chair he's supposed to sit in. There are only twelve to choose from.

"We're sitting at this end," Leo says. "Cooper, you and Imogene can sit here."

Perfect. Side by side. Cooper pulls out my chair for me, and when I plunk down in the old chair, it lets out a loud, lingering creak as if my weight pains it greatly.

"Old stuff. We probably should take these chairs into the shop and have them repaired," Cooper says to me. Then he intentionally slams his two hundred pounds of muscle down hard onto his chair to make the seat give off a popping, cracking sound. "Let's see if these will hold us through dinner."

Lauren and Leo have seated themselves across from us without any creaking from their chairs and are watching us with curiosity. I know exactly what's racing through Lauren's matchmaking mind, too.

Lauren begins carving one of the chickens. "Cooper, which parts do you like best?"

Under the table, I feel Cooper's large hand clamp down on my thigh. With a fierce squeeze, he replies, "I'm a leg and thigh guy."

While I slip my hand under the table and try to push it off me without success, Lauren looks up from her carving as though she suspects some kind of struggle is going on between us. Leo, on the other hand, is oblivious, rambling on about where we'll be camping and the gear he's bringing. I could not be more disinterested in fishing poles and binoculars.

"Are you planning on eating with one hand through the

whole dinner?" I whisper to Cooper.

"I can." He picks up a drumstick with his right hand and watches me while he eats it like a caveman. "Lauren, excellent dinner."

"Well, it's the least I could do. You're an angel for giving us that gift." Lauren smiles at Cooper as she scoops potatoes onto Leo's plate.

"Blood circulation is critical to my survival," I whisper to Cooper as I remove my hand from his and pick up my utensils. "Oh, a knife." I twirl it in my hand.

Cooper chuckles and loosens his grip on my leg then slides his hand to the inside of my thigh and lets it rest there. I exhale slowly, taking small bites of food, tasting nothing while enjoying the sensation of his warmth so close to the other parts of me I imagine him touching.

Leo and Lauren do most of the talking through the meal. There's so much to cover when planning a quickie wedding and the birth of a baby. Those two chatter, talking over each other, gentling touching each other's arms like an old married couple, laughing at their own inside jokes, almost as if Cooper and I are not in the room. Cooper gives obliging grunts and nods throughout as he finishes his dinner and a slice of chocolate torte.

"Cooper, you didn't drink any wine," Lauren says, refilling Leo's and my glasses.

"I never drink when I'm driving. I'm fine with water."

"You don't have to drive home. Stay in one of the extra guest rooms. Seriously, have a glass of wine and relax, Coop," Leo suggests.

Sweet, stupid Leo. He might as well have suggested Cooper sleep in my room since I haven't gotten laid in— oh, who's counting? *Me!*

My incredulous expression at Leo gets Lauren's attention. She bites her lower lip, and I know she's thinking the same thing.

Cooper leans back in his chair and pats his stomach—

with only one hand, of course—and gives me a mischievous grin. "That's a good idea. I'm going to take you up on your offer."

"Fa-boo-us," I say dryly.

Lauren fills his wine glass. "Why don't you two take your wine outside, and we'll join you after we clean up."

"I'll do the dishes," I volunteer. "You and Leo go with Cooper to the porch. I'll take care of the kitchen since you did all the cooking."

"I'll help you," Cooper says.

Lauren tosses a serving spoon into a plate with a loud clank. "Would you two just go outside already? Leo and I have this."

Cooper releases my leg and stands then puts his arm out for me. He's actually going to escort me to the porch? I sigh and pick up my wine glass, resigned to the fact that Lauren is indeed trying to push us together as much as possible.

As we leave the table, Cooper pulls his extended arm back and quickly grabs my hand. "Don't even think of throwing your wine in my face."

"I wouldn't waste good wine like that. I need all the alcohol I can get. You know what Lauren's trying to do, don't you?" I ask as we step out onto the front porch.

"I'm perfectly fine with her trying to fix us up." He takes my wine glass and sets it on the teak coffee table along with his own glass. Then he falls down onto the wicker loveseat, pulling me with him. We sink into the fluffy cushions, and before I can right myself, he pulls my legs across his own and leans in to kiss me. I give an unconvincing, protesting yelp before my hands reach for his face and I kiss him back. His weight is partially on top of me as he lays me down, kissing me long and gracefully. *Another well-practiced stud.*

"We can't do this here," I mumble against his lips. "They'll be out here any minute."

"No, they won't," he says against my neck. "They are going to leave us alone." He nips my neck and I shiver, feeling my nipples pebble at the same time.

Did you and Lauren plot this?" As I run my fingers through his hair, my lips and tongue grazing the stubble on his cheek, he moans, sending a flurry of activity to my nether regions. I'm incredibly wet and on the verge of delirium.

"No." His voice is raspy. "This wasn't planned on my part, but Lauren knows you and I have a thing for each other."

"I've never said any such thing to her."

"She's your best friend and can read you like I can."

"Oh, stop with that goddamn reading business," I mumble against his lips.

He keeps kissing me and grinds the hard bulge in his jeans against my thigh, leaving little to my imagination of how big his erection is. I shamelessly arch into him, wanting more but expecting to come to my senses any second now. *Any second now, Imogene.*

Cooper keeps it slow, his lips and tongue so gentle they intensify every sensation for me. I'm tasting him, feeling his warm skin and inhaling his musky scent, everything about him feeling wonderful.

He slips his hand up under my tank top and reaches for a breast that is spilling out of my demi bra, fondling it, pinching my nipple as I devour his mouth. I'm certainly not coming to my senses. I want to touch him all over. I want him on me, in me, all over me.

Reaching a hand down, I palm the outside of his jeans. With him being unbelievably hard and big, I honestly don't know how he keeps his cock contained in his jeans.

He groans. "Imogene, I don't want you to stop, but I'm about to cream my pants. I want you now, but if you're not ready to go upstairs to one of the bedrooms with me this second and let me do everything I've imagined doing with you, then we have a problem."

"We have a problem," I say between heavy breaths.

"Will this help?" he asks, raking up my shirt and snapping open my bra.

He takes a few seconds to regard my breasts with reverence before his mouth closes over a hard nipple and sucks ... and licks. I'm breathing hard, thinking that, if he keeps it up, he could be the first man to give me an orgasm by doing this. He then moves to my other breast and gives it equal treatment.

When he undoes my jeans and slips his hand under my panties, his devotion to my appreciative sex amplifies. He circles two fingers slowly around my wet opening, going deeper each time, then moves back up to lightly rub my clit. Meanwhile, I manage to undo his jeans and push them down from his narrow hips. His boxer briefs are next, and he lifts his hips so I can work the snug fabric over his growing appendage. I keep one hand grasped to his firm ass while I use my other hand to stroke his length, lightly at first and then harder until Cooper's grunts increase. I reach under his balls and stroke all the way up to the tip where I play with the sensitive head.

"Christ, I'm going to come. I vote we go upstairs to a bedroom," he grits out through his teeth.

I love having his mouth and hands on me, and a lie detector would literally explode if I said I didn't want to go to bed with Cooper and engage in every sexual image my mind has conjured up over the last five minutes. I could easily have an orgasm if he keeps fondling me, but there's an older, wiser Imogene in here somewhere saying *no*. She's the one who has been tallying up the previous boyfriends and doing a thorough analysis on why they were wrong for me. In my gut, I know I want whatever I have with Cooper to be handled with care. I desperately want to screw him; I want to know every inch of Cooper and find out firsthand what he does in bed. I just don't want to mess this up.

"Wait," I utter with disappointment. I could slap myself.

Cooper stops moving, his weight on me a solid mass of heavy breathing.

"I want to do this, but …"

"But what?" His face is directly above me, his intense eyes staring directly into mine without blinking.

"I barely know you, and I promised myself I wouldn't do this again."

"You've known me for over a year," he says incredulously.

"We've been around each other for over a year, but I don't know much about you. Nothing personal, at least."

Cooper moves off me quickly and adjusts his clothing before briskly walking to the other end of the porch. "Ahhh," he growls loudly, flinging his arms out, shaking the frustration out of his system.

I sit up and secure my bra and top. "Sorry, but—"

"No, you're right. Nothing to be sorry about, Imogene." He walks back to me, squats down, and places his crossed arms on my thighs. "You don't know me the way I know you," he says solemnly.

He's extremely intense. This is the side of him that was a federal agent, the serious man with an expression that gives nothing away, and this is the real Cooper, the one I don't know.

"I like you, Cooper, but I'm not ready for this ... with you." I reach out and hesitantly place my hand over his.

His tongue darts out and runs across his bottom lip as he looks down at my hand. Then he places his other hand on top of mine, sandwiching my hand. "It's okay. For me, this has been happening excruciatingly slow because I've had months to think about it. For you, it's happening too fast. I get it."

I exhale nervously. I'm not ready to sleep with him,

though I also don't want him to walk away from this. "Do you want to go upstairs and watch a movie? I know it's not what you had in mind, and you can go home if you'd rather."

"Sure. Let's do that." He picks my hand up and squeezes it before standing and pulling me up with him.

We take our wine glasses and go up to the second floor library where Jess put in big, cozy couches and a large, flat screen TV before she left and moved in with Carson. I pop in a DVD, some thriller that I pay little attention to.

Cooper takes off his shoes and puts his feet up on the coffee table, reclining on the couch. He then nestles me against his side, and we talk quietly, speculating over what will happen to Matt Damon before I become too sleepy to care. I am snuggled into the crook of Cooper's arm, my face resting on his chest, when I feel myself drifting off. The last thing I remember is Cooper's hand mindlessly playing with my hair and lightly stroking my head.

Eleven

"Hey, beautiful." I hear Cooper's voice close by.

I'm warm and cozy and coming out of a pleasant dream I've already forgotten.

"Good morning," he says, rubbing my back.

I'm stretching against something hard when I open my eyes, finding myself on top of Cooper, holding on to him like he's a life raft. Just what I needed; my body trapped the guy on the couch while I slept.

"Sorry. I tend to hog the bed when I sleep. You should have woken me up." I roll to the side so he can get up, but he doesn't move. I realize I've given him too much information about my sleeping habits with others.

I rub my eyes and notice that he looks the same in the morning as he does during the day. His hair doesn't look like the bird's nest I'm fingering on top of my head, and he doesn't even look tired.

"It was actually very comfortable," he says. "I dozed off right after you did, and we somehow went horizontal. You have an indentation on your cheek from one of my buttons."

Sure enough, when I feel my face, there's a little groove on my cheek. I groan and Cooper smiles. I attempt to sit up, but he pulls me back down, turning on his side to face me, mere inches from me.

While I study his full lips and think of how nice it would be to kiss him again, he regards me with the same fascination. For a second, it seems like we're going to give in to that immediate desire.

"I have a surprise for you," he says, focusing on my

eyes with a renewed energy.

"Really? That's the best you can do? Every guy says that in the morning."

He chuckles and places his hand on my waist. "That's not what I was talking about, but if you think I'm like every other guy, let me show you what I've got." He begins to unbutton his jeans when I slap his hands. He grabs my hand and traps it up over my head. "Fine, we'll save this for next time, and I'll remember this position."

"Sure," I say, holding back a laugh. I'm beginning to really enjoy his persistence. "So what's the surprise?"

"I'm going to help you and Lauren out today. It's Saturday, so you have me for as long as you need."

"I don't get it." This time, I'm able to push myself up and climb over him to get off the couch and out of the sexual danger zone.

He rolls over and stands up, stretching gracefully. "Lauren said you two need someone to put the beads in something or other. She said it's easy grunt work, but time-consuming, so I'll do the grunt work."

"You told Lauren you're going to fill the bead trays?" I force a laugh.

"What's so funny about that?" He shoves his hands in his jeans and appraises me with a sexy, little smile.

"It takes hours to pick out the tiny beads and fill the trays. It's boring and annoying when the beads get messed up. Thanks for the offer, but you can't do it, Cooper. You'll hate it."

"Jesus, here we go again. Quit trying to get rid of me. Think of me as Lauren's volunteer and pretend I'm not there."

"Like I can do that," I mutter. "You take up so much room."

Cooper turns his head to hide a mischievous glint in his eye. Before I can ask what he's thinking, I hear a commotion in the downstairs foyer.

"Where's the party?" Dylan's voice rings out.

"Oh, no. What's going on?" I ask Cooper.

He exhales slowly. "Well, if you didn't like the first part of my surprise, you're really going to hate the second part."

"You invited Dylan to help with the beads?" I ask in a shrill tone. I really hate this idea. I was excited to get up early and jump right into work, but how will I be able to concentrate when the lascivious Viking from my dream kiss is going to be sitting near me? What's more, throwing Dylan into the mix is like having a wild, barking dog in your face. These two take over any place they occupy. The day will be destroyed.

"Imogene, I didn't *invite* anyone. I *insisted* they all come and help. Everyone," he explains before he leans down and kisses my cheek. "Like I said, good morning, beautiful."

Dazed, I hear the clamor of our friends filing in and heading into the kitchen.

"Let's get some breakfast, and then you can crack the whip. We all work for you today."

"God, I hope Lauren knows how to organize all of you because this looks like a disaster in the making. Cooper, you're ... I'm going to go wash my face and change clothes."

A half-hour later, after coffee and blueberry muffins that Emma and Dylan brought over, Carson and Jess are sitting at one end of the worktable, Leo and Lauren opposite them, and Cooper and I are sitting across from Emma and Dylan. Couples, again.

Emma and Dylan look rested and tan as they happily fill us in on their honeymoon in Mexico. I'm still feeling discombobulated from waking up on a bed of Cooper splendor and then receiving the news he's enlisted our friends to spend their day off working in our stifling hot

95

bead room.

Dylan opens the windows, but we're all sweating profusely while Lauren organizes trays, bead cases, and design sheets on the table. I begin working on the necklace she places in front of me while everyone else is given a very thorough lesson on picking up the beads and putting them in the tray grooves according to the color-coded blueprints provided. Lauren enunciates each word and step as if she's talking to second-graders who have been put in charge of Houston's Mission Control Center.

"So, basically, you want us to put the beads on these trays," Emma repeats slowly, pointing to her tray.

Everyone except Lauren laughs.

"Listen, people, one wrong bead, and the necklace is fucked," Lauren stresses, flicking both hands open. "Imogene, don't laugh. You, more than anyone, know what a bitch it is to fix a mistake."

Sometimes, I forget how regimented Lauren can be about procedures. When she has it in her head how something needs to be done, she doesn't like any deviation. We've been living and working together for so long I automatically follow her rules, for the most part. However, with a culmination of stress and sleep deprivation, watching her lecture the others has me laughing so hard I start crying when Dylan does a perfect imitation of her high-pitched voice and hand waving. Cooper hands me a tissue to dry my eyes as Leo puts his arm around Lauren to ease her off the ledge of beading insanity.

"Babe, take a seat. We can do this. Have a little faith in your nimrod friends," Leo says softly to her.

"Oh, I apologize, everyone," she begins crying. "It's the pregnancy. I'm so excited and scared."

"You're pregnant?" Jess and Emma shout together.

Carson and Dylan look worriedly at each other, as if it's something catching. They watch their wives run over to hug Lauren.

"I thought we were supposed to keep this a secret until after the wedding," Cooper says.

"That was never going to happen with Lauren," Leo shakes his head.

"I had a handle on it for almost an hour," Lauren manages to say between her tears and laughter.

"She did break her own record," I add. "You can't expect the town gossip to keep a secret of this magnitude to herself. No way."

"Wow, a kid." Dylan looks a little stunned at the prospect.

"Congratulations," Carson adds, giving Dylan a big brother glare.

"Congratulations." Dylan nods. "This is great. Should we help you set up a nursery, Leo?"

"Hey, that's something to consider," Cooper says to Carson. "A baby line of furniture."

"I don't know." Carson shakes his head. "Cribs have to comply with certain codes, and at our price point, we're talking high-end stuff, and most people buy their baby crap at the big mass retailers. It might not be profitable enough to take on."

"Baby crap?" Lauren snaps.

"Sorry, I meant cribs. Not crap." Carson gives me the *what-the-hell* face.

"Her hormones are whack," Leo says apologetically, receiving a really good whack on his arm from Lauren for that remark.

"You guys, show a little sensitivity," Jess scolds them. "This is beautiful news, and you're ruining it for Lauren."

"I'm okay," Lauren wipes her eyes. "Leo is right. One minute, I'm fine, and the next, I'm ..."

"The prison matron of Cell Block H," I finish for her, making Lauren laugh. "Why don't you go take a nap, sweetie? We can handle this. You drilled the instructions into them."

"No, I don't want to miss anything. I'm working today, and you people better have brought your A game."

"And by A game, she means gossip," I clarify.

As Cooper puts his hand on the nape of my neck, nudging me to look at him, his mouth curves ever so slightly. I'm well aware that he merely wants to remind me he's paying attention to everything I do and say. It's a pleasant sensation, having his warm gaze devoted to me. Lauren may be riding the roller coaster of baby fever, but she catches the look between Cooper and me and tips her chin up approvingly.

"Damn!" Dylan shouts as he drops a bead and it rolls under the table. Then the big oaf crawls under the table, knocking his back against it and causing everyone to grab their trays in a panic.

"Jesus, Dylan, you almost took out the whole table." Carson looks beside himself.

"Kcuffing-A, Dyl, be careful," I snap.

"What?" Dylan looks at me, confused.

Why am I following the advice of teenage twats? I sound like one of them.

"Imogene is trying not to swear," Lauren says in a motherly tone that even my own mother wouldn't use.

"Well, these little fuckers are hard to hold onto," Dylan says, returning to his stool. While Emma pats his back, I realize these couples are all perfectly matched for each another. They have the yin and yang going on. Neurotic Jess and Nurturing Carson, Energetic Dylan and Soothing Emma, and Bossy Lauren and Loving Leo. This is how I always think of these married couples, and it's so odd considering that, two years ago, everyone was single and very much unattached.

Cooper could be attached if he wanted—there are plenty of women vying for his attention—so that really leaves me as the odd person out. I was never this woman. I always had some type of boyfriend; either the serious kind I loved being with every day or the make-do guy I kept around until something better came along. The joke is on me. Apparently, I became a make-do girlfriend, and I didn't even know it until Jeremy left me.

"Thank you. Again," I say quietly to Cooper while he is struggling with some tiny seed beads that fall out of his large hand. These guys have fingers and hands for rough labor and lumber, not little beads. "Let me help you." I gather the beads and put them in their designated tray grooves.

He turns to me, frustrated. "Imogene, this isn't a favor or a chore. I like doing this for you. But I am having trouble reading the little code numbers on these sheets."

He reaches inside the pocket of the T-shirt he borrowed from Leo earlier, pulling out a pair of black Clark Kent eyeglasses and putting them on in order to read Lauren's tiny handwriting. At breakfast, I assumed they were sunglasses.

"I didn't know you wore glasses." I'm mesmerized by the transformation. He still looks like a biker stud, but the glasses add a new dimension of sexy, hip professor. I like it.

"I only wear them when I can't read fine print. I can't tell the difference between the C4 bead and the C6 without the glasses, and I don't want Lauren to hit the roof if I screw this up."

Lauren's head pops up at the mention of her name, and her mouth drops open at the sight of Cooper. "Oh, my God, Cooper! You look adorable in those glasses. Why haven't I ever seen you wearing them?"

"I got them a month ago, still getting used to them." He looks uneasy with everyone staring at him.

"You look so good in those. Wow." Emma grins and then looks at me.

"Right?" I ask, smiling. "Who knew?"

"Aw, come on," Dylan gripes. "They're geek glasses.

What's the big deal?"

"Hey!" Jess leans forward and points to the black nerdy glasses she's wearing. "I have the same glasses, and no one says I'm adorable."

"You're *kcuffing* gorgeous," Carson quips forcefully and with perfect timing, causing Jess to blush and kiss his cheek.

"Honey," Emma says, rubbing Dylan's back, "if it will make you feel like part of the gang, I will go down to the drug store tomorrow and buy you some fake Clark Kent glasses."

Dylan smiles at his wife. I still can't believe they're newlyweds. All of these damn lovebirds are too much.

"Copy cats," Cooper mumbles to me, making me a little giddy.

He does look adorable with his striking eyes peeking out from behind the black frames, his hair tucked behind his ear. He looks incredibly studious and hunky, making me want one more kiss before I put a stop to this for real.

"Oh, seventy million," Jess whispers to herself, but we all hear it. We're used to her odd tic and generally ignore it; however, this time, I can't.

"Why is it always seventy million? Why not thirty million or eighty-four million?" I ask.

"No, those aren't good numbers. Right, Jess?" Cooper comes to her defense.

Jess regards Cooper for a moment, waiting for him to make a joke, but then realizes he's serious. "He's right. They're not good numbers."

"Why? I want to know where this comes from," I badger.

"Leave my wife alone," Carson says without looking up.

This bead project has proven to be very challenging for him and Dylan; however, the women are already on their second set of designs, and I'm quite optimistic that

Cooper's intervention is going to help us get ahead this time.

"I don't think I can explain it to you," Jess says, pushing a completed tray forward. "When I get anxious or screw up, or even sometimes when I'm happy, the numbers make me feel good."

"I know that, but I want to know why *seventy million* in particular is so special."

Jess frowns at me. "It just is. Why do you like to wear green so much?"

"Because I look awesome in it," I reply.

"Jess needs certain numbers," Cooper intervenes. "They are patterns to her, like the computer coding she does. Even her paintings are a system of visual patterns. Seventy million is ingrained. She's probably been using that number for years as a stim."

"Stim?" Carson asks, suddenly interested.

"Stimming behavior," Jess explains, giving Cooper a long, hard look.

"It's a self-soothing behavior," Cooper continues. "Lots of people have them without knowing it. When Dylan is sitting down at a desk, he always shakes his crossed foot." Naturally, everyone looks at Dylan for confirmation or an exhibition of his foot shaking, which we've already witnessed many times over. "And Lauren often snaps her fingers. Only on the right hand, though, and then she immediately always lifts up a strand of hair and twirls it on the same fingers."

"You do," Leo confirms.

"Carson has to work a room from right to left." Carson gives him a questioning look. "You do. When we're working at a house, it doesn't matter what room we're in, you start on the right side and you coordinate your plans to fit accordingly. That one is kind of cool, but you also do the same thing at the factory. When you do your walk around, you always go in the same direction and stop and talk to people in the same order every time."

"How is that self-soothing if I'm not aware of it?" Carson asks.

"It's not as obvious or as frequent as Jess's behavior, but it's consistent, and you do it because…?"

"It feels comfortable," Carson answers.

"Oh, do me! Do me!" Emma practically jumps off her stool.

"*Do me*? Listen to yourself." Dylan almost laughs, but he still has little bouts of jealousy when Cooper commands the attention of every female in the room.

"Oh, shush." Emma slaps his arm.

"Well, Miss Emma, since I had the opportunity of tailing you and your ex for a while, I picked up a few things about you," Cooper says, referring to the period when Cooper worked undercover, following Emma's ex-boyfriend, the son of a mobster. It was all very exciting gossip last year. Said ex-boyfriend was innocent, although he obviously had to get out of the picture, even if his father is doing hard time. It's not as interesting as this newly discovered party trick of Cooper's.

"Did I do weird stuff?" Emma glances at Jess who has obvious quirks.

"Hey, now," Jess says defensively.

"Well, your tic stands out. No one has ever mentioned that I have one, so I'm curious to know how pronounced my *self-soothing* behavior is." Emma laughs. "It even sounds weird."

"You do a few different things, but one that stands out to me is that you always cross your arms behind your back and hold your elbows. You do it when you're nervous, talking to a new client in person or even on the phone. When the delivery trucks come in with the new lumber or you meet any delivery person you don't know, you do it. You look people in the eye when you talk to them, but then your arms go behind your back."

102

"That's totally you," Dylan says.

"Yours is also kind of a tell," Cooper explains. "I bet you're terrible at poker."

"I am. Lois and Archie taught me how to play, and I'm always the first one out."

"Lois is a card shark, but she's also reading you. She knows when you're bluffing," Cooper explains.

"Did you learn all of this at FBI school?" I ask.

Cooper laughs. "Yeah, I learned how to profile people when I was training at Quantico. One of my instructors said I had a special knack for it, a deeper intuition about people. I suppose I was always studying people more than others would. That's how I ended up going undercover."

"Hmm." I'm aware that everyone is probably observing us, but I can't help myself from staring at Cooper's eyes. He responds with a slight curve of his delicious lips, ones I want roaming over my body.

"Now you know something about me," he murmurs to me.

"Tell us more."

Cooper looks up at the others who are diligently aligning beads on their jewelry trays yet seeming to be waiting for Cooper to entertain them.

"There are obvious signs, like a person's eyes. When I first started at Blackard, Dylan would usually squint and look away from me. He was feeling a little threatened by me because he wasn't sure where I fit in at work and because he thought I was competition … for Emma."

Dylan rolls his eyes.

"That's true," Carson adds.

"If you say so, but I'm not like that now."

"No, now you just give me the occasional mean, low growl. Mad Dog Dylan," Cooper responds with a chuckle, the others joining in.

"This is fascinating," I say. "Really, keep going."

Cooper shrugs as though he's suddenly bashful to

show himself in this way. "Carson generally likes meeting new people. He arches his eyebrows in interest," Cooper adds.

"I didn't have that experience when we met in Archie's office for the first time," Jess says, turning to Carson for confirmation.

"That wasn't our first time," Carson says defensively. "We met when we were kids. When I saw you in Archie's office, it was a completely different situation."

"Yeah, Carson was nervous as hell that day," Dylan says, laughing.

"I think it worked out fine," Carson says pointedly to Jess.

"I suppose I got some eyebrow arches after that," Jess teases.

"But this shows you how important eye contact is to gain someone's trust," Cooper continues. "Companies like to have business meetings in person more than video conferences because it's important to observe the nonverbal behavior of the people involved. We look for universal behaviors, but we also look for idiosyncratic, nonverbal behaviors to see who we're dealing with.

"How someone places their hands, holds their head, or how they sit or stand tells us plenty about them. If you ever watch Carson in the factory, he stands with his legs positioned fairly far apart and his hands on his hips with his elbows out. His body language tells us he's open or available to talk to people. He wants his employees to feel comfortable around him and think he's approachable."

"You do have a fatherly appeal to the people at work," Leo agrees.

Carson grunts in embarrassment.

"Dylan is another story," Cooper says slyly.

"Here we go," Dylan mutters.

"Dylan is often standing as tall as possible with his arms crossed. It's intimidating to people who don't know him, and he uses that to his advantage at sales meetings, I bet."

"Oh, he does." Emma laughs.

"And then there's Imogene, here." Cooper tilts his head in my direction. "She exhibits behavior similar to Carson's when she's among women, but when she's around men, her nonverbal behavior is more like Dylan's. It's a protective, defense measure."

"I thought her mouth was her defense measure," Jess cuts in. "Her sarcasm."

"It is to an extent, but that's verbal behavior, and I'm still compiling my file on Imogene Walsh." Cooper grins devilishly at me.

I scoff because I have nothing to say; he's pretty much nailed us.

Lauren gives me one of her little knowing looks and then stands. "Okay, I need to collect these finished trays and give you new ones, so take a potty break if you need it," she says to everyone.

"I'm going to get some water. Anyone want anything?" Cooper asks the group, but there are no takers; therefore, he pats my leg under the table and stands to leave.

Lauren uses that moment to nod her head in Cooper's direction. She looks like an angry ostrich, flinching her head to get me to follow Cooper.

"Hon, is something wrong with your neck? You look like you're in pain," Leo says, rubbing the back of her neck.

"Oh, Leo, you're just missing Lauren's tells," I say, bopping an empty felt tray on his head then leaving the room to find Cooper.

"So that was very impressive," I say, entering the kitchen as Cooper pulls a bottle of water from the fridge.

"Glad I did something to impress you." He smiles. "I was going to say more, but I didn't want you to feel like I put you on the spot."

"About what?" I lean on the counter next to him and cross my arms. Then I look down at my arms across my chest and think about that for a minute. I am like Dylan when I'm around men, defensive.

Cooper chuckles and then nods at my position. "You want to talk to me, but you're already in combat mode. I didn't tell them about your eyes, though."

"What about my eyes? Are they shifty?"

"They're beautiful."

A little, happy tremor races through me.

"You do narrow your eyes at men. You're very skeptical around them, and you used to be that way with me. Now you look at me in a different way. You're still sarcastic, but your eyes give you away."

"How so?" I ask quietly. I relax my arms and hook my thumbs into the belt loops of my jeans.

"Your eyes pop wider when you see me. Instead of turning your head or averting your gaze, you stare at me. A lot. It's nice. Plus, it pretty much confirms what I've thought. You have always liked me, but now you're showing it openly."

Of course, I'm staring at him now, that handsome face with those cute, professor glasses. I want to ruffle his hair.

Without deliberating any further, I launch myself at him and plant my mouth on his. He grunts in surprise and then approval, managing to kiss me and place the water bottle on the counter at the same time. As he wraps his arms around me, holding me tightly, and hoists me up so our faces are aligned perfectly, I curl my legs around his waist. He pushes his tongue deeper in a hungry, aggressive manner that turns me on even more. I fist my hands in his hair as though I can't get enough of him, the scruff on his chin grazing my cheek, making me moan.

"Wait," he growls. "I have to get these things off." He removes his glasses with one hand, keeping the other on my ass to hold me up. He fumbles for the counter behind him and places his glasses down. Then he grabs my plump rear end with both hands and gives me another hard boost against him. "Kiss me," he demands.

I grab his face with both hands and ravage his mouth, not caring who may walk in on this spectacle. I feel us moving then realize Cooper is walking us into the pantry off the kitchen. It's an old-fashioned room with a long, butcher-block counter and tall cupboards where the cook of the house stored dishware and food.

Cooper places me on the counter, keeping himself wedged between my thighs, as I keep kissing him, savoring him. I unbutton the light cotton, sleeveless blouse I'm wearing and undo my bra clasp then push Cooper's head back so he can see me exposed for him.

His eyes leave my face and travel down to my bountiful assets as I run one hand over a breast, fondling it until the nipple hardens then palming it as an offering.

"Shit, Imogene. Your body is fucking unbelievable," he says huskily before clamping his hot lips on my nipple. He replaces my hand with his and holds my heavy breast as he sucks and nips at it.

I run my fingers through his hair again, keeping his head firmly in place on my breasts, moaning as tingles shoot through me. That lonely, vacant place between my legs is begging for his rock hard cock. I grind against the bulge in his jeans and moan again as my head falls back against a cupboard.

"Cooper," I whisper hungrily, "I turn into a cheap slut when I'm around you."

His hand replaces his mouth on my aching breasts as he works his way up my chest, licking my collarbone then sucking and biting my neck.

"I want to fuck you," he says as he kisses my neck. "But everyone is expecting us upstairs, and we deserve a bed and unlimited time."

107

He pulls away and looks at me for a moment. We're both disheveled, the heated desire overpowering, the kind that makes people commit murder.

My hands snake up under his T-shirt and my fingers trail over his firm, flat stomach and the ridges of his six-pack abs before spreading across hard pectoral muscles. Moving my hands around to his back, I pull him closer so we're skin against skin. Then we kiss again, slower and deeper, letting our bodies rub against each other, enjoying the friction that we'd like in other places.

A thump and the sound of a flushing toilet above our heads remind us that we're not alone. Our kiss ends slowly, then I slump back against the cupboard, closing my bra and buttoning my blouse. Cooper pulls his T-shirt down and runs his fingers through his hair so he looks exactly the same as before our tryst.

"I'm not supposed to like you this way," I say.

"But you do." He places his hands on my knees and regards me with a serious expression.

"I do," I say wearily, "but I have to get back to work."

"I know, and I'm coming with you." He takes my chin in his hand and looks at me with sheer determination. "I'm still holding you to our bet."

"The hike? Seriously?"

"Absolutely. I got everyone here today so you could finish your work because, tomorrow, you're hiking with me, baby. We'll see what you've got."

"So that's why you organized this, so I'd have to go hiking with you? And you assume I won't complete it and will have to go out with you? Why not just call the hike a date and then we're done?"

"No, the hike isn't a date. It's in the woods. A date is where you have to go out in public with me and be seen as my date. Everything you do with me, you hide from others. You don't want people to know that you have a thing for me, just like this kiss. You keep everything hidden."

"Cooper, we are paired up for the wedding. That's a date."

"No, it isn't. That's a duty."

"Well, if I go on a date with you because I lose a bet, then that's a duty, too."

Cooper chuckles arrogantly. "When you're on a date with me, it won't feel like a chore or a duty."

"Says the horny man. Besides, we never agreed to *when* this potential date would take place. I could hold you off for another year. "

"Not going to happen."

"What makes you so sure? A little groping today has certainly made you very cocky."

"Because you like me, and it's more than what happened in this pantry … or on the porch."

"This is a bad idea. It will get too complicated."

"No, it's very simple. I'm going to bring you to your knees."

Twelve

The rest of the day, I spend too much time thinking about how Cooper can bring me to my knees.

Everyone stays until dinner, and Lauren is very pleased that we've accomplished getting more than thirty-five necklace tray set-ups completed. Over the next week, Lauren and I will have to string beads and add in the lockets and pendants Cooper purchased for us, which is the part that makes me feel a little cheap. He gives us this extravagant gift, and I can't keep my hands off him. The two events are not correlated; however, it didn't occur to me that I should probably have brought this up with him. That discussion wasn't going to happen with everyone around, though.

The conversation in our workroom was devoted to the uncomfortable temperature and humidity level in our old house, and Lauren's wedding and her baby—and I do mean *Lauren's* wedding and *Lauren's* baby. You'd never know Leo is getting married or about to be a father with the way she went on about the decision-making process, which clearly required only her vote. We had a few laughs over that.

Cooper would pause occasionally and glance my way or give me one of his wicked grins, but we didn't corner each other in secret for another kiss or grope. When he left, his elbow grazed my arm on his way out the front door, the small gesture feeling completely erotic because it was intentional. It sent an arousing tremble cascading from my arm down to my toes. As if he knew, he looked back at me and winked before descending the stairs to his bike.

After everyone leaves, I pack a small backpack with water and some hiking essentials Leo insists I take tomorrow. I then dig out some old, high tops and lay out some light weight leggings and a T-shirt. Because of the bug factor, I need to be covered, but I also don't want to roast.

Cooper has said he will pick me up at seven to get an early start before the heat sets in. The idea of a long, sweaty hike with Cooper doesn't keep me awake, though; it's the thought of him bringing me to my knees.

So, what? Hell, I'm pretty sure I could bring him to his knees, too. However, this whole knee business is precisely what we should both be trying to avoid because this is where things can go wrong and get messy. People get hurt or angry or both. Moreover, who the hell needs that in their life? Not me. *Kcuf!*

"You're going to have to walk faster than that if we want to beat the sun," Cooper says, turning around to watch me catch up to him.

We've been trudging up the slow incline of a wooded path for five hours. I'm drenched in sweat, have blisters breeding on my feet, and two mosquito bites I keep scratching. I'm wearing two sport bras to prevent my breasts from doing their own bouncy line dance, but the bras are a bitch. They are practically strangling me and making my hot, itchy skin worse.

Cooper, on the other hand, looks great in sweat. His hair is pulled back into a short ponytail at the nape of his neck, and he's wearing cargo pants and a threadbare white T-shirt that's plastered with sweat to his chest and abs.

"I need more water, and then I need to take a piss," I say when I reach him.

I couldn't sound or look more butch, and at this point, I don't care. I hate hiking, but maybe this was a good idea after all. Maybe Cooper will see what I look like under duress. In an apocalyptic world, I would be ugly, stinky, and mean. The sight of me should be a big turn off.

Cooper lets out a laugh and hands me one of the water bottles since he's carrying all the extra weight. I grab it and gulp half of it before handing the bottle back.

"You carry it. I'm already too top heavy," I mutter as I stalk off to find another private spot where I can kill more wildlife with my never-ending urine supply.

When I return from yet another unhappy tree, I take the rubber band out of my wet hair and try to realign my ponytail on top of my head to get the sticky hair off my neck. Cooper is standing with one hip cocked, watching me and wiping his face with his T-shirt. His sunglasses are perched on top of his head, and even in all this bug-infested, sweaty grime, he looks good with his tan, washboard abs on full display for me.

It seems unfair. I'm an attractive woman, and sometimes, I even crack the beauty ranks, but I think it always takes effort. Makeup and hair are part of my arsenal, and my body is my weapon, at least when it comes to men. I'm well aware that I should be flogged for my anti-feminist thoughts, and my mother would be the first in line with the whip. Regardless, that's who I am.

I will never be one of those fun-loving athletic women who looks good dripping in sweat with twigs in my hair. However, in my defense, I don't shy away from confrontation and being slighted or wronged in any way because I'm also not afraid to use my other weapon, my smart mouth. Boobs will sag and beauty fades, but as long as I'm alive, no one will ever be able to shut me up.

"What are you laughing at?" I glare at Cooper.

"You. You're so miserable, but you haven't once asked to go home, even though I brought you to the one trail most people hike in winter when there's less foliage and insects."

"You did? You did this on purpose?" I ask testily.

112

"Yep."

"Jesus Christ, you must really like me in order to put up with this shit." As I walk past him, I consider flinging my backpack at his head.

"I do. I didn't think you'd last this long, especially when we went past that hornet's nest. There's a clearing up ahead. We can stop for lunch."

"Super," I grumble and jump back on the trail, letting him follow me this time.

A half hour later, we come to the clearing where there's rocky terrain and a view of the valley below. After I steer us towards a big boulder with a flat top, Cooper climbs up and holds out his hand to pull me up. We sit down on the warm surface and spread our lunches out.

Cooper has two apples, a sandwich on some type of rustic bread, a big bag of dried cherries, a jar of peanuts, and energy drinks. Lauren made my lunch the night before and put it in the fridge for me, so I have no idea what I'm eating. I thought she was being nice, but as I open the bag, I see she was playing with me. I pull out a bag of Goldfish crackers and a whole log of salami.

"What the...?" I say, looking at the salami.

"That's what you packed for lunch?" Cooper asks, wolfing down a handful of cherries.

"I didn't pack this; Lauren did. I guess she thought it would be funny. Ha! Jokes on her. I love salami." I peel back the casing before taking a mouthful of the greasy meat. I have to chew until my jaw aches before I can swallow. I wash it down with the water Cooper gives me.

"Imogene, share my lunch." He spreads out a paper napkin and puts an apple and half his sandwich on it then hands me the bag of peanuts and cherries. "As much as I love watching you try to eat that thing, that salami is going to make you sick."

"I've suddenly lost my appetite," I say after the third chunk of fatty meat slides down my throat.

113

"Eat the apple at least. Really. You need your energy for the rest of the hike."

"Why? Isn't it all downhill after this?"

"I might want to have my way with you on this rock," he says, slapping his hand against the flat top.

"Then you chose the wrong aphrodisiac. I'm not in the mood. Hiking makes me want to shower and sleep."

When Cooper leans over the lunch spread and kisses me, I don't hesitate to drop that stupid salami to enjoy the kiss.

"Mm, you taste like salami. I love a woman with a big stick of meat."

"Okay, enough." The apple from his tongue lingers on my lips so I pop one of the cherries into my mouth to erase him. "Tell me why you quit the FBI. I want the real story, not the one about wanting to slow down and move to a sleepy, little town. You're only twenty-nine. Adrenaline dudes like you don't move to Hera, they move out. This town is so quiet it's practically in a coma, so something must have happened for you to quit the action."

Cooper stops eating and turns to me. I can't read his expression because he's wearing sunglasses, but his mouth is stern with lips pressed closed tightly. He sighs and takes an extra T-shirt out of his backpack and bunches it into a ball before putting it behind his head to lie down. He then clasps his hands behind his head, leaving no doubt that the question agitates him.

"That bad, eh?" I shoot a peanut at him and hit him on the forehead.

"If you do that again, I'll take advantage of you here on this rock. You're tired, and I've had a boner since I had to drag your nice ass all the way up the trail."

"Really? A four-hour boner? I think you're supposed to call for medical assistance when that happens. Besides, you can't get in here," I say, snapping one of the straps of my sport bras. "It's like Fort Knox. I'm wearing a

114

straitjacket, and I could barely get these on, so I doubt you can get them off."

"Fine. I'll work on your lower half." He grabs my hands and pulls me down, trapping me on his chest.

"You're avoiding my question, and I can't read your eyes. Is that why FBI agents wear shades?"

He laughs and breaks into a grin, pinning me against him with one hand while using the other to take his sunglasses off. Then he flings my sunglasses off my face, too.

"You're lucky those are cheapos from Target, or I'd be really pissed off."

"If we're going to talk, then I want to see your eyes."

Fortunately, a large, dark cloud moves in front of the sun, and we're suddenly covered in ominous shade.

"Lie down. Stay awhile." He moves me down by his side and swiftly puts the balled up T-shirt under my head.

"Cooper, this isn't comfortable. Something sharp is digging into my neck. Oh, it's a big rock," I say sarcastically, struggling to sit up, but Cooper pins me with his leg and then shoves his arm under my head.

"There. That's better," he says.

Since there's no escape, I turn on my side and face him, snuggling my cheek into his arm. He uses the leg that's pinning mine to pull me closer to him.

"Enough lovin' here, mister. We're on a fucking rock."

"You swore." He smiles, enjoying this power struggle.

"Kcuf you, E-loha."

He laughs so loudly it echoes over the treetops. "I'm an A-hole now?"

"You have me pinned on a rock, and I'm tired and stinky, and these goddamn bras are killing me."

"Bras?"

"Lauren told me I have to wear two sport bras when I do strenuous exercise; otherwise, I'll ruin my breasts for life. I'm in so much pain right now, I'd rather be bulldozed by my own boobs than endure this stupid hike anymore."

While Cooper holds me in his arms, he laughs into my neck.

"There. Are you happy? You win. I hate this, and I'd like you to call 911 and have me airlifted out of here. Now."

Cooper is still laughing with his face buried in my neck. At least his arm is cushioning my head. He finally comes up for air and puts his other arm around me, under my back for more support. Then he leans over me with his face right above mine and my hands pressed against his chest. I'm in a Cooper cocoon, and it's really not so bad.

His laughing subsides as he looks at me sweetly.

"This is the perfect opportunity to kiss me," I say.

"I know. I planned this."

"Sure. And you're still avoiding my question."

"I'm not, but I want to get in the right mood before I talk about something miserable."

"Did you get shot?" I ask, actually becoming more curious.

"No." He kisses my forehead. "I became very jaded about people. More jaded than you are about men."

I manage to snake my hands around his neck and slip the rubber band out of his hair. While I pull his head to mine so I can kiss him slowly and thoroughly, our lips tenderly caressing, his hair fans around us. I gasp, causing him to smile against my lips. My heart flutters, telling me I'm getting all gooey-eyed over Cooper. He is beautiful, and I feel beautiful with him.

"You definitely have my attention," I say then lick his bottom lip.

"I don't want to ruin this by talking about my former job. There was a lot of ugliness in that place, and there's a lot of good here, you being the best part. Do you remember when Carson brought me to the diner for lunch on my first day?"

I blush because I remember every detail of when Cooper walked into the diner on that day. I hid nonchalantly behind bus tubs and menus, but eventually, I had to take his order since Carson kept flagging me down. I wasn't immune to Cooper's sex appeal; however, I was confident that I was in a secure, permanent coupledom with Jeremy. I'd had no idea that I would become an obsolete party to that supposed dream relationship.

"I remember it very well." His voice is deep and seductive. "There was this obnoxious waitress who was trying to ignore me. Although, I thought she was pretty and there was something special about her, so I was going to keep trying. I could only get her to look sideways at me, but I was sure that she'd eventually come around and let me ask her out."

I laugh softly at his preposterous retelling of my behavior, which happens to be quite accurate. Thank God my parents fired me.

"If you were so interested in me, why didn't you ask me out back then?"

"Believe me, I was going to. In a matter of days, Jeremy moved away, and I thought I would swoop in and nab you before that fool changed his mind. But you were so angry with him you were taking it out on me every time you saw me. I decided you needed a cooling off period, and then I'd ask you out. I didn't know it would take a fucking year for you to get over that idiot."

As I stroke the blond stubble along his jaw, he closes his eyes. "Cooper, before we kissed, what made you think I was interested in you? I was pretty nasty to you."

"That was your shield. It was the way you looked at me and still do. You never looked at Jeremy like that. In that one week I worked with him and saw you together, I figured out that you treated him more like a brother than a boyfriend. You weren't in love with him."

"Everyone thought I was heartbroken over Jeremy, and

I was a bit, but mostly, I was angry at him. Then I was angry at every guy after him."

"As you know, I see people in a different way, and I figured it out right away. You wasted too much time being angry at a guy who had already checked out. He was a nice guy to work with, but he would never be ready for you."

"We were together day and night, we never fought, and he seemed happy."

"I'm sure he was thrilled to have you, but it was going to take him years to grow up. I'm a grown-up, Imogene, and I wouldn't have moved out of this dinky town if ... He was a dork for what he did."

"I wasn't really in love with him. You got that part right," I say, hoping Cooper will say more disparaging things about Jeremy to make me feel better.

"You made a mistake being with that guy. He was a boy. You need a man."

Cooper leans down and kisses me again, angling his head to take more. All the sensations he generates are nothing I've experienced with Jeremy or any other guy, for that matter. It's as if he's consuming me in the gentlest yet most sensual way. Maybe I have only been with men who were bad kissers and never knew it until Cooper. I don't know what it is, except that I don't want to ignore him or look away from him anymore. I look forward to these secret kisses and wonder how long the game will last before we go back to being regular, non-kissing friends again.

"Have you heard anything I said?" he asks, smiling at my dreamy state. I hope I don't look as silly as the teenage girls who swoon over him.

"Yes. Jaded, obnoxious waitress, boys, men, and some other stuff."

"Huh, I guess that's a start."

"A start to what?" I ask, stroking his scruffy jaw. "Life lessons from Cooper? I don't think so, mister. Move on and tell me why you quit your big career."

Cooper groans and rolls onto his back so we're lying side by side with his left arm under my head, bent so he can hold my hand. He is quiet as he looks up at the dark sky.

"Spit it out. Those clouds look like a storm is coming in, and if I see lightening, I'm going to make you run and carry me piggyback all the way down this mountain."

"I could do that."

"Cooper, stop evading the story. Just tell me."

"You were right about me being an adrenaline junkie. But I also wanted to be different than my dad and brothers. Most of them are cops in Brooklyn where I grew up. My dad is retired from the force and owns a bar with my younger brother Peyton, who's not a cop. They all thought I should join the force, though. But I was also a good student like my mom. She's a very successful CFO at a hedge fund. I studied my ass off and took a full load each summer so I could graduate NYU in less than three years. I was twenty."

"I didn't know that," I say with genuine surprise.

Cooper smiles. "Yeah, I'm sure you had me pegged as some kind of flunkie, but you have to be a college grad and pass the tests to get into Quantico. I became a little obsessed with neural science during college. I liked studying the brain and human behavior. It was a lot of work, and I sacrificed most of my personal life to get into the FBI Academy. Some experience was required, so I was a cop for three years before I tested for Quantico when I was twenty-three.

"I was good at testing, academically and physically, and they saw me as a perfect fit for undercover work, another reason why I don't have tattoos as you so eloquently keep asking. I didn't want any identifiable marks on me.

"When we were working on the Marchetto mob case, I had two identities going. One was as a close pal of one of Vinnie's guys. My hair was dyed brown and short, and I dressed better and used a heavy New York accent. When I was on detail following Vinnie's son on various campuses, I was blond again, short hair, fake glasses, the khaki and polo crowd you referred to … yuppie, geeky student."

"I would love to see you like that." When I tweak his chin, he turns to look at me, amused.

"Never again. Now I'm just me, but for the five years I worked in CID—"

"CID?"

"Criminal Investigation Division. I couldn't get enough of that life—playing someone else twenty-four hours a day and bringing in some of the shittiest criminals ever. I knew I never wanted to do white collar cases or have a desk job. I liked being out there every day, playing a role, being smarter than those sleazy guys, and then hauling their asses in with the team.

"Some of the other men and women in my unit were married, so I'd take the most time-consuming cases, some of the real dirty ones. It left no time for my family or my girlfriend at the time, but I didn't care."

"Ah, a girlfriend."

"That was a long time ago, and my job didn't work with our relationship."

"So, bye, bye girlfriend." I sound a little too happy about that, but Cooper doesn't seem to notice.

"The job was a rush, and I didn't think I'd ever get sick of it. It was the last gig that did me in. We were working on bringing in a big drug dealer, but we were going after some of his distributors. Like any other day, I was dressed as my usual self because, well, the look works. I'd put my hair in a tail, wear a leather jacket, use the bureau issued luxury car to look like a buyer, and do my bit.

"I was going into a dealer's place, someone I had never met before. The successful guys are careful, meticulous and shrewd, and usually set up locations for our meetings or drug buys. On the last gig, when I pulled up to the location,

I knew something was wrong. The guy had us meeting at a rundown house where someone actually lived. So either it was his home or a very bad location, but the conditions told me something was wrong.

"When he answered the door, the guy was in his robe, and I could see the track marks up and down his arms and legs. I was used to meeting with drug dealers who were smart, sharp-dressed businessmen who moved large quantities. This guy was a heroin addict. He had gone off the rails. Still, I went inside the house.

"It looked like an abandoned home with garbage and filth everywhere. It wasn't even fit for rats. I had plenty of back-up people in the two-block radius, and I could handle myself if it was just this skinny strung out guy, so I wasn't really nervous.

"He walked me to a back bedroom where he was stashing thousands of bags of heroin. It was a sloppy, unprofessional set-up; I'd never seen a dealer at the top of his game operate this way. Obviously, the guy was on his way down and going fast. I didn't give a shit about him, though.

"It was then I heard someone moaning in pain. It was coming from one of the other bedrooms. This dealer was completely strung out and slow, so I just pushed past him and went to check out the other rooms. I almost threw up when I walked into a bedroom.

"There wasn't any furniture, just a dirty mattress on the floor and three emaciated toddlers. Next to them was an older boy, about ten, and he was chained to the radiator. They were starving to death. The dealer was their dad, and he said he was willing to sell the boy if it would help the deal.

"That's when it hit me. I had to fight back my instinct to take out my gun and blow his head off. That's all I wanted to do. The feeling and raw emotions were so powerful I was willing to kill someone. There was no provocation from him, but I felt myself losing control, thinking that I could fuck procedure and legal protocol and just kill the bastard right there on the spot."

"Cooper," I say softly, "that sounds awful."

"I don't know how I held it together, but somehow, I managed not to kill the guy, and the back-up team came in. The guy went down for the drugs and human trafficking— he had already sold a daughter.

"When we were clearing the house, we found his wife upstairs, also strung out. When I carried the kids out to the social services van, I almost started crying. I had never seen anything so ugly."

I inhale slowly and think about those images. "My life has been a Disney movie compared to that."

"Yeah, I think the first decade of my life was pretty sweet, too. Things changed when I hit my teens."

Cooper sighs and is quiet for a minute, and I wait, wondering if he's going to say more.

"I never witnessed first-hand what soldiers see in war," he says quietly, "but I remember seeing people jumping from the Twin Towers on a walking history lesson that day, and we were a block away when the second plane hit. The subway shut down, so the teachers were trying to corral all these high school kids towards City Hall Park and get us to walk home across the Brooklyn Bridge. We did eventually, but not before we saw people jumping to their deaths. I thought that would be the most terrifying thing I'd ever witness. It was, actually. Still, I never thought I'd see a father do to his kids …

"What that fucking lowlife did to his children was an image I'll never forget. And the seconds or maybe minutes I spent thinking about killing him and covering it up as self-defense made me realize I was done. I was too close to doing something worse."

"But you didn't. You didn't kill him. You saved those kids."

"No one saved those kids. They're in the system, probably separated. Bureaucracy isn't humane; it doesn't love children."

"So you resigned because of that case?"

"I resigned because I realized I had spent five years, twenty-four hours a day with the worst human beings. I liked the people in my unit, but most of my casework was solitary undercover work with the most disgusting side of human nature. I took a month off to get my head back on right, but all it did was confirm that my life wasn't my own. I wasn't a hero, and I didn't feel like I was helping humanity. I was hanging with the worst scum of our species, and I didn't want the rest of my life to be full of that. The rush was gone, and it all felt too sickening after a while. So, I resigned."

While I squeeze his hand, he exhales as though he'd been holding his breath the whole time he was confiding in me.

"When you decided to resign, what were you planning on doing?"

"I thought I'd take a few months and travel around the country, visiting some old college friends. I actually headed out to Colorado to do some hiking with friends. I wasn't there very long when my sources contacted me about Emma applying for a job with Carson's company. I decided to come back to see if there were any new bites on the Marchetto case and Emma's ex-boyfriend. We were losing track of him, so that's when I decided to go meet with Carson. It took some convincing, but after he heard my background and the story behind Emma's ex, Carson thought it was a good plan to have me on site."

"That was a weird situation. Lauren was just trying to help Emma get a job. We had no idea that it would drag Emma's family and past into the mix. Poor Carson, he was caught in the middle, wanting to help Emma, but I'm pretty sure he was intrigued with you."

"I had you fooled, didn't I?"

"Oh, yeah. I figured you were some lost dude who ended up in Hera by accident and Carson was being nice by giving you a job at his factory. When Emma's father was arrested along with the other mobsters and the whole story came out, I was really …" I trail off, not wanting to sound like a raving fan.

"Really what?" he urges, waiting for me to say something complimentary.

"I was amazed that you'd pulled it off. I never would have guessed that you were an FBI agent and part of this grand scheme. You played the casual goofball part really well. Everyone believed that you were one of Carson's humanitarian projects."

As Cooper laughs, the tension he was holding in recedes.

"I had no idea you were so … smart. But you must be. Carson wouldn't promote or hire just anyone to take over as his operations manager. He and Dylan have a lot of respect for you."

"Is that what made you give me a second look?"

"No. I was still trying to ignore you," I blurt out, my face heating with embarrassment.

Cooper laughs harder. "I love your honesty."

"I still don't understand why you decided to stay here after all the drama with Emma was resolved."

"I liked how Carson ran his company, and I liked the people there. Everyone seemed really content with work and their life in this little town. It seemed incredibly normal and quiet compared to where I'd come from. My neighborhood in Brooklyn was dense. My family is large and loud. My career was exciting, chaotic, and dangerous. And then, one day, I started to dislike all of it and wanted to live a different way. I was at the top of a mountain in Colorado, and the peace was humbling. I needed more of that. Then, when I met Carson and he walked me around the factory and the studio, I got a very good vibe from the people and the place."

"It's still strange. People usually wait until their sixties to hang it up and move to a little town. Hell, I was born and raised here, and I still sometimes think I'm missing the whole world by staying."

"You won't miss anything if you travel a bit. This is a good place to come home to. You should take a trip with me. We'll go hiking in the Colorado and Washington—"

"Have you not learned anything about me today? I don't like hiking. I'm lying on this rock, waiting for my airlift."

Cooper laughs again and I join in. "We could go to Istanbul. You'd love it."

"You've been there?"

"Years ago, I had a short break between college and joining the police force, so I travelled with a college friend who was from Greece. It was great. We were broke, but he had friends and family in a few different countries, so we slept on couches and in hostels and ate at open street markets. I wouldn't make you sleep on any couches, though; I'd take you to a hotel."

"It's always nice when a guy offers to take you to a hotel so he can get in your pants." When I playfully slap his stomach with the back of my hand, he captures it and rolls towards me, his lips instantly on mine in a short yet sweet moment.

"I'm not going to pressure you into anything you're not ready for," he says with his lips a few centimeters above mine. "I have plenty of time. I've already waited a year, and I figure I'm the only available guy in town you could possibly be interested in, unless you're still hot for the high school quarterback or the rich town lawyer who was born two centuries ago."

"You've also bagged plenty of women since you've been here. I hear everything in the diner."

125

"First of all, stop saying *bagged* or *banging*. I've been out with a few women, some of whom asked me out. So there. But I don't bang women."

"Okay, so you've fucked a few women because there are plenty of young, pretty women in the area, especially during tourist season. And I know all about you and the Pilates chick."

"We weren't serious or anything."

"I didn't say you were, but you kind of picked up where Dylan left off."

"Shit, Imogene. I'm twenty-nine and have a dick. I have to use it sometimes, but I'm not setting records with nameless women every week."

"I totally understand."

"I don't like the way you said that," he says with a tinge of irritation in his voice.

"I like kissing this," I say, swiping my finger against his soft lips. "But I need to stay away from this." I swiftly reach my hand down between us and cup the growing bulge in his groin.

"Ah," he grits out.

I release my hand and smile sweetly.

"You're going to lose this bet, muffin." He pulls me up to a sitting position and sits back on his knees.

"Yuck, don't call me that. And I said I'd take you out for dinner, and you don't even have to cut your hair or dress like a yuppie. Let's just get off this kcuffing mountain already. I've had enough."

I wouldn't mind going out with Cooper. It feels good to be with a man who is genuinely engaging. The conversation alone is enough for me, but the physical attraction is downright thrilling. However, sleeping with Cooper would surely upset the delicate balance of the entire universe, and I'd end up as the scorned muffin among my family and friends while Cooper could merely move out of town if things became uncomfortable.

"You deserve *muffin* for thinking I'm a sleazy jerk with women."

"You'll get over it. Another pretty blond will want you to have your way with her, and you two may even get married and have beautiful blond babies together."

"That won't work," he responds, frowning. "I've always been partial to brunettes."

Thirteen

I spend the next three days putting in eighteen-hour days, completing necklaces, uploading new inventory to our website, and talking to potential retailers for our line.

Lauren's pregnancy leaves her tired at odd hours to the point where I catch her occasionally falling asleep sitting up with beads in her hand; as a result, I encourage her to nap while I pick up the slack.

I think about Cooper constantly. Being attracted to one man in a hundred-mile radius, of course, he's frequently in my thoughts; especially when I go into the pantry where I practically stripped for him or the TV room where I slept on top of him.

Fortunately, Cooper has been busy working long hours, handling a huge shipment of lumber that came in and large delivery orders of furniture that need to go out. He called to see if I was ready for a public dinner date with him, and I managed to stall him, citing my workload and exhaustion. It was a stupid excuse and made me sound like I was eighty-five instead of twenty-five. However, Cooper didn't let my poor acting skills deter him. To rile me, he got the last word in: *see you at dance class, muffin.*

Lauren and I finish our work for the evening then put our heels in a grocery bag before heading out the door to the dance studio near New Paltz. We're dressed in our work clothes, jeans and T-shirts, but the dance instructor, Rafe, insisted that the women bring heels that will be similar to what we'll be wearing at the wedding. Since Lauren special ordered the bridesmaid dresses, I have no

128

idea what they look like, but she informed me that we're wearing two-inch strappy heels. Nice and cryptic. I wouldn't be surprised if Lauren puts us in puffy, orange chiffon dresses so we resemble pumpkins next her princess ensemble. Although, I love her enough to let her do whatever she wants with me as long as there are no tiaras or wands.

When we enter the dance studio, the men and women are there, all except Cooper. Archie, Lois, and Eleanor are seated in the chairs along the back wall.

"Oh, great, we have an audience," I say to Lauren.

"And our parents are here, too," she adds. Sure enough, sitting along another wall are my parents, Pam and Mark, and Lauren's parent's, Nina and Garth.

"They all have cameras," I grouse.

"Let it go, Imogene. I'm an only child so my parents are making a big deal out of this. It's their one shot. And your parents are probably thinking the same thing."

"But I'm not getting married."

"Maybe they think this is the closest you'll get to the altar since you're driving every guy away." She smirks.

"Funny. At least I won't have to upchuck during the dancing. Maybe they want to film that."

Lauren laughs and then surprises herself with a small belch. "God, I hope I don't get sick," she says, covering her mouth.

"Hey, babe," Leo says, coming towards us with a big, goofy grin. "Ready to dance?"

"No," I reply for Lauren.

"Yes, let's get this party started!" Lauren pumps her fists as she and Leo walk towards Rafe and the others. Our cheerleader is back.

"Oh, fun," I mutter to myself just as Cooper enters the studio, looking a little too excited.

"Happy to see me?" His arrogant smile is breathtaking, inducing that wretched involuntary smiling on my part.

"I can't wait to do the two-step with you," I say with artificial glee.

"It's a waltz, and you're going to love dancing with me."

"I think you have waltzing confused with something else," I say, making him chuckle as if that's exactly what's on his mind.

I've had a lot of dirty thoughts about you, too.

He leans down to my ear. "It's nice to see you, too," he says in a husky voice before giving my cheek a quick peck.

Before I can respond or settle my goose bumpy arms, Rafe calls us to the center of the room. Cooper puts his arm across my shoulders, leading me over to the others as though we're a couple. I pull away to join the women by the mirrored wall where we exchange our sneakers for heels.

Rafe is a very lean, thirty-something-year-old who looks every bit the professional dancer. He's quite polished in black dress slacks, shiny black shoes, and a vibrant blue oxford. He takes his ballroom dancing seriously and isn't pleased that we have arrived in jeans.

He takes one look at Carson and Cooper, their long hair and unshaven faces, and shakes his head. "Gentlemen, I hope you can make a little more effort for Lauren's wedding."

Carson looks nonchalantly at Cooper and his attire then back at Rafe. "Probably not."

"It's fine, Rafe. I'm used to them like this," Lauren adds, bubbly as a bride should be.

"Fine. Men, gather your lovely partners, and we'll take our marks."

Rafe has the four couples hold each other at arm's length. The women are then instructed to keep their elbows raised and their left hand touching their partner's shoulder without *gripping* or *clenching*, he emphasizes. He puts on Strauss to start with some easy waltzes.

I feel surprisingly at ease once we start dancing. I thought it would be awkward and I'd stumble or lose the rhythm, yet Cooper leads perfectly. Maybe I'm imagining it, but our dancing feels superb. I wonder if we look as fabulous as I think we do.

Cooper looks down at me with a mirthful smile, as if he knows I'm shocked and pleased that we're doing so well. I don't notice the other couples, but I do hear the click of camera phones going off from the peanut gallery.

"I better not see any of those photos online," Carson says loudly to the observers as he dances by with Jess stumbling in his arms.

"Don't worry," Archie says, peering through his phone, "I'm going to make it a virus."

We all turn our heads at Archie and the dancing lurches to a stop, sending Rafe into a fit.

"He meant viral," Eleanor clarifies for everyone.

"No videos!" Dylan joins in with Carson.

"Stop! Stop! Everyone, stop where you are!" Rafe yells.

"For the love of hot potatoes," Lois says loudly, shaking her head. "You're all in trouble now." She waggles a finger at all of us.

"Can we all concentrate on the dancing? Gentlemen, you have some issues here," Rafe says sternly. "Carson, I don't know what you're doing to Jessica over there, but it's not a waltz. You're swinging her around like she's a rag doll, and you're crushing her hand and stepping on her feet. You're not a circus elephant, learning how to dance."

There's an outburst of laughter with my snorts being the loudest.

Rafe walks over to Carson and taps him between his shoulder blades. "I want you to pull back, stand straighter, and be more relaxed at the same time. If you maintain good posture, you'll feel the difference."

Carson grunts an acknowledgment while Jess looks

relieved that her husband is getting some professional instruction.

"Dylan?" Rafe barks as he walks over to Dylan and Emma. "What you're doing is not dancing. It's public molestation."

I'm laughing so hard Cooper starts laughing again, Lois and Eleanor are whooping it up in the background, and even Emma is hiding a grin. It doesn't throw off Rafe's diatribe, though.

"Seriously, Dylan, with the way you're mauling Emma, I feel like I should beat you off her with a chair. This is a beautiful waltz. The dancers are supposed to glide across the room. Stop trying to tango or whatever you're doing there. You make this look like a shake-down scene from a Scorsese movie."

Dylan looks apologetically at Emma. "I don't know what that means."

"*Goodfellas*!" Lauren shouts out one her favorite mob films.

"Okay, Lauren, you're next," Rafe says pointedly at her. Her smile disappears as she shrinks back. "You have got to stop leading and pay attention to Leo. You're making him lose his footing because you're taking his marks. You may be in charge of the wedding, but the man is leading the dance. Got it?"

After Lauren nods, Leo kisses her cheek for getting a scolding.

"And you two," Rafe says, pointing a finger at Cooper and me. "Perfect. You know how to dance," he addresses Cooper.

All eyes are on Cooper who looks a little surprised to be the center of attention; therefore, I take the opportunity to take a sweeping curtsy, which garners some laughs from the parents and seniors.

"I've been in a few wedding parties," Cooper says modestly. "And a lot of dance classes. Big family, you

132

know?"

"The rest of you need to follow their example," Rafe says to the others.

As we continue with the lesson, I become rather delirious with all of Cooper's elegant twirling and gliding against the backdrop of the classical music. I thought I'd feel like a clod, but Cooper makes it easy and fun, and I'm heady as I hold onto him. It's a good thing he's leading because I spend more time looking at his face than watching the floor or the dancers in front of us.

"Damn," I say, "I didn't know you could dance."

"Hell, if I had known this is all it takes to impress you, I would have mentioned it a lot sooner."

"You already impressed me when you carried my drunk dead ass up all those stairs to my bedroom. I have no recollection of it, but it was a very noble feat."

"It would have been a crime if I hadn't carried you," he says as he sweeps me effortlessly around a studio column. "So, does this mean you're ready for more? Dinner? A movie? A trip to Target? Anything?"

"Good point, Lauren and Leo do like to stock up on those 36-roll packages of toilet paper, but that would be very difficult to carry on your bike."

He scoffs. "You're so fucking afraid it amazes me."

"I'm very busy this week."

Cooper's expression softens. I could be dancing backwards off a cliff, and I would never know because I'm completely enamored by him. How he holds me firmly yet gently and manages to guide me into the steps and turns while locking me into a seductive gaze has me practically swooning. In the background, I hear Rafe's voice, Dylan's muttered expletives, Lois's running commentary on the dancers, and Jess's hilarious chanting, *'One-Two-Three,'* to keep Carson in step. Those sounds begin to fade away until all I hear are the violins and the rest of the orchestra playing the lulling romantic melody, and all I see is Cooper

133

looking down upon me as if we're the only people in the room. I must have one of those telltale expressions because Cooper smiles as though he caught me daydreaming about us. He did. I'm seeing hoopskirts and men in tuxedos, getting all mushy over the whole corny set-up.

"We're good partners," he says, breaking my reverie.

"That's because we can count and move our feet at the same time," I reply as we catch Carson and Dylan colliding into each other's backs.

In time to the music, Rafe waves his arms like an orchestra conductor and yells in a sing-songy voice, "There are only four couples dancing, no one should be running into anyone else, people! This cannot happen at the reception."

I laugh at the others because I'm clinging to a guy who is a natural-born dancer. In fact, I'm almost *clenching* and *gripping* him. Thankfully, the mandatory space between our bodies keeps this very PG-13.

"Too bad we're so good. It makes the others look worse," I say, clicking my tongue.

"Don't feel too bad for them, at least they get to go to bed together after this," he responds, throwing me into a rather forceful turn during a dramatic moment in the music.

My heads whips left and then right as I lose control, Cooper's hands tightening instantly to keep me steady. When the music comes to a slow part and I gain my footing, Cooper gives me a wicked grin.

"You're kind of at my mercy, baby," he says, smugly.

"You did that on purpose, and don't call me baby."

"Just showing you that it takes two to make this work. Those guys are lousy dancers, but they have a few things I envy."

"You've made it very clear that dancing isn't going to be enough for you, so we'll have our date, and I'll let you watch me eat an expensive dinner. I'll even ask for extra bread and butter if that turns you on. We can go out

Friday."

"Finally, out in public when it's not mandated by Lauren's wedding plans. Exactly how will you explain this to all those inquiring minds?" he asks sardonically.

"Oh, people will assume I'm simply breaking you in so you can keep up with me at the wedding."

"Excellent. You should break me in. I'd enjoy that."

"Kcuf," I mutter. "I made that one too easy for you."

"You did, but I'm glad we're going out. I thought you'd have cold feet after the hike. Speaking of which, how are those blisters on your feet?"

"Thanks for asking. They're killing me. This dancing business is making them bleed. These shoes will have to be pried off my feet, but I think I'm putting on a pretty good show. What do you think?"

"Great show. I had no idea you're in pain, especially since you're making those eyes at me again."

"I'm making eyes at you? Forget it. I don't want to hear it." I turn to watch Dylan screw up again as he aggressively draws Emma against him.

"Got it. Nothing about sex. How's work, and what do you think of Carson's business plan?"

I turn back to meet his silvery-gray eyes as he regards me with a pleased expression.

"Carson's business plan?" I ask in confusion. "I haven't heard it. Lauren and I are meeting with Archie and Carson tomorrow to talk about a loan and expanding the business to hire a couple of people. What do you know?"

"Oh, nothing," he says, turning his head and looking down at our clasped hands. "Carson mentioned he was planning on meeting with you two but didn't give me any of the specifics."

"Well, it should be interesting and terrifying. It's kind of our do or die moment, so Lauren and I have to suck it up and do it, whatever it is."

"You're going to be fine, Imogene." He tilts his head

to the side, looking very boyish, despite his unshaven face. That sexy, scruffy jaw makes me think dirty thoughts about him again—naked and hard and in every position imaginable. I definitely can't erase those explicit images.

"Okay, I give. Go back to that comment you made about my eyes. What about them?" I ask, annoyed and trying to put the brakes on my fantasies that are growing more sordid by the minute. "I don't make eyes at you, unless you mean the daggers I keep shooting your way."

"Nope, I was talking about the other eyes you make. You can't hide those from me."

"Oh, brother." I roll my head skyward. "Here we go again. Mr. Mind Reader."

"It's okay. I'm thinking the same thing as you."

"And what's that?"

He leans down to my ear. "That we really want to fuck each other every which way until we're crawling out of bed for water and food," he whispers.

Only an unprepared woman asks a question she already knows the answer to. I should have been prepared for the response I was expecting. I wasn't. As my knees shake and buckle, Cooper violates the waltzing code by pulling me in close to his body until I'm righted again.

"I got it," I say, stepping back into position. "This is why we should not date. No one should end up deprived of water and food. Really, such drama."

"You're right. We should skip the dating part and do those things you keep thinking about. Your eyes have crazy-ass lust in them whenever you look at me, Imogene."

I'm gaping, desperate to come up with a quick retort, but my crazy-ass, lust-filled eyes prevent any coherent strategic thinking.

I'm kcuffed.

Fourteen

Carson puts his laptop on Archie's desk and swivels it so Lauren and I can both see the loan schedule he set up. My eyes widen at the number of zeros involved; however, Carson and Archie are very sure about the plan they have constructed. Carson insists we use his storage building behind his factory as our new studio, and Archie has a part-time bookkeeper lined up for us. All we need to do is hire two more people experienced in beading to work full-time with us.

"Don't let the loan scare you," Carson says, recognizing my uneasiness. "Think of it as an investment because there isn't any interest or payment due for three years."

"You won't get this kind of offer at a bank," Archie reminds me.

"I know, but can you really afford to put up this kind of money right now, Carson? You're expanding your businesses, and it's like you'll be carrying us for three years," I say.

Carson scratches the stubble on his jaw, tired of reassuring me, probably. "I can afford it. Besides, Archie is putting in half, and the building costs me nothing since I own it. The utilities there are cheap, and your monthly sales can easily cover those and more.

"I feel good about the projections you worked out with Archie. We're running everything on the low-end here, Imogene. You don't have an expensive storefront with high overhead. Even if we have a damaging storm or blizzard, we've taken extraordinary circumstances and holiday seasons into account, and the spreadsheet reflects that. I'm no expert on jewelry, but I know the retail business pretty well, so I'm confident about this."

"I think this is a solid plan," Lauren chimes in.

"I think so, too," Archie says. "All you need to do is hire the two women Lauren mentioned."

It's impossible not to trust Archibald Bixby. He's our wise Yoda, the kind that wears a three-piece suit all year round. He's also very wealthy yet seems to bank everything since he's never married or had children; consequently, he wants to help us—we are his family.

"You like Anita and Tracy?" I ask Lauren, finding as many ways to stall this process as possible. I suppose my indecision must be indicative of how little I have believed in myself for too long.

"I do," she replies. "They are both very experienced with jewelry. Tracy has very good taste and an eye for this, and Anita is very crafty and meticulous. The beadwork she showed me was amazing."

"Okay, so what's our timeframe, Carson?" I ask.

"I'll have the guys start clearing the furniture out of the shack tomorrow. All we need to do is replace the toilet and sink, give it an industrial cleaning, and a new inside paint job. It can be ready by the end of next week or earlier, depending on how much spare time the guys have."

"It's a lot of money and quite a bit of work. You really have that much faith in us?"

"I have complete faith in you. The real question is do you?"

Two days later, I'm still questioning our decision, although I'm also excited. It's something to look forward to, even if we've needed Carson, Archie, and our parents to push us in this direction. Lauren and I have spent so many years tied at the hip—growing up together all through high school and college and even working at my family's restaurant. The last thing I want is to end up being Lauren's sidekick at the diner, two seniors in our orthopedic shoes, serving burgers and fries to tourists and high school kids.

I was too busy having fun to come up with a life plan. High school and college may have taught me a few things, but they didn't prepare me for any kind of career.

After seeing how far Carson has come with his business, despite the hardships he's endured—the death of his adoptive parents, dealing with Dylan's mental health issues, and still managing to become a successful businessman—I need it to rub off on me.

I realize I had a fairly idyllic upbringing, and it's time for me to buckle down and do the real work, taking the scary risks I am unaccustomed to. I'll let any snarky thing fly out of my mouth, and I come across as confident and cocky at times. However, the truth is I must suffer from some kind of fear that has prevented me from grasping at anything bigger or at least recognizing my intentional sabotage of anything resembling something good.

Cooper is on time, of course. It's the date he has been waiting for, the one I have dreaded because of my mixed emotions regarding him. My interest is growing in all the wrong ways, and the timing is horrendous because of my responsibilities to the business venture.

He insists on picking me up in Leo's truck, and I agreed as long as I foot the bill. I can't keep letting this guy spoil me in a way that triggers my own reservations about servitude and debt.

I've had a few long-term boyfriends—handsome jocks, a few smart business types, some who were astute and funny, some not so much. Yet I always went for the popular, good-looking guy who was envied by men, coveted by women, and screwed by me. This is why I'm hesitant about Cooper. He is a combination of every boy and man I've dated, except you'd have to multiply it by a thousand. He's off the Richter scale for me, and it's both exhilarating and frightening.

Lauren doesn't say a word as I leave the house and walk out to the driveway when I hear the truck come rumbling up to the porch. You'd think I'm being escorted to my own execution by the way my arms and legs tremble and a wave of dizziness strikes me when Cooper jumps out of the cab of the truck and smiles at me. *Goddamn his good genes.*

"Hey, lovey," he says, walking towards me.

"Really hate that one."

"Okay, I'm still working on it. You're like a fine wine—"

"Drop it. I've heard it all before. You're not the only pro, remember? I've been a player for years, too."

"You make us sound like hustlers."

His eyes roam appreciatively over me, taking in my halter dress that shows off my legs and cleavage. I've worn my hair up since it's so muggy outside. He's dressed in jeans, but I forgive him since they are not threadbare. He also has on a white dress shirt with the collar open and the sleeves slightly rolled and black dress shoes which I've never seen on him.

"Well, think about it. What exactly are we doing with each other? You're trying to get me into bed, and I'm pretending to take a stand for all women who have played that card one too many times."

Cooper laughs and holds my elbow as I climb into the truck. "My cynic. Can't wait to see what you say at dinner. This should be several hours of enlightenment."

"You laugh, but—"

As he cuts me off with a kiss, the potent desire hits me at once; his hand on my cheek, the brush of his stubble against my skin, and his lips that I haven't touched in eleven days, since the hike. Sure, he gave me a peck at the dance class, but I've been thinking about his lips and

140

everything else attached to him for eleven frigging days because obsessed people start counting and replaying their own delusional video montages in their head when they get too attached. And that's exactly what's happening here. I'm stuck in Cooperville.

While his kiss is gentle and wanting, I sense his urge to carry it on longer and also his hesitation because he wants to get me away from my home and work, my safety zone. I have been through this scenario before, though not with this man. I want to hold him a little longer.

I put my hands around his neck with my thumbs skimming the stubble on his jawline. My tongue is more forceful, and he responds with a slight moan as he leans into the cab to accommodate my wanton desire. Every little warning bell that was clanging moments ago is now silent. I do want to be with him, and these kisses are not enough.

Our mouths and tongues continue to tangle, duel, and tease each other's senses for several minutes or perhaps longer. I'm not sure how long it goes on, but at some point, we part slowly and both exhale.

"I guess that was the appetizer," Cooper says, a little breathless. "Damn good."

I touch my lips and nod.

"I think you're ready for this date. I know I am," he says in a crisp tone, containing the hormonal fireworks we just set off. "You look beautiful."

"Thank you. You look very nice, too."

He closes my door and gets in the truck before driving us out of town, heading for a new French restaurant in Kingston.

When we arrive, he makes me wait until he can open my door and properly escort me inside.

"Be prepared for a major turn on," I say as I take his arm. "I'm very hungry and plan on eating extra bread and butter the minute it hits the table."

"Good. I hate when I'm the only one eating,"

"Please tell me you haven't brought dates to this place before. That would kind of ruin this dinner for me."

"I've never been here. I picked this restaurant because it's new for both of us. Of course, I was going on the assumption you haven't been here."

"I haven't, but I've heard it's very good and the reservation list has a bit of a wait."

"I worked around that. Carson and I have been renovating the owner's house," Cooper says quietly as the hostess leads us through the small but packed dining room.

We're seated at a quaint table for two by a window overlooking a garden. The white table linens and candles suit the understated opulence and decadent menu. It's a "special date" restaurant with well-dressed couples at every table, except one which has a tired-looking couple with a baby.

The baby girl looks like she is about six months old, holding herself up in a wobbly state as she tries to grasp the big sunflower headband she's wearing. She's sitting in one of those little infant dining seats that attaches to the rim of the table, and her parents are anxiously trying to entertain her with little toys so she behaves while they eat. I've seen this before; the couple that wants a night out but loses their sitter, or worse, thinks they can tote an unpredictable baby along to a fine dining establishment. I feel a little sorry for the parents. They can't possibly enjoy their meal when they're afraid their child will misbehave and draw judgment from other diners who probably want a childfree-zone.

"She's cute," Cooper says, tipping his chin towards the squealing baby.

"I can't believe Lauren and Leo are going to have one of those in a few months." The baby is adorable; however, the thought of the responsibility that comes with being a parent gives me the willies, making me think I must be a late bloomer in everything with the exception of sex, which

142

is a truly pathetic notion.

Cooper discreetly removes his glasses out of his shirt pocket and slips them on to read the menu in the dark ambiance.

"Oh, my God. You are too cute in those glasses," I say, chuckling and shaking my head. "Seriously nerdy and sexy, mister."

He looks up from his menu and raises an eyebrow at me. "If I wear them all the time, I'll walk into walls, but I'll do it if it makes you want to spend more time with me."

"I'm flattered, but you don't have to impair your vision for me."

"Just in case, I'm going to keep them on all through dinner."

"So you'll get lucky tonight?" I ask, taking a big bite of the warm roll that was placed in front of me.

"Is that on the agenda? Am I in the running? Because I am up for the challenge."

I laugh. It feels good to be out with a guy I have known for a while. The chemistry is more than friendship, although since we haven't slept together, there's no awkwardness of trying to label the relationship ... *yet*.

Cooper is someone I want to sleep with, but he's also someone I enjoy talking to. Each time we're together, I learn something new about him, or he says something witty or intelligent that makes it that much easier to be with him. The fact that he's wrapped up in a sexy package is icing on the cake. The cake I want to lick ... and then eat.

When the waiter appears to take our orders and an extra moment to compliment Cooper on his glasses, for some reason, it makes me blush. Placing a hand over my mouth, I attempt to avoid giggling until the waiter leaves.

"I wasn't exactly thrilled about needing reading glasses, but I definitely didn't expect this reaction from ... everyone," he says.

"Hand them over," I say, thrusting my palm out.

Without asking why, he takes them off and puts them in my hand. I slide the glasses on my face and blink a few times since the prescription lenses are making everything blurry for me.

"Well? How do I look?" I ask, focusing on the fuzzy blond image in front of me.

"You look hot. But you already looked hot. Those kind of make you look ..."

"Like a sexpot teacher? A sexy English professor?"

"I see your point."

I take them off and hand them back. "Put them away. You'll get a headache if you wear them for anything other than reading."

He grunts but folds the glasses and puts them back in his pocket. "I feel like I'm locking away my super powers."

"Ha," I snort.

He looks nothing short of amazingly attractive. The candlelight only makes his arresting good looks more pronounced, and it isn't just our waiter who notices, other women turn their heads nonchalantly to catch a glimpse of my date.

As I fantasize about his mouth, Cooper fills me in on the progress he and the other men have made on clearing out Carson's building behind the parking lot. His eyes light up as he talks about painting and installing the new plumbing fixtures when the crew gets off work from their day jobs at the furniture factory. I have unintentionally created extra work for him, and he's graciously telling me it's fun.

He's doing a very good job of charming the panties off me. At the very least, they're working their way down to my knees. This is the kind of magic that ends once you sleep with someone. It's the natural order of things. The predictability and boredom of routine eventually set in, and before you know it, the guy stops closing the bathroom door—*Quarterback Cody!!*—and they start wearing socks to bed—*Wanker Jeremy!*

"We'll come pick up your tables and supplies at the house whenever you're ready. I'll set everything up for you at the new place," Cooper explains as I stare at his lips. He takes a bite of his roll and regards me with amused satisfaction. "Huh. Either you want this roll or you want me."

"Maybe both," I reply.

He stops chewing and puts the roll on my bread plate. "Can I ask for our food to go?"

"No. We're having a nice meal and someone else is serving me. And … I'm still thinking about this."

His expression darkens as he leans forward, placing both of his hands down on either side of my place setting. "Think faster before I haul you off to the restroom for something else."

I let out an incredulous laugh, but am interrupted by a high pitch squeal from the baby at the other table. She's not crying, although she has her tiny arms raised as she emits a lengthy, ear-piercing shriek that shuts down every conversation in the restaurant.

All heads turn to the baby who is continuing to screech as her pink-faced parents try to subdue her with toys and fascinating table utensils. The mother notices everyone staring at her and the baby, and she huddles as if trying to make herself smaller.

"Well done, little girl!" Cooper suddenly shouts in a booming voice and begins clapping. "Bravo!"

I look around at the bewildered faces of the patrons who would look petty now if they complained about a screaming baby in the restaurant. With Cooper leading the applause, I enthusiastically join in, and soon, all the other tables follow. People begin smiling and even laughing. They'll all have a cute, little story to tell their friends.

"Good job. Crisis averted," I say to Cooper over the applause. "You spared those parents from humiliation."

145

The parents in question nod and thank the crowd for their understanding, and the baby goes back to gnawing on a rubber toy, unaware that she caused such a stir.

"I have a few nieces and nephews. My brothers and sister have been in the same uncomfortable situation. When in doubt, make people laugh. Anyone who was annoyed to be sitting next to a baby is a little less uptight about it now."

"I guess you do have some super powers."

"Hmm." He gives me a questioning look. "I only use them for good. I'll have to show you after dinner."

Our waiter arrives with salads, which I dig into immediately to keep my mouth occupied so I don't have to continue with the sex topic that was conveniently interrupted by the baby.

"Haven't you been eating since you quit the diner? You look ravenous." Cooper watches as I shove another mound of greens into my mouth.

"Tho gwood," I mumble, chomping like a goat.

"Christ, am I making you nervous?"

"No," I reply, covering my mouth with my napkin. *Yes, you're making me nervous! I'm thinking about nailing my first Viking!*

As the main courses arrive, I start talking about the dead squirrel Leo and I found on the porch and cleaning the gutters in time for summer rainstorms. I'm rambling and my heart is racing while Cooper watches me in astonishment, as if he's wondering how his date went from clever sexual banter to hyperventilating between each bite of her duck confit.

"This is so delicious," I exclaim, picking up a forkful of duck to feed to Cooper. He frowns, but takes the food between his teeth and chews slowly without his eyes ever leaving mine.

"I've seen enough. We need to go, Imogene." He's using his deep, take-charge tone. He flags down our waiter,

146

who swiftly removes Cooper's untouched lamb and my mutilated duck.

"Why? You picked the restaurant, and I like it."

"Baby, I have never seen you like this. You're on the verge of becoming hysterical. I think it's because you're nervous about us and what's running through that pretty head of yours about tonight."

The waiter returns with our food wrapped as lovely little tinfoil swans. Then Cooper pays the bill as I gather our fragile swans. He puts his arm around me and walks me out to the truck where he opens my door and tosses the swans into the cab.

"Gah, you mangled their necks," I say, reaching for the foil packages, but Cooper pulls me back. "Oh, kcuf! I was going to treat you, why didn't you remind me? Let me go put the bill on my credit card."

"Settle down." Cooper pulls me tightly against him and strokes my cheek. "It's me. There's nothing to be nervous about, Imogene."

Imogene sounds like the sexiest, most provocative word rolling off his tongue. I inhale slowly to compose myself.

"Do you know why I wanted this date with you?" he asks, gently cupping my chin.

"I guess it wasn't about the food since you hardly ate anything."

"I wanted to be out with you like regular people who enjoy each other's company. I liked going to the estate sale with you, but that's business. And I like the dancing classes, but that's for Leo and Lauren. Tonight is about you and me doing our own thing."

"Sorry I got a little strung out in there. A lot of things are happening at once, and I don't have it as together as I should."

"Come home with me, Imogene, and for tonight, let's not play these roles."

147

"What roles?"

"Where you say something funny to blow me off, and I say something funny to continue the pursuit."

"I'm tired of being funny."

Cooper sighs, looking worried, as if he's expecting me to reject him. "Imogene, you'll always be funny, sexy, and beautiful no matter how little effort you put into it. I don't want to change you. I want to be with you."

"Let's go to your house." My voice doesn't waver this time.

Cooper looks down at me with a slight curve of his mouth. Then he leans in and kisses me again. It's an erotic slow dance of lips and tongues, and everything is warm, soft, and sensual. My body reacts instantly with shivers of excitement and need.

He takes one last nip at my lower lip then slowly pulls away. "I've been waiting for you to say that."

He wastes no more time, hustling me into the truck then speeding to the interstate to get us back to Hera.

"Text Leo and tell him he'll get his truck back tomorrow," Cooper commands as he zooms onto a rural road that only the locals know about.

I'm a good faker, but I am so nervous my fingers have trouble texting on the bumpy dirt road that Cooper plows onto. I try to rewrite the text: *U get fuck tom.*

"Oh, whatever," I mutter and push SEND.

"You okay?" Cooper glances over at me. "Second thoughts?"

"Let me see. I washed my hair, shaved my legs, and I have my guy-gettin' dress on and my best panties. I'm ready for takeoff."

Cooper barks out a laugh. He takes my hand and holds it for a moment until we come to a barricade on the dirt road, then he grabs the stick shift.

"Well fuck that," Cooper hisses. "Hold on to the handle and your panties because we're going around this sucker."

I yelp, grabbing the door handle and the headrest as the truck jolts as we go off road, driving through a shallow ravine and then up a steep hill to go around the barricade.

As we come back down and hit the road on the other side, Cooper guns it.

"I guess you really like short cuts," I say, letting go of the headrest.

"I really like getting you home quickly."

Fifteen

I've never been to Cooper's house. All I know is he's renovating it with the help of Carson, Dylan, and some of the men from Carson's contracting business.

When we arrive at a log-style home nestled in the woods, there's one front light on; otherwise, the area is pitch black. I grab the foil swans by their twisted necks and hop out of the truck, hearing rushing water in the distance.

"Are you on the creek?" I ask.

"Yep." Cooper slips an arm around my waist, practically pulling me to the front door.

I yank off my heels when we get inside while Cooper flips on some light-switches.

"Wow," I exclaim. "Lauren was right. You are tidy."

"Tidy?" He winces.

"I always expect single guys to be slobs, but your place is clean, and you must be the first guy who doesn't have his furniture arranged around a TV." I take in the Blackard Designs furniture and a few prints on the walls, creating a very rustic and comfortable appearance.

"That's my sister's doing. When Greer visits, she moves everything around."

"Greer? That's nice. And how many brothers?"

"Three brothers. They're just as nosy and annoying as my sister."

"Still, it must be nice. Lauren and I always felt cheated not having siblings."

"That's why you two are so close, though." He puts an arm around my waist and kisses my temple. "Let me give you the ten-second tour. It's a small place, not much to see."

"I like it." I nod in approval as I look around the room.

"Good." He takes my hand and pulls me down the short hallway to the kitchen. It looks like something out of a 1970s sitcom.

"Oh, my," I laugh. The kitchen has a sort of deranged festive theme going on with orange Formica counters and carpeting and dated, dark brown cabinetry and appliances.

"Scary, right? It's like a pumpkin exploded in here. Even the fridge is painted orange. Who does that?" he asks as he tosses our food packages that no longer resemble swans into the fridge. "This is my next project after I finish adding the screened porch. I'm ripping everything out of here. There's concrete under the felt carpet so I'm going to polish it, similar to what Carson has at his house."

"Do you cook?"

"No, but I can't even drink my coffee in here. This is a really hideous sight first thing in the morning," Cooper laughs.

I laugh, too. It helps to calm my nerves.

"Come see this." His striking eyes are gleaming as his laughing mouth grazes my forehead.

He takes me through a door to the porch off the side of the kitchen. It's huge, practically a whole other room that could easily hold fifty people, and smells like fresh cut wood. It has three sides open to the forest and sits on stilts close to the creek. Everything except the screen and outdoor furniture is in place.

"It should be finished in a few weeks. I have to put up the screens and stain the wood. And Greer wants to help me pick out the furniture, but I think this is where I'll probably spend most of my time."

"It's fantastic, Cooper. This is where you'll be able to drink your coffee every morning." I am smiling big time because I am in awe that he's doing this. It also means he's sticking around Hera, and that gives me more joy than I've expected.

I turn to him to see he's quietly observing me with a little smile.

"Let me show you the rest." He motions for me to go back inside.

We walk through the kitchen and down another hallway that has three immaculate bedrooms, tastefully decorated with the Blackard furniture and other modern touches against the beautifully refinished floors. The bathroom still needs a gut job, he informs me, but I'm surprised at how clean it is.

"Were you expecting me to spend the night?" I ask as we stand at the threshold to his bedroom.

"No. I definitely thought about it and hoped you would, but I didn't think you'd come home with me tonight."

"I didn't, either. It was when you started clapping for the baby."

He gives me a perplexed frown.

"It was such a sweet thing to do, and you looked so … you know."

"No." He shakes his head and moves closer to me. "I don't know."

"Dashing … and …" As I wrap my arms around his waist, pressing myself against his warmth and gazing up at him, he moves his hands to rest firmly against my back.

The quiet moment between us is bewitching to me, nothing short of a waterfall of emotions. It's unprecedented for me to feel both arousal and gratitude, but Cooper triggers all these good feelings in me at once. I'm immediately thankful I am with him tonight and not some guy I brought home from a bar who I'd despise in the morning.

"So, are we going in there or what?" I nod at his large bed with the blue and gray bedding. Then I see the bookcases wrapped around two walls under the windows. I push away from him, deadly curious to know what books he reads. I drop to my hands and knees and begin reading the titles. "Kant? Oh, no, no, no. Russell Bertrand. *Crime and Punishment*? Thomas Hardy? Okay, I like him. God, Cooper, we really do not read the same books."

"That's okay, we don't need to."

"Oh, good. *It*, a demon clown that terrorizes a town. Finally, a book I can relate to. I can't believe you read Stephen King, Kafka, and *Zen and the Art of Motorcycle Maintenance*. So Kimberly was telling the truth; you are a philosophy junkie. This is so *not* what I read. For the most part, I like happy books. And you have so many books on psychology and the human brain. Yikes."

"They are happy books. We'll read later. Come here." He lifts me up and pulls me back into his arms.

"I'm surprised. I had you pegged … differently."

"Is that good or bad?"

"Good." I hesitate.

"Imogene," he croons all three syllables in a deep timbre, waiting for me to acknowledge what he has been saying all along.

"Yes," I admit. "Okay, it was not a date from hell, although you did kill our swans. But you're right; I'm enjoying this, and … I like you, Cooper."

His mouth is on mine in a flash as he walks me backwards until my legs touch the edge of the bed. One of his hands travels up my bare thigh and underneath my dress until it settles firmly on a butt cheek. He doesn't let up on the kiss while his other hand pulls the tie of the halter behind my neck. I feel it fall forward as he suddenly pulls back to look at me.

"What's wrong?" I ask, aware that my dress has fallen to the floor, my thong covers nothing, and my breasts are bursting out of my lacy demi bra. If this doesn't have his attention, then I've definitely lost my sex appeal.

"Nothing. Absolutely nothing. You are perfect," he

replies, taking a long, appreciative sweep of my body.

I try to relax my breathing as he slides my bra straps off my shoulders and unhooks the front clasp. My nipples harden the minute I feel his gaze. Running the pads of his thumbs over my nipples, he then leans down to caress one with his tongue. While I moan as that wonderful pull in my center makes my hands frantic to touch him, he pushes me back onto the bed, bringing me swiftly up towards the pillows. His tongue circles each breast before he bites and sucks the nipples.

"Harder," I whisper.

He settles himself between my legs, the erection in his jeans taunting my fresh bikini wax. I tangle my hands in his hair and hold his head against me as he sucks harder. Instinctively pushing myself against his hardness, feeling myself getting wetter, I arch up. He snaps my thong down, trailing it slowly to my feet where he flings it behind him, leaving me completely naked while he's fully dressed. With his hands firmly holding my hips in place, he kisses his way down to my stomach then below to the wetness building between my legs.

"Wait," I say softly. When he looks up at me, the stubble on his chin brushes against my sensitive flesh, sending an arousing jolt through me. "Get naked. Take off your clothes."

He smiles and runs his tongue slowly around my clit to give me a preview before standing up. He's quite magnificent, towering over me at his full height while I lie on the bed. *He's your gorgeous Viking, Imogene.*

He takes his time unbuttoning his shirt, as if he knows this is a show for my benefit. What a great show. I fling my arms above my head and let every muscle relax as I watch him expose his ripped pectorals and abs. With his golden tan and that surfer blond hair, I'm a hot mess, and he's not even naked yet.

He pauses in his strip tease. "Damn, you're beautiful."

I smile. It's been a long time since a man has admired me or looked at me with adoration. I am elated that it's coming from this man.

As a renter of Jessica's Victorian home, I've had the privilege to admire plenty of half-naked men as they did restoration work; however, I've never seen Cooper without a shirt. He's the one that gives me the silly tremors that wake up my mind and body. I've been trying to hide this from him, but I have run out of excuses when it comes to Cooper. He's the only man I've been attracted to in ages, and this is a whopper of combustible attraction.

His eyes never leave mine, and I sense he's using his damn profiling skills on me. He kicks his shoes off then unzips his jeans and tosses them, just my Viking in a pair of black boxer briefs now remaining. When he hooks his thumbs in the band and pushes them down, his enormous cock springs out, and I exhale and whistle at the same time.

"You're quite gorgeous," I blurt out. "Get your rubbers please, Mr. MacKenzie."

He strides over to the nightstand and pulls out some condoms, giving an excellent view of his long, muscular legs that lead up to his firm ass. Christ, I have been with plenty of attractive guys, but they sure didn't look or act like Cooper. He's unique. Cooper is ... *the complete package*.

"How many do we need for tonight? Five? Seven?" He dangles a strip of condoms in front of me.

"Let's start with one," I say, trembling a bit.

While he rips open a foil package and rolls it on, I watch him with fascination, as if I've never seen this before. His amused eyes are on me the whole time, roving slowly up and down my body, as though he's deciding where to start. My breath catches when he moves gracefully, like a panther, and plants himself above me on all fours.

"I have Imogene naked in my bed, and she is suddenly

nervous and mute. Amazing." His deep, raspy voice sends a ripple, an awakening, through my body with the anticipation of his touch.

I reach up and run my fingertips lightly across his cheekbone and let them trail down the back of his neck before firmly cupping it. "This is different. You seem like a new experience."

"I've been here for a while, waiting for you to notice," he says calmly.

"Oh, I'm noticing." I chuckle softly, making him smile a little.

He nudges my legs farther apart with his knee and settles his weight on his elbows with his cock pressing against my eager center, his mouth descending on my neck and leisurely kissing my sensitive spots. The sensation of his cock prodding my clit; his warm, hard abs and chest barley skimming my skin; and his tongue behind my ear causes me to moan and arch into him.

I glide my hands down his back and around his tight ass to pull him closer to me. Unable to wait any longer, I take matters into my own hands, literally. I move a hand to grip his hard length, stroking it lightly then more aggressively. Cooper moans into my ear when I rub the tip against my wetness, circling it until I sense a change in his body. There's a shock, an electric current, that's undoing his willpower as he sucks and bites my neck.

"Oh, God. What are you doing?" I whisper.

"Biting, tasting you. I'm trying to make this last, and you're trying to rush it," he says, moving his face directly above mine. His breathing and heart rate escalate, his eyes shimmering with adoration as he looks at me.

"It's natural to get very excited about someone new." I kiss his chin and lick the stubble there.

"I'm trying to hold out so I don't come in thirty seconds like a stupid teenage boy, and you're making that very difficult."

"If it helps, I feel like a naïve, teenage girl," I confide. "I'm actually shaking."

"Good. Let me take care of that for you."

He kisses me deeply, his tongue taking over my mouth as his hand fondles my breasts. I stroke him more fervently, his cock seeming to lengthen and get even harder. He retaliates by sucking on my nipples until they ache, making me writhe in need. I wrap my legs around him, gyrating my hips and rubbing his cock against my clit.

"That's it," he grits. "We'll have to save the appetizers for later." He removes my hand and takes his cock, plunging into me.

"Yes," I gasp. "Now I remember how to do this."

He chuckles and holds still. "Give me a sec." He pushes farther, and I gasp again as he fills me completely.

Gracefully swiveling his hips in smooth circles, he strikes my clit from an angle, building wonderful friction. I can't get enough of touching him and running my hands through his hair and scoring my nails down his back. He arches back in pleasure and keeps up his slow, torturous maneuvers as he teases my clit with a finger, leaving my center soaking and swollen, on the verge of a climax.

"Ah, Imogene, you're so wet," he moans, removing his finger. He looks at me, his eyes ablaze as he licks his finger. "We're both ready."

While he gains purchase on the bed and begins thrusting into me, every muscle in his arms and chest tightly drawn, I greedily run my hands over his taut planes and hard ridges. Throwing his head back to flip his hair out of his face, he watches me with an intense aggressiveness as he drives into me.

I grip his shoulders as my climax erupts and keeps cresting. My inner muscles clench and Cooper, my skilled mind reader, doesn't stop his relentless pounding until he has wrung every last tingling spasm out of me. My legs loosen their hold on him while I feel like I'm melting into the bed.

He drops back to his elbows and buries his head in my neck as he thrusts into me until he's empty. He shouts something indecipherable as he finishes, and then I feel a sharp bite on the flesh between my neck and shoulder.

"Cooper," I groan, hugging him and tugging on his damp hair.

He pulls his head up and regards me with a flushed, satisfied expression. Then he kisses me, his lips gently coaxing mine to let his tongue dart in for a sweet finale. He stays inside of me, keeping me in a snug embrace as he studies my face.

"Sorry, I got a little carried away there at the end. Did I hurt you?" He touches the area of skin he bit. It feels tender, but I don't mind.

"No. I liked it. Does it look bad?" I ask, not wanting to let go of him just yet.

"It's bruised and it's going to look worse tomorrow. Wear a shirt with a collar." He smiles and then slowly pries his body off mine.

He walks to the bathroom to dispose of the condom, and when he returns, I admire his beautiful physique as he climbs back into bed. I'm still sprawled in the middle of the bed where he left me. My muscles have that rubbery, detached sensation, as though I no longer control them.

Cooper laughs softly at my content state and props himself up on his elbow, looking down at me with an incredibly sexy grin. I catch myself staring, lingering too long on each feature of his face, memorizing where the gray in his eyes turns silver and charcoal and where the curve of his lips meets his prominent cheekbones.

"Why me, Imogene? Why were you afraid of me? And why did you decide to go out with me?"

"Afraid is a strong word," I reply, touching the stubble on his chin. "Cold, hard fear is more like it."

He bursts out laughing. "Of me? What the hell for?"

"Because I've had my share of handsome men, and they've all turned out to be duds."

"Thank you for the first part, I think, but that's a shitty thing to lump me in with all your mistakes."

"*Duds* is a strong word. I meant that, in one way or another, they severely disappointed me and failed to live up to anything that resembled what I had hoped for. And some of the jerks left me bitter and a little hurt. Can you tell?" I chuckle.

"I'm sorry you chose poorly, and I'm sorry I got in line behind all those duds," he says with conviction. "I should have been at the front of the line."

I laugh and playfully swat his shoulder before reaching for the sheet to cover myself.

"Wait, what are you doing?" he asks, flinging back the sheet. "I like the view, and we're not done here. Oh, and I'm out of nicknames since you hate them all."

Turning into him, I wrap a leg over his and cover my chest with my arm. "Imogene. I like the way you say my name."

"Imogene," his deep voice responds.

"I like that. So, no nicknames are required. And I doubt you've ever met another Imogene, right?"

"I haven't," he says, brushing my hair back with his fingers. "Imogene it is."

"I'm actually getting used to *baby*, too." I smile and close my eyes.

When you're the center of someone's attention—whether you're a twelve-year-old girl on the playground with the boy who turns your stomach into knots or a twenty-five-year-old woman who realizes the worst possible man is the only one who interests you—it's a chance to feel special and imagine you have the world in the palm of your hands. Cooper has my stomachs in knots, and at least for these few moments, he makes me feel special. I memorize and catalogue this moment in his bed, how he looks at me, because I don't know how long this will last. A night? A week? Maybe it will be a summer affair.

"So, what are you doing, baby?" He laughs. "You're scrunching your nose like you're smelling something putrid."

"No, it's nothing." As I open my eyes, his smile disarms me.

"Nothing, shit." He kisses my nose. "You're sizing me up, overthinking all of this."

"Can you blame me? I've had a few lousy dates over the last year, and then there was the unfortunate time I spent with Wanker Jeremy."

Cooper exhales slowly and drapes an arm over my waist. "Think of them as research and practice. You had to meet a few wankers before you met me so you'd know how awesome I am."

"Ah," I chuckle. "So how many women have you been practicing with over the last decade? A few hundred? Thousands?"

"Jesus, I don't want to talk about people we've slept with. They aren't ex-wives or ex-husbands, right? They don't matter."

"Good response. So, did you sleep with that Pilates chick? Because I have seen the way she admires you."

"This is very interesting. You're jealous." He nips my ear lobe. "And, no, I didn't sleep with her."

"How is that possible? You dated her for like two months."

"You kept track of that? Imogene..." He laughs and falls back on the bed, beside himself with laughter.

I'm not proud of myself; however, his joy over my blatant jealousy is annoying and embarrassing. *Kcuf*!

"I didn't sleep with her, baby. You don't have to be jealous."

"Sure," I respond.

He turns to look at me. "In that two month period you so expertly kept track of, we went out about four times, only because she kept asking me out for dinner. It's a small town, and I could only come up with so many excuses before sounding like an asshole. So, we went out a few times and talked, and that's all that happened."

"Why didn't you sleep with her? You know she wanted to."

"Jesus, Imogene. I didn't want to *be* with anyone from this town," he says pointedly to me, "except for you."

I quietly analyze this. He's right. I'm doing my own kind of profiling and mind reading. I'm trying to figure out why he's here with me and not with an athletic woman more similar to himself. A very limber Pilates woman would be perfect for him.

"I thought you'd come around and be a little bit friendlier so I could ask you out." He rolls back on his side and pins me to the bed.

"Wait a minute. You're saying you haven't slept with anyone in over a year?"

"I didn't say that. I didn't sleep with anyone from Hera. I never said I was celibate."

"Oh, of course. You and your damn bike just roamed the countryside, visiting all the little towns to find women to screw. It was your own little fuck quest."

"That's exactly what it was," he says, sarcastically. "A fuck quest. Jesus. Did you sleep with that moron who bought you a drink at the bar?"

"The guy at the pool hall? I was there with—"

"With Emma and Lauren. I know. I was there with some of the guys from the shop," he says in a very measured tone.

"Were you jealous?" I ask, surprised at how hopeful I sound.

"Yes," he hisses.

"Huh." I let my silence torture him a bit longer.

"Well?"

"I thanked him for the beer, and he and his friends talked to us for a while. Small talk."

"I know. I saw that part. I was sitting across the room," he says, exasperated. "Did you ever go out with him after that?"

"Did you try to ask Leo or Lauren about that?" I ask, tickling the corded muscles on his arm.

"Imogene." He settles himself between my legs, his growing erection pressing against my soft belly.

"I can't help it. I had no idea you were keeping tabs on me and my lousy dates." I kiss his cheek. He's still glaring at me, waiting for an appropriate response. "I did not go out with him."

"Good." He looks relieved.

"But I did go out with two other guys," I add, giving his luscious lips a peck.

"I already know about those bozos. Those dates both died an early death. Lauren said you were home quickly and complained about them being boring."

"Wow. I was joking, but you really did keep track of who I went out with."

"It's not like I had to ask anyone. Lauren gabs about you all the time to me and Leo."

"And it's not like you were suffering, right? You had women here and there."

"Can we stop talking about these other people who don't matter?"

"Absolutely."

"Are we past the uncomfortable stage where you expect me to be a jerk? Am I in good standing now?"

"I think so." While I run my hands down his back, looking down between us where his cock is getting harder and longer, Cooper also looks and adjusts his position to accommodate his erection.

He exhales slowly before fixating his aroused gaze on

162

me. "You think so? What do I need to do to convince you?"

A million dirty things go through my mind. "Ah ... gah," I stammer some gibberish which I assume is very telling to former Agent MacKenzie.

His devilish grin is followed by a quick nip on my breast, then he kisses his way down to my belly button. I jump and wiggle in reaction to his licks. I know where he's going and my body is going into hyper-drive. I fist my hands in his hair rather forcefully, causing him to jerk up and sit back on his knees.

"You're very squirrely. Don't move, Ms. Walsh." He jumps off the bed and opens up a dresser drawer, rifling through socks and underwear he just tosses about the floor.

"What are you doing? The condoms are on the nightstand."

I'm wondering if I should be concerned that he already forgot he has protection, but I'm more anxious to get him back to taking care of business with me. I was barely getting wound up and excited to watch Cooper go down on me. It's been so long I'm pretty sure my vagina has forgotten what a tongue is. It was not Jeremy's specialty; in fact, I'd say most guys have missed the proverbial mark with me.

"Found it." He opens a black box and pulls out two pairs of handcuffs. *Handcuffs!*

"Really? You're into that?" I ask, a little scared and excited at the prospect of being restrained.

"Never was before, but since you're here, it seems that I am." His smile is a little evil, making me laugh in surprise, as he grabs my left hand and slaps on one cuff so fast my wrist stings.

"Hey, I'm a delicate flower," I squeal as he yanks my arm to the headboard and secures the other cuff to the bedpost just as quickly.

I watch my hand hang limply from the silver cuff as Cooper crawls over me like a savage beast, his muscles straining with tension. It's obvious that all of his caveman blood has gone to his cock. He's in full predator mode, aggressive and demanding. I'd be lying if I didn't say my arousal is like a Geiger counter that has shot through the roof.

He secures my right hand to the opposite bedpost just as roughly. With my arms raised and pulled tightly, I try to catch my breath and ignore my aching wrists, focusing instead on the ache swirling below.

"There, my delicate flower, that should keep you still," he murmurs as he skims his chin down my chest so his beard stubble gives me goose bumps.

I buck, jutting my hard nipples up towards him, but he clamps his hands on my thighs, holding me down and spreading my legs farther apart. Open to him, I gasp when his mouth descends on my clit and works it over with his tongue, sucking, and ... teeth. *Holy mother of the universe, you've bestowed a talented man upon me who actually knows what he's doing.*

Cooper is relentless, determined to bring me to a frenzied orgasm that ignites my core and fires mind-numbing bliss to every cell in my body. Somewhere in there, among the thundering climax and subsequent uncontrollable convulsing limbs, I scream his name. I'd applaud him, but said limbs are still restrained.

I stop jerking my hands against the handcuffs and let my whole, depleted body sink into the bed. My mind is in a haze as I gaze down at Cooper, who leans forward on his fists.

"I didn't know you were a screamer." His arrogance in the bedroom is such a turn on.

"Never was before, but since you're here, it seems that I am," I say in my stupor, throwing his own words back at him.

He chuckles and gets off the bed to retrieve the key to undo the cuffs. He releases each wrist and kisses them before placing them gently on the bed. I'm too sated to move; however, he grabs another foil package and rolls it on his cock as he looks hungrily at me.

I feel like a tipsy drunk and roll on my side away from him. "Oh, my gosh, you're going to destroy me."

Cooper spoons me and nuzzles his head into my neck. "You don't have to do anything, but I have to take care of this." His deep voice awakens my sleepy nerve endings.

Lifting my leg, he pushes his hard length into my wet center. I give it my best effort to push back to help him along, but frankly, I'm still recovering from the last two orgasms.

"Oh," I moan as his fingers begin playing with my wet folds again, opening me farther so he can thrust all the way in.

"Watching you come makes my dick insane. This won't take long," he says against my cheek.

He pounds into me with urgent grunts, his pelvis slapping against my ass. His hard body envelopes mine as he synchronizes his finger action on my clit in a rhythmic motion.

"Oh, God," I whisper as I begin to come undone again. I have one arm on the bed, bracing me against Cooper's thrusts so I don't fall forward.

"Shit, Imogene," he growls, shuddering and jerking a few more times before I feel his chest relax against my back.

I put my hand on his to keep him rubbing my clit until a little explosion erupts again. Then I yelp and collapse on my stomach.

Cooper leans gently on top of me and removes the mass of tangled hair from my face to kiss my cheek. He strokes my back then palms my curvy, ample rear end. "We have to do this more often." He gives my ass a little slap.

Rolling towards him, my hands instinctively push the hair out of his face and tuck it behind his ears, as if this action belongs to me, as if I should be the only woman accustomed to this gesture.

We are covered in sweat, the sheets damp, but I don't want to leave. I cup his face and he leans in closer to kiss me. Afterward, Cooper gazes at me as though his only purpose is to offer himself as a gift to me.

Sex doesn't always provide the end result or release you want, at least not for me, and I think it's especially rare to be in a state where every imagined, desired variable comes together in one perfect earth-shattering moment. For me, it's this moment *after*. Lust, passion, and the search for devotion are a heady mix of wishful thinking, but I do have this one solitary moment where I believe they're real. In this instant, I think I could possibly take an ice pick to the glacier around my frozen heart and chisel it from its suspended, petrified state.

"I'm pretty sure I brought you to your knees at least three times, Imogene."

"You did more than that. I can't even feel my knees."

Sixteen

In the morning, my thighs are as sore as if I'd spent the night forcing my inflexible limbs to do one of Lauren's old cheerleading routines with endless splits. We used four of the seven condoms over the course of several hours, not stopping until sunrise.

I'm not surprised by our marathon session of sex. I am surprised that I could keep up with Cooper. He's no Easy Rider in bed. He's more like Robocop, and it would have taken more than a bazooka to put him down.

I look over at the beast in question. Cooper is naked and uncovered, lying on his stomach, arms and legs spread eagle across the bed. The Viking has conquered.

I ease myself out of bed, noticing the sore purple bruises on the insides of my thighs. He bit me in several places, and I'm afraid to find them all.

I use the toilet, avoiding the mirror, then I slip on Cooper's white, button down shirt from the night before and make my way to the kitchen. He's right, the ghastly orange décor is an unpleasant blast to the noggin' in the morning, but it does wake you up. I make coffee and find an orderly fridge with unexpired fixings for breakfast. Working in the family diner has taught me how to make a few comfort food favorites, and one of my specialties is a cheesy egg sandwich. I grill up a couple of them and pour two mugs of coffee before carrying everything back to the bedroom.

Cooper rolls over and stretches, eyeing me with a lazy grin. "Good morning, beautiful." He leans on his elbow, looking like he's posing for a nude photo shoot. Well,

167

except for the erection. How the hell can he be ready again?

"Breakfast is served," I say, pretending he's not in a state of arousal.

"You cooked for me?" He sits up and accepts a mug of coffee. "Damn, this is great. I'm famished."

Once I set the plate of egg sandwiches between us on the bed, he picks one up and observes it in amazement.

"This came from my kitchen?"

"It's just scrambled eggs, Wonder Bread, American cheese, and a lot of butter."

He eats it in three bites.

"Good," he says gruffly, so I hand him the rest of mine, and he polishes it off in seconds.

"Do you want me to go heat up the lamb and the duck from last night?" I ask, watching him drink his coffee as though it's also new and different. "It's just coffee."

"You make it better than me."

"That's because I've made more than ten thousand pots of it at the diner."

He clears the dishes from the bed, shoving everything on the nightstand, then picks up another foil package.

"I forgot something," he says, crawling back to me, truly looking like a hungry lion stalking his prey. He kisses me, his tongue darting between my lips. "You look very sexy in my shirt, and—"

"Cooper," I chuckle. "I have to get home and work. Aren't you exhausted from last night? We got less than two hours of sleep."

"My dick doesn't care."

We both look down at his length.

I'm turned on, too, and Cooper's energy is nothing short of intoxicating; however, my bruised and battered sensitive areas are protesting.

He lifts the hem of his shirt and inspects the purple and black splotches along my inner thighs then checks my neck. He even pulls the collar of the shirt to the side to expose a breast that has more *love bites*.

"Shit. I'm a fucking animal," he says, displeased. "I didn't realize I got that carried away. Why didn't you say something?"

"Because I was enjoying it. And this is the price I pay for sleeping with Cooper MacKenzie."

He frowns in disappointment. "I'm sorry. I need to keep my hands off you for a while, I guess. Why don't you take a hot shower and try to relieve these injuries?"

I lean forward and cup his face so I can kiss him again. "Cooper, why don't you take a shower with me?"

"Because it would be very difficult to be naked with you and not fuck."

"Get in the shower. Now," I say sternly.

"As you can see, I really need a cold one. Probably not what you want."

"Would you get in the kcuffing shower already?" I shout and push him.

He sighs, gets up, and walks to the bathroom, looking back at me suspiciously.

Once inside the steamy shower, I stand directly under the showerhead, the hot water feeling divine against my sore muscles. Cooper, on the other hand, stands at the other end of the tub, looking seriously miserable with his boner. I begin soaping his chest and arms, rubbing my slick hands all over his body.

"Imogene, you're making this worse. I'm in agony here." He grabs hold of the shower rod and braces one hand against the tile wall as he looks up at the ceiling with a pained expression.

As I grip his hard cock, he looks down at me with wide eyes. I smile coyly and begin stroking him from his balls to the sensitive tip, rinsing the soap away. He moves his legs farther apart for balance and the muscles in his arms and legs tighten.

"Ah, Jesus," he groans, letting his head fall back as my

ministrations make him harder. I fear he may come too soon.

"Hold on a little longer. I have a breakfast treat for you." I kiss his neck then get down on my knees.

I grip his ass and have his cock in my mouth before he can react. I stroke his sack while sucking his length, using a little bit of teeth and playing with the slit until he's moaning and bucking against my mouth.

"That's good," he utters hoarsely.

That was just my warm up, I think to myself, pleased that I've got a few moves which surprise him. I suck harder and take him deeper, hearing his breath escalate. Then one of his hands is on my head, urging me on.

"Don't stop. Don't fucking stop," he rasps. His other hand begins stroking his cock at the base, his hips thrusting forward, pushing deeper into my mouth. I've never seen a guy do that. I'm absolutely turned on.

I don't let up as he ejaculates and continues jerking as I milk every last bit out of him.

"Imogene," he hisses with one last, final thrust.

With him done, I stand up and retrieve a washcloth and the shower gel to soap us up again.

His head drops down against his chest as he recovers. "Did I tell you what an idiot I am for not going after you sooner?"

"I think we both waited for the right time," I say, running a washcloth over his splendid body.

This is an outdated bathroom with a tub that's much too small for him. He's like a giant standing in here, but I find it oddly cozy and comforting to be with him in this small space.

"You're fucking amazing."

"Because I just gave you a great blow job?"

"No." He wraps his big, strong arms around me so our naked bodies are squashed together perfectly. "Because everything about you fucking amazes me. I'm serious,

170

Imogene. I knew last year you were different. I couldn't get you out of my mind, and when you came on to me at Dylan's wedding, I hoped it would last after you sobered up."

"It did. You're definitely different than I imagined. I didn't give you enough credit before, but then, most guys have been on my very long, very detailed shit list."

Cooper sighs. "As long as I'm off that list now, I don't give a crap about any other guys."

"You made it well beyond the list, mister."

"So what about today, and tonight, and tomorrow, and the day after tomorrow? You have a way of escaping, hiding out of sight, and being evasive. I have to go work with Leo and Carson on your new studio today. We're finishing the paint job, and I'd like you to come along if you can take a break from work. And then I'd like to be with you again tonight. Whatever you want to do. Sex, movies, sex, dinner, sex."

"If you're working on our new studio, then I have to work on the jewelry. I can't take time off if you guys are working for free for my benefit."

"So help us paint." His large hands squeeze my ass.

"It's tempting, but Lauren has one of her militant work schedules laid out for us today. I really need to be there with her, especially since the biz and the wedding are hard to manage while she's pregnant. She's exhausted, and I have to help her through this."

"Okay, then when I'm done painting with the guys, I'm coming over to your place. We can do nothing or everything, but I'm going to see you."

"I like that plan." I lean my chin against his chest.

"Good, because you're going to be seeing a lot of me. We have to make up for lost time—fourteen goddamn months that I should have been all over you."

"Aw, well, think of that time as the world's longest foreplay."

"I'd rather have the world's longest ... what did you call it? Fuck fest?"

"I said fuck *quest*. You know, like a vision quest. Very spiritual," I add sarcastically.

"I like the idea of a fuck fest better. It's pretty damn spiritual when I'm inside of you and you scream my name loud enough to be heard across three state lines."

Seventeen

I drive Leo's truck home, catching my reflection in the side view mirror. I'm smiling. It's a beautiful summer morning, and for once, I feel free, silly, and happy, just like any deliriously brain dead woman feels after screwing a hunk all night.

I laugh to myself, thinking of the little lectures I gave Samantha and Kelly regarding men and how none of us have the market cornered on relationships. I don't even know what Cooper is thinking other than he likes my company and the sex part. I have to agree; however, we're not teenagers or college kids, and dating takes on a whole new meaning at my age. Men can still goof off for another decade or so, but I'm supposed to put more thought into the men I go out with and consider if there's the possibility for future commitment, eternal love, children, and all those other highly complicated issues.

I think it goes without repeating that my vetting process when it comes to men has been a complete failure; as a result, I may have just roped myself into another high-octane physical relationship that's like a Molotov cocktail: explosive and potentially destructive.

When I arrive home, Leo is standing on the porch like an angry father waiting for his delinquent teenage daughter to return from an unapproved night out.

I hop out of his truck and stride towards him with Cooper's dinner shirt over my halter dress.

"Finally," he says, uncrossing his arms and taking the keys from me. "You need to work on your texting skills. I spent an hour trying to figure out what you were saying because I didn't think—"

"You thought I wanted to *fuck you tomorrow*." I laugh.

"That's what it said!"

"And then you asked Lauren to decipher it," I add dryly. "And she figured it out in two seconds."

"Yes," he replies, embarrassed.

We walk into the house with me still laughing.

"It's not that funny, Imogene. I have to meet the guys and finish the paint job."

"I know. Cooper told me about the plans for today. Don't worry; I'll take care of Lauren. Is she still throwing up?"

"Like clockwork, and she won't take a break to rest." Leo looks concerned.

"Leo," I say, putting my hand on his shoulder. "I can go help finish the paint job and you can stay here with Lauren."

He sighs. "She wants me to go. You know how Lauren is; she thinks she can work all day and night. I'm really regretting that I agreed to let her throw together a wedding before the baby is born. I should have insisted on getting married in some local judge's chambers or waiting until after the birth."

"Oh, sweetie, you know you can't insist on anything when it comes to your lovely bride. She's very stubborn and thinks she's always right."

"I know. God, I love her, but the idea that she can plan a wedding and expand the business while she's growing a human being inside of her is completely insane." He sounds angry and desperate. "I'm responsible for her welfare, and I'm not doing a very good job."

"It takes two, so you need to talk to her about loosening the reins. I'll talk to her about her workload, though. I'll take over more of her To-Do list, and you focus on getting her going to bed earlier. We have to be tougher on her."

"Do you know anyone who has ever been able to boss her around?" He looks so sweet and childlike.

"No. God knows I've tried, but she's immune to my powers. We'll do it together and get the parents onboard, though."

He looks unconvinced as I send him off to work with the Viking I'm daydreaming about.

I float upstairs, and sure enough, Lauren is sitting at the computer, scrolling through vendor lists.

"Lauren, I'll do that today, and I'll pack up the supplies for the move."

She swivels the chair around and smiles when she sees Cooper's huge shirt hanging on me. "You had a great date, didn't you? You like Cooper."

"Yes, it was very nice. Now get up. I'm calling the accounts today, and I'm going to let them know I'm sending them photos of our new stock."

Lauren lets me have the computer and then plants herself on a stool at the worktable. "Give me the details," she says eagerly.

"Dinner was nice, and the conversation was fun," I say, looking at the computer monitor.

"Imogene, you spent the night at his house. Are you as crazy about him as he is about you?"

"Crazy?" I ask, turning around. "Let's not get carried away. We like each other. Have you noticed that I haven't said one snide thing about him in almost a week?"

"Yes. I think you kind of fell for him at the dance class."

"No one is falling for anyone," I say, returning to the client list in front of me.

"He's not immature like Jeremy or stupid like some of those other guys, Imogene. Cooper is a nice guy, and he's been interested in you for a while."

"Lauren, please don't sell me on Cooper. I get that he's a nice guy. I experienced it firsthand ... the gift to us and

175

on that stupid hike. And I agree that he's a fun guy to be paired up with for a wedding. Thanks for that. And dinner was fun, and being with him last night was great. I like him. But I'm not going to blow this out of proportion."

"All right," she says glumly. "At least tell me he got you out of your dry spell and you had mind blowing sex."

"The sex was out of this kcuffing world."

Lauren exhales a big sigh and smiles. "A new romance. Can I be a teeny bit excited for you?"

"If you promise to go take a nap right now, I'll let you be excited for me. You have bags under your eyes and look like you haven't been eating. I'm serious. I promised Leo I would get you to relax more for the sake of your health and the baby."

"Fine. I'll go rest, but—"

"I'll call the stores, pack the supplies, and follow everything else on your list." I hold up her notepad.

"Are you seeing Cooper tonight? Can I cook dinner for the four of us?" She's getting revved up again.

"You are impossible. Go take your nap, and you are not hosting dinner parties for the next few months. Leo and I will be doing the cooking."

For the next several hours, an uncharacteristic optimism takes over me. I pack necklaces that need to be shipped to retailers including a display set for Sasha's in SoHo. I call on new vendors, our least favorite part of the job. I update the website with new products and put together moving boxes to transport our supplies to the new building.

When I go to check on Lauren, she's half dozing in bed with a laptop next to her, unable to stop herself from working. I put the computer on her dresser and then watch as she rolls over and falls into an early evening slumber.

I'm still wearing my date outfit and hate to take off Cooper's shirt, but I need clean clothes, so I change into long shorts and a collared blouse to cover my bruises. I hold his shirt up to my face and inhale his musky, manly scent. It reminds me of last night and everything he did from the restaurant scene to his bedroom. I shiver in delight.

Thinking of Cooper makes me smile and feel thrilled in a way I haven't felt in years. It's more than a happy or excited feeling, too. My emotions are overwhelming, and there isn't one pessimistic thought to bring me back to reality, which in itself is inspiring for a skeptic like me.

I drape his shirt on the back of my bedroom chair, wanting to make sure it doesn't get cleaned and lose his scent until I have to give it back. I'm turning into one of those gushy, crazy girls that collect mementos of a man—insane hero worship. I shake that image off when I hear a ruckus downstairs. Someone slams the front door and male laughter floats upstairs to the third floor. *Cooper*. My insides do a back flip.

As I leave my bedroom, I see Cooper jogging up the stairs. I freeze and take in the sight of him: his paint-splattered jeans and T-shirt, his broad chest and shoulders that I spent a good portion of the previous night clinging to, and his magnetic smile.

"Hi!" I sound exactly like Samantha and Kelly, the high-pitched, lovelorn teenagers from the Cooper fan club.

"Hey, beautiful. Lauren told me you were up here." He closes in on me with a big up-to-no-good grin.

"She's supposed to be napping."

"She's downstairs with Leo, putting away groceries. He's making sandwiches for dinner, and I said I'd notify you. Consider this your notice." He pushes me back into my bedroom and swings the door closed.

It takes two seconds for my brain to register that I have Cooper in my bedroom. I waste no time jumping him. I throw my arms around his neck and wrap my legs around his waist. He holds me tightly by the ass, and we kiss frantically to make up for the eight hours we were separated.

"Leo said dinner will be ready in fifteen minutes," he murmurs against my lips. He smells like sweat, paint, and a hint of sun-soaked skin.

I feel myself getting wet as the lusty, crazy-ass thoughts take over my libido. I'm too busy devouring his mouth and feeling him up to respond. Cooper doesn't stop kissing me as he lays me on the bed and undoes his jeans. I wriggle my shorts and panties off and reach for his cock.

With one hand, he pulls a foil package from his pocket before letting his jeans fall to the floor. He tears it open with his teeth and quickly rolls it on his length, which is fisted in my hand.

"You have to let go of me, Imogene, so I can get this on." His tone is authoritative and urgent.

I reluctantly let go, and in seconds, Cooper has the condom on and is positioning his cock to enter me. He holds both of my legs up as he stands and plunges into me with powerful, ungraceful thrusts. Short on time and high on sexual tension, our unabated cravings send us into a flurry of flailing limbs.

I grip the bedspread as Cooper leans over me, hitching his arms under my thighs to quicken his pounding pace at the perfect angle and with the perfect amount of friction. I grab his shoulders and hold on as he slams into me with deep, ferocious grunts, his expression fierce as his gaze never breaks contact with mine. He's waiting for me to come, and just when the tornado of spasms begin to take hold of me, he loses control and jerks and shudders his way through his orgasm.

Instead of pulling out of me, he puts two fingers against my clit and helps me climax. By the time I find the rainbow at the end of the yellow brick road, I'm squirming and moaning his name. When Cooper drops down on his hands and kisses me long and slow, capturing my remaining moans, I bite his lower lip good and hard.

"Ouch," he laughs.

"That's what you get for giving me hickies everywhere."

"I can't help myself when I'm around you." He smiles and pulls out of me before grabbing a tissue from the nightstand and wrapping the condom in it.

"I had no idea how horny I was until I saw you running up those stairs." I pick my clothes up off the floor and dress quickly.

"I was horny all day long thinking about you. I even tried to get Leo to come back here for lunch so I could take you to bed, but he wanted to get the paint job done. Geez, I was ready to punch the guy."

I laugh. "His fiancée is throwing up; he's not getting any action right now."

Cooper buttons his jeans and yanks me against him. "I think our fifteen minutes are up, but you should come back to my place after dinner. You can pack a suitcase."

"A whole suitcase? Ah …"

"Why not? I thought this was the plan. We work all day and get together tonight. You can keep some stuff at my place." He studies my face with a questioning look.

"Let's have dinner, and then we'll discuss logistics," I say, leading him out of the bedroom.

"That doesn't sound encouraging," he says as we walk downstairs.

"Cooper, I can't think straight after what we just did. I need food."

"Just because I want to chain you to my bed, it doesn't mean I won't feed you."

"Quiet!" I whisper-yell as we make it to the first floor. I hope Lauren didn't hear Cooper's remark, or I'll be interrogated.

As we enter the kitchen, Lauren looks up from the table and straight at Cooper's hands that are holding my waist. She smiles and arches an eyebrow at me.

"Leo, let me help you," I say, pulling away from Cooper's grasp.

I hear him huff behind me, but I jump in to help Leo plate the sandwiches and toss a salad as though my presence is critical. Perhaps it's the sudden interest from others, putting Cooper and I under a microscope, that makes me apprehensive about this potential relationship. Dinner and sex don't confirm that it's an actual relationship, and Cooper and I are still in the getting-to-know-you stage. After fourteen months of GTKYS, no wonder we're going at it like rabbits.

The four of us have a nice, dinner at the small kitchen table, during which we stick to analyzing the dance lessons, Leo's camping plan—which I'm still against—the church plans for the ceremony, and the hotel ballroom for the wedding reception. Cooper either has his hand on my thigh or on the back of my chair throughout the meal.

When I sneak sideways glances at him, he gives me little smirks. Leo is oblivious or doesn't care, but Lauren is watching us dead on. When we excuse ourselves to go out to the porch, Lauren winks at Cooper and I catch him giving her a chin tip.

"What was that about?" I ask when we're alone on the porch. "That little wink and nod thing between you and Lauren."

"She's my friend," he says nonchalantly as he opens my collar to inspect his handy dandy bite marks. "She's been trying to hook us up for a while but didn't know how to do it without you killing her in her sleep. Those were her words."

"Is that why we're coupled up for the wedding? Was this planned? Because I kind of wondered why Dylan isn't the best man, no offense."

"Gee, none taken. Leo and I are closer I guess. Dylan has really invested all of his time into his new life with

Emma, and Dylan agreed that I should be the best man. Do you have a problem with this?" His fingers caress my neck.

"Not at all, but it's kind of strange that I didn't know you and Lauren were so close and talking about me behind my back."

"We weren't saying anything bad about you. If anything, I was pretty direct with Lauren, telling her I was very interested in you."

"It's amazing Lauren didn't say anything to me. She can't keep secrets, and I can always count on her spilling the beans."

"There were no beans to spill, really. I talked to you every time I went into the diner for lunch. You worked damn hard at responding to all of my compliments with insults. So, are you going to pack a bag and come over to my place? I need to clean up and get out of these work clothes."

I like the fact that he's thought about plans for us, and the way he says it without any reservations, but I'm also aware that for once I'd like to slow things down to a realistic pace. I can't have sex all night long and run on no sleep and try to work all day. Lauren and I have received a generous loan from Carson and Archie, and I'd feel like I'm playing fast and loose with investment money instead of learning to live with some serious structure in my life. That's one concern.

The other is that Cooper may get tired of me by the end of the week, and that would be very awkward dancing with him at the wedding along with sharing mutual friends in a very small town. I don't want to be the woman a guy takes for a long test drive. I want to be the woman who is chosen. Whether it's with Cooper or some other man I have yet to meet, I should slow this down.

"Well?" he asks, becoming agitated with my silence. "It's Saturday night, come to my place."

"But we're moving things over to the new building

tomorrow. You said so at dinner … and Cooper, neither of us has really slept."

"Shit, you're blowing me off tonight?" His nostrils flare as he glares at me.

"No, I'm cooling us off."

"It's not working," he says as he puts my hand on the very hard bulge in his jeans.

I take a deep breath because, honestly, I'd like nothing better than to spend the night in his bed, rolling around naked as he pleasures me in every way possible.

"Cooper, I've done this before, where I latch on to someone and we move like the speed of light and end just as quickly," I explain to the hulking man before me who is many women's fantasy come to life. Maybe I'm a moron, but I actually believe there's something to taking our intensity down a notch. "If this goes caput and someone gets hurt—likely me—then it would be a very uncomfortable situation for us and our friends. I want to prevent that from happening."

"First of all, you can't necessarily prevent that. People break up after one year, ten years—they get divorced all the time. Second, this is about me; you still have some doubts about me. I'm not about to hurt you, though." His tone is stern, and he sounds offended.

"It's like we've unleashed the Kraken. From now on, every time we're together, it's going to be about sex."

Cooper shakes his head. "No. I like being with you even when we're not naked."

"Me, too. I think we should spend more time getting to know one another before we decide to spend every waking moment screwing. I like them both, but they are not the same thing."

He nods and his expression softens. "I understand. It's normal to have some concerns about me or us since this is new." As he leans against the porch railing, his phone buzzes.

He takes it out of his pocket to inspect the incoming number. "Do you mind if I take this?" His tone is somber.

"Not at all."

"It's me," he says into the phone with his head down.

There is a minute of silence as he listens to the caller, his expression stone cold.

"I understand. Bye." He puts his phone back in his jeans pocket and looks out into the evening sky.

"Is everything all right?" I ask as his attention drifts off into something distant.

He turns back to me and lets a sigh of relief escape as he studies my face for a moment. "It's nothing. Just my sister with her usual complaints."

There's an awkward silence because I don't know how to respond. I don't know his sister or the issues between them. "Anything you want to talk about?"

"No, it's not important. I need to go home and shower, and you need some rest." He smiles, but it seems contrived for my benefit.

"Good," I say softly. "So we'll both get a good night's sleep." When I stroke his cheek, he captures my hand and holds it to his face.

"Yes. I'm going to get some sleep. I'll have to jerk off thinking about you, the X-rated version, but I'll sleep."

"Oh," I say, blushing.

He takes my hand off his cheek and kisses it before letting it go. "I understand the fear, and I'm also confident that I'll eventually be able to fuck that fear right out of you … Im-o-gene."

Eighteen

Cooper arrives early, freshly showered and invigorated without a trace of his quiet distancing from the night before. I also notice that he's wearing very nice jeans; clean, casual boots; and a trendy T-shirt he would not wear for painting or work. I'm guessing he's planning to do something with me after we unload everything at the new studio building.

He greets me with a chaste kiss and a dazzling smile. I'm waiting for the birds and forest creatures to sing a cheery song for us, but there's no time for that. Cooper is directing this operation. He has Leo, Dylan, and Carson load tables, boxes of jewelry supplies, display cases, and cabinetry into Carson's and Leo's trucks. Once everything is loaded, they head off while Lauren and I follow them in her car.

The building sits behind the Blackard Designs factory, next to the employee parking lot and the basketball half court that was installed recently so employees can burn off steam during breaks and after work.

When Lauren sees that the building has received a new paint job as well as the large Imogene & Lauren sign crafted out of metal and wood affixed above the front door, she slams the car into park and jumps out. She flails her arms in excitement and runs towards the door.

"I love it! I love it!" She jumps up and down.

"You've made someone very happy," I say to Cooper as he gets out of Leo's truck.

"What do you think?" he asks, gauging my response as I take in the small building that has been given a shiny, new facelift. The gray exterior has been transformed with a light blue paint job, something clean and bright that offsets it from the rustic, dark contemporary look of the furniture company that dwarfs it.

"It's amazing. I don't even recognize it. The windows look new and all the weeds and broken concrete are gone."

"We power washed everything and had all the debris out front hauled away. Wait until you see the inside."

Lauren is trying to hug and kiss Leo as he and Carson carry in the large craft table from the truck to the building. Cooper and I follow with more boxes, and when I step inside our new studio, my mouth drops open and I let out a breathy *wow*.

It's immaculate and smells like fresh paint and sawdust. They did more than clear a space; they installed cabinets below all the windows around three walls and hung high intensity pendant lighting over additional worktables they custom built. The dingy concrete floor that was cracked and discolored has been repaired, stained, and polished. The interior is painted in an off-white color, giving a very bright effect along with all the natural sunlight pouring through the windows.

As Carson, Leo, and Dylan unload the trucks and open up all of the boxes on the three large tables in the middle of the room with Lauren instructing them this time, Cooper takes the box from me and places it down before taking my hand.

"Come see this." He pulls me across the room to show me the half bath that has all new modern fixtures.

"All it needs is a bowl of potpourri on the toilet tank!" Lauren exclaims as she pops her head between us.

Cooper laughs and then shows me the only other room with a door. Fortunately, Leo calls Lauren away, leaving me alone with Cooper.

"We built a windowless office in this corner so you can keep a computer here and the vault that Carson put under the desk," Cooper says, pointing to the small safe.

"I don't know what to say." I shake my head in disbelief. "I thought you guys were just going to clean out the furniture Carson was storing here and maybe you'd sweep the floor. This is a complete renovation, and you made us furniture and installed new lighting."

"We wanted to do it right." He gives my hand a squeeze.

Carson has always been a generous friend; however, I have to wonder how much of this extra work was initiated by Cooper. How do I begin to thank him for once again stepping up to help me? If I was younger, I would immediately assume his grand gesture is a sign he's trying to win me over, although then I remember this isn't only about me. There's a lifelong bond between Lauren, Carson, Dylan, and myself, and Leo will do anything for Lauren. Cooper has joined a circle of men who are my constant reminders that not all men are selfish jerks, those men whose kindness and affections wane considerably once the relationship clock starts ticking.

With the others unpacking boxes in the main room, I have Cooper to myself; therefore, I seize this moment to brave the question I would normally avoid.

"Did you do this for me?" I study his steely gray eyes for any fight-or-flight response.

He steps closer and circles his hands around my waist. I slide my hands up his strong arms, enjoying the contact and the reaction from my brain, command central, sending out flares to awaken every single enthusiastic nerve.

"Carson offered us the use of this little building, and he mentioned some basic repairs and clean up," I say, "but this is much more than that. Those are brand new built-in cabinets out there and custom worktables. You put in a lot of work here in a very short time, and these are not things Leo would ever think of on his own, so I have to wonder if you came up with this."

"I may have made some suggestions." As he leans down to kiss my cheek, I can't take my eyes off his unflinching gaze.

"Suggestions?" I ask. "This cost money and time. It must have cut into the guys' workload at the factory."

"I was very persuasive. I may have strongly suggested we do things a certain way. After seeing your set up at the house and how you and Lauren work, I thought I could make some improvements in this space to make your job easier."

"So this was your idea? I know you've been friends with Lauren long before I would even serve you a meal... that I hadn't eaten off of"—this makes him grin—"but did you go above and beyond because of me?"

"You were definitely my motivation, yes."

"Gosh, if we're comparing notes on who is more awesome, you're hitting it out of the park. I can't keep up with your gifts. All I did was make you a stupid egg sandwich."

"It's not a competition." He strokes my cheek.

"I have to be honest," I say hesitantly, "if you keep doing things like this, I'm going to think you're my quasi-boyfriend and not just my date for the wedding."

"Oh, good. I've been promoted from date to quasi. Yeah, that's exactly what I'm aiming for, a homely hunchback," he deadpans.

Once I give him a nice hard nudge in the groin with my knee, he bowls over, laughing and embracing me harder.

"If you keep doing that, I'll be your quasi-invalid, and I won't be able to deliver."

"Let's get something straight, Cooper. I'm serious, if we're—"

He interrupts my speech with a kiss, parting my lips until his tongue takes full control of my mouth. Holy heck, my knees just want to give away. I want him to have his way with me across our new, freshly stained pine desk!

When he releases my lips, I feel like I just got a hit of too much nitrous oxide at the dentist. Cooper should come with a warning label.

"I'm tired of you being serious, Imogene. Serious to you means doubting everything. Stop doubting me." He's gruff as he holds me against him.

"I'm trying."

"Try harder. I haven't done anything that should make you question my motives."

"Maybe that's what makes me nervous. You seem a little too perfect. No one is this perfect; everyone has faults, and mine are obvious."

"We see what we want to see, so maybe you're having so much fun with me that all you see is something that scares you. I'm not perfect, and I do have faults, like anyone else. We like each other a lot, so there's no reason for us not to be together."

"So help me, Cooper, if you end up dumping me like Jeremy did, I will shoot your kcuffing balls off."

"Please don't compare me to that dope, and please tell me you don't own any firearms." He smiles.

"I don't, but I saw your gun cabinet in your bedroom closet."

"It's locked and indestructible, so don't get any ideas that you can open it with a paper clip."

"I give one warning. And I can do a lot of damage with a fork and a coffee pot. Believe me."

"Oh, I believe you. Does that mean I'm your quasi-boyfriend?"

"We'll start with quasi and work our way up from there."

"Okay, I'm your quasi-something." He scowls. "Let's get this place set up and go have lunch."

I suspect Cooper planned on having a quiet lunch alone

with me, but after we finish unpacking boxes, filling the cabinets, and watching Lauren do a few happy dances around the new studio, everyone joins us for lunch. Since Cooper and I drove in with other people and had no vehicle of our own, Dylan made everyone head into the diner where Jess and Emma joined us.

I sit at a booth with the women while Cooper sits across the diner with the men. He glances my way occasionally, clearly anxious to escape our friends for a change.

"How long have you two been seeing each other?" Emma asks me.

I drag my gaze from the other side of the room and look at her, sitting across from me. "Almost every day for fourteen months, according to Cooper," I reply tight-lipped.

Lauren snorts.

"How long have you been dating?" Emma clarifies while Jess and Lauren watch me intently.

"Officially dating? Three days."

Lauren laughs. "Please, they've been spending oodles of time together since your wedding night, Emma. They've been shopping together, hiking together, having dinner at our house together, and they had a date."

"How long have you been hot for him?" Jess's tone is studious. I expect her to start dictating notes to herself on her phone, which is a funny habit we catch her doing frequently.

"I suppose for a few weeks. Maybe closer to a month." My demeanor is cool to avoid getting carried away with flighty joy.

"Ha!" Lauren interjects. "More like six months or longer."

"If you think you know so much, why don't you answer their questions?"

"I will," Lauren says inches from my ear. She turns to face Jess and Emma. "She actually likes him and has for a while. Imogene is having a little power struggle with herself."

"I am?"

Lauren glares at me. "Yes, it's obvious to everyone."

"It's not obvious to me," Jess adds, looking confused.

"Nothing is obvious to you," Emma responds, patting Jess's hand. "You are one of the most clueless women I have ever met when it comes to men. With the exception of Carson, that is."

Jess considers this for a moment, and then she and Emma both laugh. "And you are as tactful as your husband. Fine, I missed the signs between Cooper and Imogene."

"Imogene pretended to miss the signs, too," Lauren says with a mouthful of fries.

"Does this mean you and Cooper are officially a couple and Carson doesn't have to bring an extra tent next week for the camping trip?" Jessica asks.

"That damn camping trip," I mutter.

"You have to go. Leo says it will be the last big bonding moment for all of us." Lauren reaches for my unfinished turkey sandwich. I assume she'll regret it later when I have to hold her hair as she throws up ... *again*.

"Leo is a fatalist and thinks everything we do is our last time together. What's with him?" I ask.

"I think it's impending fatherhood that has him feeling nostalgic, and don't change the subject. I am very happy to see you and Cooper together. Finally," Lauren says as she starts picking fries off Emma's plate. "Answer Jess's question. Two tents or one?"

All three of them wait for my response.

"This is exactly what I don't want, to live this relationship out in public like it's a sleazy reality show. This is too new, and I don't know where it will end up. I can't discuss details like we used to." I look down at my unappetizing food. "You have the important stuff ... I like Cooper, and that's about all I know."

190

"Is this you being scared or is this you being evasive?" Jess's confused expression is almost comical.

"Wow." Emma arches her eyebrows. "I've never seen you scared about a guy. This is a first."

"I'm not scared. I'm being cautious. All of you have done the same, so don't lecture me."

"I wasn't cautious with Dylan." Emma shakes her head. "No way. I dove right in."

"Okay, you're the exception."

"I wasn't very … cautious," Jess stammers. "I was …"

"Oh, stop," I say to her. "It's painful just reliving that whole thing with you and Carson. You were so kcuffing clueless about him. You had that thing with Dylan because your head is wired differently. No offense, I love you, but you missed every signal Carson was sending out. That whole summer should be labeled *What Not To Do With Men,*' so please, don't try to compare that to my situation."

Jess looks a little hurt, so Emma puts an arm around her. "Ignore her, Jess. Imogene is always meaner when she's hiding something."

"Really, I'm not hiding anything. Lauren has made some very good points. Yes, I thought Cooper was kinda hot when he first showed up in town. And, yes, I'm aware that he was paying extra attention to me for a while, and I probably put too much effort into being rude to him. On some level, I liked him, and on another, I wasn't ready to get involved with any guy. That's it. Big deal. We're dating and will see where this goes, but I'm not going to indulge you and the rest of the town in a play-by-play of my love life, especially since it has a way of making me look like a loser in the end."

"Jeepers, don't be so optimistic." Lauren rolls her eyes.

"No one has said jeepers since 1942," I say.

"My grandmother says it all the time," Lauren retorts.

"My point exactly." I throw my napkin on my plate. "Jess, tell Carson one tent. And, now, that is the end of the

191

Q and A, everyone."

"God, I hope you're nicer to Cooper," Emma mumbles into her napkin.

"I'm sorry." I bury my face in my hands and sigh. "Everything is happening at once. Cooper, Lauren's baby and wedding, our new building. And, starting tomorrow, Lauren and I will be employers. That freaks me out a little." I look at their concerned faces. "I shouldn't take any of this out you guys, but it's so damn easy when you hound me with questions."

"It's nice having someone else do all the freaking out for me. I have a few crying jags here and there, but I'm kind of in la-la land over all of this." Lauren shrugs.

"Rest assured, Leo's doing his own freak out for both of you," I add with a smile.

"I may not be the most astute observer when it comes to people, but I think we're all a little excited about you and Cooper. We just want to share in your happiness. That's all," Jess adds defensively.

"Thank you. All of you. And I'm sorry for the bitchy dig, Jess."

"Apology accepted," she replies softly. "I wish I had Cooper's intuition about people, but at least I can read Carson."

"And how does the book of Carson read?" Emma asks.

"He's easy," Jess explains. "Sex, sleep, sex, food, sex, work, sex, walk the dog, sex, movies, sex, and so on."

"Do you two ever talk?" Emma grins.

"Carson is the strong silent type," Lauren explains.

"Are you kidding?" Jess exclaims. "Carson talks nonstop with me. It's like he saves it all up, and when he gets home from work, he can't stop talking. Sometimes, I have to ask him for quiet time, and he actually watches the clock, waiting until he can talk to me again."

Everyone laughs. This is a side of Carson none of us have been privy to, and it's funny and sweet coming from nerdy Jessica. Her tangled, long, red hair frames her blushing face, giving her an adorable look.

I glance over at the men to see Cooper is already heading my way. My heartbeat quickens and a smile tugs at the corners of my mouth. I leave the booth, telling Lauren I'll meet her at the car and then say goodbye to my parents and grandmother.

"Longest lunch of my life," Cooper says, putting his hand on my back as we walk out the door.

Outside in the humid heat of the mid-day sun, I want nothing more than to go some place more cool and comfortable to be alone with Cooper.

"I just spent an hour pretending to my friends that you and I are no big deal. I was lying." I look up at him, feeling like I have betrayed us. I want this to be the beginning of something very good.

"Ah, Imogene, everyone knows you're full of shit. Your friends can see right through you." He leans down and gives me a soft kiss on the lips. "This town is like living in a fish bowl. It's hard to escape all the questions and gossip."

"Do the guys ask you about us?"

"Nah. Guys don't give a crap about that stuff. At least not the details. All Carson wanted to know is if he needs to bring an extra tent next weekend."

I start laughing and Cooper grins with a confused expression. "I love how direct guys are. I can totally see Carson asking for a number count on tents and absolutely nothing about you and me. Meanwhile, I get the third degree on you every day."

"Let it happen." He caresses my arm, sending more happy tsunamis my way.

"So, you don't mind living in a fish bowl?"

"In terms of people prying in my life, it's not much different than what I had in Brooklyn."

"What fish bowl?" Lois asks, surprising us from

behind. She's dressed in her yoga attire and her pretty, silver hair is styled in a perfect chignon. She is slender and tone, resembling a graceful, aging ballerina.

I throw my hands up. "You're the fish bowl. You and everyone else. This fish bowl we live in, where everyone feels entitled to know everyone's personal business."

"It's our favorite past time," Lois says, as if this is a perfectly acceptable answer.

"It is when you're not at the center of it," I say.

Cooper snakes his arm around my shoulders for a protective squeeze.

"Sweetie pie, when a love story hits town, you better believe people are going to talk about it. Hera's population is sixty percent female, and with all the grisly news on TV, dang tootin' we're talking about romance whenever we can."

Cooper smiles. "Sweetie pie. How about that one?"

"Don't even try. Only Lois can get away with that one."

"Why haven't I seen you at any yoga classes in the last month?" Lois scolds.

"You kicked me out of the class," I say incredulously. "Remember? You said I talk too much."

"You do, but I didn't expect you to never come back. You can come, too, Cooper."

"Pass." Cooper shakes his head. "No way."

"I got Dylan to take the beginner yoga and meditation class. Men do attend."

"I heard Dylan meditated himself right to sleep in that class," Cooper adds.

"He did, but that's not the point," Lois continues. "The point is I got Dylan to sit on the floor and calm down. He was so calm he dozed off. When have you ever seen him like that?"

"Never," Cooper and I both respond.

"Oh, I know you're a very calm young man. You're

194

not like the others," Lois says to Cooper. "But Imogene carries around a lot of stubborn, crabby mojo. Maybe you can work some of your magic on her." Lois may look like a ballerina, but she sounds like pure hillbilly.

"I'm doing my best." He pulls me in and plants a big kiss on my mouth, just the kind of display Lois loves.

"Very good." Lois nods approvingly. "You'll both have to come over to my house for a poker game soon."

Cooper is enjoying the attention we're receiving because it forces me to acknowledge our relationship. I'll agree to anything so we can leave, even poker with Lois, who is hardcore about cleaning out other people's wallets.

On our way back to Lauren's car, he finds a spot alone off the main street and pulls me aside in the alley that leads to my new office. He holds my waist firmly so I face him.

"I want you to go home and pack a bag. Leo is going to drop me at my place so I can get my bike. I'll come pick you up."

"No. I'll drive to your house in my own car. I don't want us to be seen on your bike with my overnight bag, parading through town, feeding the rumor mill."

"It's not a rumor if you're actually spending the night at my house, and since when do you care what people think or say about you?"

"True. Still, I'll take my own car so I can drive to work in the morning."

"Sure. Whatever makes you happy, my little control freak." He smirks.

Guilt is a powerful thing, like an unstoppable freight train or an incurable illness. Any wave of happiness I thought I was riding is immediately squashed by the big G. I have been so careful in how I handle Cooper and how I talk about him with my friends, using my sarcastic remarks to brush off questions about him or the relationship developing between us. However, my caustic words are damaging and devalue what we are and what we have, and the thought of my glib comments to downplay my feelings towards Cooper leave a pool of bitterness in my gut. For once, I truly believe my big, fat, lying mouth could erode my heart and soul forever.

"I'm not really heartless," I blurt out in a shaky voice.

Cooper studies me with a frown.

"I don't want you to really think I'm a cold, heartless bitch and hope that maybe I'll come around eventually. You don't have to hope ... I'm not really that person."

"I never thought you were." He tilts his head to the side, wondering where I'm going with this.

"It's easier to be sarcastic and sometimes a little cruel, and I may have taken it too far with you. No, I did take it too far."

"Imogene,"—Cooper shakes his head—"it's me. I'm not an idiot. I told you I know that's part of your game face. I never once thought that's who you really are inside. Besides, I think you're hilarious ... and sexy."

"My friends think my behavior has been unseemly— more than usual, that is. It has, and it's because I do like you more than I've let on."

"You're not telling me anything I haven't already figured out."

"Good," I say, nodding and looking down, feeling brave that I'm being forthright for once while simultaneously feeling the shame that comes with ugly admissions.

"Hey." He lifts my chin so I look at him. "I'm not asking you to bring stuff over to my house so we can have undisturbed rolls in the hay whenever we want. It's so we can spend more time alone together without having to be at your place where everyone likes to drop in unannounced."

"Have you ever actually rolled in the hay?"

"No, I don't think I've ever stepped foot in a barn, but since I'm living in the country now, I thought I could say that."

"Uh-huh." I lean away to get a view of our pretty, new building, looking for Lauren's car.

"Ah, damn," Cooper mutters. "You've rolled in the hay, haven't you?"

I sigh, exasperated with my consistently bad timing. One minute, I'm telling him how much I like him, and the next, I'm confessing to yet another disappointing sexual encounter as a teenager.

"It was prickly and smelled like horse dung. I discovered I'm allergic to hay, and my skin itched like hell. And the sex was terrible. Really awful experience. Really, really ..."

Cooper growls some indecipherable expletive under his breath. "Stop talking. No more barns for you," he orders. "I have to be in the city tomorrow to help Dylan set up some new showroom display. I'll be gone for two days, and when I get back, we have to go to another damn dance class after work. So today is our day. Throw your stuff in a bag and get a move on. I expect you at my house in less than half an hour."

"Yes, sir." I decide not to salute him since he's losing patience with this whole day.

When Lauren's car rolls down the short alley and she honks the horn, I give Cooper a quick peck goodbye then jump into her car to show him that I am serious about getting a *move on.*

I watch him in the side view mirror as we drive away. He's making some gesture with his arms and shouting something. I smile and wave, and he puts a hand to his forehead and shakes his head. I can't believe he's still upset about my barn story.

When we arrive home, I open my car door to find that the strap on my favorite bag is torn to bits.

"Oh," Lauren remarks as I inspect the shredded strap. "I guess you shouldn't have put your bag on the floor. You didn't even notice that you closed the door on it."

"Thank you, Miss Obvious." My tone is snippy again.

"Then again, maybe this is God's way of sending you a sign that you were really rude at lunch." Lauren raises her chin, gets out the car, and slams her door.

"Right. God is always on the lookout for discounted designer handbags that he can destroy because they send meaningful messages to the dregs of humanity!"

Nineteen

It takes me five minutes to pack and another ten to apologize to Lauren. Ultimately, she's too tired to argue with me and heads off to bed for a nap. I throw my overnight bag in the car and drive off to Cooper's home, looking forward to having some alone time with him.

When I arrive at Chez MacKenzie, Cooper's bike is keeping company with several cars and trucks. Music is blasting from somewhere outside, and my heart deflates a little at the thought of him having a house party and the guests who are intruding on my time.

I'm feeling a little selfish at the moment. I already had to endure an inquisition at lunch, and I was planning on maybe cooking him dinner and moving his living room chairs to the back porch so we can listen to the crickets and the babbling brook while we eat. I make it sound like one of those commercials for erectile dysfunction with the happy couple enjoying being homebodies, laughing over coffee and sharing a bubble bath. The sad truth is I would gladly take what the erectile dysfunction couple has over my sorry social life.

Until I gave in to Cooper's persistence, I was pretty miserable and couldn't imagine any man asking me out, not even the few uneventful dates I did have.

As I park the car, a handsome young man comes striding around the side of the house. He gives me a familiar smile as he approaches, but it's his tall, lean, muscular body that stands out. The guy isn't wearing a shirt, so I'm staring at him when I realize he's got Cooper's swagger and facial expression, but instead of blond hair, he has black hair that almost reaches his shoulders.

I get out of the car with my duffle bag.

"You must be Imogene," he says, grinning. "I'm Cooper's brother Peyton. I've heard about you. And I think we've ruined your day. At least, my brother was ready to kill me and the others when he found us here." He shakes my hand and takes my bag.

"Others?"

"Yeah, my brothers and our uncle decided to drive in this morning to help finish Cooper's extension. The porch. When we got here, he was gone, so we let ourselves in and went to work. He got home a while ago and looked a little disappointed that we chose today to surprise him. I can see why."

I can tell Cooper's brother is a ladies' man, and I don't mind the flattery at all.

"Peyton! Leave her alone and get back and finish the job!" Cooper yells as he comes out of the house. He storms towards his brother and grabs my bag from him.

"I was merely introducing myself to your lovely lass." Peyton has a sly grin. I suspect he's the real troublemaker in the family.

"Lass?" I repeat, almost laughing.

"He gets that from my dad," Cooper says, glaring at his brother.

"Is he here, too? I'd love to meet him."

"No," Cooper says quickly. "Just my brothers and my Uncle Fraser showed up. That's plenty."

I'll hand it to Peyton, he's very cute, and I'll bet everything he says works on women. He's got the same high cheekbones and beautiful gray eyes as Cooper, except he has dark beard stubble. His muscular body is either the result of a lot of physical work, or he spends a hell of a lot of time in the gym. *He's handsome, but he's not Cooper*, I think as I study his face that's lacking that special Cooper element.

Peyton chuckles as he checks me out until Cooper clamps his hand on his brother's shoulder and turns him back towards the house. "Go."

"Okay," Peyton laughs. He looks back at me and winks. "Catch you inside, Imogene. We're going to throw some brats on the grill."

"Sorry they all showed up. The house is a zoo with them in there. They've kind of screwed up our plans."

"It's okay with me. I want to meet them. I don't know any of your family, and you know mine." I am genuinely interested in meeting his brothers. I expect it will give me more insights into Cooper since he hasn't told me much about his family.

"You sure you don't mind? I understand if you want to leave, my brothers can be overbearing. My uncle is a good guy, though."

"Well, you tell me, Cooper. They're helping you finish the porch, so would you rather do that and have me out of the way? I can go back home—"

"No, I'd rather have you here. I have to work with them, but we'll get the job done by tonight, and then they're leaving."

"You're not letting them crash here?"

"Hell, no. You're staying here. They can drive back to the city. I already told them I need them out of here by nine. Besides, they'll be done before that. They got here while you and I were setting up your building, so they've made a lot of progress."

"Great. I can't wait to meet the rest of them." I don't move towards the house because, truthfully, I am nervous about meeting his family. This is fairly new for me, meeting a guy's family, and Cooper doesn't look especially thrilled.

Cooper turns towards the house and then notices my hesitation. "Are you going to come in?"

"Darn tootin'. I have to give the MacKenzie clan a

Hera welcome wagon howdy." I smile while Cooper looks perplexed.

"I thought you said that wasn't your thing." He cocks his head to the side and narrows his eyes.

"It's my new thing. It's the new Imogene, can't you tell?"

"Again?" he asks softly.

"What?"

"You're nervous around me, or maybe it's my family." He steps towards me and wraps his arm around my waist, pulling me in for a long, powerful kiss. It knocks all those hillbilly words and any preposterous notions I had about winning Hera's nonexistent Miss Congeniality award.

Then Cooper takes my hand and leads me through the house and out to the porch extension where Peyton along with the other men are staining the wood. The screens are in place and the project looks almost completed.

Cooper and I stand at the entrance to the kitchen as he introduces me to his uncle, Fraser, and his two older brothers, Neil and Evan, who are twins. They all look like the youngest brother Peyton, tall and strong with their trademark black hair, but the others wear it cropped short.

Cooper helps them finish staining the porch floor, and I rummage through the groceries they brought and offer to grill the brats and throw together some salads.

Cooper wasn't kidding when he said his family is loud. Their talking is escalated to shouting and laughing so loudly I feel like I'm in a room full of uncensored Dylan Blackards. They are energetic and good-natured, though. Even Uncle Fraser can hold his own among his nephews. He's beefy and wide with a little extra weight, yet he has the strength of an ox as he carries an extra long ladder on his sturdy shoulder out to his truck.

While we crowd around the kitchen table that really only has enough comfortable room for four, I watch them work through several helpings of grilled brats and the broccoli salad and potato salad I whipped up.

I learn that Fraser, Evan, and Neil are all Brooklyn police officers and full of NYPD stories. Peyton has part ownership in the Brooklyn bar with their dad, Stuart. They talk over each other through the dinner, boisterous and unforgiving with their tall tales meant to embarrass one another. Cooper smiles along with their jokes and comments, often directed at him.

Although they truly are hilarious guys, I can see how Cooper is the odd man out. Not only does he stand apart with his blond mane, he also doesn't belong in their exclusive Brooklyn club. He's the one that chose to join the FBI and live apart from his large, close-knit family. All those years of being separated from them is obvious; however, I cannot decide if it's guilt he feels about missing out on family times or if he's always been the black sheep in his family.

Cooper returns their ribbing with a few scathing jabs of his own towards Neil, whom I'm told has a young son, and Evan who has twins of his own. Peyton is twenty-six, older than me, but has the makings of an immature playboy. Cooper takes the opportunity to thump Peyton's head or cover his mouth entirely when he's about to say something crude. Throughout it all, it's clear Fraser holds a special place in Cooper's heart. I watch him observe his uncle with love and respect.

There are moments where Cooper is unusually quiet, lost in a thought or something else that triggers his reflective expression. My heart softens for him when I see him in this vulnerable state as I consider how little I know about his family and childhood.

Having eaten lunch in our family's diner just about every day over the last year, I'm accustomed to Cooper being around my parents and grandmother. He also works with most of my childhood friends; however, this is the first time I'm the new person and getting to know those closest to him.

"Why haven't we met you sooner?" Peyton asks me. "We've been to Cooper's place a few times."

"I never saw you in the diner," I reply. "That's where I was working, for the most part. And I suppose you could say Cooper and I were not the best of friends until recently."

"Really?" Peyton asks, intrigued, exchanging a few raised eyebrows with Neil and Evan.

"We were under the impression that you two have been together a while." Neil looks questioningly at Cooper.

"Cooper mentioned you a bit, lass," Uncle Fraser adds in a deep, soft voice that reminds me of Cooper.

"I mentioned that you were the one woman who wouldn't give me the time of day." Cooper puts his arm protectively around the back of my chair. "Otherwise, I said everyone else in town was extremely nice. You were the one hold out."

"That sounds like me. The mean one."

They laugh and Uncle Fraser gives me a conspiratorial wink, causing me to wish I knew what it was for. I imagine it's along the lines of how Cooper has spoken about me, and I came across as the crazed post-Jeremy woman.

"Not true." Uncle Fraser points a beefy finger at me. "He said very good things about you. Greer really wanted to be here to meet you, but she's at Stu's house—that's Cooper's father—babysitting a house full of kids."

"A house full of kids?" I look at Cooper.

He nods. "The MacKenzies are overpopulating the world."

"Speaking of which, we have to hit the road soon." Evan looks at his watch as Neil agrees that they need to pick up their kids.

After dinner, Cooper helps them load their tools and equipment into their vehicles. They each give me a big hug goodbye, Uncle Fraser's a little too strong and Peyton's a little too amorous. Cooper pulls his brother away by his hair, sending them all off with some private words huddled in the dark while I wait at the front door. I decide to leave them alone and retreat to the kitchen to clean up the gigantic mess made by five hungry men.

Cooper returns and hugs me from behind, kissing my neck as I fill the kitchen sink with hot, soapy water.

"That was nice. I would like to meet the rest of your family and all these little kids they talked about."

Cooper rests his lips against my neck. "They can be exhausting when they are all in the same house. It's really nice when they leave. Forget the dishes; let's go to bed."

"We have to clean up now. You're leaving tomorrow for the showroom with Dylan in the morning, and you'll be gone for two days. The dishes can't sit here that long. Or I could come back and do them tomorrow night."

"I don't want you doing my dishes. But I definitely wouldn't mind if you stayed here while I was gone. I'd like that, calling you here."

"That's not what I was fishing for, Cooper. I have a home with Lauren and Leo. Yes, I'm the third wheel, but the house is big enough for all of us. You can call me there. I have plenty of privacy when I need it."

While I start washing the dishes, Cooper grabs a towel to dry them. He absently takes the bowl I hand him and begins wiping it, but he's distracted, staring out the window over the sink. I don't know if he's reflecting on something his brothers have said or if my remarks have bothered him. I'm used to him being completely focused on me, yet his thoughts are elsewhere.

"What is it?" I drop the sponge in the water and brace myself against the edge of the sink, studying his profile and his strong, clenched jaw.

He turns to me with confusion and irritation. "What is what?"

"You. Like this. Something is bothering you."

"Let's go to bed." He tosses the towel on the counter.

"Cooper, you've been acting different since your brothers got here. I don't know what's going on, but I can see that something is wrong."

"Ack. My family always has something going on. That's one of the reasons why I moved here, so I could still see them without being so close that I'd see them every day."

"That's it? I thought it was really nice that they came out here to help you finish the extension. The porch looks great. I wish I had a bigger family. Mine is really claustrophobic with all eyes on me. I'm the only kid, the only grandchild, so they put a lot of expectations on me. You have a whole entourage of siblings and relatives with their own lives. You don't feel like you're under a microscope."

Cooper's stern expression softens. He runs a hand under my hair and turns me towards him with his other hand on my waist. "You think you disappoint your family?"

"I worry that I may be a big letdown to my grandmother for not planning to take over the diner. And my parents would really like to see me settle down, get married, and have kids. It's all about the family restaurant and babies. They love me and they're very supportive, but they have not been subtle, either. I'm surprised they haven't put up a fight about my new business."

"They have more faith in you than you realize." He's using that rich, deep voice that makes me melt.

"Don't underestimate my grandmother. She once threatened to parade around the diner in a sandwich board, advertising my availability. She said she'd tell prospective husbands that offspring would be rewarded with cash bonuses."

Cooper runs his hands slowly up my sides. "She did not."

"Yes, she did. This was right before Jeremy came along. "

"She must like me, then, because she always gives me an extra slice of pie at lunch."

"She's always extra nice to single men, just in case. I doubt she knows about us."

"Imogene," he says, "everyone knows about us." With that, his lips claim my mouth.

I press my hands against his chest and let myself get lost in his unyielding kiss, which only ends when he picks me up and cradles me in his arms, striding down the hall to his bedroom. He actually tosses me on the bed and begins taking his clothes off.

"Hey," I say, looking around at the cream colored comforter and the white sheets. The blue and gray set is gone. "You got new bedding?"

"Yes. Take your clothes off." He's already down to his briefs, and I have to pause to watch his incredible body in motion.

"Wait a minute. When did you have time to go shopping?"

"I didn't. I hired Talia to do it."

"Carson's housekeeper?" I laugh. "She's an awesome cook and most of her clients are single men from the city who keep second homes in the area. Is that why this place is so clean?"

"She just started yesterday while I was painting your new office. I gave her money to buy the sheets when she said I needed a new comforter and a better thread count. I have no idea what that's about, so she went off to the mall and took care of it. Last week, I got a new washer and dryer for the laundry room, so Talia washed everything, made the bed, and cleaned the house because I thought I would be bringing you back here last night."

"Aww, you did this for me."

"Between the factory hours and running out to the new

houses Carson has been building, I don't have a lot of time here for domestic chores. Now, get undressed." He crawls on the bed and begins unzipping my jeans.

"So much for me slowing things down," I say excitedly. I'm already worked up from the kiss, and looking at an almost naked Cooper only arouses me further. I want to simultaneously zip my pants back up and rip off my blouse.

"If something is good, why would you want to slow it down?" Cooper is eagerly trying to remove my clothing while my hands make feeble attempts to stop his quick maneuvers. He yanks both of my shoes off and flings them at the ceiling. I watch one fall down and hit a lamp and the other skitter across the room.

"Why do you think some people can take a relationship slow and others move like the speed of light?" I ask as he finally pulls my jeans off in one fluid movement.

"People who move slowly don't have any sense of mortality. They think they have all the time in the world," he growls as we play tug of war with my blouse.

He regards me with a flash of irritation. "Why aren't you naked? Why am I doing all the work here?"

"I like watching you work for it, and why do you feel compelled to move so fast? Do you think death is around the corner or something?"

"Ah, shit." Cooper is on all fours glaring down at me. "Not again, Imogene. Stop overthinking this. Why are you shy all of sudden?"

"I'm not shy." Lord knows, a little shyness might have spared me a decade of wankers. "We're always jumping on each other like it's our last chance to screw before we end up at the Death Star."

"Maybe it is," he says, lowering his head to the buttons on my blouse. When he rips one off with his teeth and spits it across the room, I watch, fascinated, as he proceeds to work his way up each button.

"Good Lord. You're on a rampage, and you're ruining a perfectly good blouse."

"And you're ruining a perfectly good night. I'm making up for lost time, including last night, which you also ruined."

"Oh, fine." I push him to the side, and he falls on his back to watch me.

Once I get up on my knees and struggle out of my damaged blouse, Cooper hooks a finger under the band of my black panties and looks up at my breasts spilling out of my black bra. His eyes widen, and I realize I have trapped the wild boar. He looks like he's been shot with a tranquilizer gun.

I suddenly grab his boxer briefs with both hands and yank them down his legs with enough force that he yells in surprise and protectively grabs his straining cock so it doesn't get strangled in the menacing hold I have on his underwear.

"Jesus," he mumbles, all his beautiful muscles flexing in response. I am momentarily caught up in a few seconds of admiring his form.

"You wanted rough." I pop off my bra and wiggle out of my panties. It's my turn to lean over him like an animal. "Get ready for the ride of your life."

"Can't wait," he says, reaching for my waist to bring me closer.

Damn, I forgot to have the condom ready. While I eye the distance of the nightstand, realizing it's out of reach, Cooper tilts his head and catches the frustration in my expression. There's an intensity to his gaze as he gives me that knowing smirk, and that's enough for me to give it my best shot. I launch myself forward, stretching across Cooper's chest, trying to grab the nightstand drawer.

So much for my wannabe, sexy-dominatrix act. My buffoonery move has all my weight on Cooper as I struggle to pull a condom out of the drawer. He's growing harder by the second as my soft tummy and breasts press and rub against him. Finally, he laughs and reaches his arm out to retrieve the condom that I'm unable to grasp.

"Is this what you're looking for?" He smiles and holds it up to my face.

I take it and prop myself back on my knees to roll the condom on him, making him moan and throw his head back.

"I was hoping we could be more than the sum of our basic urges," I muse as I stroke his length. "Oh, well. I was wrong."

"This is a really lousy time to get introspective about us fucking." There's that smug smile. Then his eyes become hooded as I increase the stroking.

"True. This is nothing special. We're just going at it like animals," I say matter-of-factly, even though my pulse is racing.

"Wait a minute," Cooper grits and makes a power play, throwing me off him and quickly positioning himself between my legs. "Don't give me that bull."

"Oh!" When I knee his hands and cock away and push him over again, toppling to the floor, he manages to embrace me so his back takes the hard hit.

"Christ, Imogene. What are you doing?" he barks, trying to turn me over on my back.

"No you don't! This is mine!" I straddle him, and he lets me pin his arms above his head.

"Why the hell did I buy new sheets? You should have told me you prefer the floor."

I shut him up by rubbing his cock in the wetness between my legs. His eyes blaze with lust as I impale myself on him in one swift move. Then I am rocking and grinding against him. I release his hands, and Cooper assists by gripping my waist and forcing me to slam down on his cock as if he can fill more of me.

"Fuck, yeah." He bucks upward, going for the gold.

He thrusts harder, holding me in place so I won't catapult off him. Everything about his glowering eyes and tense expression tells me he wishes he were taking me in a way that would satisfy his baser instincts. With angry grunts and steely eyes, he moves one hand and puts his thumb to good use so I'm squirming above him, hurtling towards a nice, big orgasm. His needs don't even register with me at this point. It's all mine.

"Come on, beast," I cheer him on. "Let's bring this one on home, big boy."

And he does, more than once, thanks to a drawer newly stocked with condoms.

Twenty

"I'm not even listed in here," Cooper says as he scrolls through my phone.

We're taking my car to work since he's going to be in New York City with Dylan for the next two days and can't take his Harley.

"How is this possible? We've talked and sent texts, so how did you not save my number? And you still have Jeremy's number in here," he bellows, which makes me laugh.

"You're in there." I grin as I park the car behind the furniture factory. I look past the basketball court to my new, little office building and sigh happily.

"Where?" Cooper is glaring at my phone as if it has become his enemy.

"You're listed under *Viking*."

Cooper regards me quizzically and then looks back at the demon phone and begins scrolling furiously until he finds his number. "Is it because you think I'm a barbarian?"

"No. It's a compliment." I turn off the engine and smile at him. "*Sexy, Hunky Viking* seemed like overkill to put in my phone."

"Oh." As his tense face relaxes, he drops the phone in my handbag before leaning over to kiss me. Keeping his hand behind my neck, he moves back to study my face. I like this part—being past the hullabaloo and knowing we're a thing, a couple, or something. Okay, maybe nothing is clearly defined, but it is a pivotal moment … I think.

"I'm going to miss you, but you're going to be very busy," he says.

"With being a boss lady, you mean?" I laugh because that's exactly how I envision myself, and it cracks me up to think of myself as an employer.

"That, too. But I'm talking about that damn phone. You have a lot of guys' numbers in there that you need to delete. Either you're storing numbers from the past decade, or you've been a lot busier than I thought over the last year."

I grin and cup his jaw for one last kiss on his cheek, reveling in the sensation of his stubble against my lips.

"Sure, laugh, but Quasi is going to be thinking of you while he has to share a hotel room with Dylan. Me and Mad Dog. Real fun."

"You have me picturing a hunchback and a Rottweiler."

"There you go. So you need to call me a few times a day and maybe we can have phone sex."

"Oh, I'm sorry. I already have someone on call for that. Yeah, he's listed in my contacts as *Hot Phone Sex Dude*."

"Start deleting, Imogene."

Our first morning of business at Imogene & Lauren goes quite smoothly. Our two new employees, Anita and Tracy, both show up early. After Lauren and I give a detailed overview of our product designs and goals and the layout of our new workshop, everyone gets busy. Lauren likes to handle paperwork and administrative chores first thing; therefore, she turns the back office into a system that flows for her. I sit at the large craft table in the main room with the others, and we get into a natural groove of separating and organizing our personal areas and keep up a very good pace on the current jewelry projects.

The women chat casually as their fingers expertly handle the more complex beading techniques. It's inspiring to watch them bring our designs to life and gives me greater faith in our decision to take on this enterprise that seemed so far-fetched to me two years ago.

"Lunchtime!" Lauren sings as she sails out of the back room.

We all get up to retrieve our sack lunches from the mini fridge handed down to us from Carson's office.

"Are you always this cheery?" Tracy asks Lauren.

Tracy is a thirtyish, single woman, a granola head who moved to Hera from the city to pursue a more affordable, artistic lifestyle. She sort of floats around with her gauzy tops and skirts billowing around her, and she believes in positive mantras. She's really the perfect match for Lauren's optimism.

Anita is closer to my mother's age and a bit more serious and morose like me. We've been sharing eye rolls all morning, anything to balance out the constant giddy vibes the other two give off.

"Lauren is in the cheerleader hall of fame," I add dryly.

"I think it's nice," Tracy says. "The boutique I worked in was owned by a very miserable woman who drove away the tourists whenever she worked the cash register."

"Ha. That would be me," I say and Lauren laughs. "Lauren and I are opposites, so it creates a pretty good equilibrium, I think."

"Definitely." Lauren sits down at the small, four-person table by the window we've designated for eating and taking breaks.

"I thought I'd run over to *The General Store* and get some sushi today," Anita says, picking up her handbag. "Would anyone like me to pick something up?"

"Sushi Dan is in town?" I frown because I really can't afford to splurge on sushi rolls, but our quaint Old West-style grocery store that caters high-end gourmet foods, mostly to tourists, only brings in the sushi chef a couple of times a week. I hate to think of how much money I used to blow on Sushi Dan.

"I made you peanut butter and jelly," Lauren says, handing me a grocery bag. "And there's an apple."

"Thanks. Is there a juice box, too?" My sarcasm doesn't faze Lauren.

"No. I stocked water bottles in the fridge for everyone. It's sweltering in here. We're not getting any crosswind." Lauren ruffles the bottom of her shirt to fan herself. Her face is pink, but she still isn't showing any obvious signs of pregnancy.

"I'll be back in ten." Anita slings her purse over her shoulder. "Oh, look, someone is coming."

We all look out the window that faces the parking lot and watch a man walk towards our building, clearly holding an enormous vase of flowers.

"Ooh," Lauren squeals.

"Hello?" The man knocks on the doorframe and opens the screen door to pop his head in. "I have flowers for Imogene Walsh?" As he looks at the four of us, my eyes are riveted on the extravagant bouquet of hydrangeas and roses.

"Me! That's me." I jump up and dash to take the heavy vase out of his hands.

"I'll get the tip." Lauren signals for the man to wait.

"It's been taken care of. Have a nice day, ladies." He gives us a curt nod and leaves.

"Well?" Anita asks. "Who is it from?"

"They are gorgeous," Tracy says with glee.

"I bet they're from Cooper," Lauren chimes in.

"It could be from our parents," I say, but I'm secretly hoping these are courtship flowers and not daddy's-little-girl flowers.

"Open the frigging card!" Lauren hovers impatiently as I put the vase on our lunch table and fumble with the envelope.

"Oh, give me that." Lauren yanks the envelope from

my hands and rips it open. *"'For my favorite ball buster. Congratulations on your first day. Quasi.'"*

"Ballbuster?" Anita asks.

"Quasi?" Lauren looks at me questioningly.

I laugh and grab my phone. "I have to call him." I run to the back office and shut the door for privacy. I call *Viking,* and he answers on the first ring.

"Hey, ballbuster."

"The flowers are beautiful. Thank you."

"I should have brought these to your door a month ago instead of that ratty sandal. I'm kind of doing this backwards."

"Backwards?" I lean against the office door and smile to myself, racing heartbeat and all.

"I'm told the guy is supposed to give a woman flowers at the beginning. I'm a little late to the game, but in my defense, I'm working with a bunch of guys who seem to know less than me."

"About women? I don't think you have a problem in that area."

"About dating," he chides. "About … us."

"Hmm, you're doing very well, Mr. MacKenzie. Wooing me with big cash tips, jewelry you shouldn't be paying for, hikes that I hate, expensive dinners we don't eat, and flowers. Very nice."

"Did you intentionally leave out the all-night sex? Because I think that's kind of a biggie, and it's a low blow to a guy's ego when you skip over that part."

"Isn't this nice? We're actually having a conversation instead of sex."

"Seriously, I'd rather have both. But I'm glad you like the flowers, and that I did something right for a change. Maybe I should have tried this approach a year ago."

I'm deliriously happy to hear his voice. "No, this is the right time for flowers. The women were all a flutter. Our first delivery, and they're flowers for me. Not bad, Viking."

"You do know my family is Scottish, right?"

"You picked Ballbuster. I picked Viking, not Quasi, by the way. That's a term Jess used for Dylan when she wasn't sure about him. You're definitely not Quasi. And how are things going on your end?"

"Good. I can see why Carson sent me, though. Some of these stores are high maintenance clients. Dylan and I visited a few accounts this morning, and they all have suggestions about our delivery schedules, so I'm taking notes and trying to be very understanding."

"Oh, I bet you're good at giving them all the right expressions to make them feel good."

Cooper laughs. "I am good at this. Dylan's approach is a little rough around the edges, but I guess they're used to him. Carson sent me along to smooth out some of the dialogue and to keep Dylan centered on sales instead of dealing with shipping and delivery problems."

"You are the seasoned actor."

"I'm playing myself, Imogene, no acting any more. So did Lauren do a cheer when she got her flowers?"

"Lauren? We only got the flowers addressed to me."

"Goddammit, Leo. I told him this morning to have flowers delivered to Lauren."

"Oh, no, Leo must have forgotten, and his head is in the clouds with the wedding and baby stuff."

"I know what I'm going to do with that guy's head," Cooper grumbles. "Okay, let me handle this. I'm going to call you tonight. Are you going to stay at my place? I put the extra house key in your bag this morning."

"I think it's better if I stay at my place. I …"

Cooper growls. "Okay, while you're overthinking this again, I have to take care of Leo. I'll call you tonight. Okay?"

"Okay." I smile stupidly at the phone.

"And, Imogene?"

"Yeah?"

"Congratulations. This is a big day."

I leave the back room feeling swoony, imagining I look a little delirious when I return to eat my sandwich with the women. Anita is back with scrumptious hand rolls for herself and lemon bars for the rest of us.

"How is your *boyfriend*?" Lauren shakes me from my dreamy state.

"He's good. He's working."

"I think it's great you're dating Cooper," Tracy says. "Sometimes he'd stop in the store and pick up gifts. He's a doll."

"You'd see him at the boutique in Woodstock?" I ask, imagining him in the fancy shop that caters to women with money.

Tracy nods as she nibbles on a carrot stick.

"What did he buy?"

"Imogene," Lauren scolds.

"Well, I want to know who he was shopping for. That store only sells things for women, so he must have been buying gifts for … women. I'm curious."

"They could have been gifts for his mother or his sister. If he had been serious with anyone, I would have known."

Tracy nods again. "True."

Anita looks at me with that exasperated expression older women get when they listen to younger women gripe about men. "Why don't you ask him instead of guessing?"

"I will." The old Imogene sticks her chin out defiantly, reminding herself that she's dating a man this time and not another college jock or a week-kneed boy-man.

"Good. That's what I do." Anita picks up a sushi roll with her chopsticks. "I don't waste time dallying around with wondering. If I want to know what Harvey has done in the past, I ask him."

"You're dating Harvey?" Lauren beats me to the question.

Harvey is the middle-aged owner of The General Store. He's big and stocky, usually wearing a white apron, and looks like a butcher sans the cleaver. I've known him my whole life since his store predates my birth; however, the only thing I remember about his former wife were the lollipops she'd hand out to kids who came in to shop with their parents.

"Harvey and I have been seeing each other for six months. Best lover I've ever had," Anita says, slapping her hand on the table as if that proves her point.

As Lauren's wide eyes meet mine, I stifle a laugh. Anita, with her perfectly black-bobbed hair and sensible shoes, dresses rather conservatively in mom jeans and blouses with full-arm and chest coverage, so I'm surprised and delighted to hear her talk so casually about her sex life.

"We had no idea he was dating anyone," I say. "I saw him at Lois's party, I think."

"Yep," Anita adds. "I was sitting across the table from him. We went with a large group and left right after the couple said their vows, had to. Harvey works long hours practically every day at the store, so we like to spend as much time at home as possible. Sex at least twice a day. That's how you keep the relationship fresh."

I can't help staring.

"You're getting more action than me," Lauren says in a shocked tone.

"And me," Tracy says. "I'm not even in the ballpark."

"Don't look at me." I shake my head. "I was celibate for a whole year."

"Cooper looks like he'd be very accommodating." Anita smiles.

"Oh, my gosh, I don't even give Lauren details."

"Still, Cooper is one sexy, fine man, right?"

"He is." I blush, thinking about our sex romp that landed us on the floor.

Thankfully, we manage to put aside our gripping sex talk for the rest of the day, and I'm astounded at our productivity. We work well together, synchronizing a system that's manageable for all of us. The flower delivery guy returns with a different yet equally beautiful display for Lauren, and she gushes over the card from Leo. I'll have to thank Cooper for that when I speak to him tonight.

The whole afternoon, my mind wanders back to Cooper, and I try to imagine us twenty years from now at Anita's age, still hot and heavy for each other. I put a stop to those thoughts immediately. That's a whole other territory of the long term *what ifs*, and I've tried this type of imagery once before with Jeremy, only to be burned. I've decided to limit myself to only romantic thoughts about Cooper, moments that have occurred, nothing I speculate could happen in the future. It's safer that way.

We're about to close the windows when we see a gang of people, led by Archie, crunching across the gravel and dirt lot. Emma and Jess are carrying a sheet cake and Lois, Eleanor, Leo, Carson, my grandmother, and our parents are following.

"You can't leave yet!" Archie says as he enters. How he can wear a three-piece suit in this heat is beyond me. "We have to celebrate with the big wig business women of Hera."

"Sweet Jesus, those are lovely flowers!" Lois exclaims as she pushes past everyone to admire the vases we've put in the middle of the worktable. "From Cooper and Leo?"

Leo nods with relief.

"Cooper asked me what kind of flowers you like," my mother adds, pleased with the flower arrangement.

"I'm here for cake," Carson says bluntly. "Can someone cut the cake already?"

"Carson," Jess snaps at him.

She and Emma set the cake down and Eleanor begins slicing and serving with the utensils she's brought with her.

"Here," Jess says, handing Carson a large piece of cake on a paper plate with a plastic fork.

Carson picks the cake up off the plate and eats it with his hand in three bites.

"Or you can eat it like that," Jess mutters to him. He smiles with his mouth full of cake and leans down to give her a kiss.

I wish Cooper were here so I could feed cake to him and fawn over his superb boyfriend etiquette.

It's a big chocolate cake with butter cream frosting, decorated with words of encouragement and congratulations, and it's demolished in a matter of minutes as more people from the furniture factory walk down to get a slice. Even Harvey shows up to congratulate us, giving Anita a big smooch. I can't help thinking of their extraordinary sex life. Then I study my parents and Lauren's parents, wondering if they're as active.

They are all fairly young, very attractive, and openly show affection. They're still in love after all these years. I have parents who still act like high school sweethearts. Then again, I suppose I don't want to know if they use handcuffs or roll off the bed during sex. No, thinking of my parents in that way makes Cooper and I sound unbelievably pedestrian and predictable. I prefer my Viking on the hunt for his damsel scenario better. It makes me smile, and I take note that I have not said one mean, sarcastic remark to anyone today.

"And how was your first day?" my grandmother asks gently. She puts a swollen, arthritic hand on my arm and gives me a little squeeze.

"Exciting. It feels too good to be true, and I'm starting to think I should worry more about everything we do: our product, our sales, our workday schedule. If I feel happy, it seems like I must be doing something wrong. It's work; it's supposed to be grueling."

"That's what it means to go into business for yourself,

221

exciting and terrifying. You will go through bouts of happiness, fear, and guilt. It's natural to be concerned ... a lot. You aren't only responsible for a business entity; you're responsible for people's livelihoods. The burden is great, but so are the rewards. I'm very happy for you, sweetheart."

As my grandmother hugs me, I get a whiff of French fry grease and onions, which means she's been sneaking into the kitchen to help with the cooking. A surge of guilt reminds me that, if I had opted in to the family diner business, I could help my parents keep my grandmother away from the physical labor that exasperates her arthritis and bad knees. This is the time in her life when she is supposed to take up yoga and water aerobics for seniors.

My defection is the first time I haven't relied on my family for income and shelter. I'm a little proud of that and hope that, in the near future, I can report a certain degree of success which really does make my family extremely proud, more than the obligatory encouragement they always give me.

As soon as Carson and his crew of men from the factory polish off the rest of the cake, they help clean up the party mess, throwing everything in garbage bags and taking them back to the factory dumpster. That was rather thoughtful.

Then Lauren wizzes through the studio again, spraying down tables and sweeping the floor. Over the last few weeks, she's become quite fanatical about cleaning and putting things back in place. I stay out of her way and refrain from cracking a joke about her similarities to The Roadrunner. I envy the way Leo watches her with concern, and it once again, like everything else, makes me miss Cooper.

Lauren and I stay at work late, rearranging storage cabinets and unpacking more supplies that were delivered that afternoon. We're ridiculously happy, dancing around the studio, shouting out all of our wild ideas on how to market our jewelry line as well as the press packages and gifts we think we should send out to influential people.

We are a sweaty, tired pair when we arrive home at nine. Leo is furious and stands in the doorway with his arms folded, scolding Lauren for putting in such a long day. He expected us home at six; as a result, the salad he made is a soggy bowl of lettuce and the grilled chicken breasts are cold, stored in the fridge.

Too exhausted and hot to eat, I head upstairs, stripping my damp clothes off as I go. I turn on the giant box fan in my room and plop on the bed. Only wanting to hear Cooper's voice, I place the call.

"Hey, beautiful." I can hear the smile in his voice after he answers on the first ring.

"Hey, handsome. I survived my first day, and that crabby alter ego of mine was nowhere in sight."

"You've found your calling. Imogene Walsh, business woman and jewelry designer."

I love the way he says that. I'm not even sure I can give myself credit in that way because it doesn't seem as though I've quite earned it yet.

"I'm exhausted, but I feel like I've accomplished something. If I have the energy, I'm going to take a cool bath. It's crazy hot here."

"Are you naked?"

"Not yet. In my undies."

"Damn. That sounds good."

I tell him about everyone showing up to celebrate, how the women gushed over his flowers, and I thank him for Lauren's flowers and coaching Leo, reminding him that Leo is going to need to learn how to relax and enjoy the ride with Lauren.

"She's started eating for two, and Leo is freaking out for two," I say excitedly, still riding on a high from the whole day.

"I'll be back soon. I'll take him fly fishing or something to get his mind off babysitting his wife for a while."

"It hasn't even been a day, and I miss you already."

"I missed you the minute Dylan and I drove out of the parking lot this morning. Our jobs are only separated by feet and our homes are only a couple of miles apart, so you never feel far away. But, coming into the city this morning, I felt the distance between us. It's a lousy feeling, even if it's temporary. I did have a funny moment today when a woman passed us on the street, saying the filthiest things to the guy with her. It made me think of you."

"Gah!" I laugh. "You make me sound horrible."

"No. I make you sound like someone I miss. We had lunch at Dylan's favorite hole-in-the-wall joint, and when the waitress was giving some other customer attitude, all I could think was, shit, she doesn't do it as well as Imogene."

"Stop. You went from being romantic to making fun of me," I laugh.

"You think I'm romantic?" His tone is serious.

"Yes. Definitely. I don't know any man who would go out with me after the way I treated you," I confide. "These weren't little things. Rescuing me when I was a wandering drunk at Lois's party ... and you've invested quite a chunk of change into our business with the estate jewelry, at least getting us off to a great start. The giant bouquet of flowers ..."

"Maybe I just did it to get into your pants."

"No, you didn't. There are other women who have much easier pants to get into, and you know it."

"Yeah. I was only interested in you, and let me state for the record that I'm the first man you've gone out with, Imogene. Those tools you dated before me were boys."

"Hmm. That reminds me. Tracy says she used to see you come into the store she worked at in Woodstock. You bought gifts for women."

"Are you a little jealous? Wondering who I was shopping for?"

"Yes," I reply emphatically. "Yes, I am. So there."

"Good. Nice to hear. There are a lot of women in my family: aunts, cousins, nieces. Someone is always having a birthday or a graduation, nothing else to that story."

"You're lucky I believe you."

"I'd never lie to you."

"So smooth. You'll see me in forty-eight hours, waltzing, hot stuff."

"Ah, shit. Imogene, I can't make the class. I can't come back on Wednesday with Dylan. After we check out of the hotel, I'm going to see my family in Brooklyn. I promised my sister and brothers I'd come and help deal with a family situation for a couple of days."

"Oh. Is it something bad?"

"Nothing major. Hey, we're going camping." His voice is suddenly bright as he changes the subject.

"Okeydokey," I say lamely, wondering why he's not telling me what's going on.

"I wish I was there with you. Your little hometown that you think is so boring is paradise compared to what we're dealing with here. And Dylan is a fucking maniac. He made me go running with him in Central Park before dinner."

"Oh, see? You two get to bond more."

"Hardly. It was like chasing a Greyhound at the dog track. Hey, my phone is going to die any second. I have to find the charger. You should go to bed. I'll talk to you tomorrow."

After we end the call, there's an obvious tug in my chest, a yearning to see him, talk to him, feel his cheek against mine. It's too much like heartache because this all seems too wonderful, and I'm worried it won't last. There's a rush of sadness when you're elated about a new person, but you know something is hidden and fear it's not trivial.

I'm a small town girl who has grown up in the comfort of a tight community, giving the illusion I have a big family and many siblings. There's no escaping my friends and family.

Cooper is a city guy who actually comes from a very large family, yet I know very little about them, and he doesn't volunteer much. He subtly dances around the topic of his family in conversations, leaving a void, gaps that should have been filled in by now. Being used to talking about my parents on a regular basis and seeing them practically every day, the absence of Cooper's family—or rather, the lack of him mentioning them—concerns me, especially when his usual cockiness and humor are replaced with a sudden evasiveness.

An hour later, as I'm about to doze off, my phone pings with a text from Cooper that ends my night with a very big smile:

I know your phone has 1000 less numbers in it, right? I shouldn't be listed at the bottom under V. Put me under B for Bring Me To My Knees. Night, baby.

Twenty-One

In terms of work, the week goes fast. Lauren and I get to the studio by seven where I put in twelve-hour days, but in terms of missing Cooper, it's goddamn agonizing. Every day at two o'clock, Lauren begins to fade rapidly, a sudden drowsiness she can't control, so Leo takes her home to nap. When she returns by four, she's refreshed and wound up again. I use her naptime to call clients and make my own imprint in the back room office. I also always make a quick call to Cooper to hear his voice.

On Friday, he has to excuse himself to find a quieter room to speak to me. In the background, I can hear constant commotion, children screaming and adults shouting for them to stop running in the house.

"Whose home are you at?" I ask, overly excited that he'll be back in Hera in a few hours.

"We're all at my mom's place today." He sounds tired, and once again, he's not divulging anything new.

"Is it always that crazy around there? Is everything okay?"

"It's always loud here. Sometimes I walk across the street to go to my dad's house to get some peace and quiet in my old bedroom."

"Cooper, do you know how strange it is for me not to know anything about your family? You know all the important people in my life, and you're just telling me now that your parents live across the street from one another? That's plain weird. Maybe it's a Brooklyn thing."

Cooper lets out a small laugh. "They're divorced. No, it's not a Brooklyn thing. My family has a lot of stuff going

227

on. I'm leaving here in an hour and going right to your house. How's that?"

"How are you getting here? Dylan came back two days ago with the company truck."

"I bought my brother's old truck since the idiot decided he needed something bigger and more expensive. And I need a new vehicle because those dirt roads in Hera are killing my bike. I have to be able to haul stuff now that I have a *country* house," he says with a deliberate twang.

"Okay, I'm going to close up here at five and go home to pack. I'm giving you the heads up. I will probably complain endlessly about the camping trip, but I'm looking forward to seeing you."

"Looking forward? That's it? That's what you say in a letter you send to a parole officer. I thought you'd be climbing the walls, panting in heat for me."

"That, too. I didn't know how to say it without sounding desperate."

"Imogene, it has been a long week. I want you to sound desperate for me because I'm sure as hell going crazy, thinking about you. And, as far as this camping trip goes, we can spend the whole weekend in our tent, naked."

Everyone decides to meet at my house to follow each other on the drive to the campsite. I haul my bag outside and run down the porch steps, excited to see Cooper. I run by Lauren and Leo, who are loading coolers with food into Leo's truck, and Emma and Dylan, who are securing their bags in the back of his Jeep. Then I wave to Jess as I rush by her and Carson as they organize gear in the back of his truck. I just want to see Cooper.

And there he is in faded jeans and a fitted gray T-shirt. He looks superb. He's leaning against his new truck, smiling when he sees me huffing my way over to him with my overstuffed duffel. I drop the bag on the ground and throw myself at him. Unladylike and not so sexy, my

228

weight slams his back against the truck, and he lets out a short laugh before sliding his arms around me for a tight embrace.

"Hi." I smile and grip his shoulders, gazing at his handsome face and those silvery gray eyes that stop me dead every time.

"Hi, beautiful." It rolls off his tongue in that seductive, deep purr that gives me a little shiver.

Then he leans down, his lips meeting mine in a long, tender kiss. I let my body fall against his completely as I savor his mouth.

"That's enough, lovebirds." Jessica claps her hands to get our attention. "We have to get on the road."

Leo and Lauren drive around us and stop their truck in front to lead the caravan of couples to our destination. Cooper picks up my bag and tosses it in back, and then he opens the passenger door, staring at me as though he wants to say something.

"This is really nice for a used truck," I say as he climbs in the other side. "It looks practically brand new."

"Because my brother only had it a year before he decided he needed something else. I made him have it detailed before I drove back. It's in great shape and more comfortable than making you ride on my bike everywhere."

"You bought this because of me?" I blush, a little thrilled that he's making decisions based on us as a couple.

"You're the main reason, but it's true that my bike wasn't made for this off-road business. And I need a proper vehicle for carrying equipment. Come here." He puts his hand behind my head and pulls my face towards him for another searing kiss. If the console weren't between us, I'd climb into his lap and have my way with him.

The kiss ignites my bravado. I trail my hand down his chest to his groin and cup the hardness in his jeans.

"Nice package," I mumble against his lips.

His breath intake pauses briefly as I palm him more

firmly.

"This is going to be a painful drive," he whispers.

A sudden honking makes us both jump apart. Through the back windshield, I can see Dylan and Emma in their Jeep, waiting for us to go. Even with his sunglasses on, I can see Dylan's glower as he lays on the horn with Carson and Jess waiting in line behind them. Up ahead, Leo and Lauren have already driven down to the main road.

"Guess we better catch up," I say with a little laugh. "We're pissing off the Blackard brothers."

After Cooper starts the engine and waves to Dylan in the rearview mirror, we drive down the hill where Leo's truck waits for all of us. When Cooper shifts into high gear on the county road, I open my window and let the hot air blast my face and hair. I need this escape with him. I need to be with him away from home, family, and work. Although we aren't alone on this trip, I'm hoping to squeeze in some time where Cooper and I can have longer stretches together that aren't bound by the parameters of other obligations.

I study his profile as he drives. A long, blond lock of hair curves from his high cheekbone down to his strong jaw. Keeping one large hand resting on the wheel and the other on the gearshift next to my leg, he glances over at me and catches me staring.

"What?" he asks with a slight smile.

"You. I thought I had you figured out. I didn't want to have anything to do with you because you seemed like another playboy who couldn't offer anything more than superficial conversation and a good roll in the—" I almost say *hay*.

Cooper shoots me a look before turning back to the road.

"Sack. Roll in the sack," I mutter. "But I like talking to you. That's not it."

"But?"

"You've told me a little about your previous work, and I think I understand why you quit and why you moved here … but for someone who loves talking to people and making friends here, I find it odd that you never say much about your family. And they don't live far away."

"Not everyone is as close to their family as you are."

"I realize that, but I also felt like there was something else going on when your brothers and uncle came to visit you. It was nice to see you working with them, but in hindsight, I have a feeling you told them some topics were off limits with me. I got the sanitized version of one of your family gatherings.

"The cop stories were pretty funny, but they didn't say one personal thing about you. Usually, people like to talk about entertaining childhood stories or current family stuff when they are being introduced to a girlfriend. That's me, by the way. I'm the new girl, and they seem to like me, so why didn't I get the girlfriend treatment?"

Cooper chews on his lower lip and stares straight ahead. Then he looks over his left shoulder to change lanes and play some kind of game of chase with Dylan on the interstate, anything to avoid my question.

"Well?" I ask. "Am I wrong?"

"No." He glances at me. "You're not wrong. There's some tension in my family and some drama that I've been trying to stay away from. I don't want to drag you into it. They do like you, though. My brothers and Uncle Fraser all think you're pretty great. And you are."

"So what am I missing? What don't you want to tell me?"

He sighs with exasperation. "Imogene, I just spent two days with my family where everyone was in my face about every fucking problem in my screwed up family. I really want to be away from that and be here with you. Just you. Can we discuss my family another time?"

"Sure." I shrug and turn back to look out my window.

Cooper gently squeezes my thigh. "I'm sorry if I'm making you feel insecure."

"I'm not insecure about who I am," I say defensively. "I like me."

"I meant insecure about us. You touch your chin with two fingers whenever you're ..."

"Whenever I'm what?"

"Not being completely open," he says grimly.

"You mean, when you think I'm lying. I'm not lying. I'm *omitting* the fact that I'm a little skittish about some things. I'm asking you about your family and life because you're very vague about all of it. Maybe that's a product or symptom of your former career, but if I'm your girlfriend, I should be in a position to have the highest security clearance with you."

Cooper's laugh breaks the tension. "You're right, and in time, I will tell you more, but let me have this weekend with you, without my family drama."

"Okay. Just remember, I'm a very good listener, and I promise to refrain from making any jokes at your expense." I smile and take his hand, holding it in both of mine to bring it to my lips for a soft peck. Then I hold his hand up, pinched between my thumb and forefinger. "Here, you can have this back."

He smiles and shakes his head, putting his hand back on the steering wheel.

"Maybe you should take Lois up on her offer to learn how to meditate. If you're dealing with a lot of family problems, maybe meditation would be helpful."

"I already meditate."

"You do?" I ask, finding it hard to imagine Cooper chanting and sitting in the lotus position.

"Don't look so shocked," he laughs. "I don't do group meditation classes or any of that stuff. I learned years ago how to deal with the stressful shit I was involved with every day. Before work and every night before I go to

232

sleep, I spend about five to ten minutes putting myself in a complete state of relaxation where my mind isn't thinking about anything."

"I've never seen you do it."

"When I'm with you, sex takes care of the mind-numbing for me."

"Interesting. So when I'm not around, you meditate. Do you hum and have a mantra?"

"No. I sit down, close my eyes, change my breathing, and clear my thoughts. It's harder to do than you think. It took me a while to get into it and make it effective. In *Siddartha*, he says meditation is *'fleeing from the self.'* Basically, it's an escape from the agony of being, and it numbs the senses *'against the pain and pointlessness of life.'*"

"Well, that's a big, fat downer. *Siddartha*?"

"Herman Hesse."

"I know. I saw the book in your room. Oh, God, you're not one of those depressing guys who thinks life has no meaning, are you? That really doesn't suit you."

Cooper chuckles at my summation. "Not at all. I like to read a lot of books to get different perspectives, but I don't necessarily agree with everything I read."

"You keep surprising me. In a good way, though."

"Good. I'm no longer on your wanker list?"

"How did you know about the list?" I practically shout.

"You talk in your sleep. Kidding. You've mentioned the *wankers* before, and Lauren told me you had an *actual* list."

As the heat crawls up my neck, I look away, pretending to get caught up in the beautiful scenery, which is stunning but surely only offers more bug bites and an uncomfortable setting for sleeping.

It's not long before our caravan quickly takes an exit onto a wide, unpaved road. We travel uphill and enter a narrow, wooded, bumpy road. I hold onto the armrest and

233

my seat as we follow Leo's pick-up.

"Getting nervous?" Cooper asks with a mischievous smile.

"Why? Are these woods haunted? Am I going to have to deal with the Blair Witch or some slasher nut job in a hockey mask?"

"Wow. You've got some imagination."

"My favorite part of summer camp was the ghost stories around the campfire. Then I'd cry myself to sleep and sometimes pee in my sleeping bag, thinking every noise was a vengeful ghost."

"Sounds awful." He smiles. "I was thinking more along the lines of sharing a tent. Maybe you're getting nervous about that. It's the first time we're out with our friends as a …"

"A what? Are you afraid to say couple?"

"No. I've been gone all week, so I've been wondering what you've been telling people and how you refer to me."

"I tell them I rejected you for so long because I assumed you were a misogynistic, sleazy playboy, but that was all a misunderstanding."

"Jesus, is that really what you tell people?"

I grin. "Nope. I'm screwing with you. We are a couple. And, no, I'm not afraid of sleeping in a tent with you. I'm ready to jump your kcuffing bones, mister."

"Good, because I've built up five days of sexual frustration waiting to be with you. I didn't even cheat."

"You didn't have sex with yourself?"

"Nope. That would have been too easy. My fantasy Imogene is almost as spectacular as you, but I was waiting for the real deal."

"Aww, how sweet." I pat his hand as he slips the gearshift into park.

"When I get you naked, sweet is not what I have in mind." His expression is dead serious.

"Another hot quote from Herman Hesse. Love it."

Twenty-Two

We have a secluded camping spot for our group: a large, open area surrounded by trees with walking trails that lead to a small lake and all those unknown territories of wildlife I will most fervently avoid. Despite its beauty, there's not a bunny or Bambi in sight. The swarms of gnats that float above our heads make me shudder, and the shrieking caws of a nearby angry bird make me wish I had a shotgun to fire off and scare all the non-human inhabitants away.

I like animals, I really do, but I have a hard enough time sharing a home with humans, let alone a whole forest of different species. We're not meant to sleep in the same space, although I remind myself that we are doing this for sweet, lovable Leo who is both nostalgic and romantic when it comes to his friends and his fiancée.

The men begin setting up the four tents, placing them at the perimeter of the clearing, far enough apart so we all have some privacy if we talk in quiet voices or have noiseless sex. Yes, I'm totally thinking about sex, especially since I'm watching Cooper from my very uncomfortable spot on one of the dead tree trunks positioned around the fire pit where Jess is trying to figure out how to stack the pile of bricks left by the previous campers.

"Jess, reposition the bricks so they're in the same place as before. You can see the outline of the circle," Emma explains.

"I've never done this before. I can tell from the ash where the firewood goes, but I don't know how to do the rest." Jess sits back on her knees. "Imogene, you went to camp. How do you do this?"

"My camp had a dining hall and indoor plumbing. Stagger the bricks in a circle like Emma said. Make the wall high enough so we can rest the grill on top. You don't want it too close to the flames." I chomp on a carrot stick and go back to observing Cooper. "Look at those guys. I think they're arguing over where the tent flaps should face. It's hilarious. They look so serious."

As if he knows my eyes are glued to his backside, Cooper turns around and grins at me.

"What are you smiling about?" Emma asks, taking the plastic bag of carrot sticks from my hand before I devour them all.

"Nothing."

"Nothing my ass," Lauren chides. "She's crazy for Cooper."

"Of course she is," Jess adds. "And he's sweet on her, so it's all good. No more complaining about being single and all the dud guys out there."

"I barely said a word about the duds."

All three women stop what they're doing and stare at me.

"All right. Maybe I complained a little too much about men."

"Imogene, that's an understatement," Lauren says. "You terrified the male customers at the diner. Your parents wanted to fire you so you'd break that crabby rut you were putting everyone through, but Bonnie has a soft spot for how you give guys a hard time. She thought it would at least keep you from getting hurt again anytime soon."

"I am my grandmother's favorite." I shrug.

Emma chuckles.

"Okay, I was a beast ... to everyone. It was a bad year. But things are looking better," I say, glancing back at

Cooper as the men walk towards us with a little swagger even Leo seems to have picked up.

"Dylan, you're the chef; you set up this fire pit, grill thing, please." Jess stands and looks at her palms covered in soot.

"She's right, honey," Emma confirms. "You know it's really your area of expertise."

"Sure thing," Dylan replies, dropping to his knees and quickly constructing the bricks and the grill rack. "You guys would be eating beef jerky and trail mix if I wasn't here to cook."

"Yep, and when we catch all those fish tomorrow, we'll let you clean and cook them for us," Carson adds, cuffing Dylan's head.

I tune out their conversation, focusing on the nice, warm body settling down next to me on the big, fat log. Cooper puts an arm around my waist and gives me a delicious smile. The two kisses hours ago are not enough to hold me over. I want to go test out our tent now, but Leo is making a big deal about the steaks he brought and the dinner he and Lauren have planned for the evening. The others begin unpacking food and cookware while Cooper and I take a moment to catch up.

"I missed the hell out of you this week," I whisper into his ear.

He kisses my cheek. "I missed you, too. You have no idea."

"You'll have plenty of time to tell me about that. We're back in the wild again, and you know Mother Nature and I are not fond of one another, so I plan on being in our tent a lot. You can show me how much you missed me."

"I will," he says, nuzzling my neck. "Do you think you'll be able to turn off your work brain for a couple of days and actually relax? Because I plan on shutting out everything that happened this whole week, and the guys and I agreed that no shop talk can take place until

237

Monday."

"I get it. Very clever. You don't want me to bring up your family. I won't. Maybe."

"Let's go check out the tent," he whispers conspiratorially in my ear.

We get our bags from his truck and select the most remote tent, the one least likely to have people walking by to get to the vehicles or supplies. I'm surprised at how spacious it is inside with a fully inflated air mattress for two.

Cooper tosses our bags to the side and falls back hard onto the mattress, pulling me with him. The rubber makes a loud burp sound as our bodies hit it, but it doesn't burst as I feared. While Cooper rolls on top of me and begins kissing me eagerly, my fingers go right for his hair and then slowly trace across his solid shoulders and down his hard biceps.

"Hey, Coop!" Dylan yells a few feet from our tent. "Wanna go for a thirty minute run before dinner?"

Cooper jerks his head up. "Hell, no! Go away!"

We hear Dylan laugh then more footsteps before we hear Emma softly murmuring to him.

"I'd rather chase you through the woods," Dylan says quietly to Emma. "I'll give you a head start." That's followed by what sounds like Dylan slapping Emma's rear end.

When they're gone and I'm certain no one is within earshot of us, I start laughing. "There's no privacy here."

"Then you better keep your screaming to a minimum." Cooper keeps me pinned to the mattress and kisses the sensitive spot on my neck, triggering every erogenous zone to be on red alert.

"I expect everyone to be on time for dinner! Lauren and I are the only ones here prepping the food!" Leo shouts. "I don't care what you're in the middle of … I know you can all hear me! Dylan you better be back in time to cook all of this!"

Cooper curses against my neck, and I laugh in frustration.

This weekend is really for Lauren and Leo, but at this moment, I'm not feeling the love for my friends and their idea of fun, domestic chores we took to the great bug-infested outdoors. You can't give me a bed and a guy I'm crazy about and expect me to switch gears and get excited about grilled steak and fishing.

"We have to save this for later because I don't want to get busy and then stop for dinner." I stroke Cooper's cheek.

"Are you sure?" His lips push mine open again for a deep kiss.

I moan when he slips his hand under my shirt and undoes the front clasp of my bra to palm my breast so I can't formulate a coherent response. Then he lifts my shirt all the way up and puts his mouth on a hard nipple, sucking and nibbling until I'm writhing underneath him.

"Not fair." I grab his hair and yank his head off my chest.

"If you struggle, that only turns me on."

"Take off your shirt," I demand. "We can have topless kissing, no hands below the waist. And then we'll go to dinner."

"I'll take whatever I can get," he agrees.

We remove our T-shirts and I shimmy off my bra straps so we can be skin to skin, his weight and hard muscles providing a wall of comfort. We use every minute we have to enjoy a long, uninterrupted make out session. Other than the sound of a few pots and pans being clanked and that damn screeching bird, all I listen to are Cooper's breaths and moans.

Dylan makes a spectacular dinner with the crude cookware, grilling the rib eyes, red peppers, and asparagus with fresh herbs. When he calls dibs on Emma's steak since she's a vegetarian, Carson and Cooper gripe a bit about that

239

but then figure it's his payment for manning our stone-age fire pit.

After dinner, Leo and Lauren say goodnight and escape to their tent. The rest of us clean up the mess, and I bag everything, terrified we'll attract bears.

"What are you doing?" Jess asks, alarmed.

"Spraying down the area with the air freshener Lauren keeps in her car." I squirt the pungent fragrance around our plastic storage containers.

"It smells like cinnamon and candy canes," says Emma, sniffing.

"It's a Christmas home décor spray. It's all I have."

"You're trying to camouflage food smells with more food smells?" Jess asks.

"Bears and wolves are attracted to the steak, not candy canes."

"Bears and wolves?" Dylan laughs. "That stuff stinks, Imogene."

"My girl flips out when she's up against the elements." Cooper puts an arm around my waist and gingerly removes the spray can from my hand, tossing it to Carson.

"Now you know why we never invited you on our camping trips," Carson says to me. "You're almost as bad as Jess when it comes to leaving modern conveniences."

"I've been good since we got here." Jess playfully shoves Carson's chest. "I haven't complained once."

"Babe, you practically cried when we arrived and you lost your cell service." Carson laughs and traps her arms behind her back to kiss her.

"Losing contact with civilization isn't a little thing. At least I can handle a hike without crying, unlike Imogene." Jess grins at me.

I feel a spark of heat on my cheeks. "You told everyone about our hike?" I turn to Cooper, who drops his head with a small smile and a curse.

"That was weeks ago. Yes, I told a few people …

about the entertaining parts," he confesses. "But I told them you were a very good sport about managing one of the worst trails."

"We had to climb over thorny bushes, and there were hornets!" I say defensively to the group.

"There were." Cooper moves behind me and wraps his arms around my waist, resting his chin on my head. "If the thought of going without a hot shower for two days is too much for you, I'll drive you to the nearest motel tonight."

"Oh, shut up," I quip, but the solidity of his embrace has already cooled my irritation. I figure I should be able to handle a little humiliation among my friends, especially since I'm the one who usually doles it out to them.

We call it an early night since the sun has set, and when it's dark in the woods and you don't have a bonfire, music, or alcohol, the only other thing to do is go to bed. I wouldn't have minded if we had brought wine or something stronger to enjoy while we roasted marshmallows, but since Lauren can't drink now, Dylan doesn't consume any alcohol because of his strong meds, and Cooper doesn't really drink at all, it seemed inconsiderate to bring any alcoholic beverages. The upside is no one will wake up with a hangover, and we can connect with our early pioneer roots by going to bed before nine and entertaining ourselves the old fashioned way— with sex.

Cooper turns on the LED lantern in our tent and zippers the two sleeping bags together on the air mattress.

"Why didn't we bring sheets and blankets instead of the sleeping bags?" I ask, admiring how his arms flex and look taut even while doing a simple task like working a zipper.

"Sleeping bags are better at keeping snakes out of your bed."

"Snakes?" I panic and jump up on my knees while I

241

search the tent floor for anything that moves.

Cooper chuckles. "I'm kidding. Kind of. Make me happy and get naked."

"Hello, you can't mention snakes and think you can seduce me at the same time."

Once he flips back a corner of the sleeping bag, I climb into it fully clothed. Cooper strips off his T-shirt and jeans and then crawls towards me with a sly smile, wearing only his boxer briefs.

"Baby, you need to take off your clothes, and then I'll help you relax."

Taking a deep breath, I decide, if he can hypnotize me with that voice and that body, he can certainly coax a snake out of our bed. Then I undress so fast I cause the rubber mattress to bounce like a waterbed and crash into Cooper. My clumsiness doesn't obstruct his careful choreography as he settles himself between my thighs and hooks my legs over his shoulder.

For a fleeting moment, I realize I am naked in the scary dark woods, but then I'm riveted on Cooper's expression. He meets my eyes with a mixture of fierce desire and adoring tenderness, the effect heady. I give myself over completely, relinquishing every muscle and limb for Cooper to do as he wishes.

"I missed you," he says seductively to my vagina, not me. He's studying it appreciatively, as though he's contemplating what he'll do next. It could be embarrassing, but my vagina is open for business and ready to dance on the tables to get this sailor to go to town on her.

"She missed you, too. Now get busy!" I whisper. "And don't talk to my genitals like you're a pubescent boy."

"I was talking to you, Imogene." He rises on his knees, hoisting my legs and hips with him.

"Oh." Now I feel embarrassed. What woman goes off on a guy she's excited to see just because she's horny as hell? Me, that's who.

"Christ, I'm going to take care of you. Don't you know I've been going out of my fucking mind waiting to be with you again?" He licks my clit and looks down at me.

"Yes, you missed me. Yes, keeping touching me like that," I say with a tremble.

Cooper trails soft kisses along the insides of my thighs, sending arousing heat directly to the center of my physical being. At this moment, it's a slow odyssey to the palace of everything holy and gratifying.

While my hips naturally undulate, seeking more from him, he takes his time with teasing caresses, his lips and fingers pleasuring me until my thoughts are a frenzied blur. Then I begin reaching for the crescendo, and my thighs tense and tighten around Cooper's head. I don't care if I'm strangling him as long as I get my first class ride to Wonderland. However, his strong hands keep my legs up and apart so he can finish the task at hand, and boy, he doesn't miss a step, even with my wild, bucking hips.

"Yez, yes, yez," I mumble frantically.

I feel his hot breath against my thighs, and then he goes in for the finale, sucking so hard my arms flail around, pounding the mattress. He successfully hits the trip wire and the rocket launches, my whole body thrumming with pure ecstasy. I scream his name as I fall into oblivion.

It takes me a moment to come out of it and gather some semblance of composure. My legs are still hooked over Cooper's shoulders as he kneels, looking down at me with a bemused expression.

"You screamed," he says with a smile. "You screamed my name. Very. Loudly."

"Oh," I exhale. "It was worth it."

I don't know when or how he put the condom on; I must have been paralyzed in that splendid rapture for longer than I thought.

"My turn." He slides partially into me, holding my legs up and angling himself into position.

His cock stretches me and stops midway.

"I think you've grown since I last saw you," I say, amazed that he can feel too large.

"Mmm, it'll fit." He thrusts his hips hard, his cock filling me. We both moan, and then he pulls out slowly before pushing back in slowly and methodically.

I watch him, fascinated with his graceful hip thrusts and swivels as he moves in and out of me with incredible control and restraint. What this man can do on the dance floor is nothing compared to the erotic, graceful slides and glides he does with his hips and cock. He keeps it up for a while, filling me completely as my core grows wetter, begging him for more.

"You're so beautiful." He looks at me then his eyes close and his head rolls back, enjoying the friction between our bodies. I wonder how long he can hold out and keep his climax at bay.

Not long.

It's like someone flipped a switch; Cooper begins pounding into me with savage desire. He watches where our bodies connect, his expression turning feral as he goes on a raging crusade to fill me, striking the sensitive target. I appreciate his precision, and in a matter of seconds, I'm falling through another rabbit hole, a mindless mess as he hammers into me.

His climax is explosive. He inhales and exhales loudly with intermittent grunts and then loses his grip on my legs. He drops to his hands and finishes coming with a few short jerks.

"Damn." He's breathing hard, his eyes consuming me like they own me. For this moment, I feel like I own him. I know lust when I see it, and this feels like love.

If I ever thought I could fully love a man, I hope that man is Cooper. I hope this eventually leads to more.

Twenty-Three

"Rise and shine!" Lauren sings outside our tent as the morning light barely breaks.

"No," I mumble.

"Is she always this peppy in the morning?" Cooper asks, half-asleep.

"Yes. It's the only reason I ever made it to classes or work on time."

Lauren begins another round of our old Rise and Shine camp song with the addition of banging pots.

"Shut up!" Jess's voice shouts angrily at Lauren from another tent.

"We have to get up." Cooper kisses my cheek and does a push up to spring to his feet. I find myself staring at his nakedness longingly. "I promised Leo we'd hit the fishing early this morning."

"So why do I have to get up early?"

"To entertain Lauren. It's her day, too."

"I suppose, as maid of honor, I should be grateful that I got off easy with no bachelorette party. I think we're walking down to the lake for swimming and sunbathing."

"I hope we make it back in time to witness that. I'd like to see you in a bikini."

I search for a pair of shorts and a shirt. "I think you want to find another place to have sex with me," I say as we both get dressed.

"Damn, you're on to me."

Everyone except for Lauren and Leo looks exhausted and disheveled. Jess appears in pajamas and fluffy slippers, getting a chuckle out of Dylan who is already cooking up breakfast. Jess shuffles over to Carson and sits on his lap, looking as if she's falling back asleep.

I sip the strong, bitter coffee Leo hands me and perch myself next to Cooper on the same log from the night before, leaning sleepily into him. Dylan and Emma hand out plates of eggs and bacon, and then Dylan settles himself next to me with a little too much energy.

"For a moment last night, I was worried you were being attacked by a bear," Dylan says to me, trying not to smile. "But then I assumed Cooper came to your rescue. Yes, I'm quite positive that's what I heard."

"Never talk to me before six in the morning. I'm tempted to cause you physical pain."

Cooper smiles and kisses my temple. "You tell him."

"When did you know it was the real thing with Carson?" I ask Jess. I'm flat on my back, basking in the morning sun as Jess applies a heavy layer of sunblock to her fair skin.

After the men left with all their fishing gear, we spent another hour sitting around the campsite, drinking coffee. Then I led the lazy charge down to the lake with our lounge chairs and beach towels.

Jess props up the wide, flimsy brim of her sun hat and looks at me, stunned. "You're asking me for relationship advice?"

"It's hard to believe, I know, especially since I recall lecturing you about Carson two years ago. Times have changed, and you appear to be the epitome of a happy marriage, so I'm curious as to how you knew he was the one."

"Oh." Jess puts down the sunblock and looks out at the quiet lake. "For me, it was after a few arguments with Carson that left me feeling kind of sick. We could say something and unintentionally hurt one another. I didn't want to hurt him; I wanted to love him. I wanted to fix everything I felt I did wrong. One day, I stopped being afraid to let myself fall in love with him. The minute I did that, it felt right, and I was so much happier."

"Is it easy, or do you still have big fights?"

"Sure, we argue. A while ago, we had a ridiculous argument over mustard."

"You argued over what kind of mustard to buy?" I ask testily. I should know better than to ask Jess about her marriage. She's off the charts when it comes to everything atypical.

"No, we argued about where to put the mustard. Carson is a foot taller than me, and I tend to put everything at my eye level in the fridge. Then he can't find things. The mustard fight was really about other stress in our life, but that didn't come out until we said a lot of stupid things about mustard and condiments in general."

"What are you two stressed out about?"

"Carson wants me to quit my job with 5 Alpha and take a license deal on a software package I wrote the code for to sell it myself."

"That doesn't sound like Carson, asking you to quit working."

"He didn't. He wants me to spend more time on my painting and make it a full-time career, even if the work doesn't always sell."

"So how did you two make up after that fight?"

"Carson said something brilliant. He told me to stop chasing money out of fear and start believing in my passion because he's there to catch me if I fall."

"That's sweet."

"And he's right. He said marriage isn't one-sided; we're both in it and need to help each other through anything and everything. It's easy to laugh about the mustard fight now, especially since being married means you're going to have a lot of issues like that."

"You already work from home, so what happens when

you don't have any contact with all those tech people you work with? Won't you get lonely?"

"I have freelance work with Carson's company and other businesses, but he's cutting back, too. That's why he turned over a lot of his responsibilities to Cooper. Carson plans to get his work schedule down to four days a week, no more working six or seven days. Then he can be home at least three full days and I can do the other four."

"What are you talking about? What is Carson going to be home for?" Emma asks from her lounge chair she has sitting several feet away in the water.

"We want to start a family in a couple of years, so we're trying to put together a work schedule where one of us is always home with the baby."

"What baby?" Lauren wakes from dozing.

"There's no baby. I'm not pregnant," Jess confirms. "We're just planning as much as we can. We only have control over our work, so that's what we're discussing at this point."

I study Jess for a moment, envious of what she has and how much she has changed in the last two years since I met her. She has always been wicked smart and made great career choices, but she's had no confidence when it comes to men.

She moved to Hera and had a short fling with Dylan before realizing how ill-matched they were. After that little tryst, it took her a few months to discover that the man she was in love with had been standing silently by all that time. Carson and his stupid, stoic silence. What a messy drama they all created back then. I was with Jeremy at the time, feeling pretty secure about how nice and easy it was working for us. My smugness certainly backfired on me.

"What about you and Dylan?" I ask Emma, who is now fully interested in our conversation. "You fit perfectly together, too. Did you feel that when you met him?"

"Not at all," Emma replies with a laugh. "We didn't

have a choice, though; we had to work together. The first week was uncomfortable, and I thought Dylan was a jackass. A cute one, but still, I thought he wanted Carson to fire me. You've all seen how emotional and uncensored he is."

Lauren laughs. "Understatement."

Emma kicks her feet in the lake and sends a sprinkle of water our way, the cold water feeling wonderful on my hot skin.

"We had an instant attraction," Emma continues, "but we were surrounded by my family problems, and Dylan was still in the beginning stages of his therapy after rehab. Emotionally, we were both a mess, but after a month of being with him, I didn't want to keep fighting about our problems; I wanted us to fix them together. And, like Jess said, that's when you know you love the person and want to keep loving them."

"You make it sound easy. Actually, all three of you do."

Emma scoffs. "Yes, it's easy for me to love Dylan. But, no, living with someone and merging your lives isn't easy. We all have those moments when we get angry and say dumb things. When I asked to go to one of his therapy sessions, Dylan and I had a huge fight because he said it would make him feel like a loser to do his weekly confessional in front of his shrink with me there. We were engaged, and I thought I should be a part of his therapy, at least see what goes on and get to know his doctor."

"Yeah, too bad you couldn't just fight about ketchup," I add with a laugh.

"Mustard," Jess clarifies.

"Whatever," I reply. "Props to Emma. Any battle of egos with the Tasmanian Devil over his therapy has got to be right up there with teaching a hippo to do cartwheels."

"Don't let Dylan hear you say that," Lauren laughs.

"Oh, he's heard Imogene say worse," Emma retorts.

"And going with him to the doctor was not what I expected. Dylan managed to talk about me as if I wasn't even sitting next to him, and we exchanged some colorful tidbits of criticism about one another, which then escalated into a bigger argument. The doctor ended up refereeing as if he was our marriage counselor. But, hey, we got Dylan's fears out in that first session, and after that, whenever he leaves for his appointment, he always asks me if I want to go with him. I rarely do, but it's nice we got over that scary hurdle."

"I'll say. And you certainly didn't lollygag about like Lauren and Leo. It took months for one of them to make a move."

"Look who's talking? You and Cooper took a year!" Lauren touches her flat stomach, checking to see if she is showing signs of a pregnant belly yet. I catch her doing this throughout the day, every day. I don't think she's aware how often she rubs her belly like it's a magic genie lamp.

"Cooper and I were not crushing on each other for the past year. We barely had civil conversations."

"Your fault," Jess quips.

"Probably, but the point is I remember Lauren was crushing on Leo in June, and they didn't have a date until December."

"I needed to see how he danced before I could go out with him." Lauren snorts at her own statement.

"He's not that great a dancer," I say dryly.

"No, he's not," she admits. "But after Carson's holiday party, it only took one date for me to know Leo was the one. Okay, it took six months of mooning over him, eight dances, and one great date night. Now, here we are, almost two years later and still going strong. What about you and Cooper? Think he could be the one?"

"We're hardly at that point. We're having fun." I sit up and consider running into the lake to cool off. "Besides, sometimes I feel like I've known Cooper for a long time because he's been in town for a while now, but then … I met his uncle and brothers, and Cooper seemed like a new person to me, someone I hardly know at all. It's as if he plunked himself down in town one day and started a new life."

"But that's exactly what I did when I moved to Hera," Emma says. "What's wrong with that?"

"Nothing, but I already knew you from college. I thought I'd figured Cooper out over the last year … but, as it turns out, I know very little. Sometimes he surprises me."

"He's congenial for sure," Lauren says. "I do think he's a very private person, though."

"Have you all noticed that we're all only children, and we're with guys who are not?" Jess asks.

"I think my independence was one of the reasons why I chose Dylan," Emma explains. "I was dependent on my parents then an ex-boyfriend until I finally felt free. That's when everything became clearer for me, and I could see what I really wanted. My marriage still makes me feel very independent and free. I didn't have that with anyone else before Dylan."

"I know what you mean," Jess says, walking into the lake's edge to splash some water on her arms and legs. "Once I let go of what I was dependent on—hiding behind my job and my overall skepticism—I let myself fall hard for Carson."

Lauren looks at me with a kind smile. "It's okay if it takes time, Imogene. I like seeing you and Cooper together. I think you're a very good fit."

"Physical chemistry isn't necessarily enough, though, is it?"

"Don't most relationships start with physical chemistry, and then you build friendships and love after that? Maybe it's just me," Emma mumbles.

"I agree," Jess says. "In my case, the physical attraction was definitely the catalyst for the pursuit."

251

"If that's what it's based on, you're saying we're basically very superficial."

Jess shakes her head at me. "Not exactly. Physical attraction is one element of the chemistry you have with someone else, and then emotional attachment comes from the growth of the relationship."

"You sound like a science teacher. I'm expecting you to explain reproduction to me."

Lauren sighs and does another belly rub. "I think Imogene is concerned that she and Cooper are not in the same place as us."

"I'm not concerned. I'm not rushing to get married any time soon. We have a business to run, and this is the first time I've taken a whole weekend off from work since I was sixteen. I'm more worried about making payroll and sales figures. This is a very crazy time for me, for us. I like being with Cooper, but I don't want to get my hopes up and spend time with someone who may not be the one. It's easy for all of you to see things in hindsight and tell me how you knew you were in love with Mr. Right."

"I get it. You want to make sure Cooper is marriage material even though you're not interested in getting married any time soon," Jess responds.

"Something like that!" I laugh.

"Sorry," Jess says. "I'm going to sound *sciency* here. You need to do a few trial runs to come to a conclusion."

"Definitely." Lauren nods. "Mr. Right becomes Mr. Right after you've gone through some unglamorous ups and downs. Let him see you with a bad case of food poisoning when you're hugging the toilet and you've got stuff coming out of both ends, see how he handles that. Then you'll know if a man is marriage material."

"So gross, and yet, so true," Emma agrees.

I decide to end the conversation about Cooper and me by taking a dip in the lake. I stand and adjust my bikini which is more snug than usual. I can probably attribute that

252

to sitting on my ass all day at the workshop. Since I'm no longer running around the diner with heavy trays, I'm going to have to start a regular exercise regimen to get rid of this extra flab I'm carrying.

The water is chilly as I walk in, letting my toes squish into the slimy, murky bottom. I plunge in with a shallow dive and swim all the way to the stationary diving dock.

We have the small beach to ourselves and no motorized boats are allowed on the lake; I only see a few canoes in the distance. Somewhere across that lake, our men are sitting in those little canoes, trying to catch some fish for dinner.

I wonder if they talk about us as much as we talk about them, although I'm guessing jock itch is a more appealing topic.

"Hey, sleepyhead," his low voice rumbles in my ear. He kisses my nose as I struggle to open my eyes against the bright sun.

"Ow. My head hurts." I blink a few times before Cooper's face comes into focus. His hair is wet and slicked back. "What time is it?"

"It's three. We got back a while ago and came down here to swim with you. You've been asleep for a long time according to Lauren."

He rocks back on his heels and helps me sit up.

"Ouch, ouch. Everything hurts. Oh, no." I hold out my arms that are pink from my hands to my shoulders.

"Babe, you've got a bad sunburn." Cooper touches my thigh, his finger leaving a white impression, the flesh turning red when he pulls his hand back.

I touch my cheeks. "Oh, God, how bad is my face?"

"Didn't you reapply the sunblock after your swim?" Lauren asks, alarmed as she walks over to us.

I shake my head. "I came back from the swim and laid down on the towel. I guess I fell asleep pretty quickly. How long was I out?"

"Three hours?" Lauren guesses. "Emma and Jess left earlier, so I stayed with you. I dozed off, too, but I was completely covered by my sombrero."

"I was going to swim longer. Good thing I woke you up," Cooper says with concern. "Let me help you back to the camp, and we'll get some lotion for your skin."

Cooper stands up and graces me with a glorious view of his golden body glistening in the sun from his recent swim, his hair and board shorts dripping wet.

"This is terrible. The wedding is next Saturday. I can't walk down the aisle in a strapless dress with sunburn marks."

"You have a nice, light shade of brown under the red. I think it will heal in the next few days," Lauren says optimistically.

"And then I'll peel." I try to stand, but even my knees are burned. I let out a howl from the friction against the beach towel.

"Here," Cooper says, scooping me up in his arms. "I'll carry you back."

"Are you insane? It's an uphill walk to the camp," I say, trying to figure out the least painful position for my arms. I decide to drape them loosely around his neck.

"Oh, quit your griping," Lauren snaps. "I wish someone would carry me back to my tent. I have brain-fry from the heat. I'm ready to go back to sleep."

"How many times have you done this for me?" I ask softly as he weaves me through the trail brush, making sure rogue branches don't scrape my tender skin.

"I've done this enough with you to be very good at it, wouldn't you say?"

"Yes. You're very good at this."

"You can reward me later."

"Um. I can barely move. Don't expect any action tonight."

"You have a one-track mind. You think everything is about sex."

"Fine. I'll sing some delightful camp songs for you, a personal show of my wide repertoire in all things Kumbaya."

Dylan has a whole operation going with cleaning the freshly caught fish when we arrive. Everyone is helping him, giving us a cursory greeting without noticing Cooper is carrying the world's largest lobster. He swiftly takes me to our tent where I lie back on the air mattress with my arms and legs stretched out so they aren't touching other singed body parts. I don't want to move and feel too lousy to eat; as a result, I insist that Cooper join the others for a quick dinner and help them pack everything up before the predicted forecast of rain comes our way.

When Cooper returns to our tent with a bottle of lotion and some books, it's already getting dark. He turns on the lantern and kneels down next to me.

"This should help." He holds up the aloe and then begins to dab it gingerly all over my body, gently lifting the edges of my bikini where the red lines are severe. He takes his time, blowing on the gelled flesh to create a cooling sensation that gives me goose bumps.

"That feels good. Where did you get it?"

"Jess. She's a cornucopia of every weird thing no else thinks to bring. And she has provided this evening's entertainment."

"What is it?"

"You'll have to wait until I'm done here." He lies down alongside me then swirls some of the clear gel on my arms and continues to blow lightly on it.

"You're very good at this, too." I close my eyes as he massages my neck with the goopy gel.

When every part of flesh is covered with aloe, Cooper puts on his glasses and lies next to me with a couple of books. "I'm going to read to you tonight. Jess gave me two very thrilling books."

"Oh, boy. I can't wait. Is there anything sexy?"

"I think this must be the sexy one. It's *Freakonomics*." He holds up the book and smirks.

"God, you look unbelievably gorgeous in those glasses. If I wasn't burned to a crisp, I'd try to do something freaky with you. And you're not reading that book to me. What's the other one?"

"*Programming Perl*. I'm assuming it's a mystery about a cute red-head who likes to write code."

"Jess brings work books on her vacation? I want something fun."

"Sorry, phones are dead here; otherwise, I'd buy a book for you. We don't need to read." He takes off his glasses and puts them aside.

Damn, I love those glasses.

Outside, the rain picks up, the pattering of raindrops on the tent creating a soothing backdrop to our dimly lit environment. Cooper props himself up on one arm and lifts his other hand as if he's trying to decide where he can put it without inflicting more pain on me. He settles with placing his palm face up under my limp hand with our fingers are touching. He rests his head on my pillow, his warm breath on the side of my face, the simple, light caress from his fingers all it takes to make me feel content.

Twenty-Four

Lauren anxiously paces the back room in the church. She's nervous that the bridesmaid dresses were supposed to arrive last Monday and had to be overnighted to make it here this morning. With only two hours before the wedding, Leo and his groomsmen are in another room, changing into their rented attire, no mishaps for them. We're waiting for Lauren's mother who stayed behind for the bridesmaid dresses to be delivered to her home and is racing to the church with dresses that we haven't tried on yet.

"What did you expect when you asked Dee Dee to make these dresses? She's a nut," I say.

"She went to Parsons. She's a real designer."

"She wore a top hat and purple clogs all through high school. She does costumes for performers. If Elton John or Lady Gaga need a new bedazzled jumpsuit, Dee Dee is your gal."

"She and I agreed on the design, and I approved the fabric swatches. She had all your measurements, so there shouldn't be any surprises."

Emma and Jess remain silent through our little spat. They don't want Lauren to get more frazzled than she already is; therefore, they help my mother set up her sewing machine and supplies on a table, ready to do her seamstress magic to our dresses. Eleanor and Lois choose that moment to usher in the two women from the salon who are going to do our hair and makeup.

"On the bright side, at least you bought your dress in the city," I say to Lauren. I'm supposed to be her reassuring maid of honor. "The only dress that really matters today is yours, and you're going to be beautiful." I hold out the strapless, ivory bridal gown that hangs from a chandelier.

"It is perfect, isn't it?" Lauren admires the expensive designer dress her mother bought her.

"I'm here!" Nina comes bursting through the door with a large, battered cardboard box. "I have the dresses!"

"Was the box dropped from a plane and run over by a train?" I ask.

"Who cares? Pam, you should get started on these, and I'll help Lauren get into her dress." Nina hands the box to my mother and then grabs Lauren and her gown, hustling her across the room to one of the bamboo dressing screens.

"But I want to see their dresses." Lauren looks back at the box with a frightened expression.

"No. It's out of your hands. Pam will take care of their dresses. You need to get ready." Her mother directs her behind the screen.

My mother opens the box and pulls the first dress out and holds it up. Jess and Emma step closer.

"I thought these were supposed to be champagne-colored silk. This looks like Band-Aid brown," Jess whispers to us so Lauren can't hear.

"It is a dull beige," Eleanor remarks. "And that isn't silk."

"No, it isn't." My mother grimaces. "It is what it is, and this is what we have to work with. Put them on, girls. This is a size four so this must be Jess's." Jess takes the dress and holds up the muted, lifeless gown that looks like way too much fabric for her slight figure.

"I'm the six," Emma says, taking the next dress and holding it up. It looks significantly smaller than Jess's.

"And you're the ten, honey." My mother hands me the last dress. In my hands, it feels like a cheap costume from a Halloween catalogue.

We strip down to our underwear and put on the

strapless gowns, realizing the wardrobe situation is much direr than we've originally suspected.

Lauren comes out from behind the screen with her stunning gown sweeping across the floor. "Oh, my God!" We haven't looked in the mirror yet, but her horrified expression says it all. "Jess, that doesn't fit you. It looks like you're wearing a bedspread!" Lauren exclaims,

Jess clutches the top of the dress to keep it from sliding down her chest. She has absolutely no curves to fill the gown.

Lauren turns to Emma whose dress is too short and too tight. "Oh." Lauren lets out a small, high-pitched gasp. "You look like a hooker."

Lauren looks at my dress and her mouth drops open. My dress is longer than Emma's, but the cleavage problem is much worse and totally inappropriate for a church wedding.

"Don't say it." I try to pull the dress up to cover my breasts better, but there isn't enough material.

"You look like the madam that runs the brothel where these two work," Lauren says angrily. "And these aren't champagne. It's poo brown!"

"It's Band-Aid brown." Jess can't help herself.

"I will fix them, Lauren," my mother says calmly. If anyone can take charge in a room of girls gone mad, it's my mother. "Go over there and let them do your hair and makeup. I'm handling these dresses."

"What if they run to the outlet mall and just get some new dresses? The J. Crew store, anything. Someone will have dresses ready to wear," Lauren says frantically.

"We have ninety minutes until the service. There isn't enough time to shop for new dresses. I will repair these, and you all will look lovely for the service and the photos. Please, go sit."

Nina takes her distraught daughter over to the stylists, who wisely turn her around so Lauren will face the window and not be able to watch her dysfunctional bridesmaids.

"This is when a shot of whiskey really comes in handy. Too bad we have a pregnant bride. I can't even give her a joint." Lois sighs, shaking her head.

"Maybe we need that joint to go out in public in these dresses."

My mother shoots me her fed-up look.

"You're going to need chicken cutlets," Emma says to Jess.

"What?" Jess asks, confused.

"You don't have any boobs," I explain. "You're going to have to stuff rubber boobies in your bra to fill out your dress."

"I'm not stuffing fake poultry in my dress. Pam can take in the top."

"I can't take it in that much," my mother mutters.

An hour later, after my mother cuts ample amounts of material from Jess's dress and adds it to Emma's and the top of mine, we have somewhat presentable attire.

Lauren walks across the room with the statuesque grace of a runway model, her natural beauty shining through with her long, blond hair swept up into a simple chignon and her honey-colored tan that is complemented by the ivory silk. She chose a minimalist approach to her makeup, a little blush and peach-toned eye shadow. She doesn't need much since her megawatt smile is breathtakingly beautiful.

"Oh, Lauren," I stutter. "You are the most beautiful bride. I might cry."

"Don't you dare because then I'll cry and my wedding will really go to shit."

"What do you think?" my mother asks Lauren, who is studying our dresses.

Each dress has been given its own unique twist, whatever my mother had to do to make all three work together. They are all the same length and all strapless, of course, but each one had to be altered in a way to fit Jess's skinny body, Emma's athletic form, and my voluptuous shape.

"I'm still not fond of the color, but the dresses actually look nice." Lauren smiles and claps her hands together. "They're each a little different, but they go together, and you all look great."

Jess gave in to stuffing her bra and is showing off a little cleavage. Her dress has been shortened so it sits below the knee and is gathered along the sides with ruching. Emma had material added to lengthen her dress and to give her more room in the bodice, so she has an interesting seam of asymmetrical ruffles. My dress was given some extra bands of both ruffles and ruching to cover my chest and flatter my hourglass figure.

As the stylists apply our makeup and work the curling irons to give all three of us long, loose curls, my mother huddles with us while Nina distracts Lauren from all the busy details.

"Listen," my mother whispers to us. "Whatever you do, don't sit down quickly or move fast in any way. The polyester mesh material shreds very easily, and when I repositioned the zippers, I noticed the material pulling away. It practically disintegrates, so be very careful."

"How are we going to dance in these things?" Jess asks.

"It doesn't matter," I say. "We just have to make it down the aisle and then pose for the photos. Then who cares what happens to the dresses. By the time we're at the reception, everyone will be drinking and won't give a flying kcuf what we look like."

Emma laughs.

"Seriously, at the end of the night, we're going to burn these crap-brown dresses with the unity candle so we never have to see them again," I explain.

My mother chuckles. "After all the work I just put into these dresses, I'm going to pretend I didn't hear you say that. But I am worried about those zippers tearing out."

"I have an idea," I say.

The stylist holds up a hand mirror so I can see my hair and makeup.

"Super. Thank you," I say flatly. "Are we done here? I need to take care of something."

"You're done," Lois nods approvingly.

I walk quickly out of the room, mindful of the fragile fabric, and find the men's changing room. I barge in to find them all dressed, shooting Nerfballs at a net hanging from a high beam in the ceiling.

"Whoa! Hey, you." Cooper smiles, striding towards me, looking gut-wrenchingly handsome in his black tux. His hair is pulled back in a low, short ponytail and he is clean-shaven. I've never seen him without the stubble.

On their own volition, my hands reach up for his face. "Wow."

"Hmm. I clean up pretty good. I think I deserve a kiss for this. And your sunburn is gone. Your skin is glowing. I want to bite you."

"Can't do," I inform him, still cupping his smooth cheeks. "You'll ruin my makeup, and we have an emergency. I need your help."

"Is something wrong?" he asks, resting his hands on my waist.

"We're wearing disposable dresses, no time to explain."

His gaze sweeps down to my strappy heels and up to my cleavage in appreciation. "You look amazing. I want to find a coat closet and show you how many ways I appreciate this dress."

"Very sweet. Is that a quote from a Pablo Neruda love poem?"

Cooper grins. "What do you need?"

"I need a stapler. And fast. I know there's one in the secretary's office in the rectory, but it's locked. I need you to go in there and get at least one stapler, if not more."

"Why don't you ask Father Pat for the stapler? He can open the office."

"He's in the middle of the service before Lauren's, and we need the stapler now. I know they have one because, one summer, I worked in the office as an assistant. I need you to do this because we are having issues with these dresses, and ... just do it, please."

"You want me to break into the rectory and steal staplers?" He feigns disapproval. "If I do time for this B and E job, you better be there for my regular conjugal visits."

"You got it." I give him a thumbs-up and get a whiff of his soap and deodorant mingling together in the best *kcuffing* aphrodisiac. "I will do anything you want in that coat closet tonight. I'll do it on a train, in a plane, in a boat ... whatever you want."

"Excellent."

"Meet me back at the women's dressing room." I do a fast, robotic wiggle-walk to our room where I find Lauren pacing again.

When Cooper is there in less than ten minutes, I don't bother to ask how he broke into the church's office. He hands me two large staplers and four mini ones before I push him back out the door.

"What are you doing?" Jess asks as I unzip her dress and begin stapling the zipper trim onto the flimsy fabric, hiding the staples under the seam.

"Giving us extra protection and a little extra time before the dresses rip apart."

"Well, be careful back there. Don't staple my skin."

"Brilliant," Lois adds.

"Not my first choice, but not bad, honey." My mother picks up a stapler and works on Emma's dress and then mine.

Lauren watches nervously. "I really wish I could have that whiskey," she mumbles.

"Sweetie," I say, putting down the stapler and walking over to Lauren. "Your wedding is going to be beautiful. It already is."

Lauren smiles. "I love you for saying that."

"It's true, though. And I love you." I give her a light hug without crushing our dresses. "And I have something for you."

"Don't make me cry," Lauren warns as she steps back and blots her eyes with a tissue.

I pull a small, silk pouch from my bag and drop a dainty necklace into my palm. "I don't want to ruin your neckline and minimalist approach with your gown, so I won't be offended if you don't want to wear it."

Lauren takes the necklace with the tiny gold heart-shaped locket and holds it up.

"I made it for you. The locket is marked with 1914 and faded initials on the back, but you can make out the word *love*. It has the original baby blue velvet backing inside of it. It's something old and something blue, and I thought it would be subtle enough to wear with your dress. I used very small chain remnants with a few of those itty bitty rosary beads you found."

"Imogene, it's lovely. I had no idea you were making this for me. Of course I'm going to wear it." Lauren looks weepy as she hands it to her mother.

"Don't cry!" I point my finger at Lauren as Nina laughs and clasps the chain around her daughter's neck.

By the time we walk down the hall to meet the groomsmen, we're each wearing at least a few dozen staples in our dresses and itching from a few poorly placed ones.

"Carson, you shaved!" Jess shrieks happily.

He gives her that same smug smile that Cooper gave me, although Carson didn't tie his hair back. His eyes glaze over as he notices his wife's new bosom.

"Don't get too excited." I lean in towards him. "They're not real. Jess needed a little extra padding and lift."

"I'm wearing rubber breasts," Jess mutters to him.

"Sorry, babe." He's still staring at her chest. "You still look like a goddess."

Cooper puts out his arm for me, his gray eyes serious. "Ready?"

"Yes." I take his arm as we line up behind Leo and his parents. As Eleanor hands out our bouquets, my fingers tremble so much I drop the flowers. Cooper catches them before they hit the floor and returns them to me with a wink.

I can't stop looking at Cooper as I hear the chamber quartet begin to play a beautiful, classical piece while Leo joyfully walks down the aisle with his mother and father, high-fiving people along the way, which makes everyone laugh.

The rustic, old church is exquisitely decorated and the pews are packed with half the town, but I'm giddily holding onto Cooper and so excited to be with him I don't recognize a single face as we walk down the aisle. He looks down at me and gives me a small smile before releasing me to the bride's side of the altar. Emma and Dylan come next, looking perfectly relaxed and happy, as any newlywed couple would be. Carson and Jess follow, Jess twitching as if she's trying to adjust her dress without using her hands. I glare at her and try to subtly shake my head *no*.

"The cutlets are going south," she whispers angrily as she passes me to line up next to Emma.

As the joyful music heightens and everyone stands for the bride, I put aside my worries and failure as a maid of honor to watch my best friend walk down the aisle, holding on to both of her parents. Ugly bridesmaid dresses and staples aside, she is a beautiful bride, and I'm so overcome with happiness for her I have the urge to weep. I do not cry at weddings or births of babies, but something has changed intrinsically, making me want to weep at the sight of Lauren's beaming smile.

When she turns to Leo and his face breaks open into a wide grin, I almost lose it. With Cooper staring at me, raising a questioning eyebrow, I take a deep breath and pull myself together until the service is over.

When the photographer herds us outside for an extensive photo shoot, I clutch tightly onto Cooper's arm.

"Are you all right?" He looks concerned.

"A little light-headed from the excitement, I guess. I didn't eat breakfast."

"Then we need to get you to the reception before you faint. Just keep holding onto me."

I sway a little like a drunk when the photographer pulls me away from Cooper and has me pose with Lauren and the bridesmaids. Then we do more group photos where I gladly cling to Cooper's arm with a death grip.

Archie appears with a very attractive, older woman who looks closer to his age and isn't someone who is part of Lois's circle of friends. He is absolutely bouncing with delight as he wrangles the wedding party into three different limos. I ride with Cooper, Emma, Dylan, Jess, and Carson while Lauren and Leo and the parents ride in separate limos.

The reception is held in a historic hotel, and as Cooper and I wade through the tables of party guests to the head table, I glance around and notice familiar faces. Well, more like familiar ex-boyfriends. Oh, God, Cody Aasland, Mr. Quarterback, is here and Jeremy! I see a couple of more mistakes from high school and college. It's a kcuffing wanker convention.

I take my place at the U-shaped head table between

Lauren and Emma with Cooper across from me between Leo and Dylan. Lauren is going with an unconventional reception, letting a few of us give the toasts. Leo is going to speak first, then me, and then Cooper. I pull out my little notes from my cleavage, but they're smudged from my perspiration.

"Oh, great," I mumble.

When I down the glass of champagne the minute it's poured, the waiter does a double take and quickly refills my glass that I promptly empty again. "I will be your best customer tonight." I tip him with a twenty, two fives, and four quarters, two dimes, and six pennies. It gives him a good laugh.

Leo is already slap-happy buzzed when he gets up to do his toast. "I just want to say something for my beautiful wife. I tried to find the right poem or words, but I know my Lauren. She's a mob movie addict. So, be warned, she's probably the only person in this room who will appreciate this quote, and I apologize in advance to Father Pat. Really. Cover your ears, Father."

Everyone laughs and then quiets down for Leo's toast.

" *'She was beautiful! She was young. She was innocent. She was the greatest piece of ass I ever had, and I've had 'em all over the world!'* "

"*The Godfather!*" Lauren shouts with a fist pump, causing people to laugh despite looking confused.

Cooper, Carson, and Dylan are whooping it up and pounding the table.

I stand and feel a few pops in the back of my dress as some staples spring free when Leo hands me the microphone.

"Well, it will be hard to top Mr. Romance there," I address the guests who laugh as Leo stumbles back to his chair. "And I'd like to point out that I trump the rest of this supporting cast because I've known Lauren since we were babies. So, tonight, I am the best bestie of this couple, just so you're all clear on how important I am to these two fabulous people."

"Hear! Hear!" Lauren claps as the crowd laughs.

"I also want to thank Father Pat for holding his tongue when the bridesmaids showed up at the ceremony looking like *Charlie's Angels* decked out Vegas style."

Father Pat gives me a smile and nod from a nearby table.

"But I'm not here to talk about me and how great I rock this hideous dress; I'm here to toast my best friend and her wonderful new husband. They are two of the most beautiful people, and I love them dearly." I choke back the tears that begin to pool in my eyes. I look away from Lauren's teary eyes and catch Cooper's intense stare, his steely, gray eyes watching me. I blabber on with more sentimental words and a bit of humorous nostalgia about Lauren before taking my seat and blotting my eyes with my napkin.

"What the hell was that?" I mutter to Emma.

"You got a little emotional, so what? Everyone gets that way at weddings," she says, patting my back.

"Not me. I don't cry at weddings. I'm the fun one, the woman who parties it up."

Cooper is handed the microphone next, and as he stands to give his toast, he looks at me with a sexy smile, and my heart races. I'm definitely falling for him. Falling hard.

"I need help!" Jess whisper-shouts, leaning behind Emma's back to get my attention. "The fake boobs are falling down to my stomach and the top of my dress is caving in."

As I rifle through my bag for the staplers, I don't hear anything Cooper is saying, but he sure is working the room like a nightclub comedy act. Emma crouches behind Jess and attempts to retrieve the runaway rubber breasts while I scoot over to Emma's chair to assist by covering Jess's front with a napkin.

"And I am in awe of Lauren and Leo and their marriage," Cooper continues. "I could never do this."

I could never do this. That's the only thing I hear before Cooper sits down, and the quartet begins performing the first waltz. Leo takes Lauren's hand and walks her to the dance floor.

"Carson!" Jess hisses in an angry whisper.

Carson looks over at us with concern and then quickly heads into the space between our tables to stand in front of Jess.

"Why are you feeling up my wife?" he asks Emma who has her hands in the back of Jess's dress.

"She's trying to reposition my boobs," Jess snaps. "Just stand there, Carson, and block people from seeing us."

"You're what?" Carson is completely mesmerized as Emma fumbles with the cutlets and Jess struggles to keep the front of her dress from falling down.

"I look like one of Picasso's freaky three-boobed women. These rubber chickens fell out of my bra, and the whole dress is collapsing," Jess explains.

While Carson leans over the table, tall and broad enough to hide us from view, I stand and begin stapling Jess's zipper again.

Dylan and Cooper both jump over their table like cowboys swinging over a fence. They jog over to see what all the excitement is about.

"Hey, it's our turn," Dylan says. "We have to get out there and dance, boys and girls."

"Just a second, honey," Emma says as I give Jess one last staple in her back and she adjusts her bra.

"Jesus. What's going on here?" Dylan looks as captivated as Carson with our wardrobe adjustments that look more like an erotic strip club dance.

"Two seconds," I say to Dylan. I glance at Cooper, but

then look away and take extra time putting away the staplers and our bags to gather the whirlwind of thoughts racing through my mixed up brain.

I was completely excited to show off my dance moves with Cooper, but his words, *"I could never do this,"* keep resonating through me in a sickening way.

Cooper comes around the table to my side and holds out his hand. "Ready?"

With the others already gliding across the dance floor around Leo and Lauren, I take Cooper's hand and he sweeps me into the waltz. As he leads me gracefully through the other couples with powerful moves that make me feel like I'm floating, I keep my eyes fixated on our clasped hands.

"Your toast was very funny. Lauren really enjoyed it," he says finally to break the silence.

"Hmm." I keep looking at our hands and other couples.

"Why won't you look at me? What's wrong, Imogene?"

"I don't want to mess up the waltz. A lot of people are filming this."

"This is the last one and then the DJ comes on. Do you plan on looking at me then?" he asks.

Right then, "Dyslexic Heart" starts blasting, and Lauren bops by us, singing along with the song like a spastic groupie. Leo's arms are flailing about and Cooper has to pull me aside from a flying fist.

"I forgot that Lauren planned on playing a bunch of her parents' old tunes." I put on my best fake smile.

"Then let's show these goons how to dance." He takes my hand and drags me to the middle of the crowded dance floor.

"Imogene!" Cody intercepts us and Cooper frowns.

Cody still looks like a hunky high school jock, and I can tell Cooper is sizing him up.

"Cody, wow. Nice to see you," I say flatly.

"Hey, do you mind if I cut in and dance with her?" he asks Cooper.

"Actually, yeah. She's not available. There's a table of women over there, waiting to be asked to dance." Cooper nods with his chin.

"Seriously?" Cody chuckles. "Imogene and I go way back, and—"

"Great. We just missed the fun song." I stand between the two men as The Human League comes on.

"Slow song," Cooper says. "Sorry, buddy, you'll have to catch up with Imogene later."

Cody scoffs as Cooper pulls me in for a snug embrace.

"Cody, snag a bottle of champagne, and I'll meet you at the fountain lobby. We can talk then," I say over Cooper's shoulder.

"Sounds good!" Cody slaps Cooper's back before he walks away.

His expression grim, I feel Cooper's arms loosen as though he's about to turn and throw a punch at Cody's head. I press my hands hard against his back to hold him in place.

"What the fuck was that, Imogene?"

"Watch your language. We're at a wedding. He's an old boyfriend who asked me for a dance. Big deal."

"I hate him already."

"It was years ago. He's from my high school days. Get over it."

"Why aren't you all over me? What happened between the church and the reception? You're acting strange, like you're mad at me. And I'm not the one in a room full of exes. Yeah, I saw Jeremy."

"It's not my fault these guys are here. Lauren and Leo invited them."

"I don't care about those guys. What's going on with you?"

"Shoot. I like this song," I say as The Duhks's

271

"Annabel" starts playing. "And you're ruining it for me."

"Me? Why?" he growls.

"Did you mean that? What you said during the toast, that you could never do this? Never get married?"

Cooper shrugs. "Yeah. I never saw myself as the marrying type."

"And you still feel that way?" I'm not hiding my anger.

"Why? Are we getting married?" he asks, equally angry.

"No. We're dating. At least, I thought we were." I push away from him. "You know what? I don't want to have this argument here on the dance floor. In fact, I can't talk to you right now. I'm going to go cool off."

"I'll go with you, and we'll talk some place more private."

"No. Really. I need to be alone," I snap. As I turn to walk away, I feel a loosening sensation on my back as several staples pop and the fabric gives. "Kcuf!"

"Imogene!" Cooper grabs my arm and turns me back around to face him. "You're being childish. Come with me and we'll talk this out now."

"Childish? You really know how to win me over. I can't talk to you. I'm pissed as hell and my dress is shredding … Soon, I'll be pissed and naked."

Cooper takes off his tux jacket and swings it around my shoulders. "Wear this. Please," he says calmly with a tight jaw. "Whatever I did, I'm sorry. I don't want to piss you off. Why don't you go sit down with Lois and Archie, and I'll give you twenty minutes to calm down, then we're talking."

I open my mouth to say something; however, I struggle to think of a single word that docsn't make me feel like a fool. Instead, I storm off the dance floor and wade through the dining tables until I spot Archie and his entourage. There are two open seats between Lois and a woman sitting next to Archie, so I plop myself down in the chair next to Lois and pull the lapels of Cooper's tux around me.

"Oh, no, is the dress a goner?" Lois frowns. "I noticed all the girls are wearing the men's jackets. Did your backside make a big showing?"

"Something like that."

"That didn't stop them from dancing. Why are you sitting here with the old folks?"

"I suddenly lost interest in dancing." I take a sip of champagne from an unclaimed glass and notice two distinguished looking older men across the table in a very serious conversation. "Are those your dates?"

"Yes. The silver fox is Ben. He's my date. Nice, right? The tall, dark, and handsome one came with Eleanor. He's Steven, a widower and very successful in some kind of retail franchise."

"How do you manage to meet men? Women my age complain about it all the time, and somehow, you and Eleanor always find these nice, available guys."

"We're more resourceful." Lois finishes off a glass of water. "We make a point to go to as many social functions as possible, whether it's a funeral or a bake sale at the library. I met Ben at a swanky cocktail party at Mohonk. I had an appointment at the spa there when I stumbled upon his group of friends. Next thing you know, he's asking for my phone number. Eleanor met Steven at the gas station. How's that for dumb luck? So where's your handsome date?"

"He's around here ... somewhere." I fling my hand in the air.

"Why do you young women use every party as an opportunity to create unnecessary drama? Is it part of the chase? Does it really make it more fun?" Lois regards me with a serious frown.

I shrug. "Sometimes things don't become obvious until we're in the middle of one of these massive social functions. Sometimes we're stupid, and ..."

"You've had a disagreement with Cooper." Lois sighs and sits back in her chair.

"Yes." I cross my arms and slouch in my chair.

"Stop pouting. I hate when grown women do that. It's so unbecoming."

"You're so understanding I can't stand it."

"You are at your best friend's wedding and have a wonderful, young man who lavishes great attention on you. What do I not understand?"

"Did you hear his toast?" I say in a shrill voice that makes others glance over at me.

"I thought he was absolutely adorable."

"Well, I must have missed that part," I snipe.

"Do you see that woman on your other side, the one Archie can't take his eyes off of?" Lois asks in a low voice.

I turn to my right to get a better look at the attractive woman I noticed earlier.

"That's Emily Weston," Lois says.

I shake my head. "So?"

"Before she was Emily Weston, she was Archie's Emily. *The* Emily." Lois smiles as my eyes go wide.

"You mean the woman we thought was a myth, a farfetched story Archie made up?"

"That's the one. She broke his heart fifty years ago and married someone else, and Archie said he'd never get over her."

"So what is she doing here?"

"Her husband George died six months ago, and Archie ran into her at some county planning meeting, save the rain forest or something."

"We don't have a rain forest."

"You know, one of those public meetings to stop development on someone's land or some owl's tree. They ran into each other, went out for lunch, and they've been together ever since."

274

"That's wonderful. I'm so happy for Archie. What luck."

"Right, like the luck you had at my party," Lois slips in, "hooking up with Cooper." She smiles.

"We didn't *hook up* at your party, and since when do you say things like that? My mother doesn't even use that expression."

Lois shrugs. "I'm more hip. And I did see Cooper carrying you off that night."

"I believe I was unconscious at the time, so it doesn't count."

"Imogene, I wish you would understand that loving someone doesn't have to be impossible or even difficult, *unless* you are looking for reasons to make it impossible. I'm not saying everyone is worth loving, but you did find someone good. I hate to see you foolishly waste time on being upset over some silly tiff."

"Who says it's silly?"

"Me. You're sitting at the geriatric table instead of dancing with that handsome, young man."

"What if the love isn't equal?"

"Love is a bitch if you love someone who can't give you what you want. And time is cruel. It goes too fast when you're happy, and it seems like an eternity when you're miserable. Love and time are both cruel bitches. They're also necessary."

"Then I'm screwed either way. Why do I bother talking to you about this?"

"Because you're the dumb broad that is fighting with her boyfriend in the middle of a party. You couldn't wait until it was over?"

"Do you ever give any advice that's helpful?"

"If I have to be responsible for giving advice, I want four hundred dollars per hour and a good bottle of Scotch."

"Perfect."

"Imogene, you have two options: love the person you

love and live with the compromise, or you can find someone else to love. The options aren't complicated."

"It sounds very difficult to me."

"Imogene."

I look up to meet the familiar voice.

Jeremy.

"Oh, sweet Jesus H. Christ," Lois says. "That's my cue. Ben, let's dance! Everyone, let's hit that dance floor!"

"You're leaving me?" I ask pleadingly.

"I've helped you enough. I need to go live my life."

And, just like that, the whole table of seniors evacuates and leaves me alone with Jeremy.

"Would you like to dance?" he asks me.

"Not really."

He looks different—better, healthier, thinner—as if he's been exercising in the Southern California sun. His hair is cut shorter, the curls completely gone, and his face looks more defined.

"Can I sit with you?"

"Sure." I'm not making this easy for him, and why should I?

He unbuttons his suit coat and sits down. He even dresses better than when he was with me. "You look really nice," he says shyly. "Beautiful as always."

"Huh. You look good, too. Guess the new job worked out really well for you."

He nods and looks uncomfortable. "Imogene, I'm really sorry."

"That's nice, but you're a year too late."

"I still have to say it. I owe you a huge apology."

"Save it, Jeremy. We've both moved on."

"But that's just it. I didn't want to leave you. I thought I'd get settled and come back and ..."

"No. No, you don't. I spent a lot of time being angry at you. I think I hated you for at least six months after you moved away."

Jeremy nods. "It was my fault, and I want to fix it."

I look at him like he's crazy. "What?"

"I was getting a new job and thought I could convince you to come out once I was doing well."

"You hurt me. You never called. We're over and done with forever. You get that, right? We haven't spoken in over a year, and since you weren't away fighting a war or imprisoned in some undisclosed location, that means we have been over for a very long time."

"How do I explain this?" Jeremy mutters to himself and then gives me a wounded look. "I didn't break up with you, Imogene. I was just hitting the pause button."

"I'm not a kcuffing DVD player, you wanker!" I stand up and the chair falls back. I really want to slap him, but he already looks confused and scared, so I bolt from the table and run right into Cooper's chest, my lipstick making a perfect imprint on his white dress shirt.

He looks down at the mouth-print I branded him with and then regards me with a weary smile. "How is it going with the ex-boyfriends?"

His tie is gone and his shirt collar is open, revealing one of my favorite parts of his body. Who am I kidding? I love every part of him, and he seems to be oblivious that his little toast gave me a huge sucker punch.

"It's a nightmare. I'm having the worst time. I'm going to ask someone to give me a lift home."

"Ah, no you're not. You're coming to my place tonight, remember? We need to talk."

I push by him and keep walking, but in a split second, he's by my side with his arm around my waist. In the next instant, there's hollering from the dance floor as Lauren launches her bridal bouquet over the heads of a crowd of jumping women. The bouquet flies right over everyone's head and smacks Cooper in the face.

"Damn!" He palms his injured head with one hand and catches the bouquet in the other.

There's an audible gasp in the ballroom as the eager, single women realize a man caught their coveted flowers. Cooper looks at me helplessly and then at the bouquet in his hands.

"Oh, how ironic!" I bellow angrily, loud enough for everyone to hear. "Give me that!"

I grab the bouquet from his hand and lob it back across the room to the women who scream, jump, and tackle one another for the prize. Kimberly, our cute librarian, jumps up from a mound of women on the floor, holding up the bouquet with a triumphant smile.

I make it to the grand lobby of the hotel and see Cody and his friends hanging out by the fountain. He has a bottle of champagne and stands up from where he is perched on the fountain edge when he sees me.

"Hey, Imogene." He smiles and holds up the bottle.

"Sorry, Corey. You'll have to find another woman," Cooper says as he places his hand protectively on the back of my neck.

"It's Cody." Cody looks Cooper up and down as if he's judging whether to take him on and turn this into a genuine replay of a pathetic high school prom with a drunken fistfight.

I scowl at Cooper and then Cody and keep walking until I'm outside the hotel. Cooper remains glued to my side, silent yet ever so present. We cross through the valet parking zone and head into the large gazebo of the hotel garden. Usually, the gazebo would be booked with another party or a musical group, but the light drizzle of rain has moved all parties to the inside ballrooms.

I wriggle out from underneath his grip and walk away from him to lean against the wood railing, pulling the tux jacket around me. I suddenly feeling naked in my dress that has the consistency of cotton candy.

"This is all because of my toast?" he asks. "Because I was trying to say something nice about Lauren and Leo?"

"It was enough to make me consider that this isn't as good as I thought."

"Us? Are you kidding?" He walks angrily towards me. "This is the best I've ever been. Being with you, it's the best."

"We want different things. I had no idea you were someone who shunned marriage … and family. God, this all makes perfect sense. This is why you've been so vague about your family."

"I didn't know you were thinking about marriage." He stands closer and glares at me.

"I wasn't until you took it off the table. Then it became perfectly clear to me that I want to be with someone who is keeping all options open. I don't want to think I'm falling in love with someone who can't commit."

"Wait. Do you *think* you're falling in love with me, or *are* you in love with me?"

"That's not the point."

"It's a really big point."

"No, the point is you can't commit. By saying you'll never get married, you're telling me and the world that I'll never be anything more than a girlfriend. I'm the side dish, not the entrée. I'm the coleslaw you get with your steak, and sometimes you want the slaw and sometimes you don't."

"That is the stupidest analogy," he says with an angry laugh. "And, for the record, I can commit. Marriage isn't the only way to show commitment. I want to be with you, and I thought you could move in with me. That shows commitment."

"That shows you want a live-in booty call."

"Do you really believe that? Have I treated you in a way that makes you feel less important? Because you are the most important person to me."

"Then we have different ways of showing it. I can't settle for being a live-in girlfriend. I'm not ready for

279

marriage, but I know I do not want to be the eternal girlfriend. I want my future to hold the possibility of more, but you're shutting the door on all of that."

"Let's have one of the limo drivers take us back to my place. We'll talk there."

"I don't want to go to your house where I'm the houseguest. I'm going to my place tonight."

"You actually think I'm the wrong guy for you because I don't give a shit about a marriage certificate?"

"I do. It says a lot about who we are and what we want. Someday, I want a man to put himself out there for me, no matter how embarrassing it may feel or look to others. I want him to love me enough that he's willing to propose to me in the middle of the street. I want him to drop to his knee and stop traffic. That's not the same man that asks me to move in with him because it's convenient."

Cooper shakes his head in disbelief. "You just made that up. That's not the Imogene I've been with over these past weeks and months."

"Then I thank you for helping me see the light of day."

"Christ, if you really saw my family and saw what I grew up with, you'd understand why marriage doesn't work with a MacKenzie. Every single marriage in our family has ended in divorce. My mother has been married three times! My father twice! Even my sister and brothers are divorced. I've got a boatload of stepbrothers and sisters and nieces and nephews and no one has married parents. Marriage and MacKenzies don't mix. They cheat on each other, they divorce, and the cycle continues."

As much as I'm shocked by his revelation, I keep my poker face on. "You know divorce and infidelity are not genetic, right?"

"I think there's an exception with my family."

"You believe marriage would make you cheat?" I stare in disbelief at him.

"No. I wouldn't …" He looks down and is quiet for a

moment before it dawns on me what he's saying.

"Oh, you believe *I* couldn't be faithful," I say in a measured tone.

"I didn't say that."

"It sounds like you are implying that, Cooper."

"I think people who marry a MacKenzie are bound to end up divorced. We drive people away. I don't know how or why, but it happens every single time."

"That is a horrible outlook on life and relationships, and I can't be with someone who feels that way." I push away from the railing and walk briskly to exit the gazebo as I fight back tears.

"Imogene!" Cooper tries to block me from approaching one of the dozens of limo drivers parked in front of the hotel.

One of the drivers sees me charging towards his car. When he gets out and opens the back door for me, I get in without moving over to let Cooper in.

"We're not breaking up over this," he says furiously, holding the door open.

"We just did." I yank the door from his hand and slam it closed.

Twenty-Five

Avoidance is easy. Humans invented it. I excel at it.

I listen to Aimee Mann's "That's Just What You Are" at least two hundred times to justify my anger and refusal to answer Cooper's calls and texts. Yes, as the song goes, we could talk to each other until we're blue in the face, but we would end up in the same place because I will not settle for less than what my parents have.

Lauren and Emma both lived with their husbands before marrying them. It worked for them because each couple knew they would eventually get married. Even Jess and Carson lived together during their engagement, but it was only thirty days! I'm no longer the dumbass that fell for Jeremy's insincere innocence. I'm pretty sure, if I try really hard, I can talk myself out of all those feelings I built up for Cooper. All those vivid, overpowering emotions that made me feel happy and beautiful inside and out.

With Lauren and Leo off on a weeklong honeymoon at a nearby spa resort, I wander around the house in my ratty, old football jersey some guy gave me in college and cry myself stupid until my face cracks with dried tears and my head feels like it has a bullet lodged in it. My self-therapy is going like gangbusters.

Monday morning, I have to open the workshop without Lauren. On the early drive over, I plot how I'll get through the day without running into Cooper. I arrive to the parking lot before six in the morning to find his Harley is already there. I drive slowly over the gravel, hoping he doesn't hear my car, and park on the grass to get as close as possible to the front door. In the early light, the area is very quiet.

Just as I get out of my car, I hear fast, loud, crunching steps on the gravel. I turn to see Cooper, angry as all hell, walking my way like a man who has been wronged and is out for justice. *Kcuf* this small town life!

"I pounded on your door for a good ten minutes last night! I was ready to break in, but then you only approve of me breaking and entering into churches."

I have never seen him so pissed off.

"I was sleeping. Resting," I say, thinking about the headphones I never took off.

"At seven o'clock at night? And what about all my messages? You couldn't bother to return a single call?"

"I needed to rest, and I wanted to take advantage of the day since I didn't have to work and had the house to myself."

He slams my car door closed and follows me inside the workshop where I proceed to calmly flick on the lights and walk around, pretending to check on miscellaneous objects around the room.

"Imogene, knock it off." He stands at the door and crosses his arms.

"Cooper, if you think I haven't given this a lot of thought, you're nuts. All I've done for the last two days is rack my brain over how we got to this shitty point. I'm so miserable over this."

"Then you can stop being miserable," he says, closing the distance between us quickly. He wraps his arms around me and pulls me in for an urgent kiss, his hands holding my head and back as his mouth takes over mine.

As our tongues fight for control, I reach up and hold his face, caressing the stubble that has returned. This is the kiss I wanted when I first saw him shaved, polished, and decked out in a tux at the church.

The kiss ends slowly, and my gut reminds me that nothing has changed, nothing has been resolved.

He cups my face. "I want to be with you all the time. I'm fucking crazy about you, and you're crazy about me. I see it in your eyes every time you look at me, Imogene."

Of course he's right. I look at him with crazy, lust-filled eyes every time. I feel it, too, but he's also not amending his earlier arguments. Like Jeremy, Cooper is waiting for me to change for him, to go along with his plan, follow his will.

I believe in compromise, but I will not drop everything to be with a man if it means giving up a part of myself. There's a big part of me that is a traditional-thinking woman who occasionally imagines herself as one day getting married, maybe having a child, and maybe even having a bunny rabbit because, if we're going to dream big, why can't I have that damn bunny my parents refused to get me when I was seven? However, conceding and giving up on an actual marriage contract isn't something I can do. I can laugh about my loose convictions when it comes to premarital sex, yet it doesn't change how I respect and desire the union of marriage.

"Cooper, being crazy about each other isn't enough. If that's all we're doing is being crazy for each other, we can get deprogrammed," I say, trying to lighten the mood so I don't cry.

"That's not funny."

"No, this isn't funny. It hurts, and I don't want to go through this again. I don't think people should try to force change on others. Change has to come from within ourselves— blah, blah, blah. I'm not going to try to get you to accept something you don't believe in, and I'm not going to settle for what you're offering. Ultimately, it wouldn't work, and we'd both end up being miserable."

Cooper drops his hands at his side, looking stunned. "My family's record-setting gold medals in divorce happened because people lied to each other. One of the reasons I worked all those hours in the FBI was to escape the insanity of my family, all of their lying and cheating. But my work with the bureau involved a lot of similar people. Do you know how many people looked me in the eye and lied to me?"

I shake my head nervously.

"Hundreds. Thousands. Day after day, I had to talk to liars. When I decided to quit and had the chance to move here, I did it because Carson and everyone I met were decent people. But you were the prize. You were the one I noticed above all else. I value your honesty. You've never lied to me."

"No. I may not have been the nicest person, but aside from sarcastic fibs, I have never lied to you." My voice falters. I need him to leave so I can barricade myself in the back office and cry alone.

Cooper gives me a solemn nod. "I have to get back to the factory. I left a project unattended," he says somberly. "When or if you want to talk to me, please do because this is going to be really shitty being near you every day and not being able to be with you."

Over the next five days, Anita and Tracy are very understanding. After witnessing my tirade during the bridal bouquet toss, they assume I am in relationship fallout mode and keep all conversations on work. I am quiet and overwhelmed with fatigue. I wish Lauren were here to help me get through this; however, she won't be returning for two more days.

I have managed to become my own worst, wimpy nightmare. I stay late at work to avoid possibly running into Cooper in the parking lot, and I arrive earlier and earlier each day to the point that there's no point in going home to sleep the four remaining hours. I brown-bag lunch and hide in the workshop, keeping tabs on the comings and goings of Cooper's bike. I'm developing a nervous tic of hunching and diving from the window every time I hear the roar of a motorcycle.

On Friday, as we work in silence, outside the open front windows, Dylan begins dribbling a basketball on the half court. He's followed by two other employees, Noelle and Gemma, and then I see Cooper heading out of the factory and making his way over to Dylan. They chat for a moment, and then they start a game against the women.

"How can they play in this heat?" Tracy asks, staring out the window.

I glance up from the beads I'm stringing and notice Dylan and Cooper taking off their T-shirts and tossing them off to the side before getting back in the game.

"That's how," Anita replies with a big sigh. "Cooper's trying to get your attention."

"I'm well aware of that."

After twenty minutes of listening to the ball hit the pavement and bang against the backboard, I can't take it anymore. I put down the necklace I'm working on and decide to take action against Cooper's little plan. I whip off my T-shirt and head outside. At least I'm wearing my full-coverage, underwire bra today so I don't have too much on display. As the screen door to the workshop slams behind me, Dylan looks over and breaks out laughing. Cooper is less amused. He stops dribbling and Noelle snatches the ball from his hands as he stares at me.

"Excellent," Dylan says, unfazed by my attire. "Join the game!"

"Imogene!" Noelle shoots the ball at me, and I take the jump shot. It circles the rim before going in, and Noelle and Gemma cheer.

I'm elated. If I'm going to make a statement and jump around with my breasts bobbing, I better get in some good shots.

"Put your shirt on." Cooper hasn't budged. He's still glaring at me, and unlike the others, he doesn't find this hilarious at all.

"No. You put your shirt on," I snap back.

Dylan passes the ball to Cooper and it bounces off his chest as he stalks towards me and gets in my face.

"This isn't funny, Imogene. Go back inside and put on your goddamn shirt."

Hands on hips, chest out, I lean forward and look up at his pissed eyes. "No. You started this by banging that ball around. You're giving us concussions over there." I nod my head towards the workshop where Anita and Tracy are watching everything from the windows. "If you can take your shirt off and play during your lunch hour, so can I."

"Everyone in the factory can see you." He moves to block me so no one other than my employees can see me.

"So what? My bra covers more than my bikini. I'm not anymore indecent than you are. You wanted my attention, you got it."

"I wouldn't have to try to get your attention if you'd talk to me. Instead, you've been cowering in there all the time. I can't see you before or after work, because you're hiding from me."

"You said *when* or *if* I want to talk to call you. Obviously, I don't want to talk."

"Then why did you come out here?"

"To play topless basketball because I have absolutely nothing better to do!"

Gemma and Dylan laugh loudly at that.

"Cooper MacKenzie!" Daisy shouts into a bullhorn from the factory door.

Cooper turns around with a grimace.

"Cooper MacKenzie, you are needed in the factory! We've got another snake!"

"I see you got the bullhorn I suggested," I say wryly.

Cooper turns back to me. "This isn't over."

"Hey!" Carson yells as he comes our way. "Can I get my management team to get back to work?"

"We're coming," Noelle says as she and Gemma

follow Carson back to the factory.

Dylan puts his T-shirt back on. "Come on, Cooper. You're on snake duty."

Cooper grabs his Blackard Designs T-shirt off the ground and quickly shoves it over my head.

"Hey," I fumble into the shirt that smells like Cooper and sweat, spitting out some sawdust that's clinging to the shirt.

"You're coming with me," Cooper says as he grabs my wrist and leads me towards the factory door.

"Why? It's your problem. I hate snakes." I struggle to get my wrist free, but his stride and grip are too forceful.

"Because I said so."

When we enter the factory, all the employees are standing on the far side of the room, looking up at the high rafters. On the middle, flat beam, there's a big, fat snake curled up. Carson is standing directly underneath the beam, looking up as if he can talk the snake into coming down.

"Sorry, but it's your turn, and you're the best at walking the beams," Carson says to Cooper.

Cooper lets go of me. "Don't leave."

"Let's stand over here," Carson says as he guides me over to where the others are standing. "We wouldn't want it to drop on our heads."

"Why are you sending Cooper up there? What if he gets bitten?"

"It's not poisonous. It's just a regular, old garden snake."

"It looks like a boa constrictor."

"No. We get these fat, lazy snakes all the time. You might have them, too."

"You're kidding? Is that why we get to use your building for free?"

Carson smiles. "Watch him. He's good at this."

Silly Carson, of course I'm watching Cooper. He's shirtless. Why would my eyes not be riveted on his gorgeous body? Seriously, even in heartache, I can't tear my eyes away from the guy.

Cooper leans a metal ladder against the wall and climbs to the top. Then he grabs onto a beam and does a monkey swing and grab routine until he's hanging from the beam with the snake.

"Careful," Daisy says, forgetting she still has the bullhorn up to her mouth so her intended whisper booms through the whole warehouse. As everyone, including Cooper, looks at her, Carson gently removes the bullhorn from her grasp.

Cooper lifts his legs up and wraps them around the beam and pulls himself up until he's upright, squatting on top of the beam. He stands and then begins to walk the narrow strip of wood, one foot in front of the other as he slowly approaches the snake.

"Shouldn't you have a safety net under him in case he falls?"

"Shh," Carson dismisses me. "He does this all the time."

I continue to watch with a morbid fascination. It's like watching an Olympic gymnast when you're tense and worried that they'll take an embarrassing nosedive off the beam.

"Hey, little buddy," Cooper says to the snake. In a flash, he has a hand at the base of the snake's head, holding him up before grabbing the squirming middle.

"Yuck," I mutter.

Dylan and two other guys hold an industrial sized burlap sack open and stand under the beam so Cooper can drop the snake directly into the bag.

"Are you going to kill it?" I ask.

"No. We release them down the hill, but they like us. They keep coming back," Carson says.

Cooper does his whole beam walking and swinging routine in reverse until he's climbing down the ladder.

Then he approaches me, and I can tell a lot of the steam has gone out of his engine. I'll have to remember that snake wrangling is a good way to calm down an enraged person.

Carson and everyone else leave to go back to work, but Cooper stands in front of me as though he's waiting for me to say something.

"I give. Why did I have to see this?" I ask.

Cooper shrugs. "It was an excuse to get you to talk to me."

"Nice job. Fine work there with Mr. Slithers. I have to get back to work."

"Wait a sec." He reaches into a bin, pulls out a clean company T-shirt, and slips it on. "I'll walk you back."

"I'll walk myself. Really, Cooper, I don't have anything to say, and I don't want to have another argument."

"You might have snakes."

That shuts me up. He casually puts his arm on my shoulders, and I don't hesitate to let him walk me back to the workshop.

Anita and Tracy act uninterested as I walk in with Cooper. He does a slow, careful walk around, checking behind and on top of shelves while I stand in the middle of the room, waiting for him to finish.

"No snakes," he says calmly.

"Good. Thanks."

"I want to ask you something," he says. "Walk me to the door?"

"Sure." I follow him, glancing at Anita and Tracy who both raise their eyebrows.

Cooper steps outside the threshold and closes the screen door gently behind me.

"I have to go out of town for a while," he says with some trepidation. "I have to hang with my family, and I don't know how long I'll be gone, but—"

"Something bad?" I ask softly, instinctively putting my

hand on his arm.

His expression is wistful, giving me a powerful urge to hold him. He nods. "It's not good. And maybe you're not ready to talk to me, but I was hoping that, if things are really bad for me there … I could call you, have someone I like to talk to."

"Yes." I put my hand back at my side. I think of asking him to divulge the issue; however, it may open the door for more heartache if I let myself get sucked into his family's problems. "Yes, you can call me if you need a friend to talk to."

"Okay, thanks." He steps off the threshold and pauses. "You can call me anytime, too."

"Got it."

Cooper forces a weak smile.

"Good luck." I wonder what other worthless things I can say as he turns and leaves.

I hug Cooper's T-shirt around me, his lingering scent sending a riot of emotions that floor me as I watch his back disappear through the factory door.

Twenty-Six

He doesn't call.

For fifteen days, I sleep, work, and think of Cooper. Not once do I fall for the temptation to send him an innocent *'How are you doing?'* text, either.

Lauren and Leo keep the atmosphere in the house upbeat with all their discussions about the baby nursery and names they cannot agree on. They don't pry into my miserable condition, and I assume Leo already got the details from Cooper and informed Lauren … and the rest of the town. Lauren treats me with care and more sympathy than usual from either her unpredictable pregnancy hormones or from sensing that I'm more fragile than I let on.

I set the table for the lunch we're having with Carson, Jess, Dylan, and Emma and help Leo put out his famous lasagna. It's only famous because he always manages to dry it out and burn the top of it. I also help Lauren with side dishes and make three loaves of garlic bread, each saturated with a stick of butter.

"Are you going to eat that whole thing?" Jess points to the basket of bread sitting next to me at the table.

"Probably. If it had bacon on it, I'd marry it." I pick up a slice and rip a big piece off with my teeth, but the butter isn't as enjoyable as it should be. I pass the basket to Jess and continue to chew and swallow to look like a participant, though, while everyone else chats about work, Archie's new girlfriend, and anything else that I tune out.

When Carson's phone vibrates next to my water glass, I pick it up and hand it to him, noticing the display shows

292

that it's an incoming call from Cooper.

"I'll take it outside," Carson says to the table and leaves to step out on the porch.

Seeing Cooper's name is enough to make my heart race. The blood is pumping through me, and surely this is my heart actually breaking, or the garlic bread is sending me into cardiac arrest.

I want to scream and tell everyone to shut up so I can hear what Carson is saying to Cooper. Instead, I put my silverware down and rest my head in my hands.

"Are you okay?" Dylan asks, putting his hand on my back.

"No, she's not." Jess comes around the table and places her hands on my shoulders.

Carson returns and I look up from my hands to search his expression for any clue about Cooper.

"Cooper is going to be out next week," he says to Leo. "This is it."

"That's too bad," Leo says softly.

"What is it?" I ask Carson.

Jess and Dylan flank me like two protective sentinels.

"Can I talk to you outside, Imogene?" Carson beckons me with his hand.

When I stand to leave the table, I notice the looks cast between Jess and Dylan and the rest of the table. They all know what's going on with Cooper. It's me; I'm the clueless one.

An early autumn chill blows across the porch as I follow Carson. I stand behind him as he looks out at the majestic view of hills that will be changing colors soon. I wrap my arms around myself, shivering, thinking about the summer fun that was short-lived. I'm already depressed, thinking about the upcoming cruel winter.

Carson turns around and looks glum.

"What's wrong with Cooper?" My voice sounds tiny.

"How much did he tell you about his mom?"

"She's an accountant or CFO … She's divorced from his dad and lives across the street—"

"He didn't tell you that she was diagnosed with ovarian cancer a few months ago?" Carson looks past me as if he's debating on what he can say to me.

"No," I utter in disbelief. "He told me there was family *drama*. That's basically how he put it. His family had some issues, and he went there to help out. He didn't give me any details. He said he was frustrated with his family."

"It's more than that," Carson says. "His mother is dying. That's why he's been staying with her in Brooklyn."

"Oh, no. I didn't know any of this."

I feel both sad for Cooper and selfishly hurt that he didn't share this with me. If my mother was sick or dying, I'd like to think I'd turn to my friends and Cooper for solace. In all the time we were together, he didn't once mention his mother's illness or show any signs of grief.

"That was him on the phone," Carson explains. "She's had months of treatment and had a brief period of remission. Then she became sick again. They opened her up a couple of days ago to find the cancer had spread everywhere. Nothing more can be done, so they sent her home, and Cooper and his family are going to sit with her until the end. All they can do is minimize her pain."

As I shiver, Carson puts his warm hands on my arms. "I broke up with him,"—my voice breaks—"but I really do care about him."

"I know."

"I should be there with him. I want to go see him now. Do you think I can do that?" I ask, almost pleading.

"Yes." Carson nods as though he expects this from me.

"I haven't been kind to Cooper over the past few weeks, and I haven't called him once. Would my appearance be an intrusion on his family or his time with his mother?"

Carson grips my bare arms and looks down at me in

294

earnest. "If I was sitting by my mother's side, watching her die, I'd want Jess with me. If I was Cooper, I'd want to see you. I'm betting doing all the necessary things with his family, being strong and holding others up, is hard."

"But we're back to being friends again, friends that don't speak," I say quietly. "Are you sure?"

"Whatever is going on inside of him has to be hell, so he definitely needs you. I think you should go."

"Good because I wasn't going to change my mind." A surge of relief and strength empowers me. "I need my jacket and car keys." I turn to head back into the house.

"Wait." Carson fidgets. "There's something else I want to tell you, even though by doing this I'm breaking a promise to Cooper. I don't give a shit anymore. You should know."

"Know what?" I ask, unprepared for something more awful.

"The business loan—the investment money, I mean … It didn't come from the venture capital group I belong to. They don't invest in businesses as small as yours and only match funds."

"I don't understand. Lauren and I were with you and Archie in his office when we signed the papers. Why are you telling me now? I need to leave."

"This is about Cooper. That's why I'm telling you now so there are no more surprises. He approached me months ago about funding your business expansion. You kept putting Archie off about the loan, and Cooper thought he could help by fronting the money himself."

"Cooper owns our business?" I ask, shocked.

"No," Carson laughs weakly. "Archie is a sneaky lawyer, but he's on your side. He wouldn't let you sign contracts that could potentially hurt you. He agreed to Cooper's plan because you and Lauren retain ownership, and it wasn't a loan. Archie didn't have you read the fine print. Remember that next time. Business 101: read the fine print. We set it up so, if it's not paid off, it's forgivable. There's a hardship clause that relinquishes any liability. Archie drafted it. Well, Cooper set it up. It was his money."

I'm awestruck that Carson and Archie kept this from me and that Cooper never mentioned it. While I can't be angry with them for helping me, I am upset with my own poor business skills. Of course I should have read the fine print, but I trust Archie completely, and to him, he was doing Lauren and me a huge favor. He did.

"That was over fifty grand. Cooper has that kind of money?"

"Apparently. Guess he put away money for a rainy day."

"That's a big rainy day fund."

Carson shrugs. "He did have a nice government job, and before he moved here, he worked non-stop and didn't spend much on himself. You've seen his orange kitchen, haven't you?" Carson barely smiles.

"Yes, but when did he come up with the idea to be the main investor?"

"Early spring. It was before Dylan and Emma got married. Cooper approached Archie and me about it. He also told Leo because he didn't want any misunderstandings. Cooper thought it would give you two the kick in the ass to take your company seriously."

"That's before we started dating. I was kind of mean to him back then."

"Kind of?" Carson looks at me pointedly.

"Fine. Very mean. What was the advantage of him doing this if the profits don't come in for another year or so or if we fail and lose everything?"

"He gets the satisfaction of helping his friends, I suppose. It isn't just you. He's very close to Leo and Lauren. But I think you were the driving force behind his scheme. He is very … He really likes you, Imogene."

"I'm going to go now."

"Good."

I head back into the warm house and search for my purse and car keys, grabbing a leather jacket while Carson fills the others in about my decision.

"Do you want me to drive you on my bike?" Dylan asks.

It's adorable that he's serious. I almost laugh at the thought of me holding on in terror to my favorite maniac as we speed down the interstate to New York City. "Thanks. No. I'd like to make it in one piece." I pull his head down and kiss him on the cheek.

"Hey," he says, wrapping his arms around me. "Go do what you have to do, Imogene. Cooper could use some of your strength."

"Don't you want to pack a bag?" Lauren asks.

I don't want to waste time changing clothes. I'm wearing my nice jeans and a red, short-sleeve blouse under my leather jacket. My ballet flats will have to do. I just want to get on the road.

"No, I don't want to be presumptuous and invite myself into his family's home. I may be back tonight. I really don't know."

"I programmed the address of his mother's home into the GPS," Leo says, handing me my phone.

"Thank you." I'm becoming nervous again as they all stare at me with compassion and worry. "I'll be fine."

When Carson walks me to my car, I can't get to it fast enough. I've never been so happy to see my shit-mobile. For once, this crappy little car is my ticket to freedom, to see the person that has my heart in his ironclad fist.

"You sure you don't want to take my car?" Carson looks dubiously at my car and kicks the front wheel. "Everyone borrows the Beemer. It would be a better ride."

"I don't care about the ride. I just want to get there."

"Okay, but use the GPS. Don't get lost down on Canal Street again, and pay attention to the bridges."

"I will. You won't have to rescue me again."

"I don't mind, but I want you to drive safely. Focus on the road. And, if you have any problems, you call me right away. You got it?"

"Yes, Dad," I reply as I buckle myself in.

Carson leans in and gives me a peck on the cheek. "It's good you're doing this. Don't worry. No matter how much shit you've given Cooper, he's going to be glad to see you."

"Coming from a big, dopey guy, that means a lot to me." I shoot Carson a hopeful smile before I drive away.

Twenty-Seven

By late afternoon, I'm circling the Park Slope block, looking for a parking spot. I haven't been to Brooklyn or anywhere, for that matter, in a long time, and I have forgotten that every place outside of little Hera has lots of people, lots of cars, lots of traffic, and absolutely no parking spots.

I wedge my car between two high-end luxury cars and walk the two blocks to Fiona MacKenzie's home. I'm fairly certain that I'm parked illegally and may get towed, but I don't care.

It's a beautiful neighborhood of historic brownstones, and the cars and exquisitely renovated homes signify new money. As I walk by each home with its black iron gate, I peer in the windows to get a good look at what a three million dollar house in Brooklyn gets you. From what I can see, there are designer kitchens and living rooms that would make anyone drool. There are a few homes that haven't been renovated, making me suspect the residents are older and have owned the home for generations.

One of the MacKenzie homes stands before me, four imposing floors towering tall and narrow above me. I have no idea what lurks behind the white shades that are drawn.

Drawing in a deep breath, I take the intimidating walk up the steep, front stoop. The door has a glossy black finish with a massive antique doorknocker. I'm thinking of how silly I would feel pounding that knocker when I spot the doorbell off to the side. I push it and wait, looking around at the pretty, tree-lined street.

The door is opened by a young woman who looks a bit

older than me. She has long, dark hair, but her gray eyes and face resemble Cooper's.

"Hello," she states, her jeans and food-stained T-shirt suggesting that I'm not underdressed. The dark half-moons under eyes and the gaunt cheeks also give away the duress of the circumstances.

"Hello. I'm Imogene Walsh, a friend of Cooper's."

Her eyes glint with recognition of my name. "Imogene, hello. It's so nice of you to come. I'm Greer. Here, come in." She opens the door all the way and steps aside.

"Sorry, I should have called first, but no one has ever accused me of having good manners," I blurt out.

I'm not trying to be funny, but Greer smiles anyway, her whole expression creasing with exhaustion. Of course, considering the noise level of the home's inhabitants along with taking care of her mother, she must be running on nerves and caffeine.

"It's no problem. We wouldn't hear the phones, so it's good you showed up." She points her finger up and circles it in the air. "It's so noisy here. All the relatives are hanging out at my mom's house and the kids have taken over the place, as you can see."

The living room to the left of the door is tastefully decorated with contemporary furniture and art work, and the couches and chairs are occupied by men and some teenagers who are watching a pre-season football game on the flat screen TV mounted on the far wall. At least a dozen children are running in and out of the living room and down the hallway.

"Hi, Imogene." Peyton waves somberly from the couch.

I wave to him and the others I recognize, Evan and Uncle Fraser.

"Let's go find Cooper for you," Greer says, leading me up a narrow staircase to the right of the living room. "He's on the second floor, helping Neil take care of the little kids so I can get some chores done."

We enter a large room that seems like an all-purpose kids' room with toys, a changing table, and two cribs. In the middle of the floor, Cooper and Neil are face down with their heads buried in their folded arms, small children walking up and down their backs. Three other kids are pushing toy cars over their heads and around their arms.

"Owen, stomp harder," Cooper says gruffly. The little boy who must be about two begins jumping on Cooper's back.

"Perfect, kiddo."

A little girl is walking gingerly on Neil's back to keep her balance.

"Massage time is over," Greer announces. "Cooper, you have company."

He looks up. "Imogene," he says softly. "Owen, off."

The little boy tumbles off his broad back as Cooper slowly rises to his knees and then stands up and hands Owen off to Greer. Neil acknowledges me with a head tilt.

"I have to go finish working in the kitchen," Greer says to Cooper. "Why don't you take Imogene down to the study so you can talk in private?"

"Who's with Mom?" Cooper asks.

"Dad is still sitting with her."

After Cooper nods at his sister, she leaves, and he studies me for a beat then gives me the faintest of smiles. A screaming wrestling match between two of the kids crawling on Neil prompts him to finally react.

"Come with me."

I follow him down the hall to an empty office, decorated with feminine touches. It has two windows that overlook a tiny backyard. Cooper shuts the door behind us.

"Hi," I say, hovering next to the tidy, modern desk.

"This is a nice surprise," he says, staying close to the door.

I don't know what the protocol for enemies-to-loversto-friends should be during a time like this, but I'm not going to waste this trip by pretending to be a shy, ridiculous girl. I step forward and throw my arms around his waist, pulling him in for a hug. I feel the tension release from his body, and then his arms wrap around me firmly.

"Hi," he says, nuzzling my head.

"You didn't call." I hug him harder.

"You didn't call, either, and there came a point where I thought maybe it was too late, that I should leave you alone."

"I told you to call me if things got bad. *This* is bad, Cooper. It's my fault, though. I should have been the one to check on you."

"You're here." He pulls back and looks down at me. "Thank you."

"Carson told me everything right after you called today. I wasn't going to miss this chance to be with you, and ... and I want to meet your mother. If she wants to, that is."

"She'll want to meet you."

"Carson didn't tip you off that I was coming?"

"No. Maybe he didn't want to say anything in case you decided to turn around and drive back home. I'm not crazy about the idea of you driving all this way and trying to find your way around Brooklyn."

"I wasn't going to change my mind. I had no doubts about what I was doing. I wasn't sure how you'd react, though."

"I'm very glad you're here. Everything just got a little bit better. Where's your bag?"

"I didn't bring anything."

Cooper looks at me questioningly. "You're driving back tonight?"

"I'm not sure what I'm doing. I came to see you and your mother. I didn't think beyond that."

"You can borrow some of Greer's stuff and anything

302

of mine. My mom gets really groggy at night, so let's try to see her now. Is that okay?"

I nod, eager and nervous as hell.

I follow Cooper up another narrow staircase. It's quieter up here, no running, boisterous children. Fiona's room is at the end of the hall, towards the back of the house.

The door is open as we arrive, and a young man who I assume is a nurse is checking an IV line in Fiona's arm. Propped up in her bed, I can tell she is taller than me but shrunken. Her bald head is wrapped in a mint green scarf, and she's wearing a bulky, hand-knit sweater over a pajamas set. She, more than any other family member, resembles Cooper. He clearly has her face. I imagine she once had long, blond hair, as well.

On the other side of the bed is a large armchair with a big, burly man with dark, cropped hair sitting and leaning over, holding Fiona's frail hand. With her other hand, she pushes the sweater off her shoulders to adjust to the overly heated room. She's wearing the necklace Cooper bought from me that one day back in my home studio when I became aware of my awkward crush on him.

"Mom, Dad, this is Imogene," Cooper says, taking me by the hand and leading me into the cozy bedroom to the empty chair next to his father.

"I'm Stu," his father says, standing to shake my hand. "This is Fi." He looks lovingly at his former wife. From how Cooper described his family, I was expecting some shouting or at least cruel indifference. However, these are clearly people who care for one another.

"It's wonderful to finally meet you," Fiona says with an exhaled laugh.

"You, too." I smile with relief.

"I'm done here, Fi," the young man says, picking up a clipboard and taking notes. "I'm going to go eat dinner. I'll send Greer or Cooper up with another shake. Then I'll be

303

back."

"Great, another shake." Fiona makes a disgusted face, and the man smiles. "Thanks, Nishant."

"I'm going to go help Greer with feeding the kids. Cooper, why don't you take my seat?" Stu kisses Fiona's hand then heads for the door where Nishant is picking up a medical case.

"Actually, Cooper can help you, Stu." A curious smile passes between Fiona and Cooper. "I'd like to speak to Imogene alone."

Cooper gives me an extra long look. "She doesn't bite." He leaves with the other men, glancing back at me as I move to the chair closest to Fiona.

"Cooper looks brighter. Was he expecting you?" she asks me in a tired yet friendly voice.

"No. I only heard about ... I decided today, just jumped in the car and drove."

"Then it's a nice surprise for all of us. I get to talk to someone new who isn't stabbing me with needles or trying to make me drink another revolting nutrition supplement."

"You've hit the jackpot with me. I hate needles, and I was a terrible waitress. Cooper may have informed you about that."

"You made this, right?" As she hooks her thumb in the necklace, I nod.

"Cooper gave this to me a couple of months ago when I got sick again. After all we had been through—years of him not really speaking to me ... or Stu—and then he showed up with this beautiful necklace. He had changed, and he was ... happy. Who doesn't want to see their son happy? I think it's because of you."

"I don't know if I can take credit for that. I think Cooper is fairly happy living in Hera because of his friends and his job there."

"Yes, he's told me about that, although it took months to get that out of him."

Fiona coughs into her fist, and I can't take my eyes off the emerald ring she's wearing. It's an emerald in an emerald cut, beautiful and simple, the way I like gems. She notices me staring at it.

"It was a gift from Stu when we got married. I've always worn it, even when we got divorced."

"It's lovely. Green is my favorite color, and the emerald cut is my number one choice."

Fiona adjusts her headscarf and then tries to push herself up straighter, as though she's suddenly self-conscious of her appearance. She groans slightly, and the pain crosses her face in a tight grimace.

"May I help you?" I lean forward with my arms outstretched, ready to assist her tiny body.

"I'm fine. Thank you." She leans back against her pillows. "When Nishant returns, he's going to dope me up again. I don't want to waste this brief time we have together on small talk. I'm not much of a small talk kind of woman."

"Neither am I."

"Good, then I'll cut to the chase. I haven't met one of Cooper's girlfriends since he was with Sofia. Did he tell you about her?"

I shake my head, hating this topic already.

"She was his girlfriend in high school and college. She broke up with him after college graduation. It was years ago. She went off to med school, and Cooper joined the police force and then the FBI and was absent from our lives for most of the last six years. He showed up for family weddings and births, but he has kept his distance from Stu and me. Until a few months ago."

She gives me a good hard look. "Do you love my son?"

I thought I was a direct person, but she certainly surprises me. I feel the heat rise on the back of my neck, my hands fidget, and I let my eyes roam the photographs on

305

the wall.

"It's a simple yes or no."

I meet her stern expression. "Yes, I love Cooper. Technically, we're not together any more, though."

Her expression relaxes. "Pity. It's difficult to love someone you think you can't be with."

I nod, and sit back in the armchair.

"And yet you came all this way to see him?"

"And to meet you."

"Good. It's good to meet the mother of the man you love, especially if she's dying and you want to see what makes him tick."

It's mortifying to think she considers me an opportunist, and my expression must reflect that because she lets out a weak laugh. "I didn't mean to sound crass. I genuinely think it's admirable that you came to meet me. I am pleased that you feel it's important enough to know me since I have very little time left. You must care an awful lot about Cooper to come to the MacKenzie house when everyone is on death watch when you and Cooper are not even *together,* as you say."

"You said it. I don't know what will happen, if anything, with Cooper and me, but I wasn't about to miss the chance to meet you."

"I like you, Imogene. And I like you more for saying that." She smiles. "Then it's my duty to tell you about Cooper and all those little pieces of the puzzle that you may be missing."

"You read my mind. How did you know?"

"Because, when my son comes back into my life after a long absence and is happy about a young woman, and then the next time he's sad about her, I know something is up. I have to take a lot of responsibility for what happened in his life and the effect I've had on him and this family. I don't know how much he told you."

"Very little. He said his family was full of liars and

cheaters and divorce is inevitable for anyone who marries a MacKenzie."

"Ouch," Fiona says then looks around the room at all the photographs of her children at different stages. "It was foolish of me to think all of that was behind us. Cooper still harbors a grudge. I didn't know. I'm grateful he chose to return, and I've been given a second chance to see the old Cooper, the one who used to be my most sensitive child and most loving."

"I am, too. This big family suits him."

"It always did. He loved the family togetherness. It was when Stu and I divorced that Cooper became disenchanted with all of us. I was very cavalier about the divorce. I thought kids, especially teenagers, were resilient and Cooper would get over it, and in time, we'd be close again. I was very wrong about that. But, because Stu and I were not faithful to one another, in Cooper's eyes, it was a betrayal to the whole family. It was. And it only got worse when we both remarried and had more failed marriages. I didn't realize the effect I had on my kids until three of my children also had marriages that ended up in divorce. Cooper took everyone's failings personally and blamed his parents, rightly so, for the disintegration of the very safe, loving world we had initially created. Stu and I have talked about this a lot."

"You two seem very close, considering you're divorced."

"We still love each other. The mistake we made all those years ago was that we chose to give up instead of working on our problems. It seemed so easy to divorce and start over with new people, and I loved my corporate job. All I thought about was how my life wouldn't change much.

"This house was our investment property that we bought relatively cheaply before the housing boom, and we rented it out in those days. After the divorce, I moved here and brought in a new husband, and Stu remarried and had more kids. Cooper's world was turned upside down. Two houses, more siblings, separate households, constant fighting between Stu and me and the new spouses, and when you mix that in with my kids' teenage hormones, it was a disaster."

"I thought he was lucky for having a big family." I shrug. "I didn't think it could be as bad as he claimed."

"I'm optimistic that he thinks his family is getting better. I'd like to think I'm leaving him with some hope."

"I believe he wants to help his family, but I don't think he has much hope of his own."

"Ah. That is what's keeping you two apart."

"We have different ideas, yes."

"Behind you, in the bookcase, would you get that photo album on the bottom that has Cooper's name on it?"

I get up from my chair and peruse the bookcase which is jam-packed with photo albums on every shelf. I find the albums with the kids' names and pull out the one dedicated to Cooper. I hand it to Fiona, who opens it to the first page and holds it up for my viewing. It's a full page photo of her holding Cooper as he bounces on her lap. His white blond hair matches hers, as does his wide-tooth smile.

"He was two here. Adorable, wasn't he?"

"Very. He still is."

"Take it." She hands me the heavy album.

"You want me to put it away?"

"No, I want you to keep it."

I trace Cooper's name with my fingers, feeling an itchy desire to greedily take the coveted photographic archives of the man who has me in an emotional quandary.

"I can't. This is too precious to leave with me. Shouldn't you give it to Cooper or Greer to keep safe?"

"You'll appreciate it more." Fiona closes her eyes tightly with a sudden expression of pain, taking a deep breath. "I hope you don't let Cooper lead you to believe in that MacKenzie curse nonsense. It was one thing when he felt betrayed as a teenager, but he's a grown man and has to adapt like everyone else. He can be happy … Don't back down on where you stand, Imogene."

Oddly, her indirect and somewhat cryptic statements make perfect sense to me.

"And I have to ask one last favor of you, and I do not want you to be offended."

"Okay. What can I do for you?"

"Please, don't stay here. Don't attend my funeral. I want you to remember me like this and our nice conversation. Go back to Hera and be there when Cooper goes back. He'll need friends. He's a very capable man, but under that tough exterior is a very vulnerable man, and it makes me happy to think that you'll be there … as his friend or more."

"Oh … all right," I say with some dismay at being sent away.

Before I can say anything more, Nishant arrives and immediately recognizes Fiona's pain. He begins fiddling with the bags hanging on the IV pole and then administers a syringe into one of the tubes.

"Is that better, Mom?" Cooper suddenly asks with concern from the doorway. With his hands shoved in his jeans pockets and his hair hanging in his face, he looks like a big, shy kid.

"Yes. I love Nishant." She smiles at the young nurse.

Nishant chuckles, his boyish good looks making him look like he could be twenty or forty.

Fiona's eyes close and I assume she's drifting to sleep until her hand shoots out and grabs mine with a gentle grip.

"Imogene." She smiles, opening her eyes briefly before closing them again.

I stand and look down at her, knowing this is the last time I will see her. Then I say goodbye to Nishant, who will be with her when she takes her last breath, and I meet

Cooper in the hallway.

"What have you got there?"

"Your mother insisted I take this photo album for myself. It's all about you." I hug the album to my chest in case he thinks he's going to put it back in his mother's room.

"Why does she think you'd want that old thing?"

"Because it's when you were a happy family, and it was the most important part of your life."

"*Was* being the operative word. The present is more important."

"I'll take good care of it unless you would rather have it."

"No. You keep it." He taps the book with a finger, contemplative for a moment. "You must be hungry. Let's have some dinner together."

My thoughts hang on that word *together*.

Twenty-Eight

Every room on the first floor is overcrowded. More relatives and friends have arrived with covered casserole dishes and bags of food that they hand off to Fiona's sister Beth, who is running the kitchen. People fill plates, taking food from the mysterious aluminum covered trays and the beverages and desserts scattered across the kitchen island and table. They eat standing up, leaving their dirty plates and dishes on any available surface before they move into the living room to visit with Fiona's immediate family members.

I watch Beth and Greer trying to clean the kitchen and organize food, astounded that they can keep up with the traffic of bodies in their way.

Two giggling little toddlers I saw earlier in the playroom are naked except for their diapers. They latch on to Cooper's legs.

"Someone smells really ripe," Cooper's voice booms as he looks down at the two cuties jumping on his leg.

Cooper picks up the girl. "Is it you, Nikki?" He sniffs her diaper and then puts her down.

"I dumped!" the boy says gleefully, standing with his chubby, baby hands behind his back.

"Owen," Cooper feigns disapproval. He picks him up, the foul odor overpowering. "Whoa! You've got a big bomb in there, kiddo." He puts Owen under an arm and hoists up Nikki with his other arm.

"Evan said he'd put them to bed for me," Greer says.

"Okay. I'll change them and then hand them over to him." Cooper laughs as he holds the floppy gigglers at his sides. "Wait here, Imogene. I'll be right back."

I take my jacket off and hang it and my handbag on the back of a kitchen stool.

When Cooper returns, he greets a few more people, and then we sit at the messy counter island.

"What would you like to eat?" Cooper asks me with a serving spoon poised above a tray of macaroni and cheese. There are eight other similar trays with unidentifiable casseroles.

"Whatever you're having." Among all these strangers and under the circumstances, I'm not at ease, and filling my empty, nervous stomach has little appeal.

Cooper fills my plate with goopy concoctions and then makes one for himself with enormous proportions to satisfy a giant. Greer passes us bottles of cold water from the fridge.

"This place is a disaster," she says to Cooper. "It's not just this kitchen, the downstairs bathrooms ... and that living room is trashed." Behind her, Beth stacks the unopened casserole dishes on top of one another and leans back against the counter with an exhausted sigh.

"I doubt Mom cares," Cooper says solemnly as he chews.

I take a few bites of food, but my heart isn't in it. I put my fork down and watch Cooper and Greer discuss how to get the house organized and keep people moving in and out for the next few days.

"Cooper?" A very pretty woman stands at the entrance to the kitchen. At the sight of her, my stomach lurches as if it's about to expel the few lumps of noodles and lettuce I managed to swallow.

"Sofia, hi." Cooper gets up from his stool and strides across the room to give her a big hug.

Sofia, my brain whispers to me. Sofia, the girlfriend from high school and college. Sofia, the doctor. Sofia, a gorgeous brunette with green eyes; long, straight glossy

312

hair; and a perfect figure. She's taller and slimmer than me, dressed casually yet very chic in a white, silk blouse under a fitted leather jacket and a gauzy blue scarf wrapped around her neck. She looks like a model who stepped off the streets of Paris. She's utterly breathtaking. Beth and Greer obviously know her well and both step forward to give her hugs, too.

I feel rather plain, dumpy, and invisible next to her. I'm still holding the photo album in one hand. No way am I giving this back. While their little love fest is going on, I jam the album in my handbag that's hanging on the back of the chair. I remind myself that Sofia is Cooper's ex-girlfriend. She's in the past. I'm the present. *I'm the present ex-girlfriend.*

"Sofia, this is Imogene," Cooper says, smiling with his hand out towards me.

"It's a pleasure to meet you," Sofia says, displaying a sincere smile.

"Hello." I jump off the stool and put my hand out for a quick shake while sizing her up. I have at least thirty pounds on her. Not to sound petty and jealous—*I am!*—but I could take her.

"I'm going to take Sofia upstairs to see my mother. Hopefully, she's awake," Cooper says to me. "I'll be back down soon."

"Okay, sure." I try to sound confident.

After they leave, Greer regards me with a sympathetic smile. "She's an ex. But it was years ago," she says to reassure me.

"No biggie," I lie with a nonchalant hand wave. "I have a great idea."

"What?" Beth asks wearily.

"You two sit down, eat, and relax. I'll clean up here. I have a lot of experience in this area of food service."

"You're a guest, Imogene. We don't expect you to do anything," Greer says flatly.

313

"I'm a friend. You're both going through a tough time, and I want to be useful. Sit down," I demand. Both women oblige me by coming around to my side of the kitchen island and sitting down on the stools.

I give Beth and Greer two nice ceramic plates from the cupboard, not the flimsy paper ones, and they serve themselves from the buffet set before them. Then, for the next two hours, I put the giant pots of stews into small, individualized serving containers and break down all the casseroles into smaller plastic and glass containers I find in the cupboards.

I label and stack everything in the fridge to make it easy to find and serve them. I re-plate all the desserts and place them on the kitchen table along with stacks of paper plates and plastic utensils so people can serve themselves. I find Peyton and have him set up lined trash cans at the entrance to the kitchen and by the table so it's obvious to anyone eating that they must clear their own garbage. Then I set up a beverage station at the end of the island with bottles of soda, water, juice, and disposable cups.

When the rest of the kitchen island and all the counters are cleared and wiped down, I wash all the big pots and pans by hand and put them away. I clear one shelf in the fridge for any new incoming food brought by visitors while Greer and Beth watch me in silent appreciation. I have to admit, it feels good to put my diner skills to use.

After all the food is organized, the kitchen is immaculate, and I've created a flow for making serving, eating, and cleaning easier, I plunk down on the stool between the two women.

"Thank you," Beth exclaims with some renewed energy. "The kitchen hasn't looked this nice in weeks."

"It was my pleasure. Thank you for letting me be with your family today."

I don't have to mention that part of my lengthy visit and industrious kitchen endeavor is due to wanting to see

314

Cooper who has been upstairs all this time. I'm losing hope that he will return any time soon.

"My mother and Sofia were close for many years," Greer says, as if she can read my mind. "They haven't seen each other in a long time, and Cooper hasn't seen her, either. They're just catching up."

"I need to get going." I stand and pick up my bag and jacket, the precious photo album making the bag rather heavy.

"You can't drive back tonight. It's too late," Greer says, standing up to take their plates and glasses to the dishwasher.

"I didn't plan on spending the night. I'll be fine driving back. There's less traffic now."

"No. You have to stay. My dad's house is across the street. Evan took my kids over there and put them to bed in my old room. I can set you up in the boys' old room. They're bunk beds, but I can loan you a T-shirt to sleep in, and you'll have the bathroom to yourself. It's just my dad, me, and my kids staying over in that big house. Cooper and the others are camping out here on couches and whatever bed they can find."

I contemplate this for a moment, sleeping in Cooper's childhood room. I really am too tired to take that confusing drive back to Hera tonight, and with my mind obsessing about Cooper, I'm liable to crash my car.

Imogene, you want to stay near the Viking, my inner voice nags.

315

Twenty-Nine

The decision to not leave right away gives me a tinge of hope. Greer walks me across the street to her father's brownstone a few houses down. When we enter, I notice it hasn't been renovated. It has the musty scent of older furniture and décor used by a big, bustling family years ago. The home is dark and quiet.

"My dad is asleep and hopefully my kids are, too," Greer says as she leads me up a narrow staircase similar to the one in her mother's home. The rows of houses all built during the same Victorian time are attached side by side and have the same layout unless they have been renovated by new, wealthy owners.

We peek in Greer's childhood room and look towards the big, pink bed where Owen and Nikki are fast asleep. Then she leads me down the hall and flips on the light switch in the boys' old room. It's painted blue, has two bunk beds with plaid comforters, several posters of heavy metal bands, and dusty models of ships and planes.

"The bedding was cleaned a few days ago and no one has been using this room. Cooper sleeps on one of my mom's couches or on the floor in the kids' playroom, and my other brothers stay at their own homes every night since they live nearby. So, you have the bedroom to yourself. Do you want to borrow a night shirt?"

"No. I'm fine."

Greer leaves and returns with a package of toothbrushes. "Bathroom is right through that door," she points. "I'll see you in the morning."

I brush my teeth in the dated, blue-tiled bathroom, turn

off the overhead light, and lie on top of the comforter of one of the bottom bunks. Then I turn on my side and face a window, staring at the branches of a tree for what seems like hours before I close my eyes and try to meditate the way Cooper has explained it to me. That's a big fail. I'm too restless to fall asleep, and I can't clear my brain from thinking.

I pop my eyes open when I hear the click of the door opening and heavy footsteps on the rug.

"Imogene," Cooper whispers. I feel his hand gently rest on my hip and the mattress sink as he sits on the bed. "Are you asleep?"

"No." I turn over to face him.

His sculpted features look more severe in the moonlight yet still handsome and beautiful. I yearn to touch his face and kiss his lips, but I don't move.

He studies me for a few seconds then leans down and kisses my forehead. I smell Sofia's floral perfume on him. "Can I stay here with you for a bit? I need to get out of that house for a while."

"Sure. I turn back to my side, and he lies down and spoons me, but there are a few inches of space between our fully clothed bodies to keep it innocent. It doesn't temper the desire surging through my veins, though. The yearning has turned into a burning lust. I cross my arms in front of me and keep my hands to myself as Cooper moves his head closer to mine until I feel his breath on the back of my neck.

"My mother is dying," he says in a low, sad voice. His arm snakes around my waist, and I take his hand in mine and bring it to my lips. We hold each other like that until I hear his breathing change and his body leans into mine, heavy with slumber.

Perhaps he wears Sofia scent because of simple hugs or maybe there's more between them. It doesn't change how I feel about him, though. In fact, seeing him tonight

317

makes it harder to stop myself from falling deeper and deeper in love with him.

I think my love for him must be an endless pit. I keep falling, and I don't know how I'll find my way out.

I wake before him when it's early and barely light outside. I untangle my body gently from Cooper and slip out of bed. I brush my teeth and grab my shoes, bag, and jacket then tiptoe down the creaky, old staircase.

"Good morning," Greer says, coming down the hall from the kitchen. "Dad and the kids are still asleep. I made coffee and eggs. Will you join me?"

"Thank you, but I need to get on the road before the traffic gets bad." I slip on my shoes and slink towards the front door.

"Oh," she says, disappointed. "Okay. Well, I hope I get to see you more often. Next time I come to visit Cooper, we should get together."

"I'd like that." Against my typical protocol, I give Greer a hug. "I'll be thinking about you and your mom."

"Thank you."

She slouches against the front door, waving goodbye as I cross the street to find my car. Fortunately, it wasn't towed. I toss my bag and jacket in the car and drive out of the tight parking spot.

I roll down my window for fresh air and drive slowly down the one-way street that takes me back past both Fiona's and Stu's homes. Greer is gone when I drive past. A sickening wave of melancholy begins to swirl in my gut and work its way up to my chest where it sits there like a dead weight. Everything about leaving Cooper here feels wrong.

"Imogene!"

As I glance over my shoulder and see Cooper running down the sidewalk, I slow down and check for him in the side mirror. He jumps on a car and runs the length of it before landing in the street. I stop, blocking the cars behind me, and Cooper runs around to the driver's side and flings open my door.

"You didn't even say goodbye!" he says, out of breath.

"I didn't want to wake you. You need the rest, Cooper." I glance back at the cars honking at us and then take in his tired yet determined eyes that regard me with disappointment.

"You thought you could sneak away?" he asks.

"I'm not sneaking away. Your mom asked me not to be here for the funeral. She asked me very nicely to leave," I explain in a shaky voice.

"I know," he says. "Damn, I hate this."

While I nod, our eyes lock, and we both move in for a kiss. A real one. A needy one. His tongue pushes between my lips, and I meet him with the same hunger, thankful there's no trace of Sofia's perfume, just Cooper's musky, manly scent. The kiss ends when the fed-up morning commuters lean on their car horns all at once.

"I'm not leaving. I'm going back to Hera. I'll be there when you come back. You'll need friends to lean on." I take all the romance out of that kiss in a matter of seconds.

"Friends," he says. "Right … okay … Bye, Imogene."

Once he closes my door, I drive away, watching him in the rearview mirror as a caravan of cars follows me.

Thirty

Four days after I return home, Fiona passes away with her family at her bedside. Three days after her death, the family holds the funeral. I receive all of this information secondhand from Leo. Cooper and I haven't spoken since that morning I left him standing in the street.

When he returns the following week, pulling his truck into the parking lot, I stop what I'm working on and look out the window to watch him. He unloads a box from the back of his truck, holding it in one hand and closing the gate with the other. He pauses and looks directly at me. With a single wave, he looks away and walks inside the factory.

"Kcuf," I say softly.

"What's wrong?" Lauren asks from the table where she's working with Anita on a complicated necklace.

"Nothing." I return to my seat.

"Cooper is back," Tracy says for Lauren's benefit.

"Good," Lauren says as she searches for a bead that fell from her hand. "We'll have to invite him over for dinner soon. He needs his friends around him."

With Lauren's baby bump finally showing, she has taken on a more motherly tone overall, as though it's her duty to act older.

"He has a lot of friends at work. He's very comfortable in that factory," I remind her.

If she invites him over for dinner too soon, it may be awkward for him, for us. I feel like I've rejected him twice, although my heart would disagree. Does he really want to be around me when he's still grieving? My presence may spark some hostility on his part, or maybe I'm jumping ahead again. Maybe Sofia is back in his life and my feelings for him aren't relevant. Considering my position on future commitments is entirely the opposite of Cooper's; it would be easier to suffer the heartache now rather than later, get him out of my system and love him like a brother.

I can't stand our separation; as a result, two days later, I get up the nerve to take a homemade pie to Cooper's house. I have to see him. I have to talk him. I have to know if this is all there is or if there's more for us.

My nerves and emotions have gone haywire since Lauren's wedding. A thousand times, I've talked myself into pursuing him and then talked myself into forgetting him. You can't pursue someone who doesn't share the same basic fundamentals about being a couple, and worse, you cannot forget someone if your heart is holding on with a Titan's grip.

I drive up to Cooper's house, the surrounding autumn colors giving me a little boost. I'm wearing my new, tall boots and a fitted, leather jacket while hoping I don't come across as trying to look like Sofia.

As I lift the apple pie off the passenger seat, it's still warm in my hands. Cooper's front door is open and I hear pounding, the sound of some type of construction. I only see his bike and truck, no other vehicles, so I'm hoping he doesn't have visitors, namely one beautiful doctor. I walk through the doorway and head down to the kitchen where I find Cooper smashing his cupboards and counters with a sledgehammer.

I'm too enthralled with the way he throws his whole body into the destruction of the woodwork and orange Formica to say anything, and besides, nothing can be heard over the deafening sound of the splintering wood. When he turns for another swing, Cooper notices me. He stops mid-swing and lowers the sledgehammer.

"Hey," he says in a neutral tone.

"Hi. My grandmother made you an apple pie." I hold it up higher. "You're working on your house again. That's certainly one way of removing the old cabinets. Or is this a Dylan Blackard method of working off aggression?"

"It's a good release, yes." He tosses the sledgehammer into a pile of debris. "But if Bonnie makes me pie, I'm eating pie." He walks towards me and takes the pie then pulls two forks from the silverware drawer.

I notice boards with swatches of stones and wood, so I peruse them more closely. "I like this stone for the tiles, and I like the cherry wood for the cupboards."

Cooper looks at my color scheme choices and then holds up the pie. "Let's eat this thing." When he nods towards the porch, I follow him.

Since I was last here, retractable glass panes have been added over the screens. "You made it a full-season porch?"

"Carson convinced me to do it. The screens are removable and the glass opens like a gas station door."

"I see that. Good idea. Very cool."

He places the pie on a coffee table and tosses two cushions from the new wicker couch on the floor. They're still encased in heavy plastic, so when we sit down on them, they make a ruckus.

"I suppose it's time to set up this room," he says, looking around.

"It's time to eat pie."

He digs in with his fork and takes several mouthfuls. "Fucking good," he growls.

"I should have brought vanilla ice cream to go with it."

"Pie this good doesn't need ice cream. You better have some of this, or I'm going to eat it all."

I take a bite and the warm, soft apples ooze together with the cinnamon and brown sugar, a familiar taste from my grandma's home.

"Culinary perfection. I love your grandmother's food."

He polishes off half the pie without my help and then puts his fork down. "Why couldn't anyone bring this kind of food to the grief buffet?"

"Oh, I'm sorry. I should have thought of that."

Cooper smiles. "I'm joking. I can't remember what we were eating at my mom's house. It was a never-ending supply of food. It was nice that all those people came through the house and brought us food, but I don't think any of us could really taste anything. We were eating because we were supposed to. I feel like I'm tasting food for the first time. This pie is incredible. And so is the woman who brought it."

That feels good to hear, and I shiver like a little girl. At least I don't giggle. "How is your family doing?"

"Better. It helped to have my mom at home and everyone in the house every day. It was tiring, though. We all talked until we were sick of each other, but it made the funeral easier. And it's better knowing she's not in pain anymore."

"I like your family. Greer is really something. She was taking care of everyone. You, too. You're a natural with people. The big ones and the little, poopy ones."

"Yeah," he says with a laugh. "I've changed a lot of diapers over the years. Greer liked you, too. So did my mother."

I toy with another bite of pie, pushing it around in the pie tin.

"What's wrong? You're not talking as much as you usually do, and you haven't said anything snarky yet." He quiets my fidgety hand and removes the fork.

"Being snarky to someone who just lost his mother isn't really appropriate. Am I that bad?""

"I need someone to make me laugh. I've been fucking miserable without you these past few weeks."

"Me, too."

As I reach out to stroke his cheek, he catches my hand,

holding it against his leg.

"I didn't think I would ever feel that way about you," I say. "And I didn't think you could do it. But you did—you broke my heart."

His expression darkens. "You ripped my heart out, Imogene. How many times have you walked out on me? The last time I saw you, you left me standing in the street."

"Then let's make each other feel better. I won't mention how much you love your family and how everything you do revolves around them and that your opinion on marriage is bullshit."

Cooper scoffs with a faint smile.

"I won't mention any of that." I get on my hands and knees and crawl a breath away from his face. "For tonight, you can have my body, and we'll make each other feel good. Tomorrow, we'll go back to being frenemies and won't mention it."

"You've propositioned me when I'm at my weakest, and I want you more than anything I've ever wanted. I accept your terms, only because I'll most likely renege later. But you know that."

"I do, and I'm willing to take my chances because …"

"Because you want me inside of you."

"Yes." I'm unsteady at the thought of his naked body.

Cooper unzips my boots, pulls them off, and then strips my jacket and blouse off as he kisses me hard. I fall to the floor where he straddles me, helping me to remove the rest of my clothing. I undo his zipper and discover he's not wearing underwear. Then, after he removes his work boots, T-shirt, and jeans in a matter of seconds, I wrap my hand around his hard cock.

"I'd carry you to the bed, but I recall that you have a thing for the floor."

I shut him up with my mouth, pulling him down by the neck and kissing him until I have control over him. My other hand strokes him and rubs him against the wetness building in me. He's ready to push into me, and I want him to. I want it hard and fast, and I don't want to think about words like *love* and *forever*. My legs have him where I want.

As he's about to enter me, he jerks back. "I don't have a condom. Shit!" He's instantly a bundle of tense, knotted muscles above me.

"I've been on the pill since I was seventeen, and I've never had sex without a condom."

"I've never done it without a condom, either," he grits as though his composure is hanging by a thread.

"What about the pretty doctor?" I ask mostly to toy with him, although also out of a warped, jealous curiosity.

Cooper looks like he's being strangled. "Sofia? It's been at least six years. I always used a condom. I haven't been with anyone except you in the last six months."

That makes me smile, and I stroke the tip of him until he's slick and pulsing in my hand.

"Christ, can we do this?" He watches my hand fondle him. "Now?"

"Yes."

With the magic word, he thrusts into me with enough force to push the rug a foot backwards. I yelp as he fills me.

"Ah! God," he bellows. "This feels better than I expected. Jesus, why did I ever use condoms with you?"

"Because I told you to."

"Right." He smiles at me as he gains stability on his arms and tries out a few thrusts. "It's very different without armor. Let's make use of this." He lifts one of my legs and throws it over his shoulder. "You're very flexible, and I can think of quite a few things I want to do with you."

He adjusts his body so he's thrusting into me at an angle, slow at first with a circular motion. While I'm so wet and delirious with lust that my limbs feel detached and lifeless, Cooper is lost in his own nirvana over his newfound discovery, the raw contact between us as though

325

he's losing his virginity … to me.

He kisses his way down to my breasts and takes one peaked nipple in his mouth, sucking until I feel the sensation in my wet core, making me writhe against him. Then he moves to the other nipple and sucks it even harder before biting his way back up my throat. I shudder and moan and finally move my hands to grip his shoulders.

With him getting harder and stretching me, it sends me into a hysteria of need. I buck against him as he begins pounding into me, hitting that sweet spot. I cry out as the orgasm builds.

"Like that," I say breathlessly. "Harder … faster. I'm almost there."

Someone or something growls; it's either Cooper or a bear in the woods. I hold on as if I need to get closer to him as he keeps striking that beautiful spot. Then I arch up as the eruption builds in me. Cooper drops to his elbows and furiously pounds into me with short, fast thrusts that send me over the edge, spiraling into bliss.

He shouts my name and empties into me with three more thrusts before collapsing on top of me.

"Home run," I whisper, feeling spent.

Cooper chuckles but doesn't move.

"You're getting heavy," I say dreamily.

"Sorry. This feels so good. I don't want it to end."

"The night's not over."

He props himself up and puts his weight on his arms again then slowly detaches himself from me as if we're a fragile coupling. Then he looks at me with that beautiful, forlorn expression that makes me swoon for him. I close my eyes to shut out his beauty. I don't want a broken heart tonight; I just want to feel him again.

"I'm going to get us some water." He kisses me then grabs his boots.

"I'm going to run to the bathroom."

"You have to put on your shoes if you're going to walk

through the kitchen. There are nails and sharp broken things everywhere." He stands up, wearing only his steel-toed boots. I stare at him.

"Kcuf. You look hot like that."

"Hold that thought." He grins and goes into the kitchen.

While he rummages in the fridge, I slip on my knee length black boots and make my way across the kitchen to the bathroom. When I return, Cooper is leaning against the counter, chugging from a water bottle. As he sees me, he spits up some water and practically chokes. His eyes travel from my boots up my naked body, his cock springing to life and giving me a full salute. I put my hands on my hips and watch him with amusement.

"Shit, Imogene. You look like a naked Wonder Woman."

"It's the boots."

"It's the woman."

"Thank you."

He puts the bottle down and strides towards me, climbing over a pile of debris. Dressed, Cooper can be an intimidating figure; naked, in his big heavy boots, he looks like an imposing god who misplaced his toga.

He cradles my face in his hands and kisses me with a loving gentleness, as though something he lost has now returned. Those romantic thoughts swim through my head, and I should shut them off, tune them out. However, I may only have this one night with him, and I damn well am going to make the most of it. I will suffer the consequences later.

"Put your hands here," he commands as he places my palms on the edge of the remaining countertop. "Step back and bend over."

I do as he says, and he pushes my legs farther apart with his knee, his erection pressing against my ass as he palms my wet clit. It doesn't take much for him to make my legs weak in the knees as he circles and plays with my wet folds slowly, tauntingly, and with expert control considering how hard his cock rubs against me.

When he slips his fingers inside me, my head flops down and I grip the counter and let my hips go wild, undulating in ecstasy. I gasp as a sharp spasm of pleasure ripples from my center to the tips of my breasts. I am so close to climaxing, but Cooper is keeping it slow and steady, torturing me so I can't reach my happy ending.

"Cooper!" I say desperately.

He thrusts in from behind, almost knocking the wind out of me. I'm holding onto the counter at a ninety-degree angle as he holds my hips and jerks me back towards him with each thrust. The gentle giant is gone. Cooper is all power, forcefully gripping my hips to the point of pain and pulling me harder to bury himself deeper.

As his need grows and I feel him getting harder inside me, he begins to lose control, grunting and exhaling in a fury. Just when I think this goddamn beast is about to cheat me out of an orgasm, his fingers begin caressing my clit, and before I know it, he's rubbing the perfect spot with the perfect rhythm, making me wetter.

It's a good thing our brains don't have to work at this because I'm in a trance. Every nerve is tingling, my inner muscles clenching, trying their mightiest to hold on to him and the intoxicating joy as our bodies slap together. I scream some incoherent gibberish when I reach the pinnacle, and then I'm free falling, happily in a tailspin.

I'm mush; my brain, my muscles. I can't hold myself up any longer. Cooper leans against my back and wraps one strong arm under my waist and puts the other against the counter so I don't bang my head. Then he goes to town on my accommodating body, pounding into me and yelling appreciative remarks of satisfaction.

Standing me up, he holds my back against his chest so I feel his heart beating rapidly. He's still breathing hard, and I'm still in a boneless stupor. Finally, he kisses my neck and rests his chin on my head.

"This is great," he says. "Pie, boots, and oh, yeah, my favorite naked woman."

I laugh and turn around in his arms to kiss him again.

"Want to try out my new shower?"

"Actually, I want to try that new soaking tub I saw."

"Ah, you saw that, did you? I got it because you mentioned how much you like bubble baths. I've never seen the appeal of a bath myself."

"Then let me show you."

He grins and leads me back to his bedroom to the newly renovated master bath. The thirty-year-old combination shower and tub unit is gone. In its place is a glass-enclosed shower stall for two, and under the window is an enormous half-egg shaped soaking tub. For the next hour, I wash every part of him and show him how spectacular a bathtub can be for slipping, sliding, riding, and coming.

When we make it to the bed, Cooper rewards me by worshipping every part of my body with his mouth and skillful tongue. By the end, I'm another tired mess, ready to sleep, but Cooper has other ideas, more unfinished fantasies he wants to explore.

By three in the morning, we're falling asleep ... on the floor, tangled in the bedding that has been stripped from the mattress. We're surrounded by handcuffs, a couple of expensive ties, two cans of empty whipped cream, a bottle of honey that was a complete miss, and condom wrappers.

We wake up when a screeching bird smashes into the glass of the bedroom window, and I about piss the sheets. After we have one more round of sex in the shower, I feel like Cinderella—my time is up.

"Can I take you to the diner for breakfast?" Cooper's damp hair falls forward over his face as he buttons his jeans.

"No," I reply as I watch him cover up his sexy chest and abs with a clean T-shirt.

"Don't tell me you're spending another Saturday working."

"I'm helping Lauren with the nursery. I think I offered to paint it today."

"I can help. It will get done faster." He eyes my solemn face with suspicion, and rightly so.

"Cooper," I sigh. "We're back in the same place, and I told you I'm not settling for this. It's not good enough for me."

"I thought we weren't going to talk about this ..."

"This is bullshit. You thought that, after a night of sex, you'd skip back into my life and we'd carry on as if that little incident at the wedding never happened. It happened. You said you're never getting married, and I said I can't accept it."

"Last night, you said you weren't going to mention this—"

"Call me a liar!" I blurt out angrily. "I can't help it. I saw you with your family. All that stuff about them being unfaithful to their spouses has nothing to do with us. And I'm sick of you hiding behind your excuse that no one can be trusted, that everyone is a liar and a cheater. I don't buy it and neither do you."

"Hold on a minute," he says sternly.

"No, you hold on." I start crying. The woman who doesn't cry at weddings or over men is opening the flood gates for Cooper. "You are a good son; I heard it firsthand from your mother. You are a good brother; Greer and your brothers love you and depend on. You love being part of that family, and you gave everyone strength and love during a very sad time. I didn't think much about marriage before, but since I've seen what you want to take off the table, I'm furious about that. I love you, and I want all of that with you. The marriage with the noisy family, the

330

squabbling siblings, and the poopy diapers. And, yes, even the funerals when everyone has to come together."

"You love me?" He jumps forward to take my hand, but I slap his hand away.

"Is that all you heard? Because the rest of it is pretty important." I glare at him to hide my embarrassment that he can't return my heartfelt sentiment.

"We can still have that without a marriage certificate."

"No. What is your problem with paper—notarized certificates? Didn't you need one for your gun permit? Jesus Kcuffing Christ. Under your loose definition of living together in *your* house, I get a few drawers, we go off to work, and meet up at night for sex. But, if things get tough or even boring, walking away is an easy out."

"I'm not like that. And you love me."

"Stop saying that." I swat my hand blindly in front of me, but he jumps out of the way this time.

"But I'm *not* like that," he says more loudly.

"You're setting us up to both be like that. I want to build a life together, while you'd rather live side by side. It's not the same."

"If you really believed that, you wouldn't be with me."

"I'm not with you, right? We just hooked up for a night." I dab my eyes with my sleeve and head for the front door.

"Are you leaving me again? Seriously?" Cooper shouts as I stomp through the dirt driveway to my car. "Last time, you left me standing in the street!"

"Yes, I'm leaving. Again. This time, I'm driving off into the sunset!"

As I swing open my car door too hard and it bounces back and hits me in the ass, Cooper stands in his doorway with his arms crossed and that smug expression like the Jolly Green Giant.

"I've got news for you!" he shouts. "Sunset doesn't happen for another eight hours!"

331

Thirty-One

"Exactly what did you say to him?" Lauren asks two weeks later after she gets tired of seeing Cooper and me giving each other the silent treatment every day in the parking lot.

"That I love him and we're done. Something like that."

"You said you don't want to get married anytime soon, so why are you fighting about this?"

"Because he took it off the table."

"Oh, you and your stupid table."

"You know I'm right. If Leo had said that a month or two into dating, you would have dumped him."

Lauren purses her lips and looks down at the gravy she's stirring for the pot roast. "You're right. I would have broken up with Leo if we weren't on the same page. But I'm kind of sad about you and Cooper because you two are so great together. He went through a really tough time reuniting with his mother, and then he had to watch her die. This isn't the time to talk about if you're on the same page. This is the time to be together and let him heal or grieve. Then maybe the other things you want will come later."

"What if they don't? What if I fall more in love with him and then face a more devastating rejection later?"

Lauren gives me her sad, puppy dog frown.

"Don't make me feel worse. I already feel terrible. I would rather be consoling him. I want to be that special person who makes him feel better when he's grieving, not this whiny woman I'm turning into. But every time we're together, we want to sleep together. I can't be his sex friend."

Lauren pinches her nose and sighs. "You *are* the special person who makes him feel better. He's crazy about you, Imogene, and it's not just the sex and pie."

"Crazy isn't the same as love." I take the pot roast out of the oven and uncover it. "I know you think I'm being unreasonable, but I think I'm doing both of us a favor. Cooper doesn't have to put up with my demands. I'm giving him all the space he needs. We'll be friends again ... eventually. It will be good." I lift the pot roast out of the pan with two spatulas.

"Great, you keep telling yourself that because you're going to get to practice being friends when he gets here in about ... oh ... ten minutes."

"You invited him for dinner?" I drop the pot roast on the serving platter and broth splatters everywhere.

"Leo did. Today at work." Lauren gives an apologetic eyebrow raise. "Next to me, Cooper is his best friend, and he wants to have him over. Leo feels like he hasn't done enough for Cooper."

"Leo should have his best friend over, and I should start looking for a new place to live so I don't make things awkward for all of us."

"No! You're my built-in babysitter."

I laugh. "As appealing as that is, you and I have been living together for a long time. It's time to cut the strings. You and your husband need a home that doesn't have me invading every room and every meal."

"Where would you go? Back to your old, My Little Pony bedroom in your parents' house?" Lauren asks.

"I haven't slept in that room since I was ten; I turned the basement into the cool room. Besides, my mother turned the pony room into her sewing hideout, and the basement is full of junk. I can find a nice rental. Maybe I could move in with Yadi and Kimberly."

"I would miss you so much."

"You see me every day at work."

"Hello," we hear Cooper shout from the front hall.

"Hey, Cooper!" Lauren replies.

"Kcuf, kcuf, kcuf, kcuf," I mutter to myself.

"Did that help? Is it out of your system? We good to go here?" Lauren looks sympathetic at my anxiety over this man.

"No, but I don't have any choice. He's my friend, right? We're all friends."

"Right." Lauren takes me by the arm, then we walk out to meet Cooper.

He's leaning against the balustrade instead of making himself comfortable in the living room, which is what he'd typically do.

"Hi." My hesitation is obvious, my smile sad.

"Imogene." There's a fluid warmth to the way he says my name. I don't think I could possibly ever get over the way it makes me feel.

"We're having my awesome pot roast tonight," Lauren declares.

"Excellent." Cooper smiles faintly. "Where's Leo?"

"He ran to the store to get a couple of baguettes. I'm craving bread and gravy," Lauren explains. "He should be back any min—oh!" Lauren puts her hand on her belly and leans over, her face contorting with pain.

"Lauren?" I put my hand on her back and see small droplets of blood on the floor between Lauren's bare feet.

"Oh, God, no," Lauren moans and more blood spurts out.

"Shit!" Cooper bolts to Lauren and picks her up, cradling her in his arms.

"Is she having a—"

Blood seeps through the white apron over her billowing baby-doll style dress, spreading wider.

Holding Lauren with one arm, Cooper pulls his keys out of his pocket. "Imogene, get the truck started. You're driving us to the hospital!" He tosses the keys at me.

334

I don't bother to think, I dash out the front door and race to Cooper's truck. As I start the engine, Cooper is already opening the passenger door, sliding into the seat with Lauren in his lap. Her eyes are closed tightly as she moans and cries.

"It's too early," she says weakly.

"Drive!" Cooper yells at me. "Drive fast."

Lauren grimaces again. "A cramp," she moans.

"Don't push, Lauren," Cooper orders. "Try to take slow breaths, but don't push."

"Do you know what to do?" I ask, stunned that Cooper seems fairly collected despite our panic.

"No. I have no idea what I'm doing, but I think she's supposed to fight the urge to push."

Once I speed out of town to the hospital and swing through the emergency room drop off, screeching to a halt in front of an ambulance, Cooper jumps out, holding Lauren's floppy body against his chest. He runs through the sliding doors of the ER entrance while I park the truck in the visitor lot and run into the waiting room where they are nowhere in sight.

As I'm about to inquire at the admissions desk, Cooper comes through a pair of swinging doors that are locked to the public. His jeans and the bottom of his white T-shirt are covered in blood.

"How is she?" I ask.

"I don't know. They had me put her in one of the beds and the doctor was there. They told me to leave." The worry in Cooper's voice terrifies me. "I'm going to go call Leo. Can you call her parents?"

"I didn't bring a phone. I didn't bring my purse. I drove without my license."

"It's okay." Cooper touches my shoulder. "I'll go outside and call everyone. Why don't you sit here and wait to see if the nurse or doctor comes out to talk to you."

I nod then find an unoccupied chair in the waiting

room. Sitting anxiously on the edge of the seat, I watch the double doors for any signs of a doctor or nurse.

Cooper returns and takes the chair next to me. "Lauren's parents and Leo are on their way. I called Carson, too. Sit back and try to relax, Imogene. It could be a while."

I move back in my chair and take a deep breath, unable to calm down. It's impossible. My gaze keeps racing back and forth between the clock on the wall and the doors. Someone needs to tell us what's going on.

"I shouldn't have let her work so hard." I shake my head.

"This isn't your fault." Cooper stares at me without blinking. "You didn't cause this. No one did. It happens." He picks up my hand and holds it against his leg.

"She wouldn't slow down," I continue. "I should have made her leave work earlier. I should have done a better job at the wedding. I should have ordered the dresses and prevented that whole fiasco. I shouldn't have let her cook and clean—"

"Stop it. You didn't do anything wrong, Imogene."

He squeezes my hand as we sit in tense silence until Leo comes running through the sliding doors, followed by Lauren's parents. Leo goes right to the admitting station and they open the double doors for him, a nurse leading him to see his wife. Lauren's father sits with us while her mother paces the waiting room.

"Try closing your eyes for a while," Cooper says softly so only I can hear. "It may help you."

I close my eyes and listen to the sounds of muffled conversations, beeping machines, and the whoosh of the sliding doors, over and over until there's a synchronized rhythm to my breathing and the surrounding sounds.

Forty minutes later, Leo comes out and we lunge out of our chairs together. Leo hugs Lauren's parents and then me. "Lauren is stable. The baby is okay, but they have to monitor both of them," he says, excited with panic.

Leo notices the large patches of blood covering Cooper's jeans and shirt. "They stopped the bleeding," he says. "Her blood pressure spiked way too high."

When Emma and Jess arrive, Leo repeats everything to them. Then Carson, Archie, Lois, and Dylan arrive, and Leo starts to explain everything again when he's interrupted. A nurse comes out and whisks Leo and Lauren's parents through the mysterious double doors while I sit silently next to Archie. Cooper takes charge and updates everyone on Lauren's status.

As Nina and Garth finally return, it makes me feel a little better to see their hopeful faces. "She's doing better," Nina says. "They've moved her out of the ER to a regular room. They'll let two visitors in at a time with Leo. I thought you and Cooper would like to go."

"Yes," Cooper replies for both of us. He then takes my hand and walks me towards the door a nurse is holding open for us.

We continue to hold hands as we follow the nurse down a hallway, up an elevator, and down another hallway to Lauren's private room. The lights are dimmed, but it's hardly restful. There are plenty of flashing colors, beeps from the monitors, and a buzz of conversations from other rooms and the nurses' station across from Lauren's door.

Lauren looks frail in her hospital gown. She's hooked up to a monitor, the wires protruding from the top of her gown, and her arm has an IV in it. She's partially covered by a thin blanket and sheet and doesn't look pregnant at all. As Cooper and I approach her bed, Lauren opens her eyes and regards me with a sad, tired, ghost of a smile.

I look at Leo sitting in a chair against the wall, showing my confusion.

"She's going to be okay, Imogene. The baby is okay … so far. It was the placenta …" he says, but then seems to forget the other details. "Lauren will have to stay on bed

337

rest until she delivers. She's tired and a little out of it."

"Okay," I whisper.

I let go of Cooper's hand and walk around to the side of the bed without the IV pole. I slip under the heart monitor wires and slide into bed next to Lauren. Then I put my arm gently across her waist, and she tilts her head to touch mine. I lie next to my friend as she closes her eyes and drifts off to a state of semi-sleep.

Leo motions Cooper over to the door where they stand and talk in hushed tones for a few minutes. Then Leo leaves and Cooper leans against the doorway, watching me hold on to my friend with a possessive, sisterly love.

"Imogene," Cooper whispers and lightly shakes my shoulder. "Babe, visiting hours are over. We have to leave."

I wake up to Cooper's lovely gray eyes above me. Lauren is fast asleep and the room is darker.

"Visiting hours ended at eleven. The nurse let you stay a bit longer since you were both asleep. It's one o'clock now."

"Where's Leo?" I ask groggily.

"He's sleeping in the waiting room. He doesn't want to leave, but I need to take you home."

"All right." I sit up and Cooper helps me off the high bed so I don't stumble and knock down any of the equipment surrounding the bed.

A nurse comes in to check Lauren's vitals as we leave quietly.

We don't talk on the drive back to my house. I try to think of things I can do to help Leo and Lauren over the next few weeks, but nothing spectacular comes to mind other than the usual domestic chores.

When Cooper parks in front of the house, he turns off the engine and hops out of the truck before I can tell him not to bother. I climb the porch steps slowly and then sit down on the top one.

"You need to get some sleep," Cooper says, standing before me. "Visiting hours start at eleven. I'll come pick you up."

"They only let three people in. Lauren's parents will want that time. I'll go later in the afternoon. I want to sit out here for a while, but you can leave."

"I don't want to leave." He sits down next to me, leaning his elbows on his knees. He is silent as he steeples his hands.

"Thank you for your fast thinking," I say, studying his profile as he looks up at the stars in the clear night sky. "I don't think I could have gotten Lauren to the hospital on my own. You're good at managing emergencies."

"I hope everything really is okay. I hope this doesn't happen again."

"Leo and Nina seem pretty sure that everything will be fine."

"Yeah." He glances at me and then sighs as he looks down.

As we sit in more silence, I want to say something because I don't want to let go. I'll hold onto this stillness between us as long as I can if it means it will somehow change this, *change* us. Cooper looks just as conflicted.

"I am in love with you," he finally says, turning to me. "Every time I said I was crazy about you, what I really meant was that I am in love with you."

"Oh," I stammer with a nervous smile of surprise. "Thank you."

"Thank you?" Cooper lets out a little laugh.

"Thank you for telling me. And thank you for all the other nice gestures. Buying that necklace and giving it to your mother."

Cooper looks at me as though I've discovered one of his secrets.

"You didn't think I'd notice your mother wearing a

necklace I made, the one you said you were giving to your sister?"

"Oh," he mumbles.

"Thank you for getting our business off the ground and up and running. We wouldn't have that workshop or those employees if it wasn't for you."

"All I did was buy you a few beads."

"Carson told me about the money, Cooper."

Cooper closes his eyes and exhales slowly. "Shit."

"He thought I should know. I'm really astounded that you did it."

"You're a good investment."

"That's it? You mean my business, right? You're not talking about me, personally."

"Both. I fell for you long before you'd even go out with me. I couldn't separate that woman from the businesswoman. All I saw was you. I love you, Imogene."

Hearing that makes me happy, sending my heart racing, but another part of me that is more scared overpowers the lovesick woman.

"I've been thinking about us a lot, Cooper. I've been trying to figure out why I love you and couldn't feel that way about Jeremy or other men."

"Good. You only love me, so stop wondering about those losers. Jeremy, Cory ..."

"Cody. And I don't think about them. I've been thinking about *why* I love you. It's exhilarating and passionate, and I feel amazing when I'm with you. I can call it love because it's also frightening. It's frightening because love is unpredictable, emotionally unstable, and uncontainable. It's a real love, and ultimately, real love leads to unintentional pain and loss. But I still want that kind of love, knowing that there's a certain amount of suffering that comes with loving someone because it also comes with the greatest amount of passion and joy.

"I suppose it seems premature for me to be so bull-headed about marriage and family, but being with your family only confirmed my feelings about this. I'm willing to live every exhilarating moment with you, even if it means that someday one of us will be sitting at the bedside, watching the other one leave this life."

"I want that, too." Cooper slips his arms around my waist and kisses me, causing me to momentarily lose my train of thought.

"No. Let me finish." I stop the kiss. "I accept the unpredictable aspects that come attached with love. You don't. You think that, if you don't get married, it makes life and love easier to control, to contain. I don't want a manageable, containable love, Cooper. I want it to explode, and I want everything that comes with it." I remove his hands and stand up.

"How do I keep ending up in the same argument with you?" He stands up and towers over me with an exasperated expression.

"Because we are not on the same page about anything. You pursued me relentlessly, and you got me. You got me, Cooper. But love is a like a top-secret government project with you. You want containment, to make it safe. It's not about safety!"

"I told you I love you!" he shouts angrily, causing me to step back. "I'm sorry. I didn't mean to yell at you, but you don't understand what my life felt like when my family fell apart."

"Then tell me."

"I was young, and I experienced years of degradation living with people who said they loved me but betrayed everything that our family was built on. My parents were horrible to each other and weren't much better with us. And then I chose a career that kept me in a continuous circle of violence, deceit and violence."

"It must be very difficult to reconcile those two things that ruled your life for so long." I open the front door, but

341

Cooper blocks me with his arm. "I think I'll go to bed now."

"I'm sorry I'm not the man you want me to be."

"I don't think you're the man *you* want to be. Why did you and Sofia break up? After all those years together, you must have loved her."

"She broke up with me after college. She was going to med school in Chicago and wanted me to apply for a job there."

"Why didn't you go?"

"She wanted to get married first."

I snort and lean against the doorframe.

"The truth is I wouldn't have gone to Chicago with her anyway." He presses against me until I meet his eyes. "I've never loved anyone the way I love you."

Thirty-Two

Lauren has been on bed rest since she was discharged from the hospital three weeks ago, and I have taken it upon myself to be her main caregiver. I run home during lunchtime and make her a tray of food, or I bring home soup and sandwiches from the diner. I change her linens, bring her dinner, and make sure she has entertainment every night. Leo does laundry and dishes and listens patiently while I talk to Lauren with my endless stories about work and town gossip.

When friends come over to visit Lauren, I chaperone each session as though I'm her mother or hired medical staff. I'm less clingy when Cooper comes over. He'll hang out and talk with Lauren and Leo in their room on the top floor, and I'll excuse myself to work in the studio below. Sometimes, when he brings over a movie, I'll join them, but I sit across the room from Cooper and talk in a breezy tone as my insides shatter at the sight, sound, and smell of him. He always gives me an extra smile and takes an extra moment to acknowledge me. It's excruciating, but I gladly accept the pain because I love him.

I make a point of greeting him every morning in the parking lot and no longer try to hide as a means to get over him. Cooper seems to look forward to these happenstance moments of coincidentally arriving or leaving work at the same time, too. Sometimes, I see him lingering by his truck or bike as if he's waiting for me. I confess that the same thing crosses my mind when I stand by my car and pretend to look for the car keys in my purse or take another fake phone call.

Leo finally steps in and tells me I'm trying too hard to be everything for Lauren and it's okay to take it down a notch. He encourages me to stay at work during my lunch hour and eat with Anita and Tracy. Lauren convinces me to take up yoga again, so three times a week, I take a class with the new yoga instructor Lois hired, Anima-Christi. She's surprisingly bitchy for a yoga teacher, and I suspect that's why Lois adores her and why I enjoy her class. She's an intimidating little powerhouse who spends an inordinate amount of class time correcting my uncoordinated yoga positions or talking about finding your Zen. I'm all for finding some Zen, which is why I keep attending her classes even though I'm constantly being singled out as the worst student in the group.

"Can I have the other half of your burger?" Anima asks me from across the booth after she polishes off a grill cheese sandwich and soup.

"I thought you were a vegetarian. You berated me in front of the whole class the other day for wearing a Ms. Piggy T-shirt."

"It said *'I Love Bacon.'* It's not appropriate for my class." Anima takes the burger in her skinny fingers and wolfs it down like one of Carson's big, burly dudes.

"Kind of hypocritical of you," I say.

Emma and Jess laugh.

"I like bacon, too, but I don't make fun of animals that are slaughtered for our benefit," Anima explains. "And Ms. Piggy is a beloved national treasure."

"Oh, here she goes." I sigh.

"You're both full of crap," Emma states. "I'm the only vegetarian here."

"You're wearing leather shoes and your bag didn't skin and tan itself." Jess holds up Emma's purse as evidence.

"This was fun as always, but I have to get back to

344

work." I look around the crowded diner, but I still don't see Cooper. I was trying to stretch out lunch as long as possible in the hopes that I'd run into him.

We pay our bill then visit with Archie and his sweetheart Emily at the next table before heading outside into the sunny November day.

"Imogene!" Cooper shouts from across the street. He's coming from the General Store, walking slowly, looking down one side of the street and the other with some apprehension. "Come here!"

I don't move. I notice Carson off to my right in the middle of the street with his hands out, making the oncoming cars slow down to a stop. To my left, Dylan is in the middle of the street, stopping cars coming from the other direction. They are about a hundred yards apart from one another and cars are at a standstill, waiting for them to move. Cooper keeps looking at me as he steps into the street and walks to the middle and stops.

"Imogene, come here, please."

A crowd assembles behind me.

Anima pushes me forward. "Go!" she demands.

"That's not very Zen of you," I shoot back at her, noticing everyone, including Archie, my parents, grandmother, Lois, and the whole diner pretty much standing behind me or next to me, waiting for this show to begin.

"Is this going to happen?" Dylan shouts to me and Cooper. "I see the sheriff's car and a bunch of angry tourists!"

"Imogene?" Cooper says loudly as he hooks his thumbs in his belt loops and takes a casual stance, waiting for me.

"Seventy million big ones," Jess whispers to herself. Then she takes my purse from me. "Go, Imogene."

I begin to slowly walk towards him, glancing from side to side at Carson and Dylan as they hold back the growing

345

traffic.

It's too chilly not to wear a jacket, but Cooper stands before me in his standard black BD T-shirt and jeans with a sexy smile, looking as handsome as ever.

"Do you know what you're doing?" I ask him nervously.

"You said the right man would stop traffic for you."

"I think I meant it metaphorically."

"I don't think so," he says with a faint smile.

While my insides churn with excitement, making me suddenly glad I didn't finish that burger, Cooper smiles as he gets down on one knee. He slips a ring from his pocket, and I immediately recognize his mother's emerald ring.

I hear gasps and giggles from the crowd.

"Finally!" Dylan throws his hands up and turns back to face the cars he's blocking.

"I don't understand, Cooper. What changed your mind?"

"You, of course. Being away from you gave me plenty of time to think about what my life is with you and what it would be like if I let you go. You taught me some very important things about myself, that I *do* need my family, and I do love them. The time I spent with my family reminded me how good it can be to have them, especially under the worst circumstances. I hadn't felt that in a long time, Imogene. And when you showed up at my mother's house, I felt stronger. It felt good to belong to a family again, but I also want to belong to you."

"Oh," I say nervously. "Are you sure you've thought this through? Because I will never be one of those people that takes things in stride. Cooper, I'm a mess of emotions all the time."

"I love you because you are a mess of emotions. You're overly dramatic, strong willed, incredibly funny, and fiercely loyal and faithful to the people you love. I want to be one of those lucky people to be loved by you."

346

"You are."

"Will you marry me, Imogene?"

He gazes at me expectantly, taking my breath away. I look at the quiet crowd of people watching us with anticipation then turn around to look at Carson behind me. He nods as though I'm getting approval from my big brother.

"Imogene!" Cooper snaps in a friendly tone. "I'm on my knee in the middle of the street. I stopped traffic because of you. Will you marry me?"

"Yes. Of course I'll marry you," I reply with a laugh. "Did you really think I would say no?"

"You have a way of making people work for your attention." He smiles.

He puts the ring on my finger, and it slides into a hard, pinching stop at the knuckle.

"Kcuf!" I whisper-shout. "My finger is too fat for the ring!"

"We'll have it sized," he says, laughing as he puts it on my pinky.

As Cooper stands and kisses me slowly, sweetly, and thoroughly in front of everyone, there's applause and some cheers from my family and friends. Then Cooper puts his arm around my waist and walks me back towards the diner so Carson and Dylan can let the cars go through.

"Why don't you take the rest of the day off to celebrate, and I'll take care of closing up later?" Anita asks as she wrestles through the crowd to see my ring.

"Excellent idea," Cooper exclaims.

I agree, and after a few more hugs from friends and family, Cooper drives me back to his home because he says he has another surprise. I'm about to make a crack about ribbons tied on male appendages, but when he walks me through his house, I'm speechless. The kitchen has been completely renovated and is pristine in natural stone and polished concrete with cherry wood cabinets. I selected this color scheme. The slate tile and fixtures in the bathrooms are complete, and the full-season porch is set up and ready for lazy afternoons.

"I brought in Carson's crew to help get it done," he says, looking at my amazed expression. "Two years ago, I didn't know how to use a table saw. Over the last year, these guys brought me up to speed and taught me everything. I worked on the house every day. Lauren told me you've been thinking of moving out... I was hoping you'd come here. Unless you want to be married first."

"We're engaged, close enough." I look down at the ring on my pinky.

"She wanted you to have that." His voice breaks a little. "My mother really liked you, Imogene. She didn't get to tell you how important it was to her that you came to see her. She told me several times that her ring was meant for you. I guess she expected I would propose eventually. She gave the necklace you made to Greer. I thought you'd like to hear that."

"I do. It makes me feel closer to your family."

"So when are we getting married?" he asks.

I snort a laugh. "Are you serious? You proposed thirty minutes ago. We have to decide this minute?"

"I assumed you have some idea of when you want to get married and start a family and buy minivans and all of that other stuff."

"No, not at all."

"Huh. Okay, well, can you move in today?" He puts his hands on my waist and looks down at me with an eager grin.

"Wow, you kind of want to do everything at once. I have to pack, and we have to do some planning."

"Let's not, just stay here, and we'll get your stuff next weekend. I'm sick and tired of living with that feeling of missing you. Every day, I've missed you. When you would say hi to me in the morning and walk into your office, I missed you. When you would say goodbye to me at night and drive away, I missed you. I've been feeling so lousy I actually considered stashing some snakes in your workshop to have an excuse to come spend the day there. I was going to let them slither around, and I'd pretend to catch them so it would take days."

I laugh. "I missed you, too. Every day. Every minute."

His hands slide up my back, and he strokes his fingers lightly against my neck. "I'm sorry I didn't tell you I love you when we were arguing at the wedding. With the way you talked about marriage, I realized I wasn't the person you thought I was. I wasn't the person who was fully committed to my family, not the way you are. I realized that, before we had our big blow up when you kissed me— at the other wedding last spring—I was missing an important element, something you wouldn't overlook. You are the reason I went back to be with my mother and family. It was all because of you, Imogene. I wanted to be better."

"You are. You're the best." I step up on my tiptoes to kiss him. "I'm madly in love with you, Cooper."

"When are we getting married?"

"I haven't planned past today."

"Fine. You're forcing me to bring out the big guns." Cooper removes his glasses from the inside of his T-shirt collar and slides them on his face.

"Yep. That'll do it."

"There's more. I've got Pablo Neruda, hand cuffs, bubble bath, whatever the hell you need," he says, picking me up and carrying me off to the bedroom.

Epilogue

The video Leo made of the proposal was meant for Lauren since she was bedridden at the time. We had no idea that it would go viral and spark over a million hits along with a bounty of proposals for Cooper. I received my share of messages from strange male admirers; however, it was nothing like the racy videos and explicit handwritten letters and email messages directed to *'Hunky MacKenzie.'* Cooper shrugged off the calls from media and fans and put Daisy on gatekeeper duty, junking all emails and disposing the offers of matrimony when packages and flowers were sent directly to the Blackard Designs shop.

I took a different approach. I adored the local and national attention, and when New York TV stations called us to do interviews for their human interest fluff segments, Cooper of course gave a *"hell, no,"* while I decided to take advantage of the opportunity and make as many guest appearances as I could on local and national morning news shows in the city.

I made sure to wear Imogene & Lauren jewelry and hawk it in every interview. Lois and Eleanor were my unintended entourage and acted as my overly zealous, bitchy handlers behind the scenes. Lois declared me the best media whore she has ever witnessed. I admit I was enjoying the attention, having Lauren dress and accessorize me for every appearance, and I practiced using a television voice and mimicking the TV hosts' body language. Cooper thinks my sarcasm, improvised one-liners, and the ability to ham it up on live television was a major attraction; as a result, my fifteen minutes of fame had a nice two month tail.

We got more clients, more orders, and hired another employee. If I thought I was working hard before, I learned quickly that a growing business means a lot more work, but I embraced it with a new enthusiasm.

Once my big head deflated, Maisie Penelope Adams made her appearance one bright January morning. She came by way of a C-Section and was the pinkest, pinched-faced, tiniest baby I have ever seen. Maisie was born with a large salmon-colored birthmark on the back of her neck and on top of her forehead.

When she was finally swaddled and handed to her mother, Lauren exclaimed, "She's perfect!" Leo was so happy he cried more than his baby.

Unfortunately, Archie and his new bride Emily missed my glamorous foray into the television publicity circuit and the birth of Maisie. After living more than fifty years without the love of his life, Archie couldn't wait any longer and certainly couldn't continue to live vicariously through the rest of us. Therefore, shortly after Cooper proposed to me, Archie and Emily got married at the old farmhouse that Archie had purchased all those decades ago in preparation to propose to his lovely, young Emily. That is, before she went off and married George Weston and had a litter of children. This time, Archie went all out to romance his sweetheart. After their nuptials, he whisked Emily off for a two-month honeymoon in Italy where my mature friends have informed me people of any age will feel young at heart, immersed in the romantic culture and history.

Leading up to our own wedding, Cooper's house became *our* home, and his housewarming gift to me was a fluffy bunny, Serpico. That was Cooper's doing. I haven't seen the movie, but Cooper assures me that our bunny is the spitting image of Al Pacino. Cooper also refuses to put him in a cage. I can't say I am terribly excited to have a free-range rodent in the house, but Cooper has become attached to him and doesn't seem to mind the rabbit turds that cunning little furball leaves around the house.

I'm also not the one that jumped into planning our wedding. I left everything up to Cooper. He selected a date in May, and to humor me, he arranged to have the ceremony and party at his family's bar in Brooklyn to accommodate the whole MacKenzie clan, babies and all, and every friend and relative from Hera.

Gun shy after Lauren's dress debacle, I wasn't interested in going down that road again; however, Cooper was pretty sure I could *staple* something together at the last minute. I did him one better. I took the girls out for a day in Manhattan for some much needed spa therapy at Bliss, and then we went shopping and each bought the first *kcuffing* dress we loved and wore it out of the store. Cooper hired a limo to drive us around and bring us back to the bar after all the guests had arrived.

When we walked into the beautifully decorated "Scottish" pub, the first thing I noticed was Lois and Eleanor behind the bar, managing the bartenders and concocting who knows what. The second sight left me speechless and smiling: Cooper, leaning against the bar like a cocky gunslinger, or rather, a groom. He wore a striking, tailored black suit, the perfect cut for his broad shoulders and trim waist. He didn't blink twice or look dismayed in the least when I appeared in a blood red dress with a plunging neckline in both the front and back. He smiled appreciatively, taking me in slowly from the tall black heels, the red lipstick, and settling on my smoky dark eyes.

With drinks in hand for the guests and food catered from an Italian restaurant owned by one of Cooper's Brooklyn friends, the wedding ceremony was stress-free. Within minutes of saying our vows in front of the minister, the party started. It was everything I wanted—a celebration without an agenda and the boisterous, unfiltered MacKenzies shaking up the more conservative Hera guests.

As Cooper nestles his lips against the sensitive spot under my ear, his scratchy stubble sends shivers of lust and love through me. I asked him not to shave so I could experience that little thrill during my wedding dance.

"Are you happy, Mrs. MacKenzie?" He has the relaxed baritone of a man who didn't experience any wedding day jitters.

"I am very happy, Mr. MacKenzie. And you?"

"I'm insanely in love with you. I was expecting some virginal-looking white number, but this dress is spectacular. It's you."

"Red is for love, passion, and good luck. And I look awesome in it."

"Yes, you do." He kisses me, and I hear Lauren cheer and make everyone clink glasses.

I snuggle in his embrace and sway to the music, amazed that I am now part of this huge family. Instantly, I have become an auntie and cousin to all these toddlers and teenagers ransacking the bar.

While Jess and Carson dance nearby, I notice her reach up and touch Carson's face as she says something that makes him laugh. Dylan and Emma are slow dancing in their own world, holding on to each other and kissing as if they are alone and blind to the rowdy people around them. Lauren and Leo hold little Maisie between them and dance as one happy family.

"Cooper," I say, reaching up to hold his face. His eyes open lazily. "Thank you for not giving up. Thank you for being persistent and hounding me to go out with you. I wouldn't have had the nerve, and we never would have ended up together if you hadn't seen through my ... abrasive side."

He smiles. "My pleasure. You couldn't have stopped me from hunting you down. I doubt I could have ever let up. I want to be with you, Imogene MacKenzie."

353

"See? You like saying that. You like that we *sound* married."

"I do."

"Good, because as soon as we leave here, we get to have married-people sex."

"Let's leave now."

"Drive back to Hera, now?"

"No, I booked us a room at a very nice hotel for tonight. Then, in the morning, we're flying out of JFK. I'm taking you on a honeymoon."

"Where are we going?" I ask. "And what about work?"

"Lauren and Carson are the only ones who know what I've planned, and they are not telling you. I'm taking you someplace that requires flying over a very large body of water, someplace that has beaches and ports, good food, lots of beautiful things to see, and a very big bed."

"Another surprise," I laugh. "You're good at those."

"Anything to make you happy." He kisses me tenderly.

Six months later ...

"You're fat."

"I am fat," Jess replies, looking at her pregnant belly.

"I thought you'd carry the baby like a basketball, like Lauren did," I add, not trying to be mean, but I'm curious and concerned about how pregnancy changes a woman's body.

"Lauren is tall," Jess explains. "Tall women carry it easier. I'm short. Everything is smooshed and fat, even my ankles.

Jess lifts up her swollen legs and tries to point to her toes so we can all see her puffy ankles. She's seven months pregnant and looks terribly uncomfortable.

"I feel like that girl from *Charlie and the Chocolate Factory*. What was her name?" Jess asks.

"Vicky?" Emma asks.

"Violet," Lauren confirms. "She blew up like a piece of blueberry bubble gum."

"Yes, that's how I feel. Like I'm blowing up. My skin is even a little blue." Jess pulls up her maternity T-shirt to display the fair skin stretched across her belly. Her pink-white skin does have a bluish tinge to it.

"Are you okay, Jess?" Carson asks from across the room.

He's sitting at his dining room table with Cooper, Dylan, and Leo, going over the new line of BD baby furniture they will be shipping out this week. Cooper's idea for a line of baby furniture from last summer went into production when Carson found out he was going to be a father. All of a sudden, Carson became fascinated with baby products and had Cooper help do the research and work with the design team on creating mid- to high-range cribs, toddler beds, changing tables, play tables, and storage armoires for toys and clothes.

"I'm fine," Jess groans. "You ask me every ten minutes."

"I can't help it. You look like you're in pain."

"No, you look like you're in pain every time you look at your pregnant wife," Dylan cuts in.

Jess and Emma laugh, but Carson looks seriously scared.

"Oh, no," Jess gasps as she reaches for the bowl of tortilla chips on the coffee table.

"What?" Carson shouts.

"I … I can't reach the chips." Jess falls back against the couch, laughing.

"Hilarious," Carson mutters.

"You make me look like a pro," Leo says to Carson. "You are really freaking out over nothing."

"Carson, look at me." Jess waves. "I'm reaching for a chip. Oh, I have the chip!" She holds it up and Carson scowls. "Now I'm dipping it in the guacamole. I sure hope

355

I don't break my water doing this."

We're all laughing. It's entirely too easy to tease Carson about his overprotectiveness.

"He's worse at work," Dylan says, standing up to do one of his Carson impressions. "Where are you?" Dylan yells into his cell phone for effect. "Why are you putting away groceries? Who said you could make waffles? Why are you standing up? Are you in labor? Are you having the baby today?" Dylan shouts as he performs Carson's posture and expressions perfectly. I laugh so hard, rolling on the floor next to Maisie, that she laughs in response and that gets Bert, the Bulldog, rolling around on the rug, too.

"Man, give the guy a break," Cooper laughs.

"Carson, I am now getting up to walk to the kitchen." Jess stands and grins at Carson's stony expression. "I'm walking. I'm walking, and I'm walking," she repeats, moving her hands and legs in slow motion. "Oh, I'm stopping." She looks down at her belly.

"This isn't funny in the least," Carson says with a tense face, wondering why Jess is pausing.

"Oh … it's just heartburn. Now, I'm walking again." She chuckles as she walks into the kitchen.

Carson's face visibly relaxes.

"Wow. She had you going there." Cooper observes Carson. "Maybe you need a vacation."

"Maybe you should see my doctor," Dylan chimes in. "No one is this nervous or uptight unless there's a real reason to be worried."

"Dylan is right, Carson." Lauren shakes her head. "Honey, you are a wreck, and your wife is having a perfectly normal, healthy pregnancy. What are you going to do when she actually goes into labor?"

"When that happens," Cooper explains, "I'll give Carson a good knock-out punch, and then I'll take Jess to the hospital. Lauren and Imogene can be her coaches in the delivery room. When Carson wakes up, the nurse will hand him the baby."

"And then Carson can freak out about putting the baby seat in the car and getting up at night to check if his baby is breathing." Leo shrugs. "Sorry, Carson, but you're going to be one of those dads that always freaks out.

"Can we stop talking about this and get back to these orders. These shipments have to go out this week." Carson fumbles mindlessly with the papers in front of him.

"Hey, my crew is ready," Cooper responds. "We're loading the local trucks at six o'clock tomorrow morning, and we have two national shippers picking up the California orders Tuesday afternoon. By Friday, we should have our numbers in for you."

"I think, by the end of next month, we'll have a good idea of where this line will sell well," Dylan says, closing his laptop.

"Carson!" We hear Jess shout from the kitchen.

"What?" He sounds angry, but he looks alarmed, as if this is the real deal.

"I'm opening the refrigerator now. If I go into labor, I'll let you know," Jess says in a sing-song, teasing voice.

"Goddammit." Carson gets up from the dining table.

"Where are you going? We haven't finished the inventory list," Cooper says.

"I have to go check on my wife," Carson growls as he heads to the kitchen.

"Ha!" Dylan shouts and lets out a loud, belly laugh.

The rest of us can't hide our laughter, either.

"The guy is going to kill himself with worry before his kid arrives." Leo shakes his head.

Lauren and Emma are sitting on the couch, knitting baby blankets or something babyish while I get my daily baby fix. Maisie is only wearing a diaper as she gets up on her chubby knees and crawls a few feet before plopping down on her belly. We make a game of it, and I follow her and then pull her back to her starting position, which makes her giggle. Cooper comes and joins us on the floor.

"Hello, little beautiful." Cooper rolls the baby onto her back, kisses her forehead, and then gives her a big, loud raspberry on her belly. She screams and laughs in delight and pulls his hair, so he gives her more farting sounds on her sensitive tummy.

"That makes her pee every time. I bet she just filled her diaper," Lauren says.

Lauren has been very relaxed since having her baby, nothing like a hyper cheerleader anymore. She's more like Mother Earth as she shuffles around in Uggs at work and carries Maisie on her hip.

"I'll change her," I volunteer.

"Oh, you want to get in some practice?" Emma asks. "Something you want to tell us?"

Both Cooper and Lauren raise their eyebrows at me. Maisie is the first baby I have ever paid much attention to. Perhaps it's because Cooper and I are her Godparents, or maybe it's because I'm quite enamored with this little girl who can't speak or walk and poops and pees all the time, but she brings so much joy to her parents and the rest of us.

"Is there something you want to tell me?" Cooper asks me in the guest bedroom where I'm placing Maisie on her changing pad. Cooper pulls a new diaper out of the baby bag as I wrestle with the baby's flailing legs to get her wet diaper off.

"I'm not pregnant," I say with a laugh.

"Okay."

"You look a little sad about that? Or are you relieved?"

"Nah. But I've been getting used to the idea. I've thought about it."

When she has a clean diaper on, he picks up Maisie and holds her above his head until she laughs again.

"I thought we could be married a bit longer before we have kids," I say. "I see how Leo and Lauren juggle work and parenting, and that's with grandparents helping out.

Before we get caught up in that life with all those people involved, I kind of want you to myself for a while. I like when the two of us are alone."

He holds Maisie with one arm and puts his other around my waist.

"I like running naked through the house with you, too. Babies change schedules and take energy, and I'm pretty happy with our spontaneous sex." Cooper kisses me.

I sigh as our lips part and the kiss ends. "I think I could eventually manage two pregnancies, tops."

"Well, a MacKenzie woman can get pregnant by thinking of babies. Two pregnancies could actually be four babies. Remember, twins run in my family."

"Four kids?" As I shudder, he chuckles.

"God, what if we do have twins? I can't even narrow it down to one baby name."

"Easy, we call them Thang 1 and Thang 2." Cooper says it with a straight face as he kisses Maisie again.

"I love how easy going you are with kids," I say with a smile. "Really, it's nice that you've had so much practice with your nieces and nephews."

"Let's give this baby back to her parents so we can go home."

"And be alone?"

"Yeah, I want to be with my wife."

We walk back to the living room where Cooper hands Maisie off to Leo. Dylan is setting up a movie for the theater screen that rolls down from the ceiling, and Emma and Lauren are putting more snacks on the coffee table. Jess is snuggled up to Carson on the couch, apologizing for teasing him while she continues to taunt him with his baby fears. He looks happier and at ease as long as he has Jess next to him. We say goodbye and leave, taking Cooper's truck back to our house.

"You're really thinking about us having children, aren't you?" I ask, studying his profile as he drives.

"Of course," he replies, glancing at me. "Imogene, I paid attention when you gave me your speech about marriage and family. Whenever you're ready, tell me when and where."

"My go-to stud, how romantic."

"We can make it more interesting, maybe go to Portugal again. Algarve. Or maybe the Amalfi Coast or Provence. What do you think about that?"

"We could have a destination conception," I laugh. "Someday. Not now."

"Whenever you're ready."

"Well, it doesn't always happen when you want. It might take us a few months or years."

He scoffs. "Excuse me, but my dudes know what they're doing."

"I beg your pardon. I didn't mean to insult your swimmers."

"Home," he says as we arrive and he parks the truck. "Did I tell you how much I love you?"

"Yes. And I love you."

"Are we going to go inside to practice so we're really good at this?" As he takes my hand, I can't stop laughing.

"Maybe." I grin as we walk inside. I've been a grinning fool since the day he proposed.

"Well, at least we'll make it fun." He picks me up and cradles me in his arms as he barrels into the house. "Did I tell you I love you?" he asks again, smiling.

"Every day."

Acknowledgments

A big thank you goes to Michelle Carroll, Emma Corcoran, and Becky Korte. These women were more than my beta readers; they were the friends who cheered me on through some less than stellar days. Michelle also gets a special shout out for all those fun teasers she creates for me to post on social media.

Autumn Hull's keen eye for content helped me fill in plot holes and smooth out a number of scenes to make Cooper and Imogene's story so much better.

Alizon Duckwall and Kristin Campbell are my amazing editing team who make my eyes bleed with all the revisions and corrections they send my way. However, their detailed edits are the necessary polish.

Aaron Campbell maintains and updates my website, and I'm pretty sure he's happy that I don't have time to run a daily blog.

Alisha and Damon at Damonza did an amazing job on my cover. I'm always impressed with their creativity and professionalism.

Finally, I would like to thank all the readers and bloggers who have enthusiastically supported my books. I appreciate everything you do for me whether it's a personal message, a review, talking about my books online, or sharing my books with friends.

Thank You!

Sara

About the Author

S. A. Wolfe lives with her husband and children in New York City. When not writing or reading, she loves hanging out with family and friends. Unfortunately, she is also great at procrastinating.

Dear Reader-

If you are interested in finding out when my next book will be published, or you'd like to be an early reviewer for my next book, please subscribe to my mailing list at:
http://www.sa-wolfe.com/

I love interacting with readers, please contact me at:
https://www.facebook.com/sawolfe24

https://twitter.com/sawolfe_

sawolfe24@gmail.com

The FEARSOME SERIES:
FEARSOME (Book 1)
FREEDOM (Book 2)
FAITHFUL (Book 3)

Thank you!

S. A. Wolfe